Cambridge Girl

A Novel By

PEG MADDOCKS

Trefoil Books
Rancho Bernardo, California

Published by Trefoil Books. *Cambridge Girl* may be purchased from Trefoil Books, P.O. Box 501323, San Diego, CA 92150-1323.

Edited by Sandy Pasqua
Cover design by Mary Scott, Maddocks & Co.
Page layout by Kenis Dunne, Dunnes Publishing

10 9 8 7 6 5 4 3 2 1
ISBN: 0-9674339-0-8

ACKNOWLEDGEMENTS

J am immensely grateful to my many friends who have contributed their time and effort to making the publication of this book possible.

Mrs. Catherine Kilkelly, who vividly remembered historical events and facts about the early years of this century. In memory of Sgt. Fred Rhode, a brave soldier and survivor of The Bataan Death March. My editor, Sandy Pasqua, *Metropolitan San Diego Magazine,* who was so helpful and wise. Dr. Dennis Hensley, author and teacher, for his encouragement in my early years of writing.

Mary Scott, creative director at Maddocks & Co., who designed the cover of *Cambridge Girl.* Kenis Dunne, a good friend who prepared the cover text and helped design the mechanicals of the book.

My readers, for their suggestions and encouragement: Dr. Joseph Buckley, Gerry Egan, Rita Jansen, Marty Judge, Evelyn King, Emma Kocenko, Camille Lane, Virginia Linnehan, Margaret McManus, Carmaline Murphy, and Claire and Bill Spaulding.

Special thanks to the "Club Girls" for the memories and lasting friendships.

I am grateful to Attorney Marshall F. Lippman, General Counsel of the Hudson News Company.

December 16, 1999

To Gail —
Hope you enjoy
a look back in history.

My Best Wishes

Peg Maddocks

DEDICATION

To my children, Frank, Peg, Nancy and Bill, and my grandchildren,
Frank, Erin, Sarah, Meghan, Jesse, Jaime and Aaron.
Thanks for your love and caring.

And to the most important person in my life, my husband, Gene,
who really deserves to be called my co-author. Without his patience
and guidance, I never would have conquered the computer or
finished this novel.

FORTHCOMING TITLES BY PEG MADDOCKS

The Santorini Odyssey

Beach Walk

FOREWORD

*I*t is never necessary to explain Cambridge, where it is or what it is. And if an explanation is attempted, it falls short of telling the whole truth. Listeners hear the accent, "Pahk the cah in the Hahvahd Yahd," and mimic it with exaggerated glee. They sense the special ambiance of Harvard Square and equate it with Picadilly and Trafalgar Squares. It is neither of these, but the aura of Harvard Square is inescapable.

Say "Cambridge" and people envision an ivy-covered colonial Harvard University grown to worldwide prestige or MIT (Massachusetts Institute of Technology), alma maters of presidents, Nobel Prize winners, the rich and the famous. What happens at Harvard and MIT flows down the Charles River and touches every shore of the world.

Finally, consider the cosmopolitan atmosphere created by the large mix of ethnic groups who are descendants of the thousands of immigrants who arrived in the mid to late 1800's. They were Irish, Italian, Polish, Jewish, Portuguese, Lithuanian, Swedish, French, African American, Greek, Armenian, German, Chinese, and smaller groups of other nationalities. These early ethnic groups settled in areas of the city where double and triple-decker tenements abounded. There they established enclaves where they could speak their native language, buy their native foods, and build their own churches where services could be conducted in the dialect of their homeland. These enclaves still exist today. This fact alone adds a fascinating international appeal to the city and also draws a line of an explicit difference between the Cambridge worlds of "town and gown."

On a recent visit to Cambridge, I heard that Cambridge should be known as "The People's Republic of Cambridge." The Harvard Square area's zip code, 02138, is now considered the most prestigious address in the country, outclassing Beverly Hills' 90210.

ONE

ambridge, Massachusetts, 1929. Torrential rain that had flooded the streets for seven days, subsided occasionally now. Then, without warning, a sudden cloudburst would send more with unrelenting force making it impossible to see even just a few feet ahead. On the eighth day, during a lull in the storm, Mary O'Meara and her four-year-old granddaughter, Meghan, hastily put on rubber boots, raincoats and hats and trudged up Athens Street to the corner store where Bill O'Meara worked.

Listen to my boots squish, Nana." Meghan giggled.

"Step carefully, darlin, or yer might go fer a swim," Nana warned, now struggling to plod through the deep water without falling. She thought to herself, maybe this wasn't such a good idea.

When they reached the corner store, Nana pushed open the screen door and yelled, "You whooo, son, look who's here."

"Ma!" Bill was startled. "What in God's name are you doing out in this weather, and with little, Meg too? It's dangerous with the streets flooded and all."

"Aw, we weren't afraid, were we, darlin?" Nana boasted, putting her arm around Meg.

Meg grinned up at her father. "We're brave, Daddy. We like adventures, don't we, Nana?"

"Yer right about that, darlin. Yer see, Bill, dear, we're desperate fer a quart of milk, because we're making an Irish pound cake, and me helper here drank the last of me milk, and we can't finish it. Oh, and I needed a loaf of bread, too."

"I'm completely out of bread, Ma. I haven't had a delivery for two days because of the rain. But I'll get your milk right away, and you two get back to the house before a downpour starts up again."

While Bill was in the large wooden ice chest getting the bottle of milk, the screen door opened. "Well, well, will yer look who's here, Meg?" Nana said, smiling broadly. "It's yer little pal, Dorothy Mulroney and her mum. Quick, Mrs. Mulroney, put that umbrella down, don't yer know it's bad luck to keep an umbrella up indoors."

"Aw, go on with you and your superstitions, Mary O'Meara," Mrs. Mulroney quipped, closing the umbrella and shaking the rain off. "Glory be to God, is it ever going to stop? My Mike says he's going to start building an ark."

Bill, stepping out of the ice chest, heard the remark and laughed. He put the bottle of milk in a double brown bag and joked, "Tell, Mike, I'll help him if he'll take the O'Mearas aboard too." He handed his mother the milk and said, "Now get going home, Ma." Then he asked Mrs. Mulroney, "Now what can I get for you today, dear?"

Mrs. Mulroney put her hand alongside her mouth and whispered to Bill, "Before I give you my order, I've got some juicy gossip to tell you and your mom." She raised her voice, "Dorothy, you and Meg be good little girls and go stand at the front door and let us know if it starts raining hard."

The two four year olds took each other's hands and giggled as they flopped in exaggerated fashion across the floor in their rubber boots. The screen door, covered with water, made it difficult for them to see outside.

Looking back at the adults, Meg mischievously whispered, "Let's open the screen door and look out, Dorothy."

The grown-ups, now huddled together at the counter, paid no attention to what the girls were doing. Mrs. Mulroney spoke in a soft confidential tone, "Wait 'til you hear about the goings-on at the Burke's last night 'til after two in the morning. And it went on 'til the patrol car came and put a stop to it." Then her voice dropped to a murmur. The adults, deeply engrossed in her story, didn't notice that the girls had now begun running in and out the swinging screen door.

But that was not adventurous enough for Meg. Boldly, she began running up and down the three steps to the flooded sidewalk.

"Come on, Dorothy, don't be a sissy," Meg urged.

Reluctantly, Dorothy followed Meg's lead. They held their faces up with their mouths open to catch the heavy rain that now began falling. They splashed their feet in the deep water on the sidewalk, soaking each other and laughing.

With each trip down the stairs, Meg became more reckless. In a daredevil move, she left the safety of the sidewalk and ran a short distance out to the flooded street. Instantly, she disappeared in a swirling vortex of water.

A few seconds passed before Dorothy fully realized that Meg had actually disappeared. When the reality hit her, she raced up the stairs into the store screaming hysterically, "Meg's gone! She drowned in the street!"

Looks of disbelief passed between the adults as they raced out of the store and down the steps. Meg was nowhere in sight. Terror covered their faces. Their eyes frantically searched the street now being flooded by a torrential downpour.

"Jesus, Mary and Joseph, the sewer!" Bill cried, pointing to the sewer cover lying under water near the steps. He splashed rapidly toward the telltale swirling water flowing into the open manhole. He looked down and screamed when he saw Meg's head bobbing in the deep water. "Oh, Holy Christ she's been swept into the sewer! She's down there, Ma!" Oh, dear God, don't let her drown, he prayed. Her hands were clinging to the rungs of the rusty metal ladder mounted on the sewer wall. Bill's first impulse was to jump into the narrow hole, but he was afraid his large body would crush Meg. He hollered down, "Hang on tight, darlin, Daddy'll get you out."

Meg, frozen in terror, looked up at the sound of his voice, and thought with relief, My Daddy will save me. I just have to hold on tight. But panic seized her when her nose and mouth suddenly filled with fetid water.

Because it hadn't rained for several hours prior to the current downpour, the level of sewerage and water had gone down about four feet. Yet now, with the force of the heavy incoming rain, it was rising quickly and Meg's head soon would be under water.

Meg kept reliving the moment when her feet suddenly went out from under her, and she fell downward into the deep water. Although it seemed like forever to her, within seconds her head shot up out of the water. It was at that very moment that she saw the rusted rungs of the ladder and grabbed at them. Am I dreaming?, she thought. But the heavy rain pouring over her made her realize it was not a dream.

While continuously calling down words of encouragement to Meg, the three grown-ups, kneeling in the flooded street and looking into the sewer, tried to think of how they could save her.

Bill stretched out flat on the flooded street and lowered his head and shoulders into the hole as far as he could go without toppling in.

His mother and Mrs. Mulroney held his legs tightly. The volume of the rain increased.

Bill stretched his hands in as far as he could.

Meg reached up to him with one hand. Their fingertips were just inches apart.

"Be brave honey; hang on!" Bill urged. He jerked his head out of the hole and yelled to Mrs. Mulroney, who stood helplessly by. "Quick! Call the fire department from the phone in the back of the store." He looked at his mother. "Ma, start praying hard, I've gotta go down the ladder. I don't have a choice."

"No! Bill, it's too rusty. It'll break from the wall with yer weight. Can't yer see that! Meg'll drown fer sure. Bill, listen to me. Let's try to talk her up the ladder."

Both Bill, and his mother, a diminutive sixty-year-old woman, lay out flat in the flooded street and put their heads into the sewer. Their bodies were now almost submerged in water.

Meg's pathetic face looked up at them, and she wailed, "Get me out, Daddy. Hurry!"

Nana leaned farther into the sewer and yelled to Meg in a crisp tone, "I thought yer were me brave little girl. I never knew yer to be a sissy before. Feel around with yer feet and see if yer can find some more rungs of the ladder that yer can put yer feet on and then yer can climb right up."

Meg was exhausted and on the verge of giving up, but her Nana's voice gave her courage. Her hands, cut and stinging from her frozen grip on the rusty ladder rung couldn't hold on much longer.

They could see she was slowly swinging her legs in search of the rungs.

"That's it darlin!" Nana yelled excitedly.

Bill coaxed, "See, there's some rungs above you and more below you. Come'on, darlin, you'll find them!"

Nana again stretched out her small body in the swift-flowing water and stuck her head and shoulders into the sewer while Bill held her tightly. "Now yer listen to me Meghan O'Meara. We can't come down because the ladder won't hold us. We're too heavy! Yer have to climb up!" She tried another tactic. "Glory be to God, darlin, I can see yer good fairies all about yer now. They'll help you up!"

Meg looked around. "Where?" she sobbed.

"I see them, too, darlin!" Bill yelled excitedly. "Come'on now, they'll come up the ladder behind you. Hurry! Find the ladder rungs with your feet and start climbing."

They could see her feet fumbling to find the rungs. Her body twisted, and she whimpered, "I found a rung."

"Ah, that's my girl!" Bill yelled. "Now get both feet on it."

When they saw her body straighten, they knew she had both feet on the rung.

"Now comes the easy part!" Nana said with great exuberance. "And, because yer Irish, you'll make yer way up here without a bit of trouble. Ain't it so, Bill? The Irish never give up, do they?"

"That's for sure. Now Meg, all you have to do is to hold on tight with one hand and reach the other hand up to the next rung. One hand after the other."

Meg turned her head and looked down behind her. "I can't see my good fairies," she sobbed.

Nana responded quickly, "Oh, child, they're there, believe me. Yer can't see em because they're under the water pushing yer up."

Meg moved her hands so slowly that Bill and Nana were frightened that she might pass out. Her face was white with fear.

In a compelling voice, Nana ordered, "Hurry now! Climb! Help the fairies. They're only wee, yer know. We can see they're trying to push yer up."

Meg reacted. She brought her other hand up to the next rung and moved her feet up.

Bill stretched his hands down to hers. "I've got her!" he cried, grasping her tiny hands tightly. His perilous position caused his upper body to teeter dangerously on the edge of the sewer rim.

Nana realized that the sudden thrust of Meg's body was pulling him into the sewer. She laid herself across his legs. Their bodies were completely under water.

At that very moment, the Wonder Bread delivery truck, about to pull up in front of the store, stopped suddenly.

"Oh, my God! Look!", the driver yelled to his helper, "Isn't that two drowned bodies laying under water in the street?" The men jumped out of the truck and raced towards the bodies just as Nana lifted her head up out of the water to catch her breath.

"Help!" she screamed when she saw the men and frantically pointed to Bill's body, which was now slowly slipping into the sewer.

The two men grabbed Bill's legs, just in time to stop his downward slide.

"My little granddaughter fell into the sewer and it's me son trying to pull her out."

"Holy Mother of God!" the man shrieked. With all their might, they slowly dragged Bill, now holding Meg's hands, out of the sewer and up to the flooded surface of the street.

Gathering Meg's limp body into his arms, Bill rushed into the store, followed by the deliveryman who put a bracing arm around Nana and led her up the slippery stairs.

Pandemonium filled the store. Mrs. Mulroney, sobbed uncontrollably, and ranted hysterically at Dorothy, "See what happens when children don't obey! Look at poor Meg laying there dead."

Nana, now cradling her semi-conscious granddaughter in her arms and wiping the slime off Meg's face with her soaking wet apron, shot a fierce look at Mrs. Mulroney and snarled, "Shut up!"

The humid air in the store mingled with the sewer stench and brought bile to everyone's mouths.

Bill took Meg from Nana's arms. He peeled off her grimy raincoat, and laid her on her stomach. Putting his hands on her back, he pressed in and out. Within a minute, a gurgling sound came from Meg's mouth, and she regurgitated a thick flow of dark brown slime. Slowly, her eyes opened and she screamed, "Mama!"

Everyone cheered. "She's alive," Bill shouted and grinned broadly as tears streamed down his face. He picked up Meg, shook the deliveryman's hand and then put his arm around his mother, hugging her close to him. The bells of the ambulance sounded in the distance.

Meg's pretty flowered dress was beyond recognition. Her slime-caked legs and arms shivered as she laid across Bill's shoulder. "I feel sick, Daddy. I want to go home. Where are my fairies?" she moaned pathetically.

Nana replied quickly, "The little ones have gone back to their secret place, honey, and we'll go home soon. All you need is a good tubbing and..." She whispered in Bill's ear, "...a good dose of castor oil."

The ambulance driver and his helper rushed into the store. Meg looked up at them in fright and buried her head in her father's chest.

Bill sat her on his knee, and the two men knelt by her side and talked softly, reassuring her that she was going to be fine. They examined her and wrapped her in blankets.

The ambulance attendant whispered to Bill, "I think we better take her to the hospital and let a doctor look at those cuts on her hands." When they learned how the rescue was accomplished, they praised Bill, Nana and the bread men for their quick action and bravery. They gently laid Meg on a stretcher. Bill held one hand and Nana the other. The ambulance driver said to Meg as they carried her out of the store, "Meghan O'Meara, you're one of the spunkiest kids I've ever seen. Bet you'll never be afraid of anything again in your life after this adventure, huh?"

Meg smiled weakly at him and glanced at her Nana who gave her a wink and their secret nod of agreement.

ø * ℺

Meg's rescue made the front page of the *Cambridge Chronicle*. Bill and Nana became local heroes to everyone except Meg's mother, Margaret, who was furious at them for not taking better care of Meg. She was plagued for weeks with nightmares.

The O'Meara's family and friends attributed the rescue to good luck that had followed Meg ever since her unusual stroke of midnight birth, between September the 11th and 12th, 1925. It was recorded in the hospital as a midnight birth. The church recorded the birth as taking place on the 11th and the city recorded it on the 12th.

According to an ancient Irish legend, the small people, the fairies, are in attendance at midnight births, filling the newborn with either good or evil and casting their magic powers on the infant for life. In Meg's case, everyone was sure she was filled with good, for she announced her arrival with a healthy howl, had all her fingers and toes, lots of curly blond hair, green eyes that seemed to twinkle and rosy cheeks. She was the answer to her parents' prayers, for Margaret had miscarried a baby girl six months after their son Joseph was born.

ø * ℺

A few weeks after the sewer event, Margaret O'Meara, still fretting about Meg's near drowning, made an appointment with Bridget

McGinty, the tea leaf reader. She needed reassurance that Meg was filled with "good" at birth and not "evil."

The tea reader served the tea in a garishly painted cup. Margaret and Meg took turns sipping and when it was gone, Bridget McGinty put one hand on Meg's head, and with the other, turned the cup upside down in a saucer and spun it around three times, then righted it.

"Now, Meg," Bridget said solemnly, "I'm going to tell yer all about what kind of luck the fairies gave yer at birth and what life holds for yer in the future."

Meg was fascinated. Bridget looked steadily into the cup, then a startled look covered her face. "Glory be to God, there it is right off. I can see without a doubt yer a child who was filled by good fairies at birth."

Meg smiled broadly at her mother and the tea reader. "Can I see the good fairies?"

The tea reader ignored her. "No wonder yer didn't drown, child. The truth of the matter is right there in the cup, Margaret. See! See the figure of a girl? That would be yer Meg!"

Margaret and Meg were only allowed a quick glimpse inside the cup at the scattered tea leaves clinging to the sides before Bridget pulled it back.

"I didn't see me. Can I look again, please?" Meg begged.

Bridget ignored her. "Well look at her! Like she's flying happy as a bird. That means she'll travel." She again flashed the cup by their faces.

Once more, Meg and her mother tried to look inside the cup.

"Oh, and look at the stars, a good sign!" Again the cup passed in front of them swiftly while the reader pointed to scattered tea leaves around the top of the cup. "That means good health and happiness, Meg. Oh, Jaysus, Mary and Joseph, will yer look at the way the leaves have piled up on the bottom of the cup? Means they'll be excitement piled on top of excitement all her life." Raising her eyes skyward, then looking back down at Margaret, she said in an ominous voice while jerking her thumb towards Meg, "Oh, brace yerself, dearie. This one will drive yer wild 'til she's off on her own. She'll be different than most for sure. She'll have no fear of saying what she thinks. You'll find that out. Maybe she was born ahead of her time. Not at all like yer pride and joy, Joey, who's always so quiet and well behaved."

Meg frowned at Bridget McGinty, then looked at her mother.

Margaret was miffed. She put her arm around Meg. "Meg's my pride and joy, too, and I'm sure she'll grow up to be a very special young lady." She handed Bridget one dollar, stood up, took Meg's hand and left.

TWO

*M*eg and her brother Joey were as different as a brother and sister could be. At seven, Joey was quiet and thoughtful, whereas Meg, at four, couldn't sit still a minute and continuously sought attention. While she was fair like her mother, Joey had inherited his father's dark skin tone and blue eyes. Although Meg was too young to play neighborhood games, Joey often included her in spite of the fact that the other boys teased.

Meg adored him.

✄ * ✄

Athens Street in Kerry Corner where the O'Mearas lived was an Irish area in St. Paul's parish off Harvard Square. They had a cold water flat on the second floor of a three-family tenement. In 1929, Cambridge was a bustling cosmopolitan city accentuated by Harvard and MIT, alma maters of famous statesmen and Nobel Prize laureates. But strong lines that were fixed and rigid had been drawn between "town" and "gown" long ago. The academic community and wealthy Brahmins lived in ivy-covered dormitories along the Charles River and in stately homes around Harvard Square. The less affluent ethnic groups like the Irish, lived in their own enclaves.

Meg and Joey, second generation Irish, were often reminded by their father how special they were, "You're Irish, you're Catholic and you're an O'Meara; you couldn't ask for more! We know we're descended from the kings of Ireland, because there are so many O'Meara castles in the old country. Now, can you get any ritzier than that?"

Then following their father's lead, they'd stick their thumbs under their armpits, put their noses up in the air and strut around the room saying, "Aren't we grand?" in uppity voices.

The children believed the royal tale because Nana always promised, "I'll take yer both back to Ireland, and we'll visit our castle... when me ship comes in, that is."

When they were older Meg and Joey learned that most Irishmen of their parents' generation claimed to have royal heritage. It helped sustain their Irish pride.

✝ * ✝

The O'Meara's Irish ancestors' immigration to America began in the middle 1800s along with hundreds of thousands of other poor Irish families who were starving because of the potato famine. Bill's parents, Joseph and Mary O'Meara, were from County Clare. Margaret's parents, Tom and Delia Sullivan, were from the Cladagh district, on the shores of Galway Bay. Both families emigrated in search of better lives in America, where they were told, "the streets are lined with gold."

No royal yacht brought them to their new homeland. Their voyage began by steamer from Cork to Liverpool where they waited in shabby boarding houses until they found an emigrant packet ship. These ships, often referred to as "coffin ships," carried both cargo and as many as a thousand passengers in steerage class.

Living conditions during the twenty-five to thirty days at sea were close to inhumane. Bunks, three-tiers high, used up almost every inch of the lower deck space. There was no privacy and very little room to move around.

Within a short time, the atmosphere was stifling as the passenger's food supplies became rancid and maggot-ridden. Because of the shortage of water, personal hygiene was non-existent, and the stench that was created, mixed with the rotting food, made conditions insufferable.

It was a joyous occasion when passengers were allowed up on deck for a breath of fresh air. Unfortunately, this didn't happen often, because the North Atlantic seas were seldom calm.

Jammed as they were below decks, with crying children and sick and wailing elderly passengers, tempers often got out of control. Fighting, a familiar pastime of the Irish, was an everyday occurrence.

But, in spite of all the hardships, most survived and arrived in Boston with a few shillings and all their worldly possessions tied up in a large bundle.

Within a decade, both the O'Mearas and Sullivans had large families. Thomas and Mary O'Meara had five children: James, Daniel, Joseph, William and Mae. Bartholomew and Bridget Sullivan had six children: Thomas, Joseph, Grace, Nell, Margaret and Bartholomew.

Bill's mother, Mary, was the only surviving grandparent that Meg and Joey ever knew.

⚘ * ⚘

Meg loved the attention Nana lavished on her, and spent almost every day at her house, which was next door. Her Nana's sweet round face was creased with deep cheek dimples. She wore dentures, but they were out more than in. She brushed her gray hair neatly into a pug that was held in place with tortoise shell hairpins. Her freshly laundered house dresses were always protected by a full apron. Meg loved to watch Nana when she took her "elixir." In the pocket of her apron, she always carried a small, wrinkled, brown paper bag. Two or three times a day, she'd put her thumb and index finger in the bag, bring out a pinch of brown powder, hold it under her nostrils, then sniff. Meg would hop up on Nana's lap and deeply inhale the peppermint aroma while Nana sneezed.

Nana would laugh and say, "I'll save yer some snuff fer when yer a grown up, darlin, but I doubt yer'll be needing it. Yer won't have any problem with yer nerves, I'll bet."

⚘ * ⚘

In less than a month after the sewer incident, Meg and Nana encountered another frightening situation while walking down Cowperthwaite Street near the Charles River. At a bend in the road, they saw the ragman's horse lying in the street thrashing violently and whining. The ragman was cursing and tugging at the leather harness to release the horse from the wagon.

"Glory be to God, what's the matter with Sam's horse?" Nana cried in alarm.

"Nana, I'm scared!" Meg whined, watching the horse turning and twisting wildly on the street.

Neighborhood men were running to help. One called out to the bystanders loudly, "Sam's horse broke her leg. You ladies stand back. Hang on, Sam, O'Hara's coming with a strong rope!"

O'Hara appeared around the corner running fast. "I'll loop the rope over that metal bar up on the light pole." It took three tosses before he was successful. Then he shimmied the rope until the two ends came back down. He quickly made a noose on one end and put it over the thrashing horse's neck.

Nana and Meg stood mesmerized on the sidewalk. "What are the men going to do, Nana? Are they going to hurt Rosebud?"

"Well, darlin, she's broken her leg and when a horse breaks her leg, it's all over fer her."

What does that mean? Meg wondered, clinging tightly to Nana's legs. She wanted to look away but felt compelled to watch.

A burly man grabbed the other end of the rope and signaled the male bystanders to form a line behind him. With a commanding voice he ordered, "Now men, when I say three, pull hard! We have to do the hanging quickly, or the old nag's gonna die a slow, painful death. Ready, one, two, three." When the men lifted the horse off the ground, the terrified horse's eyes bulged out, and her mouth spread wide open in a ghastly grin and her tongue hung out. Within seconds, the horse was suspended fifteen feet off the ground.

The ragman quickly pushed his wagon under the limp horse, and the men slowly lowered the strangled animal into the rag-filled wagon. The horse's foam-covered mouth emitted one final whinny, her body shuddered, then she was still.

Sam's voice cracked as he said, "I'll have to get another horse and wagon to take old Rosebud to the slaughterhouse."

Meg's heart pounded with fear; now a familiar sensation. She knew nothing about hanging, but she knew that once the men hung the horse up on the pole, Rosebud seemed to be asleep. That the men chose death by "hanging" as a solution to end the horse's agony, did not occur to her.

Sam, the ragman, gave a robust slap on the horse's rump, tipped his cap and said in a muffled voice, "So long, old Rosebud. You were a good old gal."

Something in the tone of Sam's voice and the way he looked at the scrawny nag with tears in his eyes, made Meg sad again. She looked to Nana for reassurance but saw that she too was crying and biting her lower lip. The lump that had been building in Meg's throat exploded. She burst out crying, burying her face in Nana's skirt. "Oh, Nana, poor old Rosebud. Is she...dead?"

Nana wiped her eyes with her hanky. "Now, child, don't be sad. They had to hang her. Poor old thing is at peace in horse heaven, and she didn't suffer too long, now did she? That's the way I want to go." Then, switching her voice from a consoling tone to a matter-of-fact pitch, she knelt in front of Meg and held her hands. "It would be cruel, darlin, to let her lie there in agony while someone went to town to fetch a policeman to shoot her. When I was a little girl in the old country, I learned when I was just about yer age that when a horse breaks his leg, yer have to hang 'em or shoot 'em quick, 'cause they can't live with a broken leg."

Meg relieved her anxiety by envisioning Rosebud with a smile on her face racing through a heavenly field of roses. She usually imitated everything her Nana did, so now she decided to try to be brave and stop crying.

Later that evening, after Meg was asleep, Nana was chastised by Bill and Margaret for allowing Meg to witness such a gruesome event.

"How could you have let little Meg see something so frightful?" Margaret cried.

Nana responded to the tongue lashing with, "Gotta learn sometime that yer can't last forever. Good thing for the child to learn about death from a dead horse instead of a human."

Bill looked at his mother and shook his head slowly, "Well, I guess there's some wisdom in what you say, Ma, but..."

Margaret gave him a dirty look. "First she lets Meg almost drown in a sewer and now she let's her see a horse being hung! What next?"

ɒ * ɒ

In the autumn of 1929, Bill gave up his job at the Athens Street corner grocery store because he was offered a much better job as the manager of a First National store on Huron Avenue, a "lace curtain Irish" area of Cambridge. To be close to his work, the O'Mearas had to move from Kerry Corner. They rented a three bedroom flat on the top floor of a triple-decker on Grandville Road, which was close to the trolley line that went to Harvard Square. They now were in St. Peter's parish.

Meg missed her Nana and begged her Mom to let her go and stay with Nana for a few days.

Nana didn't let on how much she missed Meg, but she was very lonely. Bill talked Margaret into letting Meg go for a visit with his mother. But Margaret warned Nana that she'd never see Meg again if she involved her in any dangerous situation.

When Meg arrived, Nana hugged her tightly and cried. "Oh, how I've missed yer, darling."

Bill said, "I've got to get right back to the store, Mom. Now remember, no adventures."

Nana and Meg looked at each other and grinned.

Bill shook his head and said, "You two make a peach of a pair."

After he left, Nana said, "I've got some tea on for us. Sit down, darlin and tell me all about yer new house in that fancy 'lace curtain Irish' neighborhood?"

"What's lace curtain Irish mean, Nana?"

"Well, darlin, I'll tell yer. Long ago in the old country, before we lost everythin' in the potato famine and came to America, we all had lace curtains, especially in the parlor windows that faced the street. Lace curtains were the tradition, yer know. Everyone who had any sense of pride had them; always starched and white as snow they were."

"Are your parlor curtains lace?"

"Yer bet they are, darlin. When times got better here, it was the first thing I bought to keep the tradition, yer know."

Meg nodded as if she understood. "You like things pretty, don't you, Nana?"

"That I do, darlin. Look at this pretty dress I'm making fer yer doll. Would yer like me to put a little lace on the collar?"

"Oh, it would look beautiful, Nana!"

"Find a pretty little button in me old box I brought from the old country."

Meg loved exploring through the tin box that held hundreds of buttons in different colors and sizes.

Nana picked up her flat iron from the coal stove, spit on her finger and touched it to the hot iron. It sizzled. She began to iron a wrinkled piece of lace when suddenly she moaned, and fell to the floor.

Meg jumped down from the chair and ran to where Nana lay, yelling, "Nana, Nana!" Nana's eyes were open and staring intently. Meg shook Nana's shoulders with both hands. "What's the matter, Nana? Can't you talk?" Chills ran through Meg when Nana didn't respond. Meg felt Nana's forehead the way her Mom did when she was sick. It was cold. She stood up, frightened. Tears filled her eyes. She knew something was seriously wrong with her Nana. "I'll go find a grown-up to help you, Nana. Don't be afraid, I'll come right back." She leaned down and quickly kissed Nana's forehead; it felt strange. Panic seized her and tears streamed down her cheeks. She ran out the screen door to the front veranda. She looked up and down the street screaming, "Help me, someone help me! My Nana is sick and can't talk."

A couple walking on the other side of the street heard Meg's frightened pleas and hurried across to her. They followed her into the house. The man knelt besides the lifeless body on the floor and put his head to Nana's heart. He closed Nana's eyes, looked up at his wife and shook his head.

Meg was confused. "Leave her eyes open! Why are you shaking your head "no"? My Nana's going to be okay in a minute. I think she's just tired from making my doll's dress. I want my Daddy!" Meg burst into tears and lunged at the man, hitting him with her little fists. She sensed that something was seriously wrong with Nana.

The woman put her arm around Meg's shoulder and spoke soothingly, leading her into the parlor. "Honey, my husband will get help and your daddy. Just sit here with me 'til he gets back," she whispered. The ominous tone of her voice sent shivers down Meg's back, and she broke from the woman's hold and ran towards the kitchen yelling defiantly, "I want to see if my Nana is better. I want to stay with her, not you."

The woman ran after her. "No! Wait, dear," she pleaded.

Meg stopped abruptly when she reached the kitchen door.

Nana's whole body was covered with the man's coat.

The woman put her hands on Meg's shoulders and tried to turn her around.

Meg resisted and screamed, "Why did he put his coat over my Nana and cover her face? I want my Nana to wake up. Please, please wake up, Nana....Nanaaaaa!" She was hysterical, but something inside her kept her from going any closer to Nana's silent body, and she returned with the woman to the parlor where she sat stoically.

It was almost half an hour before a police car screeched to a halt outside, and Bill flew into the kitchen. He tore off the coat covering his mother. He looked down at her and fell to his knees. Grabbing his mother's stiff body into his arms he cried, "Oh, sweet Jesus! Not my Ma! Not my Ma, please dear God," he begged.

Meg ran to the kitchen when she heard her father's voice. He was crying so loud. He was always so brave. The ray of hope she still held that her Nana would be all right now faded. She knew, somehow, that her sweet Nana was dead. She didn't look dead, just asleep like Rosebud. But Meg now knew the truth.

                      ø * &

Nana was waked in the O'Meara's front parlor. Joe went to Meg's side each time she climbed up on the kneeling step and softly ran her hand over the satin lining of the casket and looked lovingly at her Nana's lifeless face.

"Meg, let's say goodbye to Nana now, because Aunt Grace is going to take us to her house for a couple of days."

"I wish Nana could open her eyes and see all the beautiful flowers people sent to her." Meg said forlornly. And before anyone could stop her, she leaned into the casket and kissed her Nana's cheek and said, "Bye, Nana. I love you."

Joe put his arm around her and led her out of the room. "Mom says that a big black car will take Nana and all the flowers to the cemetery where Nana's husband and all her other children who died are buried. She says Nana will like being with her family again."

Meg accepted that happy news but wished so much that her Nana was still alive. Something about Nana's death puzzled her. She had been told that Nana died from a shock, and that was all. She never got a satisfactory answer when she questioned her mother. "Nana was using her flat iron that she heated on the stove, not an electric iron like you use. So how could Nana get a shock if there wasn't an electric cord on her iron?"

Her mother always gave her the same answer, "It was a different kind of shock. I've told you that a hundred times. Now she's an angel in heaven, just say a prayer to her."

THREE

$\mathcal{E}$very Sunday afternoon, Bill and Joey wheeled Meg in her wicker stroller up the hill to the corner of Huron and Concord Avenues. Meg loved these walks because they all dressed up in their Sunday clothes.

When they started out from home, Bill always asked them, "How do you think we look, kiddos?"

"Like a million dollars!" they'd answer in unison.

The O'Mearas were happy in their new neighborhood. Bill seemed to know everyone, because most of the people they passed were customers at his store. He'd tip his hat to all the ladies, even those he didn't know. Some would nod, but others would flutter their eyelashes or blush. Bill O'Meara was an exceptionally good-looking man, full chested with a soldier's bearing. His crooked smile was captivating, and made more so, because he had inherited the deep dimples of his departed mother. His thick black hair, neatly parted in the middle and brushed back, had an unmanageable cowlick on the left side that always fell across his forehead. Margaret teased him about it, claiming he created it on purpose to look like a "dandy."

Reaching their destination, Fitz's Drug Store, Bill parked the stroller, put on the brake and told Joe, "Stay with Meg 'til I get back with your surprises. It'll take me a few minutes to pick out just the right things."

He'd return promptly in five minutes, holding his hands behind his back, and asking, "Which hand has the surprise?" Whether they picked the left or right, they always won. But before they could have the little brown bags of candy, Bill pinched their cheeks and made them promise, with a "cross your heart and hope to die," not to tell their mother about stopping at Fitz's Drug Store. The children loved this Sunday ritual although they wondered why their Dad's breath smelled funny when he came out of Fitz's. Meg and Joe whispered about it secretly, because now they began to smell it more often, especially when he was late getting home from work. Their mother called the smell, "that damn bootlegged beer." She claimed it was illegally smuggled in from Canada. Joe found out from friends that Fitz, the druggist, and others, sold it in the back rooms of their store.

❧ * ❧

Within the next few months, the O'Mearas lives began to change dramatically. Times were getting tough for everyone because the nation's economy was heading towards an all time low while unemployment was nearing an all time high.

Margaret cried often, and Bill drank more than usual. They fought constantly over trivial things. Usually after the children were in bed, they'd hear their parents arguing loudly.

Bill had heard rumors that his store might be closed. He worried that he'd never find another job.

When Bill came in the door at night, Margaret always asked, "Any news today, Bill? Did you hear from the district manager?"

When the black day came, Margaret didn't have to ask; the answer was on Bill's tormented face, and he was drunk.

He tried to say something, but he was so despondent he just sat down at the kitchen table, pounded his fists and buried his head in his arms. His body convulsed with sobs.

Stunned, Joe and Meg began crying and wrapped their arms around their father. They hated to see him cry. He was always so strong and brave.

In a choked voice, Joe said, "Dad, we love you even if you don't have a job."

Meg, ever the optimist, sobbed, "I betcha he'll get another job tomorrow."

Margaret motioned the children to leave.

Reluctantly, Joe led Meg out of the kitchen and shut the door. They sat on the stairs in the hallway just outside the kitchen door and heard their mother trying to console their father. Joe sobbed quietly. A strange hollow feeling filled Meg, and she cuddled up to Joe.

"You see, Meg, Dad's real worried because we won't have any money to buy food and things."

"I can give Dad the fifty cent piece that Uncle Bert gave me. Maybe that will make him feel better."

Joe put his arm around her shoulder. "You're a good kid, Meg." Joe led Meg outdoors, away from the sad sounds.

ᘍ * ᘗ

From that day on, the word "depression" dominated everyone's conversation. It was a grim time for the O'Mearas and millions of Americans. No jobs were available, and overnight the O'Mearas joined the ranks of the poor.

Some Sundays, following Mass at St. Peter's Church, children from the now over-crowded Catholic orphanages were lined up at the back of the church, hopeful that a family might take them in. Some came from homes whose parents could no longer afford to feed them, while others had been deserted. Their parents just walked away from them. Each Sunday a few were taken in by parishioners until the depression was over. Only a few were adopted.

Meg always looked with pity at the shabbily dressed children and was frightened by the thought that her parents might have to put Joey and her in the back of the church. She prayed every night it wouldn't happen.

Lately now, once or twice a week, other victims of the depression knocked on the O'Meara's door. The shabbily-dressed foul-smelling men were looking for a handout of food and shelter. These homeless, out of work, hungry men were called "bums" in the east, "tramps" in middle America and "hoboes" and "okies" out west. They shared a common state of destitution, but unlike Bill O'Meara and millions of others looking for work in their own area, these discouraged men had deserted their families and took to the road to find work.

"Don't ever turn those poor souls out, Margaret," Bill strongly cautioned her. "Because there but for the grace of God go I."

Margaret, frightened by the bums, was reluctant to share what little they had. Sarcastically, she'd comment, "And there, but for the generosity of my sister, Grace and her husband, Frank, we'd be starving, too. Her fright at their new state of destitution seriously depressed her.

Charity from her sister caused many arguments in the O'Meara's house. It hurt Bill's pride deeply to take assistance, even from a relative, although they couldn't have survived without it.

The chore of giving the bums handouts of food when Bill or Joe were not at home became Meg's job. When one knocked on their door, Margaret opened it a crack and told the bum, "Go down to the bottom of the cellar stairs, and I'll send a plate of food down with my little girl." She would then lead Meg with a dish of warm food to the top of the cellar stairs and yell down, "You-who, here comes your food. Meet my child at the top of the stairs where I can see you, and she'll hand you the food and come right back up to me." This way she could protect Meg in the event the bum was a bad one. Occasionally, there were troublemakers.

One day Margaret feared that a bum was about to hurt Meg, because when he took the food, he put his hand under Meg's chin first, then placed it on her shoulder.

Margaret screamed, "Take your filthy hands off my child! Meg, quick, run up the stairs!"

The poor man was shocked. He tried to apologize and mumbled, "It's just that she reminds me of my little daughter. I haven't seen her for so long." He ran out of the cellar with the plate of food and disappeared.

Meg wasn't frightened. She had no fear of the dirty men. Most of them were so thankful for the food, they'd gobble it up the moment she handed them the plate. Many said, "God bless you, little girl." It made her feel good to help them, they looked so sad. She remembered that her Nana always told her to help people in trouble.

♌ * ♌

Most every evening now, Bill went to their locked, private cellar room. Whenever Margaret asked what he was doing down there, he'd answer curtly, "It's none of your business." The sarcastic statement hurt her feelings, but she never pushed to know more. If she did, Bill got angry and yelled at her. Sometimes their arguments were so loud, the people on the floor below banged on the steam pipes to quiet them down. These daily clashes began to frighten Joe and Meg. Now they'd hide under their beds until it was over.

One evening after "Amos and Andy," Bill told Joe and Meg to come down the cellar with him. The children looked to their mother for permission. Margaret hesitated just a moment, shrugged, then nodded at them to go. Maybe now she might find out what he did down there. She suspected it had something to do with beer, but she couldn't prove it. She would never go down there now. A bum could be sleeping there.

When Bill unlocked the door to their section, he turned to the kids, "I want you both to promise not to say a word to your mother or anyone else about my project down here. Understood? If you disobey, I'll never let you help me again."

They nodded their heads and tried to see beyond him when he turned on the overhead light. The smell of beer was overpowering. Wooden boxes filled with brown bottles were stacked in the corner, and a huge crock stood in the middle of the room.

"Are you making beer, Dad?" Joe asked, an embarrassed grin covering his face."

"I sure am, son, and I don't have to tell either of you kids what your Mom would say if she knew about it."

"Boy, she'd be mad at you, Dad!" Meg said, thinking about all the times she heard her mother yelling at him for drinking too much. "I'll never squeal, Dad!"

Bill put his hands on his hips and looked down at the kids. "Beer is a magical brew that makes me feel better, what with my job gone and all. And because of the Prohibition law, you can't buy it in stores anymore. So, I'm making a little money by selling it. See that crock? Well it's filled with hops, yeast, malt, and water, and it's been brewing for a long time, and I think it's ready to be bottled. But I needed a couple of smart kiddos like you two to help me bottle it. So what do you say, are you with me or agin me?"

Joe and Meg both reached out and hugged their Dad, laughed and said, "We're with you!"

"Then let's start bottling."

Meg's job was to stir the pale brown liquid in the large crock with a big wooden stick. White foam rose to the surface.

Joe was in charge of the enema hose. He squeezed one end of the hose tightly until his Dad was ready to siphon the beer from the crock into the bottles.

When Bill said "Ready, aim, fire," Joe placed his end of the hose in a bottle, which he held at an angle, then slightly loosened his hold on the hose so the liquid flowed at a slow rate.

"Remember Joe, the trick is to know when the bottle is filled with beer and not foam, and to shut off the supply quickly so none of it spills."

The kids loved everything about their Dad's project; the smell, the excitement of secretly doing a grown-up job, but most of all, sharing this secret with their Dad.

Joe said, "You're much happier in the cellar than upstairs, aren't you, Dad?"

Bill made a funny face and said, "Ain't that the truth!"

When it was time to cap the bottles, Bill did it alone. He placed a fluted flat cap on the top of the bottle, put it under the capping press, brought the capper handle down with lots of muscle power, and presto, the fluted edges were squeezed securely over the top of the bottle, at least most of the time. Occasionally the caps popped in the night and the explosive noise woke everyone. Most of the neighbors knew what the noise was. They too made beer in their cellars. If they got caught, they'd be arrested and sent to prison. But the extra money they made was worth the risk.

& * &

Cambridge, 1931. Meg was six and in the 1st grade at St. Peter's school. Joe was ten and in the 5th grade when he won a Holy Picture of St. Joseph for a composition he wrote about Meg.

My Sister Meg

She's six years old. She's perpetual motion. She always runs, never walks. She can't sit still for more than a minute. My Mom has timed her. She hates to lose in a game. She's a tomboy and a daredevil. My mother and my Aunt Grace are always trying to make her be more lady-like, but without success. She has the best sense of humor in our family! Her personality is like my father's, but she looks like my mother. She hums like my mother when she's doing her chores. She has blond hair. She only comes up to my shoulder. I like her a lot, but sometimes she's a real pain in the neck.

--Joseph O'Meara, Grade 5

Meg and Joe were very close, and in spite of their state of poverty, they both found small ways to make their parents smile and be proud of them.

ࡄ * ࡄ

There was one small ray of hope on the horizon that might make things better for them. Bill, like thousands of other veterans, waited and counted on the promised World War One Veteran's Bonus to come soon. For years, veterans had pleaded with the government to pay them, but their appeals fell on deaf ears. Then a nationwide veteran's movement, called The Bonus Expeditionary Force, was formed. Veterans from all parts of the country were urged to converge on Washington, D. C. in June to lobby for the bonus. The response was overwhelming. Thousands came by every means of cheap transportation. Some even brought their families. Herbert Hoover's administration viewed the movement with hostility.

Bill desperately wanted to lend his support, but there was no money for the trip until one evening when the O'Mearas were having supper with Margaret's sister, Grace and her husband, Frank Regan. Frank, also a veteran, turned their conversation to the veteran's movement.

"We ought to go, Bill," Frank said. "But I can't get away. How about you going for both of us!" With that, Frank handed Bill twenty-five dollars, saying, "This ought to get you there and back. Those damn...Republicans don't give a...," he paused and looked at the women, "hoot about what's happening in this country."

Bill was both stunned and thrilled at Frank's generosity. Margaret protested the idea vehemently. She was terrified that Bill would get into trouble. But there was no stopping him.

"You have to fight for what you want, Margaret, for what's owed to you, when you deal with an idiot like Hoover," Bill said fiercely.

Frank gave Bill a strong slap on the back. "Atta boy, Bill O'Meara. Go get em!"

They all took the subway into Boston to see Bill off at the bus station. On the way home, Margaret recanted over and over all the reasons why Bill should not have gone: "He'll get into a fight. And, if there is any beer around, he'll probably get drunk and insult some government official. He'll be arrested for sure!" Her litany frightened Meg and Joe.

Trying to pacify her, Joe teased, "Gee, Mom, you make it sound like he's gone off to war.

"My Daddy's brave! He could beat up anyone." Meg bragged.

Margaret glared at her children.

Joey nudged Meg with his elbow and muttered. "Shut up, Meg."

♋ * ♋

When Bill arrived in Washington, he took a bus to the location of the protest. The sight of thousands of veterans and their families stretched along the banks of the Potomac startled Bill. My God! All those men are veterans. And look how many brought their families, too. Tears welled in his eyes, and a fierce sense of pride enveloped him. "God, I'm glad I'm here!" he said out loud.

A man standing close by heard Bill and gave him a left-handed salute, his right arm was missing. "Right you are, buddy! Here, have an American flag."

Bill shook his hand, stuck the small flag in his lapel and asked, "What outfit were you in?"

"The best! The Third Division!"

"Me too!" Bill said, smiling broadly, immediately feeling a warm camaraderie with the man. "Your D.A.V. cap says you're from Cambridge, Ohio. How about that, I'm from Cambridge, Massachusetts. Name's Bill O'Meara."

"Nice to meet ya, Bill. I'm Charlie McNamara, "Mac." Let's walk around and see what's happening."

It was hot and muggy. Ice cream vendors were everywhere. Agitated voices had reached a crescendo. Cars driving by honked in support. Babies cried. Children played. Women fanned their faces. The smell of onions cooking made Bill hungry. Tents and field kitchens had been set up by the Army. Large amounts of food were donated by the District Police Department, many of whom were veterans. Like most of the veterans, Bill and Mac's spirits were high with hope. They were confident the government couldn't refuse them now.

But they were wrong. In spite of their monumental lobbying effort, the Senate voted against the bonus, and many of the disillusioned went home, but not everyone. Close to 10,000 veterans stayed, including Bill and Mac who fell in with a group of other Ohio veterans. Every night in their tent, now called their "foxhole," they drank home brewed beer and rotgut whiskey, singing over and over, "Round on the ends and high in the middle, O-HI-O." The more they drank, the more boisterous they became. The police often had to quiet them down, but overlooked their illegal drinking.

After several days, Hoover became incensed at the brazenness of the veterans, and on July 28th, the Chief of the District Police

Department was ordered by "the highest authority" to move all the protesters out.

Because the Police Department had been so good to them, the veterans slowly started evacuating the grounds. But they didn't leave fast enough to suit the President. General Douglas MacArthur, Chief of Staff of the United States Army, with Major Dwight Eisenhower at his side, marched up Pennsylvania Avenue towards the veterans. They were followed by armed infantry, cavalry, machine guns, tanks and trucks.

This monumental show of force, along with the use of tear gas, bombs and sabers, convinced the veterans to flee the attackers. Discouraged and defeated, they dispersed and went home.

Bill had been given a pint of beer by his friend Mac for the long bus ride home. They promised to keep in touch.

ଢ଼ * ଢ଼

"You look terrible, Bill!" were the first words out of Margaret's mouth when he came through the door. He hadn't shaved for days, his Sunday suit was stained and the brim of his straw hat had a piece missing. Meg and Joey hugged their Dad, relieved that he was safe.

The O'Meara's relatives and neighbors, many of them veterans, wanted to hear Bill's first hand version of what happened. The whole nation had followed the story every day in the newspaper.

A crowd gathered that evening on the first floor veranda of the O'Meara's triple decker. Meg and Joe sat beside their Dad. To them, he was like a returning war hero.

Pale and exhausted, but eager to share the shocking experience, Bill began, "I still can't believe that our government could treat us the way they did. There we were, thousands of brave men who had willingly fought for our country, only asking for what was owed us. The banks of the Potomac were lined with thousands of people, many living in tents with their families. It would break your heart to see how shabbily many of them were dressed. There were so many veterans with only one leg or one arm, and some with no legs in wheel chairs. We waited, hoped and prayed everyday that good news would come. When the bad news came that our appeal was turned down, you could hear the most awful tragic sound of mournful sorrow and disappointment. Thousands of humans crying in despair, hopelessly deserted. It was unimaginable to me that we were forced out of our own capital by our own kind, U.S. soldiers."

Frank Regan asked. "Bill, did the veterans realize that the country was angry at the way you were treated? Hundreds of thousands of sympathizers from every State across the country wrote letters to their Congressmen, rallying to the veterans' support and condemning the President's action."

"Ya, we heard about it. It sure made us feel better. Of course, the worst moment of all was when we saw that General MacArthur arrogantly coming toward us veterans with all those weapons behind him. It's strange, but none of us were afraid at all. We just felt so damn powerless and angry at the brutality of them attacking their own kind: helpless veterans. How could they do that to us? Geeze, just a few short years ago, we fought like hell for our country. We were all willing to give our lives, and now all we wanted was what was coming to us?" Tears ran down Bill's cheeks as he relived that moment. "Oh, we stood up to them though! We all locked arms. My buddy Mac from Ohio only had one. But that tear gas stung our eyes so badly, we were forced to retreat." Bill's voice choked up. He couldn't go on. He got up and walked quickly into the cellar where he got drunk and passed out.

That night when the children were ready for bed, Margaret told them a story about their Dad's heroics in World War I. It was a story they had not heard before. They had seen his medals and knew his arm was badly disfigured in the war, but Bill didn't like to talk about it.

"No man loved his country more than your father, and this Washington experience was more than he could bear. He's bitter now, kids, but he'll be okay in a little while. Your father did more than his share of defending his country. In 1916, he fought with the National Guard in the battle on the Mexican border against Pancho Villa. He was one of the 12,000 troops sent there under the leadership of General John Pershing. In 1917, he enlisted in the Army and served overseas in France. He was seriously gassed while fighting in the front line trenches of the Lorraine sector and was hospitalized. When he recovered, he was right back in the fight. In the battle to save Chateau-Thierry, he was severely wounded. A large piece of his right arm was blown off by shrapnel, and there was doubt his arm could be saved."

Both children looked at each other in horror.

"Fortunately, there was a skilled team of surgeons in a field hospital near the front who grafted skin from his thigh to the section of his arm that had been shattered. He was awarded the Purple Heart. You've seen his terrible scar. Always remember, your Dad was a very brave hero."

ø * ৳

The veterans eventually were avenged when Hoover was not only not re-elected, but became one of the most despised presidents in history.

The O'Meara's spirits were lifted on March 4, 1933, when Franklin D. Roosevelt was inaugurated President of the United States. The President instituted a number of "New Deal" programs to get men back to work. One of the first of these programs was the Public Works Administration. Bill came home one day smiling broadly and calling out to his family in excitement, "Margaret! Kids! Guess what? I applied for a laborer's job and got it! I'll be digging ditches for $900 a year." Margaret was thrilled, but felt sure that the strenuous labor would cause severe pain in Bill's weakened arm, and he might even lose the use of it.

In spite of Bill's steady income, the O'Meara's financial situation was still precarious; they were behind in so many bills. Once a week, Margaret's sister Grace, gave them extra money to buy food and other necessities. Bill kept accurate records of these "handouts" as he called them. "I swear, Margaret, I'll pay back every red cent, although, God knows, Frank Regan doesn't need it! He was damn lucky that his 'spirits' business was never discovered by the authorities and shut down. He'll be a wealthy man now that they've repealed the Prohibition Amendment."

FOUR

*T*he O'Mearas had to move again. Margaret broke the bad news to the children. "The landlord raised our rent, and we have to move. I've found a nice low priced flat on the other side of Huron Avenue, on Oliver Street. It's not as classy as this neighborhood, but it'll be fine."

"Why did our landlord raise our rent, Mom?" Joe asked.

"Everything's going up, Joe," Margaret explained. "Milk went up to 10 cents a quart today. Yesterday, butter was up to 28 cents a pound, bread's five cents a loaf, and potatoes were two cents a pound. Where's it all going to end?" she lamented.

The O'Meara's new neighborhood was quite different from the Irish one on Grandville Road. Although the majority of their new neighbors were Irish, there were several "foreigners," as Margaret described any person who was not Irish. She never thought about the Irish as being "foreigners."

She told the children, "I think our new landlord must be English, with that name, Carver. That must mean they're Protestant. Be nice to them but don't get too friendly with them. They're not our kind."

Meg and Joe were not old enough to understand the parochialism of their parents, especially Margaret, who held it against those who were not Irish. It probably resulted from the years of drilling into each successive Irish generation, the watchword, "pride," pride in being Irish. In the O'Meara's case, they carried their feeling to extremes at times.

Bill would say, "There are only two kinds of people in the world: the Irish and those that wish they were." He often reminisced about the old days with Meg and Joe, repeating stories his mother had told him. "When the first large groups of Irish immigrants came to America in the 1800s, oh, boy, were they hated! I'll show you how they were treated. There's an old sign that's packed away in your Nana's trunk in the cellar. It says, 'Irish need not apply.' It was a stinging way to let the Irish know nobody wanted to hire them."

Joe asked, "You mean they could never get a job?"

"They could never get a good job. They were hired only as servants or coal carriers. But, by 1930, when you kids were little, lots of Irishmen had positions of importance in America. And, that helped to make the rest of us Irishmen look good, until the Depression, that is."

☲ * ☲

The O'Meara's new landlords, Mr. and Mrs. Carver, had three sons and two daughters. Helen, who was Meg's age, became Meg's friend immediately. Joe made friends with Bobby Carver, who also loved baseball, and they practiced together at nearby Raymond Park every day.

Meg, now eight, was allowed to go to the Saturday movie at the Porter Square Theater with neighborhood kids. "Mom, imagine this! For only ten cents today, I saw a cartoon, a serial and two main features. And look, Mom, on our way out, I got this beautiful pink dish for you, for nothing!"

Meg was exuberant about everything and especially so about making her First Communion. Every day she discussed all the wonderful details of her preparation for the sacrament with her new friend, Helen, who was enthralled with the idea.

"Oh, I wish I could receive the body and blood of Jesus Christ in the little magic wafer like you're going to do, Meg. We don't do that at our church, but I wish we did. Then I could wear a white dress and veil like yours," she moaned, again trying on Meg's elaborate net veil.

Meg felt badly that Helen couldn't share this miracle. But she came up with a solution, three weeks after she made her First Communion. "Helen, I have a plan so you can receive communion. Next Sunday, we'll meet in the back yard at eight-fifteen, and we'll go to St. Peter's together. We'll go in the side door just a few minutes before Mass starts. The nuns won't notice us because it's the children's Mass. I'll have to teach you how to genuflect, bless yourself, and how to keep a straight back when kneeling. If you don't kneel up straight, the Nuns will whack you. If anyone asks who you are, I'll tell them you're my cousin from Boston."

Helen was frightened when they entered the church that Sunday morning, but Meg held her hand and kept promising her they wouldn't get caught.

Joe sang in the choir, which was in the back of the church, so Meg knew he couldn't see them. She chose the second pew at the end of the row near the door in case things didn't work out.

At communion time, Meg whispered to Helen, "Follow me and do what I do." They stepped out of the pew, went to the communion rail and knelt. Meg muttered out of the side of her mouth, "Keep your head down until the altar boy puts the gold plate under your chin."

Helen became extremely nervous as the priest drew near. She wanted to run. She whispered, "What if the priest guesses I'm Protestant?"

"Don't worry, you don't look it."

"What if my teeth touch the host by mistake?"

"Don't do that! It'll bleed, I told you."

"Do I have to swallow it whole? What if I choke on it?"

"You won't. It's thin."

Suddenly the altar boy put the gold plate under Helen's chin. She kept her head down but stuck her tongue way out. The priest placed the host on her tongue, and she quickly pulled it inside her mouth, but too frightened to swallow it. She was terrified it might bleed. It slowly melted, and she gulped it down. I'll never do this again! she swore to herself.

When Mass was over, Meg felt a great sense of pride. "I'm so glad you were able to receive communion, Helen. Wasn't it a wonderful feeling?"

Helen stopped short, "No. I don't feel good at all."

Meg put her arm around Helen's shoulder. "I'll tell you what. When we get home, I'll fix you some nice cinnamon toast and tea. You're probably hungry from fasting."

Helen looked at Meg in horror, "Oh, Meg, I forgot to fast!"

Meg looked alarmed. "You ate! Oh my God, that's a sin. Do you feel sick or anything like that?"

Helen quickly felt her forehead and looked down at her body. "No, I think I'm okay. I feel good, honest I do, Meg."

Meg, ever the optimist and quite self-assured at eight, made a logical assumption. "Hummm. God must like you, Helen. I don't think he's going to punish you for not fasting." Meg looked pensive, "But, maybe I should confess what we did, just in case."

"Oh, don't Meg," Helen begged. "You promised never to tell anyone."

"Okay, I won't. Besides, God knows everything anyway, and I don't think he'd mind your receiving communion even if you are Protestant. The nuns are always telling us it's our religious duty to bring converts into the faith."

It was true, the nuns constantly preached that the children of St. Peter's School should strive to be soldiers of Christ and bring converts into Catholicism. Meg sincerely believed that what she had just done was what the nuns wanted her to do, and the slight pangs of conscience she had about it quickly disappeared, but she never confessed it.

Helen never went to church with Meg again, "It made me too nervous, Meg. But I still want to be your friend, Okay?"

"Sure," Meg said in a thoughtful voice. "That is, if you'll run away to Ireland with me."

"Run away to Ireland!" Helen was shocked. "Are you crazy?"

"It will be easy. We'll pack a few clothes and take along some cookies, candy and fruit. That will be enough until we get to Boston where we'll sneak aboard a ship that's going to Ireland."

"You're loony, Meg! How would you know which ship is going there?"

"That's easy, we just walk past ships where people are going on and listen to see if they talk with Irish brogues. If they do, we'll follow them and pretend that we're their kids."

After much pressure from Meg to share this great adventure, Helen reluctantly agreed. But her confidence weakened as the day of their departure drew near.

The day before they were to leave, Meg showed Helen a framed map of Ireland that hung on the O'Meara's living room wall. "See, here's County Clare where my Dad says there are lots of O'Meara castles. We can visit them, or we can go down here, (she moved her finger down to southern Ireland) where my mother's family, the Sullivans, came from."

Meg sounded so confident and knowledgeable, Helen believed that the journey was really possible, but didn't believe the part about capturing a live leprechaun.

"We'll meet at midnight, in the back yard, under the big tree, next Saturday, okay, Helen?"

Helen, still uncertain about the trip, answered a weak, "Okay."

"Don't worry, Helen. Midnight is a good time for us to go. I'll have my 'good luck' that the fairies gave me at my midnight birth."

At midnight, on Saturday night, Meg sat patiently on her small suitcase and shivered from the cold, damp air until one o'clock. Helen never showed up. When she tried to sneak back into her house, her suitcase fell open, and the noise woke her parents.

Bill and Margaret stood in the kitchen looking at Meg in disbelief. Margaret screamed, "You were going to run away to Ireland?"

They were shocked that Meg would try something so bold and dangerous. Bill agreed with Margaret that Meg needed a severe punishment, but he cringed when Margaret put Meg across her knees and spanked her bare bottom soundly.

Meg was screaming when Bill carried her into her bedroom and put her into her bed. "That's enough, Meg. Quiet down now. You'll have the whole neighborhood awake. You know, kiddo, I'm disappointed in you for doing something as foolish as thinking about running away to Ireland. I want a promise that you'll never do anything like that again, or you won't be my pal anymore."

Sobbing quietly now, Meg looked up at her father and choked out, "I'm sorry, Daddy. I just really wanted to see our castles in Ireland. Please still be my pal!"

"Okay, but you're rooted on the veranda for two weeks."

The next morning, Bill and Margaret had to suppress smiles when Meg told them of her elaborate plans to get to Ireland. She never mentioned that Helen was supposed to go with her; Joe had taught her not to be a squealer.

Helen's only excuse was that she didn't wake up until morning. Their friendship cooled considerably after that.

৯ * ৯

When the Kelly family moved in next door, Meg immediately made friends with Barbara, who was in her class at St. Peter's school. Meg thought Barbara was beautiful. She had long curly, reddish brown hair, dimples and the bridge of her nose was spotted with freckles.

Meg pleaded with her mother to allow her to let her hair grow long like Barbara's, but Margaret was emphatic about Meg's hair style.

"Don't fuss with me about it. You're going to keep your Dutch clip. It's more practical and besides, you don't have any curl in your hair." The Dutch clip was short, shingled up the back, and cut into bangs on the forehead. It was the most common hairstyle of the day for children.

Now each day, Barbara and Meg walked arm in arm to school. Barbara, a quiet girl, soon became a loyal fan of Meg's and was always agreeable to whatever Meg suggested, although she was a bit in awe of her new friend and her adventurous spirit.

Joe, who had a part-time job at his Aunt Nell's penny candy store near St. Peter's school, got a better job selling newspapers. Nell offered his job to Meg and Barbara if they promised to obey her strict rules. "I'll teach you how to sell candy and make change. You'll work before school, during the lunch hour and after school, and I'll pay you five cents a day, in candy. If I catch you snitching candy, God help you!" She raised her fist to them, then grinned broadly.

Aunt Nell, unmarried and in her late forties, was the kid's favorite aunt. Meg always wondered why she wasn't married. On their first day of work, she asked her aunt.

"Unfortunately, I'm destined to be an old maid. I had a boyfriend once," she'd told the girls. "But my sister, Grace, felt he wasn't good enough for me and made me break off the romance. She made me give his ring back even!"

Meg sympathized, "Oh, you must have felt so bad, Aunt Nell. Was the ring beautiful?"

"Big, but not beautiful. I think he got it in a Cracker Jack box!" she laughed.

"Did you ever meet another man that Aunt Grace thought was good enough for you?" Barbara asked.

"Nope. But they all looked good enough to me!"

Nell had a wonderful sense of humor and never complained about her dull life. Everyone loved her. Frank Regan, Grace's husband, had bought the candy store for Nell so she could earn a living. She had a room of her own in the Regan's house.

Meg and Barbara loved working at Nell's store, and without too much of a conscience, they tested, as they called it, extra pieces of candy every day.

✍ * ✍

Meg and Barbara became inseparable. Barbara allowed Meg to make all the decisions about what to play, where to go and what to wear.

After seeing many movies, the girls decided to be actresses when they grew up. To practice acting, they wanted to put on shows for the neighborhood kids.

To help them, Aunt Nell promised, "When I change my window displays, I'll give you the faded crepe paper to make costumes and scenery."

The girls were thrilled.

"What made you girls decide to go into show business?" Nell asked.

"We think we'd make good actresses when we grow up." Meg bragged.

"Oh? I thought you already were!" Nell quipped.

The girls found a stage in a deserted garage without doors. No one knew who owned it, and no one seemed to care.

Their biggest show was about Hawaii. About fifteen kids who had paid a penny, sat on the floor watching. Meg was Dick Powell, and Barbara was Ruby Keeler. A blue crepe paper sky and an orange moon was the backdrop. It was a romantic setting, the girls felt. Dick opened the show singing *Night and You and Blue Hawaii* to Ruby. Dick paused and kissed Ruby on the lips, the audience howled with laughter and booed the stars.

Totally embarrassed, Meg and Barbara ran off the stage, out of the garage and to Meg's back yard where they consoled each other while counting the admission receipts with satisfaction.

Their flop did not deter them from continuing in show business. They went on to perform a series of Dick Tracy mysteries that the girls wrote. Their small audiences seemed to enjoy the mysteries more than romantic plays.

❧ * ❧

Meg's adventurous spirit often had her dreaming of far away places, and it made her restless. When she was in this mood, she and Barbara often explored beyond their neighborhood. Leaving their tenement area was like stepping into another world. Walking down Garden Street, they passed beautiful, large brick homes, the Botanical Gardens, Observatory Hill where astronomers worked, and Radcliffe College. They'd always stop at the Cambridge Common to look at the statue of George Washington, erected on the site where he took command of the First Continental Army. Then they'd cut over to

Brattle Street to visit Longfellow's house, which was open to the public. They had been taught his poems in school and recited them as they walked through his home.

On their way home, a few blocks from Harvard Square, they came to a very old gray stone Protestant church, built in 1790 according to a pitted brass sign.

"Let's open the door, Barbara, and see what it looks like inside."

"No, Meg, you know it's a sin to go into a Protestant church. Sister said God would strike us down dead!"

"We'll just open the door and look inside, not go in."

Barbara relented, "Well, okay, but let's just open it a little. What if a Protestant sees us?"

Meg looked around the church yard and saw no one. It took all their strength to pull the big brass ring hard enough to get the door open. They then held it open by bracing their backs against it. The dimly lit cavernous interior was spooky.

"Let's get out of here," Barbara whispered, moving past Meg.

The temptation was too great for Meg. She pushed Barbara forward into the vestibule. Barbara screamed. Her voice reverberated off the walls of the empty church with such a terrifying sound, the girls panicked. They raced from the church, and up the street for a half a mile before they stopped.

Barbara whimpered, "That was God yelling at us, Meg!" Her face was ashen.

"Do you really think so? Are you going to faint?" Meg asked in concern.

"I hate you, Meg O'Meara! You're the meanest person I know. I could have been struck dead for all you care. Don't ever speak to me again." She walked away from Meg.

Meg felt sorry, but following so closely behind Barbara in a single file, she also felt silly. Softly, she began calling out a cadence, "Hup, two, three, four, hup, two, three, four." By the time they reached their street, both girls were giggling hysterically and collapsed on Meg's front steps, the fear of God's punishment forgotten.

ⅆ * ⅈ

Barbara's father, Dick Kelly, had a much better job than Bill O'Meara. He was a driver for the Cambridge Sanitation Department. Bill's favorite joke was, "Dick's a G-Man, a garbage man!" Bill was still working on outdoor projects: digging dirt walls for ice-skating rinks at city parks in the winter and repairing the fairways at municipal golf courses in the summer. Bill and Dick met regularly every night at Paddy's tavern for a few "how do you do's" with the lads, and to enjoy the fellowship of the Irishmen who gathered there regularly. Paddy Fennell, the owner, was everyone's friend. If you didn't have a dime for a brew, he'd run a tab, and you'd pay him when you could.

According to Margaret's orders, Bill was only to spend a dime a day for beer, but on paydays like tonight, he always spent more.

"It's six o'clock and your father isn't home yet, Meg. Go get him."

"Why don't you make Joe go?"

"Because Joe has lots of homework. Look there goes Barbara after her father, I'll bet."

Meg caught up with her. "I hate to go to Paddy's, don't you?" she groaned.

Barbara looked mournful. "I hate it! And tonight I have to try and get the car keys out of my Dad's pocket if he won't leave. My Mom's afraid he might kill someone, driving his machine when he's drunk."

The smell of booze and tobacco overpowered the girls when they opened the front door of the tavern. Men turned to look at who came in. When Paddy spotted the girls, he yelled loudly, "Now watch yer language, me bays. A couple of little darlin's just came in the door."

Men turned from the bar to see if it was their child. Bill spotted Meg and called, "Come over here to the table, Meg darlin."

Barbara's father was also there, along with other men. "Ah! Here's my girl, Barbara," Dick said as he held out his hand to her.

The girls hated it when they had to stand and wait and plead with their fathers to come home.

Meg whispered in her father's ear, "Dad, Mom sent me after you. You're already an hour late for supper. She's mad! I don't want you to get in trouble." Meg was always on her Dad's side even at times like this.

"Well, darlin, I have to finish me pint, don't I. Can't leave it here on the table, or Dick Kelly will be drinking it and get drunk. Oh, what a terrible thing that would be, eh!"

All the men laughed. Bill always talked in a brogue when he had too much to drink.

Barbara's father had put his arm around her waist. When she leaned down to whisper in his ear to come home, she reached into his jacket pocket and got his car keys without him realizing it. Meg saw her do it and smiled slyly.

Standing back from the table, Meg folded her arms across her chest and looked sternly at her father. "Dad, are you coming home or not? I'm leaving right now."

"Okay, honey, I'll just chug-a-lug me beer and we'll hit the road. Come on, Dick, let's all ride home in your machine."

Dick Kelly stood up, tipped his cap to the others at the table and began patting his pockets and pulling the linings out when he couldn't find his keys. "Jesus, I can't find my keys, Bill."

"You probably lef 'em in the car. Let's go, ol' pal." Bill put his arm around Dick's shoulders and they followed the girls outside.

The girls were relieved that their fathers had come so willingly tonight. If they came home without them, they'd be sent back. They hated that humiliation.

The two men searched the car for Dick's keys. Meg and Barbara stood by suppressing giggles until Bill convinced Dick that he must have left them home. Dick couldn't figure out how he did that if the car was at Paddy's, but accepted it. The men supported each other as they staggered home behind their daughters.

FIVE

Cambridge, 1935. Meg had always been intrigued with her non-Irish neighbors who were Swedish, Armenian and French, but she particularly liked the Cardillos, a large Italian family that lived in a big single-family house around the corner. The father, Big Tony, was a handsome heavy-set man, close to seventy years of age. His grape arbor covered a quarter of an acre of the property. In warm weather he'd invite passing neighbors to stop for a glass of homemade wine. Mouth-watering smells of Italian cooking always filled the air near the house.

Often, Meg would stand at the Cardillo's kitchen screen door, inhaling the delicious aromas, and call out, "Hello, Mrs. Cardillo. Your cooking smells wonderful today."

As usual, Mrs. Cardillo, a heavy woman, would waddle over to the door with a large wooden spoon filled with bubbling tomato sauce. "Heya, you little Irish girl. You wanna trya my sauce, huh?"

Meg would slurp the delicious thick liquid and say, "That's the best sauce you've ever made, Mrs. Cardillo! I really mean it!"

"Youa always saya that. Don't cha your mama feed you?"

One day after being given a delicious meatball, Meg told Mrs. Cardillo the truth about her mother's cooking. "My Mom just cooks plain things. We eat the same food on the same day of every week: On Sundays, it's roast beef. Mondays, we eat leftovers from Sunday. Tuesdays it's boiled chicken. Wednesday is liver and bacon day. Thursday, we have corned beef and cabbage. Fridays are fast days, so we have to eat fish, and on Saturdays, it's beans and frankfurters."

Mrs. Cardillo laughed at Meg. "You tella your mama to comea over to seea me, and I'll a teacha her how to cooka spaghetti, okay?"

"Wow, that would be great! I'll tell her. Thanks Mrs. Cardillo." But Meg knew her mother would never go into the Cardillo's house. Big Tony Cardillo ran the illegal neighborhood numbers racket. Meg's parents called him a gangster.

Although the O'Mearas never bet, they enjoyed guessing which numbers would win. The daily winning numbers were published evenings in the racing results in the sports sections of the *Boston American, Advertiser* and *Record.* The middle three digits of the win, place and show payoff results in the 7th race at Suffolk Downs, or another track when Suffolk was closed, determined the winning number.

One day in July, Big Tony called to Meg from the grape arbor. "Heya, kiddo, comea here."

Meg joined the old man on the rustic bench under an arbor. "Hi, Mr. Cardillo. Can I have some grapes?"

"Sure, kiddo, helpa yourself. Mya rheumatism isa bad today. Maybe you helpa me, huh? Wanna maka some money?"

"Sure!" Meg was excited. "What do I have to do?"

"The firsta thing is to keepa your moutha shut. Don't tella nobody whata you do for me, kapeesh?"

"I know how to keep a secret, for sure." She knew her parents wouldn't like her to be around Mr. Cardillo, and she wondered what she'd tell them about how she got the money. "What do I have to do?"

He smiled broadly extending his hands forward in a common Italian gesture, "Heya, it'sa nota much. Justa pick up somea money and somea notes from all the nicea neighbors who do the business witha me."

Relieved, she asked, "You mean, like just run errands for you?"

"That'sa right. Youa smart kiddo."

"Can my best friend Barbara help me with my job?" She asked hopefully.

"Heya, heya. What I'ma tella you. You don'ta tella no one," he growled, sticking his chin out and squinting his eyes, making his face appear ferocious.

Meg, worried that he might change his mind, quickly assured him, "Okay, Mr. Cardillo, I'll do it. When do I start? What do I have to do? And how much money will I get paid?"

Mr. Cardillo chuckled at her directness, patted her head, and put his hand out. "You knowa somethin, youa one smarta kiddo. Let'sa shake hands ona the deal. A nickel a day, and youa starta worka righta now."

Meg had never given a handshake before. She had only seen men do it, and it made her feel grown up. She thought, I guess this is what people do who are going into business with each other.

Several weeks went by, and amazingly so, not one neighbor told Meg's parents what she was doing. She carried out her daily assignments with great success, running from house to house picking up little pieces of paper with numbers on them and coins wrapped inside. She'd deliver them to Mr. Cardillo in the grape arbor where no one could see them make the exchange. When she had saved fifty cents, she surprised her parents with gifts. A White Owl cigar for her Dad and a pack of Lucky Strike cigarettes for her Mom who said she smoked to calm her nerves.

Her parents were stunned. Margaret asked, "Meg, where did you get the money to buy these?"

Meg had prepared and rehearsed her answer to make it sound convincing. "I've got a job!. I run errands for the neighbors, lots of neighbors!" She smiled enthusiastically.

Bill and Margaret looked at each other, silently questioning the truth of her answer. The same thought came to them simultaneously; no one in their neighborhood pays children to do errands except, maybe Mr. Cardillo.

Margaret took Meg's face between her hands, questioning her sternly, "Do you run errands for Mr. Cardillo. Do you pick up notes and money from the neighbors and deliver them to him?"

Meg was flabbergasted! How could her mother guess? I was so careful. I better not lie. I've got a hunch my working days are over. She whispered the truth, "Yes."

"Jesus, Mary and Joseph," Margaret cried. "Our ten-year-old daughter is the neighborhood runner for the number's racket!"

Bill stormed over to Cardillos and came very close to beating the old man. "You stay away from my kid, or I'll let the police know what you're doing!"

Mr. Cardillo looked at Bill with raised eyebrows. "That'sa nota good idea, Mr. O'Meara. Youra kiddo wasa collecting for me, kapeesh?"

Bill understood his meaning. He never spoke to the old man again.

Meg was spanked soundly on her bare behind again, lectured on the evils of gambling and got two weeks solitary confinement on the veranda. She was warned never to go near the Cardillo's house again, but she did, the next year when the grapes were ripe.

ℒ * ℒ

That summer the O'Meara family spent most Sunday afternoons visiting with relatives; sometimes with Bill's sister, Mae and her family in Allston or with his brother Dan's family in Sommerville. They would all listen to Father Charles Coughlin. He had captured the imaginations of millions of impoverished people like the O'Mearas with his angry tirades against social injustice. More than five million people joined his political party, The National Union for Social Justice. But his charisma faded quickly when he accused President Roosevelt of betraying the country with his New Deal programs, calling him a dictator and a Communist sympathizer. He expressed strong anti-Semitic views and attacked labor unions and industry. Bill and Margaret O'Meara were among the first to defect. Within a short time, millions of other Americans resented what he was preaching. Because he was a priest, they had believed that what he preached must be true. When the Catholic Church realized the damage he had done to its image, he was quickly eased off the air.

ℒ * ℒ

Bill got a second job working Friday nights and Saturdays at Hymie Sullivan's Fish Market on Brattle Street in Harvard Square. "I'll bring you home a real treat this Friday night," he promised the family. The treat was a big bag of lobster legs, and they all sat around the kitchen table for an hour, sucking out the sweet meat.

"Some night I'll bring home a real treat; lobster claws and tails, which are real delicacies!" The night he did, they all agreed they liked the meager sweet meat of the legs better!

The week before school opened, Meg and Barbara visited the fish market to watch the goldfish in the big tank in the window. Hymie Sullivan's daughter, Sarah, came in wearing a Girl Scout uniform. Meg stared at her uniform bodice, which was covered with badges she had earned. Meg had always dreamed of becoming a Girl Scout, but there was no troop at St. Peter's school. Sarah noticed Meg staring and asked, "Would you like to join the scouts, Meg?"

"Oh, would I!" Meg exclaimed.

"Well, we have an opening in my troop, and I'm trying to find a recruit so I can earn another badge. As a matter of fact, I have my old uniform right here in this bag, and I'm trying to sell it. I bet it would fit you," she said taking the green dress from the bag and holding it up to Meg.

"It's perfect, just needs the hem turned slightly," Sarah commented.

Meg's heart pounded with excitement. She looked at her father who had been watching from behind the counter. "Oh, Dad, could I please buy it and become a Girl Scout?"

"I'll sell it for three dollars," Sarah said.

Bill always had a hard time saying no to Meg. "Why sure, Meg, it'll be good for you to do some of the things Sarah does and earn badges. I'll pay Hymie tonight when I get paid. What does Meg have to do to join, Sarah?"

"Just come next Wednesday at four o'clock to the hall at Christ Church across from the Common and sign up."

That information jolted Bill. "The Christ Church! Geeze, that's a Protestant church, huh?" Bill said. "I don't know, kiddo, if your Mom will let you."

"She will!" Meg said confidently, hugging her father and thanking Sarah. She and Barbara raced home. They both wanted to try on the uniform.

Meg's becoming a Girl Scout took on the proportions of a national crisis at home, in school, and with the pastor. It came to a head the following Wednesday when she proudly wore the uniform to school. Her classmates were awed when Meg described the many exciting things she would be doing in scouting. She described all the different badges she would be awarded for different tests she'd have to take. They were especially enthralled with her description of camping out, sometimes for two weeks in the summer. Actually she knew very little about the subject, but she stretched her imagination.

Sister Bartola, Meg's favorite nun, broke into the circle of conversation with a smile on her pretty face and her arms crossed and tucked into the wide sleeves of her habit.

"Well, Meghan O'Meara, just look at you. You didn't tell me you were going to be a Girl Scout," she said in a pleased voice.

"I wanted to surprise you, Sister," Meg answered honestly.

Suddenly, Sister Superior pushed her way through the group to see what was happening. "What's going on here? Well, well, well, what have we here, Meghan O'Meara? Who said you could be a Girl Scout? We don't condone scouting at St. Peter's."

"I know," Meg answered timidly. "That's why I had to join Troop Seven at the Christ Church in Harvard Square."

"The Christ Church!" the old nun sputtered. She instantly became apoplectic, stuttering, "That heathen church and their devil's doings."

The students backed away quickly, sensing trouble. Sister Bartola looked sorrowfully at Meg, but she was not allowed to speak in Meg's defense. Sister Superior took Meg's ear and led her out of the school yard and over to the priest's house next to the school.

The nun banged loudly on the front door.. Meg looked at her sideways and thought the nun's face might explode; it was red and bulging out of her stiffly starched white wimple.

The elderly housekeeper opened the door and looked from the Sister Superior to Meg, guessing at trouble.

"I must speak to Dr. Gannon immediately," Sister Superior said in a near hysterical voice.

"But he's saying his office now, and I can't be bothering him, Sister," the housekeeper apologized.

"Oh, but we must bother him, immediately. This child has been solicited by a heathen group, and the saving of her soul is at stake."

The old housekeeper put both hands up to her mouth in shock. "Oh! Come in. Come in. I'll get him right away," she said, shuffling swiftly down the hall, looking back every few steps, and muttering religious ejaculations.

Meg looked up at Sister Superior, who was still breathing heavily, and said emphatically in spite of her fear, "Sister, I'm going to be a Girl Scout."

The nun lost control and swung the back of her hand viciously across Meg's face, hitting her so hard, Meg almost fell over. In a seething voice she hissed, "You've always been a troublemaker, but this time you've gone too far, young lady. Mark my words!"

Meg rubbed her stinging cheek, and her eyes welled with tears. But she was determined not to cry and let the nun know she was hurt and frightened. Remember, she said to herself, an O'Meara doesn't kowtow to anyone. And she was doing fine until she heard Dr. Gannon coming down the hall toward them.

Everyone in the parish feared him. He was often described as being haughty and dogmatic. Many felt that because of his Rome education, he had high hopes of being elected a Cardinal, and one day, the Pope.

When the priest came closer, Meg noticed his nose was up in the air as if smelling something unpleasant. He strode slowly toward them, his fine long black cassock rustling. Then he spoke in his superior tone, "I hope you have an extremely urgent reason for this abrupt intrusion, Sister Superior."

The nun, fearful now that the reason for the intrusion might not be urgent enough, did a little curtsy then blurted out in a frenzied tone, "Oh, Dr. Gannon, this child, Meghan O'Meara, has been taken in by heathens in the guise of joining the Girl Scouts at that Protestant Christ Church near Harvard Square."

Dr. Gannon put his hands behind his back, looked down at Meg's uniform with disdain, then looked at Sister Superior,

"That's not a problem, Sister. I don't allow the children of my parish to be involved in scouting and, of course, my rule will be obeyed. Therefore, send this child home to take off that piece of clothing and have her return here within the hour with either her mother or father. That will be all, Sister. You're excused." With that he turned, glided down the hall and disappeared.

Meg ran home, crying all the way. She was frightened and her heart was broken. She wanted to be a Scout more than anything else in the world. She ran into her house, threw herself at her mother and sobbed out what had happened.

Margaret was shocked at the five welts on Meg's cheek and furious that the nun had hit her so hard.

Physical punishment was allowed at St. Peter's school, but was supposed to be confined to the hands with a thin rod called a rattan. Some nuns would pull a child by the ear lobe if they didn't move fast enough. Twice, Meg had to put the gum she was caught chewing on her nose and walk into every room in the school.

Margaret rocked Meg and soothed her with loving words and kisses. Both Margaret and Bill disliked Dr. Gannon. Since he'd become pastor, the warmth and good feeling that had existed in the parish had disappeared. He was a tyrant, and most people felt the only important thing to him was money. He harped on it every Sunday and published a list twice a year with the names and amounts parishioners gave at the semi-annual collections. It was humiliating, especially in these hard times when families had so little.

Margaret's Irish was up now, and in a determined voice she raised Meg's spirits. "Don't you worry, honey, you'll be a Girl Scout even if we have to change parishes. I'll get a cloth soaked with Witch Hazel for your face. You lie down on the divan while I get dressed. Then we'll march up to see his majesty, and I'll tell him a thing or two."

Meg could not believe that her mother was about to argue with Dr. Gannon. She never realized that her Mom could be that courageous. She looked at her with new found respect. "Gee, Mom, you're just about as brave as Dad."

Margaret decked herself out in her Sunday pongee dress with the ecru lace collar and put on her new veiled straw hat and fawn colored gloves. She checked to see that the seams were straight on her stockings, picked up her purse, and said smiling, "Okay, Scout, let's go do our good deed for today. And remember, keep your mouth shut and let me do the talking."

Dr. Gannon kept them waiting a half hour in the small reception room. When he arrived, Meg started to stand up, which was the rule, but her mother pulled her down, and before the pastor had a chance to speak, Margaret blazed at him with controlled, Irish fervor. "I'll get right to the point, Father." She knew it upset him when he was addressed as Father instead of Doctor. "I don't like the looks of my little girl's face. We'll have Dr. Walker look at it when we leave here. One of your nuns, er, employees did that to her?"

She had put him on the defensive. He was speechless at her arrogance and accusation.

"If there is any permanent injury, you'll hear from our attorney (a line she had heard in the movies). Now, what is this nonsense about Meghan not being allowed to be a Girl Scout?" she asked in a superior voice.

He interrupted her with a booming, "Madam!"

But she was too fast for him. Standing up and pointing her finger at his face, she said calmly but emphatically, "Scouting is good for children. St. Mary's and St. John's have scouting programs. I think it's too bad that my Meghan, who has never missed Mass one day since she started school, has to go to a Protestant church to be a Scout instead of to her own parish, and that's your fault. The O'Mearas are good Catholics, so have no fear of her losing her religion, and that was your concern wasn't it, Father?"

Red blotches covered his face and his fists were clenched. He turned on his heels, stormed down the hall, went into a room, and slammed the door.

Margaret and Meg looked at each other, and Margaret raised her eyebrows in a gesture of surprise and a small smile crept into the corners of her mouth. She had won the battle! Meg started giggling, and her mother put her finger to her mouth to hush her, and they left the priest's house.

Margaret took Meg back to her classroom. Sister Bartola put her arm around Meg's shoulder and walked her to her seat. Just as Margaret was closing the door, she looked from Sister Bartola to Meg and said in a matter-of-fact voice, "I hope you have fun at Girl Scouts today, honey. Be careful crossing the streets, dear."

Sister Bartola looked from mother to daughter and put her hand up to her mouth, which had just begun to form a grin and said, "Oh, my. Good day, Mrs. O'Meara."

Nothing was ever said again to Meg about being a Girl Scout. Sister Superior ignored her and never spoke to her again, except through a second party. But one winter morning in the middle of a raging snowstorm, Meg was the only child to show up and sing the Latin requiem responses. She did not carry the tune very well in her alto voice, but she did it loudly. The sister superior kept turning around and glaring at Meg.

SIX

ambridge, 1936. Bill had been told to get involved in the political campaigns in Cambridge, because politicians could pull the right strings to help him get a better job. Frank Regan had offered to take him into the liquor business, but Margaret and her sister, Grace, were afraid that would be too close to the occasion of sin, and he might begin drinking heavily again.

Bill's first involvement in politics was displaying a large poster with the candidate's picture on the front of their house. Next, he passed out campaign literature in the nearby neighborhoods, and stuffed envelopes for mailings. One evening, a coordinator for the Hurley for Governor campaign visited the O'Mearas. "My name's Timmy Ahearn. I'm the Democratic ward boss for this area, Mr. O'Meara. Your brother-in-law, Frank Regan, told me that you might be willing to organize a rally for Charlie Hurley's campaign here in your neighborhood. We'll supply the ice cream, a flat bed truck and a sound system for the candidate's rhetoric. All you have to do is to see that there's a good turnout of voters. When the coordinator was leaving, he said, "Bill, we want you to know, if you do a good job on this rally, Mr. Hurley will be happy to do you a favor, if you ever need one."

God knows he needed help. His arm ached severely at the end of each work day. He knew he couldn't dig ditches much longer, or his arm would become completely useless.

The whole O'Meara family pitched in to make the rally a success. Joe and Meg posted flyers on every lamppost for blocks around the area. They told kids that they could have all the ice cream they could eat if they brought their parents to the rally.

The night of the rally was unbearably hot and humid. Hundreds had gathered on Oliver Street, completely blocking traffic.

When the flat bed truck carrying a large insulated ice cream box came down the street, the driver couldn't believe his eyes. Hearing the patriotic music blasting from the large speaker horns on top of the truck, the crowd roared and cleared a path so the truck could slowly make its way to the O'Meara's house.

"Holy Mother of God!" the truck driver whistled through his teeth. The big black Cadillac that was following the truck stopped before it reached the crowd. Timmy Ahearn jumped out of the Caddy and stood on the running board estimating the number of people. He stuck his head in the back window to talk to the boss. "Geeze, Charlie! What a rally we have here!"

Grinning mischievously, Charlie Hurley said, "And what a problem we have here, Timmy, if you can't find enough ice cream for all these folks. Now listen, the minute I get out of the car, you hop in and have Pepper drive you to every store around here that sells ice cream. Buy it up and get back here fast! Here's a fifty."

Hurley got out of the car, loosened his tie, threw his jacket over his shoulder in a casual manner, then started through the crowd giving all the men hearty handshakes and pats on the back. The older ladies got pleasant nods, and younger women got a snappy wink especially if they were pretty. At least twenty babies were kissed before he reached the flat bed truck and hoisted his large frame up on to the platform with the help of the crowd. He raised his arms up in the air, leaned into the mike and yelled, "Now this is what I call a rally!"

The crowd went wild. Charlie Hurley's broad Irish face with its million-dollar smile always froze permanently in place when he was in public. His warm, exuberant demeanor had already won over the crowd. But Charlie's greatest asset was his eloquent manner of speaking. He was believable, sympathetic and said exactly what his audience wanted to hear. He had already won over the crowd.

His speech was continuously interrupted with applause and whistles. When he saw the Caddy returning and parking away from the crowd, he knew that was his cue to give his closing remarks, which were his trademark. "I'm not Curley, our good friend, James Michael. I'm Hurley! Charles Hurley! But we both have one thing in common; we care about you and you and you (pointing to different people in the crowd). My fellow citizens, if you want a better life in this Commonwealth of Massachusetts for the next four years, if you want a governor who cares about the little guy, put an 'X' next to my name when you go to the polls on election day. Then we'll all be singing *Happy Days Are Here Again*. I'll make that song come true!"

Then, in a splendid tenor voice, he led the hundreds of people in singing the Democratic theme song. After the song was over and the cheering died down, Hurley yelled out to the crowd, "Let's hear it now. I scream. You scream. We'll all scream for ice cream!"

And the crowd screamed! They mobbed Timmy and the driver who tossed Hoodsies, popsicles, fudgicles and ice cream sandwiches from atop the flat bed.

Hurley made his way to the O'Meara's veranda. His shirt was soaked with perspiration and his slick black hair was dripping wet. He put his arm around Bill, who was beaming sheepishly at the top of the stairs. "So, you're Bill O'Meara, and this pretty woman is the missus, and these good looking kids are yours, huh? Well, I have to tell you, Bill, this rally was way beyond my wildest expectations. It's the biggest neighborhood rally I've ever had in Cambridge." He clamped his large hands over Bill's hand and said in a confidential tone, "Bill, if I can do anything to repay you for this great turnout tonight, just say the word."

Bill, in his usual unassuming manner, simply said, "It was our pleasure, Mr. Hurley. Glad to help."

Meg couldn't believe her Dad was going to pass up this chance to let Mr. Hurley help him. She squeezed between her parents and looked directly up into Mr. Hurley's face. "Excuse me, Mr. Hurley, but it sure would be nice if you'd help my Dad get an easier job because his arm was almost shot off in the war, and it hurts because he digs ditches every day."

Shocked at Meg's brazenness, Bill and Margaret glared at her and apologized for her rudeness.

Hurley patted Meg on the head and asked in a concerned voice, "What's your little lass talking about, Bill? Roll up your sleeve. Let's see that arm."

Bill was embarrassed. He had never discussed his war injuries with anyone but family.

Charlie Hurley urged him again to show where he was wounded. Bill turned his back to the crowd and reluctantly rolled up his sleeve, exposing the severe ugly scar. "My God almighty, Bill, how can you do manual labor with an arm like that? You come down to my office tomorrow and we'll see if we can't get you into something less strenuous."

He shook Bill's hand again, nodded to Margaret and winked at Meg. "Goodbye, Bill, and thanks a million!" He walked down the stairs into the crowd of well-wishers who reached out to shake his hand.

"Geeze, did you hear the way he called me 'Bill,' just like I was a friend?" Bill was elated. Then changing his tone, he pinched Meg's cheek while chastising her for being so bold.

"But Dad, he's going to get you a soft job!"

"We'll see, we'll see," Bill said philosophically.

☙ * ☙

The next morning Bill went to Hurley's office and was received warmly by Hurley's staff who had heard about the big rally. He didn't get the desk job he'd hoped for, but he did get a much less strenuous position with the Maintenance Department of the City of Cambridge. When he got home, he threw open the door and yelled, "Hey, everyone, I'm now making a thousand bucks a year!"

A few weeks later, the O'Mearas received more good news. Bill would now be receiving his WWI disability pension of $27.50 a month for life. And, the best news of all followed shortly. The veterans' bonus bill finally passed in Congress, and mailmen all over the country delivered the long awaited bonus checks in manila envelopes. At last, they had their pot of gold: $1,200.00.

☙ * ☙

At eleven, although still spirited, Meg's attitudes and behavior changed. She became somewhat subdued. She told Barbara, "I'm not going to be a tomboy anymore, and I'm not going to let Joe or my father see me in my underwear either. And, if neighborhood boys tease me, I'm not going to punch them, I'll just snub them. When I told my mother that from now on, I'll wash and iron my own clothes like you do, Barbara, guess what she said?"

"She didn't say anything, she fainted."

Meg laughed, "No. She said if I take good care of my clothes, I can let my hair grow long!"

"Oh, I'm so happy for you. Now I can teach you how to put it up in rags every night and have curls like me."

Although now the girls played with dolls only on rare occasions, their final doll experience would never be forgotten. Meg's old Gloria, with the real hair, sat at the end of her bed, as a decoration only. The Dionne Quintuplets, which she won after a year of collecting one thousand Wonder Bread wrappers from trash barrels, were seldom taken out of their beautiful pink and white bassinet. Her favorite, Joan, had been kidnapped from the veranda, although Meg suspected that her mother might have had something to do with her disappearance. Joan was dirty and smelly. Only Beverly had Meg's attention now. Barbara had a twin boy doll named Tommy. The small six-inch, rubber dolls were both anatomically the same. Both dolls were severely disfigured from numerous appendectomies, and their mouths were grotesque from overfeeding.

Their final doll adventure began innocently.

"It's such a nice warm fall day, Barbara, why don't we take Beverly and Tommy for a walk down the Charles River?" Meg suggested.

They pretended their dolls were walking beside them by holding them like puppets with strings tied around their necks. When they arrived at the river, they sat on the grassy bank across from the Harvard Business School and ate the sandwiches and cookies they had packed for lunch.

"Maybe our dolls would like to go swimming, Meg," Barbara suggested.

"What a great idea!" Meg agreed.

Holding the end of the string tightly, they'd toss the dolls out into the water, then slowly pull them back to shore. After several swims, the calamity occurred.

When Meg tossed Beverly out, the force of the throw and the weight of the water that had accumulated inside the doll, yanked the string out of Meg's hand. Beverly sank instantly. Meg panicked, and screamed hysterically, "Help! Help! Beverly is drowning." It brought back memories of her near-drowning when she was four.

Alarmed bystanders along the shore came running toward the girls yelling, "Where did she go down?"

Meg and Barbara pointed out to the spot in the water where Beverly disappeared. "There! Right out there!" Meg cried.

"How old is she?" screamed an elderly woman.

"About two years old," Barbara answered.

The woman grabbed the two girls by their shoulders and began shaking them violently. "You stupid children. Does your mother know you took that two year old down to the river? She ought to be arrested."

By now, quite a few Harvard students had moved their sculls close to the shore. Hoping to rescue the drowning child, they yelled, "Where'd she go down? Point to the spot."

Meg and Barbara were too frightened now to tell the crowd that Beverly was a doll.

Everyone on the shore pointed to the area about eight feet out where Meg had pointed. The students jumped out of their sculls and dove down into the deep murky water.

A man with a grappling hook ran up to Barbara and asked, "Show me how tall Beverly is."

Barbara held up Tommy and sobbed. "She's the same size as Tommy; they're twins."

An astonished look came over the man's face. "Is Beverly a doll?"

"Yes," Barbara whimpered.

"Sweet Jesus, what a relief!" The man shouted to the crowd, flailing his arms to get their attention, "Everybody, listen! Beverly's a doll! Not a child!"

Everyone along the bank and in the water seemed to freeze when they realized what he'd said. Then all eyes turned toward the girls and glared at them.

The crowed dispersed. Men cursed Meg and Barbara. The scullers climbed back into their boats, angry and repulsed by the slime from the bottom of the river that covered their bodies. A man grabbed the girls by the back of their dresses and shoved them up the embankment. "You two, wait right here; someone's gone to get a policeman. If you were my kids, I'd strap you so hard, you wouldn't sit down for a week."

Meg broke away from his grip and ran back down the bank and walked out in the water crying, "I'm not leaving without my Beverly."

A sculler, about to pull away from the shore, was touched by the agonized look on Meg's face and dove back into the river. Now that he knew what he was looking for, and the sediment had settled, he almost instantly retrieved the muck-covered Beverly. Holding her up as he broke through the water, he yelled, "Hooray! I've found her. Look! I've found Beverly!" Meg jumped up and down in excitement.

The young man brought his scull close to shore and tossed Beverly to Meg's outstretched hands. "She'll be fine now. Dry her off, and please, promise me that Beverly will never go swimming again. Okay?"

Flustered, Meg hung her head while squeezing the water out of Beverly and uttered softly, "I promise you she won't. Thank you very much for saving her."

The handsome man winked, smiled at her, and said, "You're a cute little girl." He waved and rowed away.

Meg almost lost her breath. Her heart beat rapidly as she watched the sculler leave. Her body filled with a strange titillating sensation she had never felt before.

She was startled out of her reverie by a policeman who grabbed her arm, led her up to the police car and put her in the back with Barbara.

The girls were terrified when the police car pulled up in front of the O'Meara's house.

Margaret was frightened when she opened the door and saw the policeman holding Meg by the arm. When she heard what happened, she immediately dragged Meg into the bedroom. She put her over her knee, pulled down her bloomers, which at age eleven, humiliated Meg severely, and spanked her soundly while the policeman listened at the front door.

Both girls were forbidden to see each other for two weeks. Confined to their front porches, they managed to communicate in sign language or by notes carried by neighborhood kids.

SEVEN

Christmas, 1937. On Christmas morning, Meg tore the wrapping off a large box. "Oh, my God! I can't believe it! White figure skates! Wow! Oh, Mom and Dad, thanks a million."

For the past two years she had begged her parents for skates, and either they didn't have the money, or they felt skating was too dangerous for a girl. Several neighborhood children had drowned in Gerry's pit off Walden Street when ice broke. Meg would only be allowed to skate at Raymond Park, which was flooded by the city in the winter.

Sonja Henie was Meg's idol. She had seen all her movies over and over. She had pasted pictures of her idol on the back of her door. She couldn't wait to get on the ice and try the tricks that Sonja did.

She gobbled her breakfast and raced off wearing a wool jacket, ear muffs, mittens and a plaid skirt that she rolled over four times at the waist, because figure skaters wore short skirts. She wore red summer shorts under the skirt. Her legs were bare. She was the only girl on the ice. It was crowded with boys playing hockey, among them her brother, Joe.

He watched Meg teeter out on the ice and fall flat on her bottom. The hockey players jeered her. One of the boys shot the puck at her skates just as she got back on her feet. She fell again.

Joe glared at the boy and pointed his index finger. "Take five on the bench, Boudreau, after you apologize to my kid sister."

For a second, the boy hesitated, but Joe was bigger than he. He mumbled, "Sorry," and skated off to the edge and sat on the bench.

After a while, Joe dropped out of the game to help Meg. That night he bragged to his parents, "Dad and Mom, our Meg's a natural!"

His compliment warmed her as she continue to rub her legs that were by now numb and purple.

By the end of Christmas vacation she felt like a pro. Now she had speed-skated backwards, and seldom fell except when she hit a hole or a crack in the ice, which was often.

A school friend, Fran Crowley, who also got skates for Christmas, told Meg that next winter they should skate at the Boston Arena on Sunday afternoons. "Lots of figure skaters there," Fran told Meg. "We can watch them and learn how to do spins and jumps. They play waltz music, too."

"Oh, how I'd love to learn to dance on ice!" The thought excited Meg.

Both girls decided to start saving right away. Meg began doing a variety of jobs after school and on weekends. She hung out neighbors' laundry when it was so bitterly cold that the clothes froze instantly. She carried out ashes and trash. She shoveled snow. She was determined to skate at the Arena every Sunday next year.

℣ * ℣

Cleaning her Aunt Grace's apartment turned out to be Meg's best paying job that winter. The apartment was located on Oxford Street in an affluent section of Cambridge.

Grace's husband, Frank, now owned two taverns. They had only one child, John, who was severely retarded and confined to a wheelchair. No one in the family ever talked about his affliction or what caused it. Although five years older than Meg, he weighed only a few pounds more. She enjoyed amusing him. He'd almost fall out of his chair with laughter when Meg imitated his father's coarse voice saying cuss words, but that was only when Aunt Grace was out to the store.

Meg had a secret desire to teach John to walk. She prayed every night that one day he would. When her aunt went to the store, and left John in her care, she'd try various ways to get him to walk. Most of the time she'd stand with her back to his chair, pull his arms up over her shoulders and drag him out of his chair. She'd then tow him across the floor, but not very far. He was dead weight.

During these experiments when Meg tried to move his thin immobile legs, John would slur swear words that he'd heard his father saying. Then he'd laugh.

Meg would stand in front of him and lift her legs up and down as if marching. "Up and down, up and down. Lift your legs, John. Lift them. You can do it. Try, try!"

John would shake his palsied hands, and give her a big grin, while drool spilled down his chin. Meg didn't realize that only a miracle could make John walk.

One day that miracle happened. Meg was feather dusting furniture in her aunt's living room and rushing the job, because she planned to go to the movies with Barbara at noon.

Recklessly flicking the feather duster over an ornate china lamp on a small table in a corner, she hopped over the cord. Her left foot snagged the cord and the lamp slid off the table and crashed to the floor, shattering into hundreds of pieces. Horrified, she yelled to her aunt in the kitchen. "Aunt Grace, Aunt Grace, I'm so sorry, I..." Before she had a chance to finish her apology, her aunt was running towards her in a screaming rage. "You stupid, stupid clod. Look what you've done to my beautiful lamp." Her anger was out of control, and she began fiercely slapping Meg.

Meg covered her head to ward off the violent blows and cried in fright and pain, "It was an accident! Stop, Aunt Grace, please stop. You're hurting me bad," she begged. "I'm so sorry. Stop, please!"

Suddenly they froze in astonishment.

John staggered into the living room towards them with his arms flailing. His face was scarlet with anger. He shrieked a long series of curses. Then he lunged his body at his mother and collapsed in her arms, unconscious.

The dead weight of her son caused Grace to sink to the floor where she cradled the limp body in her arms.

In a bizarre quivering voice she mumbled, "Jesus, Mary and Joseph, he walked!" Then she screamed hysterically, "He walked!" She buried her face in his chest and sobbed uncontrollably.

Meg was at once both terrified and exalted. She knelt on the floor beside her Aunt and patted her back and said excitedly, "I knew it, Aunt Grace! I knew he could walk!"

Grace slowly looked up at Meg in the strangest way. Through tightly clenched teeth, she growled, "Shut up! Shut up, you stupid child. He can't walk, never, never. They said Never! Oh, dear God, my baby John." Then she sobbed so pitifully, Meg was afraid her heart would break.

Meg heard the back door open and ran through the house to the kitchen where her Uncle Frank was standing, staring at the empty wheelchair.

Meg grabbed his hands and cried, "John walked! Uncle Frank. He really walked 'cause he didn't want Aunt Grace to hit me for breaking her lamp."

Frank's eyes raced from the empty wheel chair back to Meg. Roughly pushing her aside, he raced to the living room. The sight of his wife and son huddled on the floor sent a wave of terror through his body. He dropped to the floor beside them. Tears filled his eyes when Grace looked up at him with a mournful stare. He lifted his unconscious son from her arms and carried him into the bedroom.

Meg helped her Aunt up from the floor, put her arm around her waist and led her to John's bedroom.

Meg would always be confused by what happened in the next hour. Her mother came, a priest came, and Dr. Walker arrived at the same time as the ambulance that took John to the hospital.

Later, driving home in a taxi with her mother, Meg questioned her mother repeatedly. "Why can't you answer my questions? Why isn't anyone, except me, happy that John walked? Will he die because he walked? How come?" Meg was confused by everyone's attitude and wondered why she felt guilty about what happened. It really wasn't her fault, was it?

Margaret said little in the taxi, but when they got home, she listened to Meg's version of what happened, then explained, "It was a frightening experience for Grace and Frank. They are afraid he might die because of the experience."

"You mean, because he walked?"

Margaret hesitated. "The doctor thinks his walking was just a temporary thing, and it won't happen again. I think John loves you so much, Meg, he didn't want his mother to hurt you. We must forget the whole episode. I want you to promise never to tell anyone about what happened today."

"But why, Mom? I saw it with my own eyes. It was like a miracle. It was a miracle!"

Margaret glared at Meg. "Don't ever say that again, Meg! Never again, or you'll be punished more severely than you ever have been. The priest said we mustn't speak of it as a miracle. Do you understand?

He'll be fine in a day or two, and that's the end of it." Margaret refused to speak about it again. Only Meg and Joe believed it was a miracle.

A week later Aunt Grace asked Meg to come and help clean her house. John grinned broadly at her and shook his hands rapidly in happiness when she kissed him. Aunt Grace apologized for hitting her but never said a thing about John's walking. By now, Meg knew better than to bring it up. She thought it was the strangest thing in the world that no one in the family shared the joy of John walking.

Ø * Ø

Grace, as the matriarch of the Sullivan family, always spent considerable time overseeing the lives of her brothers and sisters. Besides Aunt Nell's candy store, her husband, Frank, bought a small variety store in Central Square for Anna's brother, Tom.

Her youngest brother, Bert, managed one of Frank's taverns. Bert had been courting a girl, Kay O'Hara, for two years. But Grace felt she was not quite good enough for her brother. Although it didn't happen often, Frank interceded and encouraged Bert to get married. "I'll see to it that you get your sister Grace's blessing."

Grace and Frank were total opposites. Grace spoke and acted in a refined manner. She was often complimented on her beauty. Her clothes were expensive and elegant. Frank, blunt and coarse in his language, was a man's man. He was handsome in that dark, rugged, Irish way: thick black hair and steel blue eyes. His gold eye tooth irritated Grace. She thought it was vulgar. Since the episode of John walking, Frank changed. He was away from home a great deal of the time now. He had always enjoyed kidding with Meg and Joe, and made a point of being home if they were at the house for dinner. He'd always perform the same ritual: He'd pile up their plates with an excessive amount of food and continuously ask, "More, huh? You want more and, oh, ya, pepper. I forgot you kids love pepper. Eat every bit of it now! Pepper will put hair on your chest."

Although Meg and Joe hated pepper, they enjoyed the game and scraped the pepper off to the side when their uncle wasn't looking. His gruffness didn't bother the kids, because they knew he wasn't serious. The fact that his only child would always be a little boy in a wheelchair with very little mentality hurt him deeply. He'd roar with laughter when John imitated him and used cuss words. It was about the only manly thing the poor kid would ever do.

A year later John died. The walking event was never mentioned again; it was as if it had never happened.

Curious, Meg asked her mother, "Why don't the Irish ever talk about what causes people to die?"

"Because it's not polite to discuss the medical reasons for a person's death, Meg, but don't worry, honey, John didn't die from his attempt at walking."

"And my Nana didn't die because she was ironing my doll's dress, huh? I think about her a lot, Mom, because I was with her when she died."

"Your being with her had nothing to do with her death, honey. You were Nana's pet, and you gave her a lot of happiness. You just remember that."

EIGHT

Cambridge, 1938. Meg and Barbara looked forward with eager anticipation to becoming teenagers in the fall. They made decisions: No more May parties, the annual ritual of marching in tissue paper hats and carrying poles with streamers. No more garage stage shows. No more dolls. No more street games at night. Now they took tap dancing lessons on a large piece of plywood in the teacher's house. They borrowed each other's clothes and experimented with different hair styles. Every time they left the neighborhood, they put on Tangee lipstick.

∅ * ∅

That summer the O'Mearas took their first vacation. They rented a cottage on the ocean in Brant Rock for a week. It was called "The Jimmy." Bill and Margaret's friends, John and Alice Sheehy had a cottage nearby. In anxious anticipation of their first vacation, Meg washed, ironed, and packed all her clothes two weeks before they left.

When they arrived at the cute two bedroom cottage, Meg and Joe were ecstatic.

"Smell the salt sea air," Joe said dramatically.

"And feel the cool ocean breeze." Meg said as she threw her arms out expansively. "Isn't it invigorating?"

Bill sniffed heartily. "It's a lot better than the smells and humid air of the city, eh, kids? This kind of air is good for you."

The next morning, The two Sheehy girls, Pauline and Colleen and their younger brother Johnny knocked on the screen door.

Meg invited them into the living room. The girls were pretty like their mother. Johnny was cute and had a twinkle in his eyes. It was his ears that caught your attention though. They stood out straight from the sides of his head. Meg called him, "sugar bowl ears." He'd always laugh when she teased him.

Bill joined the kids carrying his fishing pole and pail. "Okay, who wants to go fishing with me out on the jetty?"

Joe came out of the kitchen and yelled, "Me!"

Johnny said, "Can I go, too?"

"Go ask your Dad and see if he wants to join us," Bill said.

Colleen Sheehy said, "I don't think my father can go this morning, Mr. O'Meara, because he's painting our porch today."

Bill and the two boys went over to the Sheehy's house to see if they could get John out of his job, but they didn't have any luck.

The three girls decided to take a walk downtown and buy some postcards and a frappe.

Several hours later, when the girls were walking back home along the beach, they heard someone yelling, "Help."

They looked out to the end of the jetty and saw Bill, Joe and Johnny flailing their hands. They immediately realized that the tide had come in behind them and trapped them out at the end.

Pauline said, "We've got to get help. I'll run to the Coast Guard station. You two girls yell out to them that the Coast Guard will save them."

By now, quite a crowd had gathered. This wasn't an unusual situation; it happened frequently. Within a matter of minutes the Coast Guardsmen had a boat in the water. The man on watch had spotted the trio. They rowed swiftly out to the end of the jetty that was now almost under water. The waves were splashing against Bill and Joe's knees. Joe had Johnny on his shoulders and Bill was holding a string of fish aloft.

The girls were relieved when they saw the Coast Guardsmen helping the stranded trio into the boat.

When the boat pulled into the shore, the crowd cheered.

Bill and Joe were embarrassed.

Little Johnny said, "I always wanted to be saved by the Coast Guard. I finally got my wish."

There was much good will teasing that evening as the O'Mearas and the Sheehys sat around the outdoor table in the O'Meara's back yard and ate the succulent mackerel the fishermen had caught.

The next day, Joe met some girls who invited him to go for a motorboat ride. Reluctantly, they invited Meg.

Margaret and Bill watched from the shore as their two children boarded the boat. Margaret said with pride, "Meg is developing into a very attractive young lady."

"And our Joe looks like a movie star in those black knit bathing trunks. Takes after his father, don't you think?" Bill grinned at his wife.

During their week's vacation, Meg and Joe learned to row a boat, and went riding in one of Joe's girlfriend's convertible, with the top down. They went to a dance at Fieldston, and a boy with a pimpled face asked Meg to dance. He tried to kiss her when he walked her home. Embarrassed, she pushed him away, not sure of what she should do. The year before, she might have socked him.

They came back to Cambridge tanned and relaxed. The minute they got into the house, Meg rushed to Barbara's house to tell her all about her vacation. "It was the most sophisticated experience of my life!" she said breathlessly. "I met this dumb fourteen-year-old boy who had hundreds of pimples. He tried to kiss me. I said 'No'! I even tried a cigarette. It was ickie!" Meg bragged. "I spent most of the time with Joe and the older crowd who told jokes, discussed world affairs, and constantly sang *A Tisket, A Tasket, I Lost My Yellow Basket.*"

Barbara listened intently as Meg elaborated and exaggerated each fascinating incident of the vacation.

The following week Meg woke up one morning and thought she was bleeding to death. Her mother had put off discussing menstruation and now felt badly that she had not forewarned Meg.

"It's normal for a girl your age, Meg, and it will happen once a month. It's your own business, don't discuss it with anyone else. It means you're maturing."

"Does it happen to Dad and Joe?" Meg wanted to know more about this revolting event.

"Of course not. Just women."

"Why just women? That's not fair."

"Because that's the way God made us. Now, let's forget about it and just accept it."

In time, Meg came to realize that her Mom really didn't know much more about the purpose of this female occurrence. Their discussion on sex was even more limited. All Meg was told was, "Don't you or anyone else ever touch your private part or God will punish you, and you'll go to hell."

Naturally, Meg discussed menstruation with Barbara who began her cycle shortly after Meg. She, too, had not been prepared and was glad that Meg had forewarned her. Meg's mother called it, "that time of the month." Mrs. Kelly referred to it as "your period." Some of Meg's chums called it "my friend" and others called it "the curse," a title Meg thought best described it. The rest of Meg and Barbara's sex education came from older neighborhood girls. Soon the girls' breasts began to develop, and they got their first bras. The rite of passage had begun for them.

This was the summer of the tan for Meg and Barbara. Every chance they got, they laid in the sun for hours. Their fair Irish skin burned, itched, blistered, and peeled. But eventually, they tanned and felt they looked much more attractive.

They faithfully set their hair at night with rags or bobby pins and experimented with face and eye makeup.

On hot summer Sundays, a large group of neighborhood kids took the trolley to Harvard Square, the El subway to Park Street, then a train to Revere Beach. It was always an adventure, especially when they captured the prize position on the El, the open grated door at the front of the subway train. The wind would blow in their faces as the train raced through the subway tunnels. When the train speeded up, the impact would almost blow them over as they held tight and screamed.

They sunned, swam, ate the lunches they had packed, and in the late afternoon, rode on their two favorite amusement rides, the Dodge-em cars and the terrifying Virginia Reel. Before boarding the train for home, they would buy a five-cent Sugar Daddy lollipop that lasted all the way home. Life was good.

Meg stretched out on her bed. It was the night before her thirteenth birthday, and a panorama of scenes from her childhood filled her thoughts. She looked back at the hard times her family had been through. But in spite of those bad times, she thought, I really had a happy childhood. I'll have more freedom now that I'm going to be a teenager. And if I get a bicycle for my birthday, I'll really be able to go places. She had begged her parents for a bicycle, but they were not enthusiastic about the idea. Meg was restless with a Celtic thirst for adventure. She was always looking forward to the excitement the tea leaf reader had promised.

She knew she could never settle for the kind of life her parents had. She didn't want a life like poor Aunt Nell. Nell had just died an old maid last week. Meg had been devastated by her death; she had always been close to her Aunt.

When Nell became critically ill, Meg often helped with her care. She could not be left alone. Last Tuesday, while Aunt Grace was taking a bath, Meg sat by Nell's bedside. Nell asked in a weak voice, "Will you say the rosary with me, sweetie?"

Meg put the beads in Nell's hand and helped her bless herself. She knelt at the side of Nell's bed, bowed her head and began the rosary, "In the name of the Father and of the..."

Suddenly, Nell reached out and grabbed Meg's hand. A strange gurgling sound came from her mouth. Meg looked up and saw her jaw slacken and hang open. Her eyes stared hard at Meg and a familiar terror seized her. She instinctively knew Aunt Nell was dead. She tried to scream but nothing came out. She dreaded telling Aunt Grace. She was afraid she'd be blamed. She pounded on the bathroom door, "Aunt Grace! Aunt Grace! Come out quick, something's wrong with Aunt Nell!"

Grace shooed Meg out of the bedroom. "Hurry, call the priest, your mother and Uncle Frank."

Meg, trying to be brave, held back tears until her mother arrived, then she broke down. "It must be my fault, Mom! First my Nana dies when I'm with her and now my Aunt Nell. Maybe evil fairies are around me now."

"Darling, it's not your fault at all. Dr. Walker told us she might die at any moment. We didn't want to tell you. You loved Nell so much."

Meg prayed that night that her mother was telling her the truth.

This last night of Meg's twelfth year of life was a beautiful moonlit September evening, lightly-laced with autumn's smell. She got out of bed, quietly opened the bedroom door and tiptoed out the screen door to the veranda.

She curled-up on the weather-beaten rocking chair. The sky was replete with thousands of twinkling stars. A surge of loneliness engulfed Meg as she thought, I'm not going to be a kid anymore. I'll be a teenager at midnight. I'll be doing all kinds of grown-up things I guess, like dating boys? Aunt Nell told me I could be anything I want to be, and I want to be a famous figure skater. I'll have to skate more often at the Arena. I'll have to find more jobs. I promised Aunt Grace I'd clean her house once a week and polish her silver every other week. God! I hate that job.

The thought of the long walk home from her aunt's at night in the winter sent a chill through Meg's body. But there were pleasant encounters on the long walk home. I'll talk to my old friend, the big old owl, perched in that giant Elm tree when I start up Upland Road. I can imitate his "whooo" pretty good. I love to watch him spin his head round and round. And a few blocks farther, I can smell the delicious aroma of the fresh bread cooking in Hatherway's Bakery. That keeps me warm until I'm close to my own neighborhood. I sure wish my parents had a car, then I could learn to drive.

Meg had already saved seventeen dollars for skating at the Arena this winter. Most of it she earned cleaning for Aunt Grace. She had earned a few of those dollars by doing a most unusual job. Barbara and she were visiting Harvard's Peabody Museum on Oxford Street. They loved to roam through the various rooms filled with real stuffed animals and the world-famous glass flowers. But one gory exhibit was their favorite: a gruesome head of a gorilla, encased in a large liquid-filled square glass box. He had a fierce face and huge staring eyes. One day, while they were standing in front of the bodiless creature, a museum employee stopped, looked at them and asked, "Do you girls know what that is?"

"It's a gorilla head," they answered in unison.

"Would you believe that some of us think it just might be the head of a prehistoric man? What do you think about that?" he asked, grinning.

"I'll ask our history Sister at school. She knows all about prehistoric stuff," Barbara suggested.

The man put both his hands up to his head dramatically. "Heaven forbid! Don't tell the nuns. Catholics don't believe in evolution."

"What's evolution?" Meg asked.

"Come back later when you're older, and I'll explain. I have to get back to my laboratory and my butterflies now. Ta ta." He waved and started down the hall.

"Hey, mister, can we see your butterflies?" Meg asked enthusiastically.

He hesitated at first, then relented. "Well, just for a few minutes maybe, but you mustn't touch a single thing in the lab."

The girls followed him into a room filled with thousands of dead butterflies that were pinned to boards and in jars of fluid. The girls were impressed.

"Wow, did you catch all of these?" Meg asked.

"Of course not. Many people before my time collected the majority of the rarer species from all over the world. Some of them are from Charles Darwin's famous collection. Maybe you girls would like to earn some money catching butterflies?"

"How much did Charles Darwin get paid?" Meg asked, skeptical now about business ventures since her first job of numbers' running.

"Not money, but he received great honors. I'll pay you five cents for common ones, but if you bring me a monarch, I'll give you twenty-five cents."

He showed them the monarchs with their orange and brown wings and black veined borders. The girls agreed to try, and thanked him. In fact, they did capture many common butterflies but only four monarchs.

❧ * ❧

Suddenly Meg snapped out of her reverie and realized she was cold and had goose bumps on her arms. She crept quietly back into the house and into bed. Just as she was drifting off, she heard the front door open. The smell of her Dad's cigar drifted into her bedroom. He had been watching Joe play baseball for the Cambridge Red Sox. The team was in the playoffs. She could hear her Dad bragging to her Mom about how great Joe had played. Then she heard her father coming down the hall toward her room. He always kissed her good night, no matter how late it was, even if she was asleep. He opened the door quietly, walked over to her bed, leaned down, and kissed her cheek. Meg reached up and hugged him.

"Midnight birthday girl in a few hours, huh?" he whispered, pulling the covers up to her neck. "Good night honey, sleep tight, don't let the bed bugs bite!" He'd been saying that to Meg and Joe for years. Walking towards the door, he turned and blew her a kiss.

Meg sat up quickly and whispered loudly, "Dad, am I going to get my bicycle?"

He looked at her with his only kidding, angry look, and said in a firm, but hushed voice, "A bike! A bike for a girl! I've never heard of such a thing!"

"Oh, Dad," she whined. "Let me see your face. You're kidding me, aren't you?"

He gave her a prissy smile, squinted his eyes and pursed his lips. "Would I kid you, kiddo?"

Meg smiled smugly when he slowly closed the door, whistling, *A Bicycle Built For Two.*

NINE

ambridge, 1939. Traffic on Route 2, going out of Cambridge toward Arlington, was not particularly heavy as Meg, Barbara and their new friend, Jane Baxter, pedaled their bikes up the steep incline toward their destination, Walden Pond. It would be the farthest the girls had ever gone on their bikes.

Jane Baxter, new to their neighborhood and a sophomore, was more worldly than anyone the girls had known. Her cute face was highlighted by curly platinum hair. Long dark lashes framed her ice-blue eyes. Her trim figure confirmed her athletic abilities. She played basketball, baseball and tennis for the Girl's Athletic Association at High School.

Biking to Walden Pond had been Jane's idea. She told the girls, "We'll meet lots of interesting boys there."

"How?" Meg asked.

"Easy. We swim out to the raft and sunbathe, until we're pushed off by a boy."

"Pushed off by a boy!" Meg was incredulous. Jane explained, "It's important to get pushed off, Meg. It means the boy thinks you're interesting and wants to get to know you."

Meg had a serious attitude adjustment to make the first time a boy came up behind her and pushed her in the water. Her impulse was to pull the boy in with her and hold his head under water until he nearly drowned. Learning to be coquettish did not come easily, but by the end of the afternoon, she had reconciled her feelings.

"I guess it's not so bad to let a boy think he's more powerful than you." Meg said philosophically, after two of the boys asked her for her phone number.

♋ * ♋

With Bill's new job as custodian at the main branch of the Cambridge Public Library came a fairly good pay raise.

That fall the O'Mearas upgraded their living standard by moving from Oliver Street to a double-decker house on Newell Street. Although only a few blocks from their old neighborhood, Margaret considered this move a step up because of its proximity to the more affluent streets off Upland Road.

✎ * ✎

When the first snow fell, Meg, Barbara and Jane went to visit Jane's older sister, Beth, who had married well and lived in a large home on prestigious Linnean Street.

Jane wanted Meg to meet the good looking boy next door. "His name's Roger, and he's a great figure skater, but kind of a sissy. Maybe you've seen him at the Boston Arena."

Meg recognized Roger immediately when he came out of his house and waved to the girls. He and Meg had skated together several times at the Arena. He had taught her to waltz.

Roger joined the girls in building a fort for a snowball fight with other neighborhood kids.

Later in the afternoon when the temperature dropped and the wind became harsh, Roger invited the girls into his house for cocoa and cookies. Meg and Barbara had never been inside a house this large or so elegant. It looked like a scene from a movie. They would never have been allowed to invite snow-covered kids into their homes, much less serve them food.

Meg would always remember this memorable afternoon as they sat on thick carpet in front of the large stone fireplace that glowed with crackling logs while listening to Roger play "Deep Purple" on a huge grand piano. He alternately winked at Meg, Barbara and Jane.

The girls discussed this unusual boy all the way home.

"I think you have a crush on him, Meg," Barbara teased.

"Well he's tall, dark, rich and handsome, what more could a girl ask for?" Meg laughed.

"But he's sort of strange," Barbara mused.

"Yes," Meg contemplated Barbara's remark, and that night she lay awake trying to analyze what it was that made Roger different from other boys she knew. Although he had a sissified voice and acted effeminately, she had seen him perform dangerous jumps at the Arena. She was puzzled.

⚡ * ⚡

Jane decided that Meg and Barbara definitely needed to be educated on a variety of subjects. She happily took the responsibility of preparing the girls for their transformation from the cocoon of parochialism at St. Peters to the freedom and sophistication of public high school. Her litany astounded them. "I'll teach you all the clever things to say to boys. I'll show you how to put on makeup, what to wear, what words to use, how to jitterbug, when and how to cut classes, how to hook school, what sporting events to attend, what clubs to join, and what subjects to take that are easy." Jane's concept of high school was summed up in one word: fun.

She stunned them with, "You know, lots of seniors flunk out on purpose so they can stay in school another year."

They had to wear bobby socks and brown and white scuffed-up saddle shoes. It was dumb to wear shoes that look new.

Margaret blasted Meg for ruining a brand new pair of $12 shoes.

Jane gave the girls a list of the boys who were popular and okay to date, along with those who were wolves and fast. "They're the type that might get fresh with you." She warned them not to date the intellectual type; they usually were jerks.

They absolutely had to carry their books to school in a dark green flannel bag slung over their shoulders like the Harvard boys use.

Jane promised them, "I'll meet you every day before school in Harvard Square at the Georgian Restaurant for coffee and doughnuts, and after school for cokes at Daly's Drugstore or at Hood's to listen to the jukebox."

The final phase of their "charm course" was cosmetic surgery. They must pluck their eyebrows, shave their legs and underarms, and to their chagrin, any pubic hair that might show when they wore bathing suits.

"Oh, my God," Meg said to Barbara after one of these intense coaching sessions on life as a teenager. "I had no idea high school was going to be so exciting and complicated. How will we ever learn it all? I have a feeling we better not let our Moms know about shaving you know where."

"Not in a million years would I tell my Mom about that! And where in the world are we going to get enough money to buy all the clothes we have to have?" Barbara was concerned.

"Let's try to get babysitting jobs," Meg suggested.

New words were added to their vocabulary daily. One of the most-used new word was "sexy." It was used to describe everything. Reversible coats were sexy, kerchiefs were sexy, favorite bands and songs were sexy, the way some athletes walked was sexy, cherry cokes were sexy.

Meg craved the excitement high school promised and urged Barbara, "Trust me dearie, we are going to be 'hep to the jive.' We're going to be 'solid.' We're going to have more boyfriends than we'll know what to do with. We're about to have the best times of our lives, and I'll bet the boys we date won't know anymore about that mushy stuff than we do. We'll be learning all kinds of new things: biology, bookkeeping, French, civics, and other interesting subjects they never taught us at St. Peter's. It'll be fun to have seven different teachers every day and change rooms every period. You'll probably be the 'femme fatale' of CHLS; that's what we have to call Cambridge High and Latin School. I'll get into lots of sports, and I'll skate every chance I get. I'll be a terrific ice skater even before I'm a senior. So cheer up, sweetie. We're going to have a ball! Just you wait and see."

℘ * ℘

Because they were building a new high school in September 1939, classes at CHLS were split into two sessions. Juniors and seniors went in the morning and sophomores and freshmen in the afternoon. Meg and Barbara got jobs babysitting in the morning in an apartment house on Linnean Street. Meg sat for the Hardys' two children and Barbara sat for the Turners' baby. Commanders Hardy and Turner were in the Coast Guard and attended engineering classes at MIT. The girls were paid 25 cents an hour. Now they could buy their cosmetics and daily cokes and coffees in Harvard Square.

℘ * ℘

When the last bell rang at 3:45, Meg gathered up her books and raced out of her civics class. Mr. Danahy, standing just outside the door, stopped her with a commanding voice, "Miss O'Meara, may I have a word with you?"

"Sure, Mr. Danahy. What's the matter?"

"Nothing, young lady. Guilty conscience?" he asked in his strong, cultured voice. "I wanted to compliment you on the composition you wrote on your Irish heritage."

"You really liked it? My father helped me." Meg was pleased.

"I'm giving you an A for honesty because not too many Lace-Curtain Irish admit to having had such a humble ancestry.

You know, Miss O'Meara, you could be an A student if you spent more time studying, instead of hanging around Harvard Square in the day and riding around at night with your boyfriends from Fresh Pond." He gave her a sidelong glance, folded his hands behind his back, and strode down the hall leaving Meg standing there in astonishment.

How does he know what I do? She was astonished. It was true. She wouldn't miss an afternoon after school with her friends in Harvard Square. And yes, Meg, Barbara and Jane would occasionally see the boys from Fresh Pond in the early evening when they were supposed to be studying at the library.

Meg's brother, Joe, didn't approve of Meg not being at the library where her parents thought she was studying, but he didn't snitch. He knew the boys were nice guys so he didn't worry.

The girls' dates with the Fresh Pond boys were casual affairs. The boys picked them up at the library in Bud McLaughlin's car. Bud was Jane's steady boyfriend. Mostly they followed the same routine. They would drive to Lexington or Arlington, singing along with popular songs on the car radio. Their favorites were *Frenisi, Maria Elena* and *Green Eyes*. Then they would stop at The Cup, The Old Mill, or The Brown Lodge for take-out orders of French fries, fried clams, and frappes to eat on the ride home. Just before the girls were let off at the library, the boys casually slid their arms around the girls and gave them a quick good night kiss.

Peter LeSage had twice asked Meg to go steady, but she said no. Barbara also said no to Charlie McMahan, although she was tempted to say yes.

Joe had advised Meg not to go steady because she was too young to be tied to one boy. Meg and Barbara made a pact to "play the field" at least through their freshman year.

The girls had a high moral code which came mostly from the dread of God's punishment for sins of immorality. They were taught and believed, that if you die with a mortal sin on your soul, you'll go straight to hell. They actually had been taught more to fear God than to love him. They never missed going to confession on Saturdays. They would never forget the first time they had to confess the most embarrassing sin of all, that of impure thoughts and actions. They had been caught playing doctor.

There were always stories about fast girls who let boys go all the way with them. One girl was expelled from school when she became pregnant. They had a vague knowledge of prostitutes who had sex with men and were paid for it.

Margaret constantly warned Meg about being out at night alone and riding the subway. "Don't let a man get too close to you because he might be a white slaver and drug you with a needle, then kidnap you and take you away to a foreign country to be sold." Meg had heard that story over and over.

The girls never missed Mass on Sundays or Holy Days. It was a mortal sin. But the real significance of the Holy Days of Obligation were an enigma to them. They were told that the feast of The Circumcision, celebrated on January 1, was in honor of Jesus, being admitted to the temple. The Nuns never explained what the word circumcision meant. The feast of the Immaculate Conception was celebrated to remind them of Mary's virginal purity but was not related to the birth of Jesus. It was celebrated because the Virgin Mary was born without the stain of original sin, which is imposed on every human at birth for the sins of Adam and Eve. Everyone else had to be baptized to erase original sin from their soul. Like most Catholics, the O'Mearas accepted what they were taught as truth. To question the dogma of the church would be sacrilegious. Most Catholics knew nothing of the teachings in the Bible for the Catholic church did not encourage its flock to read the Bible. Self-interpretation was not allowed. The Church wanted Catholics to know only what Rome dictated should be known. Not until the early 1940s were Catholics allowed to have Bibles in their homes.

♨ * ♨

Meg's grades in her freshman year of high school were not good. She flunked French and felt badly because she had always wanted to speak a foreign language. She was told to bring her parents to school to discuss ways they could help her with homework.

They refused to go. "Tell your teacher we're too busy," Meg's Mom said, criticizing her harshly, "Stop taking French! I don't understand why you want to talk like a 'foreigner' anyway!"

Joe helped Meg with her homework and explained their parents' reluctance to go to the school. "It's their Irish pride, Meg. You know they never went to high school and would be embarrassed to speak to a teacher."

Lately, it seemed that Margaret became annoyed over even the smallest things that Meg did. When Meg defended herself, which she always did, an angry scene followed. Sometimes Margaret would become hysterical, go to her room, slam the door and cry for an hour or more. Meg, feeling guilty, would try to comfort her Mom, but that made the situation more volatile.

After a month of scenes like this, Bill took Meg for a walk one evening after supper. "Listen, kiddo, your mother is going through something they call the change of life. It happens to women about her age, and they get real nervous, and every little thing seems to bother them. So please, honey, do what your Mom tells you to do without any lip. Okay? Just don't talk back to her."

Meg promised, "Okay, Dad, I'll try, but she sure picks on me a lot lately." Meg was strong-willed, independent and had a streak of Irish stubbornness that never knew when to give up. She always spoke her mind when she felt strongly about an issue.

Bill also was the recipient of Margaret's tirades and instead of arguing back, he'd head for Paddy's for a couple of beers. Only Joe coped well with his mother's bad disposition. He agreed with whatever his Mother said, which always made her feel better. He was a peacemaker.

Joe was an honor student and very popular at school. In his junior year, he was elected president of his class and captain of the varsity football team. Mr. Downey, the headmaster, had promised Joe he'd get a Buckley city scholarship to Harvard for sure.

ᢓ * ᢓ

"Meg, Meg, keep your back up and down, straight!" Edi Scholdan, the world-champion Viennese skating instructor at the Arena yelled loudly at Meg who was attempting a Jackson Haines sit spin. She was not his pupil. She could never afford the five dollars for a thirty minute lesson with him, but he often helped her. It was Meg's second year of skating, and Edi often complimented her on her fortitude and daring. She had the kind of perseverance it took to become a good figure skater, but she would never have the money or training necessary to compete as an amateur. Amateur skaters belonged to an elite, wealthy society in this era, especially in the Boston area.

Meg had learned recently that to enter Olympic competition as an amateur, one had to take a series of tests authorized by the United States Figure Skating Association. And, in order to take those tests, you had to be a member of a U.S. Figure Skating Club. These clubs were very costly, and members had to be voted into the club by a committee made up of blue-blooded Boston brahmins.

Discouraged, Meg knew she'd never become an amateur figure skater, but Edi Scholdan encouraged her to forget about being an amateur skater and become a professional with the Ice Follies or Ice Capades. Meg set a new goal for herself.

A month later at the Arena, she was skating the ladies' steps of the waltz to the *Blue Danube* when Edi Scholdan took her hand. Without losing a beat, they continued the waltz. Other skaters moved back to the side boards of the rink to watch and applauded enthusiastically when the dance ended. Meg was ecstatic. Her face was flushed, and her heart pounded with excitement when three little girls asked for her autograph.

The owner of the Arena, Walter Brown, complimented Meg and Edi, "That was a great show! What's your name young lady?"

Edi introduced Meg, and Walter Brown asked her, "Meg, I like the idea of a little break from public skating with an ice dancing exhibition. How would you feel about performing dances occasionally with Edi on Sunday afternoons? You'll have free admission."

Edi looked at Meg, "What do you say, Meg?"

"Anytime. Wow!" Meg answered enthusiastically. "But I don't know any dances except the waltz."

"I'll give you a book with diagrams of other dances," Edi offered. You practice and I'll help. You'll learn quickly, I'll bet!"

What an incredible opportunity, Meg thought. I can't wait to tell my family.

Dad and Joe congratulated her enthusiastically, but Margaret squelched the excitement by questioning Mr. Brown's motives.

"Maybe you're good enough to entertain the crowd, but why do it for nothing? I bet Mr. Scholdan will be paid." Meg felt there was no use trying to explain to her mother what an honor it was to skate with Edi and lost her temper. "Mom, you've never even seen me skate! And Dad, you've only watched me once at Raymond Park that first winter I learned to skate. Yet I always hear you both bragging to your friends about what a great skater I am. You don't even know what I can do!" She ran to her bedroom and slammed the door and cried. She'd show them!

TEN

ambridge, 1940. War clouds hung over Europe. Germany had invaded Austria. Great Britain and other European nations were making enormous war preparations, and the threat of a second world war became more of a possibility every day. Adolph Hitler, the Reichsfuehrer of Germany, brazenly began invading many other small European countries. He then invaded Poland, unmercifully bombing Warsaw, Krakow and other large Polish cities, killing thousands of civilians daily. The European countries that had not been invaded, mobilized their armies and navies and prepared for war.

Every night after supper, the O'Mearas listened to the radio for news about the war. Bill would later discuss what was happening in Europe. He'd get steamed up when he talked about the Germans. "Those bastard Huns are the most ruthless animals God ever put on this earth!" He predicted, "If we don't stomp down on those Heinie S.O.B.s pretty damn quick, we'll have a second world war on our hands, and this time it could be the end of the world. But my old Yankee division will beat their asses off again if they want a fight!"

"Watch your language, Bill, in front of the children," Margaret warned sternly.

"Yes, dear," he responded condescendingly.

Meg looked at her Dad with concern. "Dad, you won't have to fight again, will you?"

"Don't worry, honey, not with this arm. Geeze, I couldn't hold my rifle steady enough to hit a Kraut if he was standing right in front of me."

Joe put his arms on his Dad's shoulders. "Don't worry, Dad. If the USA goes to war, I'll be over there taking up where you left off."

Margaret, realizing what Joe had said, dashed a look of fear between father and son. "Don't talk that way, Joe! You're going to Harvard. You're going to be the first college graduate in our family."

Joe put his arms around his mother and kissed her head. "Don't worry, Mom, I'll get to Harvard." Then he thought, but I might have to wait a while.

The fear of American involvement in the war heightened daily now that England, France and other smaller nations had declared war against Germany. The American economy was the best it had been in years, and nobody wanted to upset the status quo. The O'Mearas no longer considered themselves poor. Bill's income of $1,200 a year now put them in the lower middle-class category.

In June of 1940, a bill was introduced in Congress that called for the first peacetime draft in the history of the country. At first Americans resented it strongly, but after a few months of publicizing how ill-equipped we were with only 190,000 men in our army and National Guard, ranking us 17th in the world, ahead of Bulgaria but behind Portugal, the danger hit home. The draft bill became law on September 6, 1940.

On Friday, October 4, Joe was late for supper and when he did come home, his face revealed that something serious was wrong. Margaret asked in alarm, "Joe, what's the matter? Are you sick?"

"Did you miss a pass at football today, Joe?" Bill asked in a calmer voice.

"I'm okay. I'm not sick, and I didn't play today. I have something important to tell all of you. Please hear me out until I've given you all the details, okay?"

They nodded in agreement and sat back down at the table, looking bewildered.

"What I did today has been on my mind for quite a while, and I've given it every consideration, so don't think I've rushed into it. I talked it over with Mr. Danahy, and I won't be jeopardizing my chances of going to Harvard on the Buckley scholarship, so that's not a worry. I don't want to be drafted and be in the Army as a foot soldier. No offense, Dad. I want to be in the Army Air Corps, so I enlisted today because we're going to be in this war real soon!"

A wave of shock filled them for a moment, then all hell broke lose. Margaret screamed at him, "No, Joe, no! I won't let you! You can't ruin your life like this. You're only eighteen!"

Bill stood up and held Joe by the shoulders. "Geeze, Joe, the planes! You don't want to be up there in the planes!" Bill was at a loss to understand why his son would want to fly. Flying was the most fearsome way to fight in a war. "I'm proud of you, Joe, but why the hell did you have to sign up so soon? It may be a couple of years before we get into the damn war."

"I hope you're right, Dad, but I think it's going to be our war very shortly. They told me at school that my grades are good enough so that I can take an exam when I return and get my diploma. I want to be a pilot. It's always been a suppressed desire for a long time, and I feel this is my big chance."

Bill's eyes filled with tears and Margaret ran to her bedroom crying hysterically. Meg put her arms around Joe's waist, buried her head in his chest and sobbed, "Don't get shot like Dad did, please!"

Joe fought back tears and broke away from Meg. "I'm going over to tell Eileen. I'll see you later." He raced out the door. In spite of his advice to Meg about not going steady, Eileen Smith was the only girl Joe had ever dated. The O'Mearas loved her. Joe called her his All-American girl. She was the head cheerleader and would go wild when Joe made a touchdown and cry for an hour when the team lost a game. Margaret often said, "One day I hope she'll be my daughter-in-law."

Joe was inducted into the Army Air Corps two weeks later after he had taken multiple exams to determine his possible future as pilot, bombardier or navigator. The O'Mearas and Eileen tearfully waved goodbye as his train pulled out of South Station for the long trip to the March Field Army Air Corps Post in Riverside, California. With tears streaming down his face, Bill saluted him and held the salute until the train was out of sight.

For the next nine weeks Joe would be in pre-flight school. Then, for nine more weeks, he would attend first primary flying school. Then nine more weeks of basic flying school. And finally, he would go on to advanced training for single- or multi-engine planes. It looked like it would be a long time before the O'Mearas would see Joe again. A feeling of emptiness filled the family.

❧ * ❧

Since Meg and Barbara first began high school, they had stayed friends with the same group of girls who were among the most popular in their class. They did everything together; wore the same hair styles, swapped clothes and sometimes even boyfriends. There were two Margies, a Meghan, a Margaret, a Maggie, a Peg and a Peggy. There were three Eleanors, an Ann, Annie and an Anna. There were two Barbaras. These were the more common names of the day. The less common names of the others included Virginia, Jane, Evelyn, Patricia, Nancy, Gloria, Rosamond and Carmaline. Many of the girls had been named after saints or popular movie stars of the day. Once a week they met at different homes for "club," for girl talk and food. They practiced jitterbugging and all the new dance crazes like the Big Apple, Truckin, and The Flat Foot Floogie. One of their mothers nicknamed them the "dirty dozen" because of the condition of the living room when the meetings were over. Cokes had been spilled, cookies crumbled, and candy wrappers torn into tiny pieces and scattered about. Being part of this special group of friends was important. It gave all of them that warm security blanket that teenagers crave from their peers.

The new buildings at CHLS were completed, and all classes were now on a regular schedule. When the new school year began, Meg was thrilled to be selected as an officer in the Girl's Athletic Association.

On the first day back to school, Meg's new homeroom teacher, a pretty young woman, announced humorously, "I'm Miss Boyle. As you are aware, female teachers are not allowed to be married."

The class booed.

"I agree. Thank you," she began the orientation.

Meg looked around the room to see who she knew. She caught a very good looking boy staring at her, and as their eyes met, he winked and smiled.

Meg blushed, something that seldom happened. A few minutes later she glanced over at him again trying not to be obvious, but again he caught her looking at him and laughed.

Miss Boyle, glancing from Meg to the boy, asked, "Could you two hold off getting oriented with each other until I finish?"

The class laughed. Meg and the boy suppressed grins.

The bell to change classes rang and when Meg walked out the door, he was waiting for her.

"Hi. I'm Tom Souza and you're Meg O'Meara. I always check out the good-looking chicks."

Meg tried to act nonchalant. "What are you, a detective?"

He grinned. He was unusually handsome. His black curly hair and dark eyes, shaded by thick lashes made him quite intriguing. His olive skin was smooth, unlike most boys his age who were plagued with pimples.

They walked down the hall together. "I don't think I've seen you before. Are you new in town?" Meg asked.

His answer was tinged with a trace of sarcasm. "I'm from a section of Cambridge where you Lace-Curtain Irish girls would never go. I live in the Portuguese section of East Cambridge, on the wrong side of the tracks, as they say."

Meg wasn't quite sure how to react to his churlish attitude. "Well, I hate to disappoint you, but I've been to East Cambridge many times. I always visit your church, St. Anthony's, when I'm making the Seven Churches on Holy Thursday. It's always so beautifully decorated."

He seemed at a loss for words. Then said, "I guess I'll see you around." He gave Meg a last quick look, turned and walked down the hall.

Meg looked after him in bewilderment. She wondered if he would ask her for a date. She hoped he would. There was a rough charm about him that fascinated Meg. She wrote Joe that night about Tom Souza.

Joe wrote back:

"He's an okay kid. He has the makings of a great athlete, but he's got a chip on his shoulder, which gets him into fights every now and then. When his father died, he had to drop out of sports and get an afternoon job to help support his mother. If he's good to his mother, he can't be all bad. Say 'hi' to him for me."

Meg never did have any real dates with Tom, but he'd always show up at dances and ask to walk her home, which was at the opposite end of the city from his home. Sometimes they'd stop and "smooch," as Tom called it, on Observatory Hill on Garden Street where Harvard astronomers as well as the young lovers, studied the stars. Tom regretted that he couldn't afford to take Meg out on real dates like her other boyfriends. Meg didn't mind.

Meg, Barbara and Jane still dated the Fresh Pond boys, who often invited them to go dancing at the Totem Pole at Norumbega Park. The big bands like the Dorsey Brothers or Glen Miller played there. Although Meg always had a good time, she'd often find herself thinking of Tom Souza during the evening and pretend she was dancing in his arms.

Her social life in her junior year was hectic. She was invited to both the junior and senior proms. The "club" girls always went together to local dances on Friday nights, which were held either at Brattle Hall in Harvard Square, The Cambridge Boat House on the Charles River, or at G.O.P. Headquarters. They had to crash the G.O.P. dance, via a fire escape ladder. Naturally, none of them belonged to the Young Republican Club, but Meg knew a member named Bill who always let them stay. They often crashed house parties, something the host expected and usually hoped would happen.

The "club" always went to the varsity games at home and away, and rarely missed a CHLS hockey game at the Boston Garden.

Meg never missed Sunday skating at the Arena. At sixteen, her life was totally fulfilled.

⌀ * ⌀

Cambridge, 1941. The threat of war grew greater every day. Beaches were closed at sundown and Coast Guardsmen patrolled with watchdogs. England, Australia, New Zealand, the Union of South Africa, and Canada had declared war on Germany and Italy. The Germans invaded France and entered Paris. London was bombed fiercely day and night, killing thousands.

Joe wrote regularly, always expounding on the thrill of becoming a pilot:

"I'm so excited about flying every day, and I love this great California weather and this pretty city of Riverside with its palm-lined streets. I'll be getting my wings soon and I'm looking forward to coming home on leave."

But he never made it. He was sent to Clark Field near Manila in the Philippines, flying a B 17. In his usual good natured-way, he'd written, "I guess they needed warm bodies out here, and I qualified after all those months of California sun."

⌀ * ⌀

On Sunday afternoon, December 7, 1941, at the Boston Arena, the recorded music suddenly stopped. The skaters slowed down and looked up to the large horn-shaped speakers when a voice said, "Attention, attention! Please! May I please have everyone's attention. Please stop skating! I have a very serious announcement to make. All radio stations have been interrupted with a special news bulletin from Washington, D.C. Japan has just bombed Pearl Harbor in Hawaii, and many United States ships were sunk. There are hundreds of casualties."

The national anthem began and everyone looked anxiously at each other in confusion.

"Does it mean the United States will have to go to war?" Fran Crowley asked Meg.

"Hawaii belongs to the United States, doesn't it?" Meg was unsure. A boy near them said, "Why the hell did the Japanese do that? I thought they were on friendly terms with us."

His friend bellowed, "The yellow bastards, we'll blow them to bits!"

Chills raced down Meg's spine. "I'll bet we'll have to go to war now, Fran."

The girls skated over to Alex, an usher who was just leaving the ice. "Alex, wait a minute. I want to ask you something." Meg said.

"Sorry, girls, I have to leave. This news will hit my Ma real bad. My brother Leon is stationed on the battleship *Arizona*, at Pearl Harbor." His eyes filled with tears as he ran off to the dressing room.

A sickening feeling came over Meg, and she put her arm through Fran's. "I don't feel like skating anymore. I'm scared. Let's go home. My folks are going to be really worried about Joe."

On Monday morning, December 8, Mr. Bramhall, the assistant headmaster at CHLS, called an assembly of the entire student body to hear President Roosevelt declare war on Japan in a radio address. His speech was inspiring, and every student's face was solemn. A wave of anger and fright filled them. The impact of what the President was saying now made war a reality. Then, Mr. Bramhall made a startling statement, "Any of you seventeen-year-old boys who want to leave school to enlist in the service of his country will be allowed to do so immediately. When the war is over and won, we'll welcome you back to finish your education. God go with those of you who want to leave school and fight for the honor of your country."

For a moment there was silence. Then suddenly, the full significance of his words penetrated. Loud cheers went up throughout the auditorium. Older boys jumped out of their seats and began slapping each other on the back as they ran up the aisles yelling, "Let's go get 'em, CANTABRIGIANS!"

It seemed like half the auditorium had emptied before Mr. Bramhall was able restore order.

On the evening's news, the O'Mearas heard a terrifying report, "The Japanese have bombed Clark Field near Manila in the Philippines, destroying half of the U.S. air power there. We have no information on the number of casualties."

"Oh, my God, my Joe," Margaret wailed.

"Don't worry, darlin, our Joe will be okay," Bill tried to assure her, holding her in his arms.

Meg added, "Remember, Mom, he's got his own plane and probably flew away before the Japanese attacked."

Every day thereafter, the O'Mearas prayed for news of Joe, but they heard very little news about that area of the war. They tried every way to find out if he was still in the Philippines, or if he'd been able to fly out. They went to Mass every morning.

The radio and newspapers were filled with the heroics of General Douglas MacArthur as he urged his men to resist every attack. Then, when it began to look hopeless, for his safety, MacArthur was taken off Bataan, but promised to return.

Bill, still filled with loathing for the General who had driven the Bonus Veterans out of D.C., commented, "Some General, running out on his men. He's all show! My son will do fine without the likes of him, anyway."

Desperation clouded every day of the O'Meara's lives as details of the Japanese invasion in the Philippines filled the newspapers. The stories of the Death March of Bataan where thousands of Americans and Filipinos died or were executed during the march, was front-page news for weeks. Was Joe dead or alive? Had he been captured by the savage Japanese? All the O'Mearas could do was hope and pray.

Bill would say over and over, mostly to himself but loud enough for Margaret to hear, "Our Joe's okay. He's smart. He'll survive." Then quietly, "Please, sweet Jesus, let him live!"

Meg wished she could do more for her country than knit socks for the Red Cross. A wave of patriotism swept the nation. Everyone wanted to be part of the war effort. The Fresh Pond boys signed up in the Army, Navy and Marines. Meg's friend Tom Souza tried to get in the Navy, but got caught with a false birth certificate.

On December 11, Germany and Italy declared war on the United States. A few hours later, the United States declared war on them.

When Margaret hung a little banner with a blue star in the front window in honor of Joe, she murmured, "I pray to God that I will never have to hang a gold one here."

Very few hours in the day passed without constant reminders of the war. Newsboys screamed headlines in Harvard Square from the kiosk where subway commuters came and went. At the movies, newsreels graphically showed the battles around the world. Remote islands in the Pacific became household words: Midway, Leyte, Guadalcanal, Corregidor, Iwo Jima and Bataan. World War II touched everyone's lives.

✥ * ✥

Cambridge, 1942. Sudden drastic changes were taking place daily in the United States now that the country was at war. Everyone's life changed. Never had the feeling of patriotism been as strong as it was now. Americans wanted to do their part for the war effort. New jobs were created daily for both men and women in shipyards and aircraft factories.

Every neighborhood had an air raid warden who was trained to identify enemy planes and to enforce blackouts in his district. Air raid drills were held weekly in schools. Every city had air raid shelters and shrill sirens were tested once a week.

Shortly after Pearl Harbor, enemy bombers supposedly were sighted over New York but it was a false alarm. Along the Atlantic and Pacific coastlines, sightings of enemy submarines were often reported, but none had fired torpedoes.

Because of the large quantities of food needed to feed the servicemen at home and overseas, rationing was put in effect. Every person was issued a coupon book filled with stamps that must be used to buy food. Many items such as butter, sugar, meat, and coffee became scarce, and lines were always long as people waited to get their weekly allotment. Victory gardens sprang up across the country, and city people who had never planted so much as a flower, became skilled at raising vegetables in their back yards and in public parks.

Along with the food shortage, a severe gasoline shortage developed quickly because planes, ships and tanks used millions of gallons every day. Gas ration stamps allowed the average driver only three gallons a week.

Harvard Square went through a drastic transition. Once, happy-go-lucky college students strolled to classes in their J.Press suits or cruised through the square in their flashy cars. Now most young men were in military uniforms of khaki or navy blue wool. College students were allowed deferments from active service if they signed up in programs like the Army's A.S.T.P. or the Navy's V-12. But as soon as they finished college, they would report for active duty.

Men not in uniform were either too young or too old, and a popular song was written about them. Men with physical disabilities were classified 4F and, although they couldn't be in the service, most of them helped the war effort by working in vital defense industries. As in all wars, there were men who found ways to avoid being drafted into the service. In this war they were called "draft dodgers" and were scorned by the public.

The worse the war news, the more human effort was put into the defense of the allies. Now when the *Star Spangled Banner* was played in public, voices were raised loudly in song and men always removed their hats when the flag passed by in parades.

Shortly after the war started, American women began entering the military services. They became Army WACS, Navy WAVES, Coast Guard SPARS and Women Marines. They served at home and abroad, replacing men as clerks, drivers, cooks, technicians and as medical aids alongside armed forces nurses in battlefield hospitals. There were also women's branches of the National Guard.

All across America, a nine o'clock curfew went into effect for everyone under eighteen years of age. It was felt that it would be wise to have young people off the streets in the event of an air raid. Many evening social events were canceled.

At Cambridge High and Latin, so many high school boys had gone into the service, the athletic teams didn't have enough players and had to merge with teams from Rindge, an all-boy's high school.

To keep the youth of the nation physically fit, daily exercise periods became mandatory in every school in the country. Everyone was urged to keep buying War Bonds or Defense Saving Stamps.

Letter writing to servicemen became the most popular national pastime. Hollywood sent U.S.O. shows to many of the battle areas to entertain the troops. The country's motto was "Do Your Part," and most did.

⊘ * ⊘

On August 11, 1942, The O'Mearas received a letter from the War Department:

Dear Mr. and Mrs. O'Meara:

Your son was serving in the Philippines at the time of their surrender. In the last days before the surrender, casualties were not reported. The War Department will consider persons serving in the Philippine Islands as missing in action until definite information is received to the contrary.

It is hoped the Japanese Government will provide
a list of prisoners at the earliest date.

s/ *Major General Ulio*
The Adjutant General
The War Department

It was unbelievable to the O'Mearas that the information in that letter would be all they would know about Joe. They desperately tried to find out more, but it was hopeless.

Meg's friend, Tom Souza, made it into the Navy after many tries. When he came home on his first leave from boot camp, Meg had a dilemma because she had been going steady with Rick Donnelly for the past three months.

Tom walked into Hoods' in Harvard Square and leaned down into the booth where Meg was sitting with friends. She was startled when she heard his voice.

"Hey, good looking, what's cooking?"

"Oh, Tom!" Meg cried, jumping up and throwing her arms around him. He looked so handsome in his white sailor suit.

He kissed her passionately, and all her friends laughed and clapped. They moved to an empty booth to be alone and talk.

"What do you mean you can't go out with me tonight? I've been saving my pay for months and finally have the money to take you out on a real date. I'd lie in my bunk at night dreaming about you and me going to a Boston nightclub for dinner and dancing. Hell, you sure know how to hurt a guy, Meg."

"Tom!" Meg was stunned. "I've written you at least twenty letters, and I've only heard from you twice, and once it was just a postcard. You never even let me know you were coming home. Don't try to make me feel guilty." She turned her head away, as hot tears burned her eyes.

"Hey, don't sweat it. I can get another date just like that!" he bragged, snapping his fingers in her face.

Meg was deeply hurt. She slid out of the booth, and ran outside to walk to her part-time job at Sears Roebuck.

"He's trying to con me, trying to make me feel guilty. Why does it bother me so much? I must still care for him, but I love Rick."

A car pulled up alongside her, and a voice called out, "Hey, darling, where are you going in such a hurry?"

It was Rick. He saw the faraway look in her eyes. She was looking at him but not really seeing him. "Did you forget that you asked me to pick you up at Hoods' and drive you to work?"

Meg apologized, got into the car, slid across the seat, and gave Rick a quick peck on his lips.

"Your girlfriends told me your old boyfriend Tom Souza is home on leave and gave you a bad time. He always liked to tease you. Don't get mad at him; he'll be going overseas soon."

Meg looked at Rick's profile and thought to herself, how very special he is. Ever since we first met at that dance, my instincts told me he would come to mean a great deal to me. He's so much like Joe. I like the secure feeling I have when I'm with him. She smiled at him and leaned her head on his shoulder. Then her thoughts went back to Tom Souza, and in an angry voice she blurted out, "Consideration! That's what Tom Souza lacks. I can't believe he expected me to be waiting for him."

Rick laughed and squeezed Meg close to him. "Are you sure you still don't have a crush on him?"

She looked at Rick and ran her finger over the small scar on his chin. "Nope, I love you, and I have no regrets."

Tom Souza called Meg that night. He obviously had had too much to drink and became quite maudlin. Meg tried to cheer him up by telling him about how handsome her girlfriends thought he looked in his uniform.

"I jus' want to say two things, Meg O'Meara. No, three things. One, I'm gonna keep dreamin' 'bout you when I'm off on some lonely island in the Pacific. Two, I think you still like me, and three, but if you don't, then Rick's a lucky bastard. So long, sweetheart. See you around sometime."

Those were the last words Meg ever heard from Tom. She never saw him again. His ship was sunk by a Japanese submarine and there were no survivors.

☙ * ☙

When Meg began her senior year of high school in September 1942, The girls outnumbered the boys. The males that were left would soon be going into the service. Barbara, now, Babs, and her boyfriend, Charlie McMahon, broke up. When he came home on leave after a tour of duty in the North Atlantic, Meg saw him coming up from the subway carrying his duffel bag. She ran to him and gave him a hug. "When did you get home? Does Babs know?" she asked excitedly.

"I don't know, and furthermore I couldn't care less," he answered brusquely.

"What are you saying, Charlie? What's happened?"

"I haven't had a letter from her since I went back on duty after my last leave. Not one! Do you know what it feels like to see the mail ship come along side, stand around at mail call, and not get one stinking letter from your supposed best girl?" The anger and hurt on his face exposed his raw feelings.

"I know that's not true. She wrote to you every day. I often put a P.S. on some of her letters to you. I even mailed some of them for her. Maybe you gave her the wrong address."

"Sure, sure. You girls always stick together. How can you get APO, New York, N.Y. wrong?" He quickly turned and walked away from Meg.

Chuck Loveland, a good friend of Meg, drove her to Bab's house. When she answered the door, Meg could see she had been crying. They reached out and held each other. "Did Charlie call you?" Meg asked.

Between sobs, Babs blurted out, "No, and I never want to hear from him again. Do you know he asked Anna Swenson out tonight? She called to gloat, I'm sure. She wanted to be sure we had broken up. And, she had the nerve to ask me why I stopped writing to him! Oh Meg, I love him so much, and you know I wrote every day, even though I didn't hear from him too often."

"What?"

"I only received a few letters after his last leave. I never told you or anyone. I just kept pretending he was writing to me all the time. We had a fight just before he left, not serious though, and I thought that's why he didn't write."

Meg tried to get them to talk. They both stubbornly refused to believe the other and they never saw each other again.

Thousands of letters from servicemen were lost or delayed in delivery everyday. Numerous stories circulated about mail being lost for months, stored in warehouses waiting for available ships to take them overseas. Serviceman who faced death every day and didn't hear from their girlfriends or wives for weeks, became despondent, then careless, the most dangerous situation in battle. Along with a fresh shipment of weapons and troops, mail from home ranked as the highest priority for keeping up high morale.

ELEVEN

ambridge 1943. On Sunday, January 3, a dream came true for Meg. She was one of eight skaters selected at the Boston Arena to try out for the Ice Capades at the Boston Garden on Monday morning. In spite of the excitement of this momentous event, Meg was skeptical that her mother would let her miss school to attend the audition, so she didn't tell either parent and hooked school on Monday morning.

Riding the subway to Boston, Meg wished that she could be sharing this exciting event with her parents but mostly, with Joe. This is my big chance to make something special of my life, she thought, to make my life exciting! I'll travel just like the tea reader promised. She bent her head and prayed silently that the "good fairies" would work their magic today.

Packed in her green school bag were her highly polished skates, her light blue skating dress and satin tights that her mother had helped her make, and her white gloves. In the dressing room at the Garden, she put on leg makeup and more lipstick and rouge than usual to make herself look older than seventeen. When she took a seat rinkside, she saw Roger Genet, her former skating friend waving to her as he came off the ice.

"Roger! I heard you were with the Ice Capades and hoped so much I'd see you today."

He kissed her lightly on the cheek. "I saw the list of tryouts today and looked forward to seeing you again, too, Meg. I hope you make it. It's an exciting life."

Roger sat with her while she waited her turn. He noticed she was growing more apprehensive by the minute. He took her hand and said, "Meg, try this deep-breathing exercise. It'll help you relax. It always works for me before I perform."

They took deep breaths together and when her name was called, Roger gave her a hug and said, "Break a leg!"

Meg stepped on the ice, took a deep breath, fixed a smile on her face and skated to the center of the rink where the skating director waited.

The woman smiled, introduced herself, and said, "Meg, as you can imagine, with the war on, we don't have many men left in our chorus. We are recruiting strong skaters like yourself who are willing to skate men's roles when necessary. Does that bother you?"

"Er-uh, no, no, of course not," Meg answered, trying not to show her disappointment. She had dreamt all night of performing in beautiful glittering costumes."

"Good! That's the kind of attitude we like in our skaters. You'll get lots of chances to play female roles also. We selected you, Meg, because you're a strong skater, and Edi Scholdan gave us a fine recommendation about your skating ability. What we'd like you to do, is to demonstrate the waltz." Meg breathed a sigh of relief. The waltz was her favorite dance. She took the fifth position on center ice, put a frozen smile on her face and waited for the music.

"Hold up a minute, Miss O'Meara," the skating director called to her. "Roger just told me that you two were skating partners a few years ago; I'd have no objections to your dancing together."

"Neither would I," Meg said grinning, a surge of confidence filling her now.

Roger joined her on the ice and the music began. In perfect precision, they glided down the ice. Meg felt almost giddy.

Under his breath, during the first few rolls, Roger uttered softly, "You're doing terrific!"

When they finished, the small audience applauded and Meg kissed Roger on the cheek and thanked him profusely. She knew she could never have done it as well alone.

John Harris, the owner of the Ice Capades, pointed to Meg and nodded. She was asked to sit with three other girls who also had auditioned earlier in the day. The girls all felt that they must be finalists because some of the other girls who had auditioned earlier had put on their skate guards and left. Meg's heart pounded with excitement. She had prepared herself for rejection because of her age and because she had not been taught professionally. Thinking ahead, she decided, "If I don't make it with the Ice Capades, I'll try out for the Ice Follies when they come to town."

It was about four o'clock when the last contender finished her performance and left. A short while later, the skating director came over to the girls. "Young ladies, congratulations! We'd like the four of you to join the Ice Capades family."

The girls were ecstatic! They kissed and hugged each other and cried and laughed at the same time.

The skating director calmed them down and said, "I want to tell you what must be done now. We need you to come to the office tomorrow with your parents to discuss signing a year's contract. As members of the chorus, your pay will be fifty dollars a week. I'll go over all the other details tomorrow with your parents. Now, we would like you to go back out on the ice and pose for some pictures for the Boston newspapers."

The most incredible feeling of elation surged through Meg's body. Her dream had come true.

Riding home in the subway, she had to suppress the urge to tell her fellow passengers that they were riding with a new "Ice Capet." She visualized the life ahead and had to keep suppressing smiles.

She was both excited and frightened about telling her parents. When she got off at her trolley stop, she ran the rest of the way home, raced up the stairs, burst into the kitchen holding her skates in outstretched hands and yelled joyously, "I'm a star! I auditioned for the Ice Capades today at the Boston Garden, and I made it!"

Her parents and Aunt Grace, sitting at the kitchen table, looked up at her in confusion.

Margaret asked angrily, "Where were you? Why are you so late? You've missed your dinner. We've been worried sick about you. Do you know what time it is?"

Meg looked at them in confusion. She wondered if they understood what she had said, "Didn't you people hear what I said?"

"You didn't go to school today, did you Meghan?" Aunt Grace accused her.

"No, I didn't go to school today, because I auditioned for the Ice Capades today, and they want me to skate with them. It's the biggest event of my whole life!"

Grace gave Margaret a glaring sidelong look, which caused a frown of confusion on Margaret's face. She wasn't sure how to react. Grace narrowed her eyes and looked steadily at Meg. "Am I correct in assuming that you didn't attend school today without your parent's permission? Then you went to the Boston Garden to try out for the Ice Capades without telling your parents anything about it?"

Meg threw her hands up in exasperation. "Yes, I hooked school. Aren't any of you excited, even a little proud of what happened to me today? My life-long dream came true!"

Bill glanced quickly from Margaret to Grace. "Geeze, kiddo, that's right! Hey, that's really something! Congratulations, honey." He got up from his chair and kissed Meg on the cheek. "I'm proud of my little girl. It's really wonderful news, huh, Grace and Margaret?"

"Wonderful news?" Grace repeated caustically. "A seventeen-year-old girl in a road show as a chorus girl? I certainly don't think we'd want that in our family."

Seldom had any member of Grace Sullivan's family ever done anything of importance without consulting her. She was a true matriarch. To her, what Meg had done was unthinkable.

Margaret, quite used to agreeing with whatever her sister said, now turned on Meg. In an angry tone, she yelled, "I don't want to hear any more about your foolish adventure today. We'll discuss your hooking school later. Put your skates away and come back here and eat your supper that I've kept warm for you."

Meg stood in the middle of the kitchen floor, looking at her mother and aunt. She became almost speechless by their reaction. Then she reacted violently, "Damn you both! I can't believe this is happening. What's wrong with you two? Are you out of your minds? Do you have any idea of how hard I've worked for years for this chance?"

Bill put his arm around Meg's shoulder and tried to lead her out of the kitchen. "Come on Meg, put your skates away. We'll talk later." He winked at her.

She pulled away from him. "No, Dad. This has to be settled right now. Oh, I wish Joe were here. he'd make all of you understand what a fantastic opportunity this is."

Margaret said emphatically and loudly, "There will be no further discussion, Meg."

"But I was told to bring my parents with me tomorrow to the Boston Garden to sign a year's contract. You have to come with me!"

"Sign a contract!" Margaret exploded. "You must be out of your mind. We'll have to get your head examined! You're a child, and as long as you are living in this house, you'll do as you're told. Now go to your room. I don't want to hear any more of this nonsense."

Meg was devastated. "I can't believe what I'm hearing. Don't you have any idea how lucky I am? It's my big chance to skate professionally, to be paid fifty dollars a week, travel all over the United States. Why wouldn't you want me to do it?"

Bill couldn't resist commenting on the money, "Fifty bucks a week, honey. Whewww!"

Aunt Grace glared at Bill, and Meg in turn glared at Grace.

Meg's Irish temper exploded, "For the past four years, I've had to clean your damn house every week to earn enough money so I could become a good skater. Do you think I enjoyed being a cleaning maid!?"

Margaret's face went white with shock. "Don't you ever talk to my sister that way, Meghan O'Meara! Apologize this minute, then get out of my sight."

Tears streamed down Meg's face as she turned and ran down the hall to her bedroom and slammed the door. She had never been so hurt in her life. They're cruel! They don't care about me. I'll run away. Her heart was broken.

A half an hour later, Bill knocked on her door, came in and sat on the edge of her bed. He took out his handkerchief and wiped her face. He held up her chin and said, "Listen, kiddo, I'm real proud of you, honest! But geeze, you never should have talked to your Aunt Grace that way. And, you should have asked if you could have taken the day off from school to try out. I think that's what's got those two so up in the air, your not asking permission."

"Come on, Dad, you know Mom would have never let me try out. That's why I didn't tell her."

"Yup, you're probably right there," Bill agreed. "Listen, honey, stop blubbering now. Here's what we'll do. I'll take the morning off work and take my skating champ over to the Garden, okay?"

Meg's red blotched face lit up. "Oh, Dad, Will you really? Will Mom let you?"

"She will now. I thought it was about time I stood up to the Sullivan sisters. Of course your Aunt left in a huff and your mother isn't speaking to me, but they'll get over it and if they don't, they'll just have to get under it," Bill laughed at his joke.

"Oh, I'm so proud of you Dad," Meg said hugging him tightly.

& * &

The next morning Meg and her Dad left the house without a word to Margaret who acted as if they weren't even there. At the Ice Capades office, Meg introduced her Dad. They were given all the details of the contract and a overview of what life as a professional skater involved. "Many hours of the day are spent rehearsing and then at night, doing the show. And sometimes there are two shows a day. It's not an easy life, Meg. You are continuously traveling, living in hotels, eating meals in restaurants, and taking care of your laundry. It may sound glamorous, but it's a tough life."

"That doesn't leave the kids much time for themselves, does it?" Bill asked.

"No, Mr. O'Meara. They're on a very strict schedule. We put our show together in Los Angeles during the summer, then hit the road, stopping in all major cities across the country."

"Sounds wonderful to me!" Meg said.

"I notice here on your application, Meg, that you won't be eighteen until September. I'd like to recommend that you take this summer off after you graduate, and when we come back to Boston next winter, you can sign on with us and come to Los Angeles in the spring. Would you mind waiting until then?"

Meg's disappointment showed dramatically as her eyes welled with tears. "My mother didn't call you did she? She wasn't too keen on the idea of me going in the Ice Capades."

"No, Meg. But she should be happy now that you're going to wait until you're eighteen."

Meg blurted out, "Okay. So does that mean that I definitely will be in the Ice Capades of 1944?"

"That's right, Meg, and we'll look forward to having you."

Bill put his arm around Meg, winked at the lady and said, "I think that's a good idea. Then I don't lose my best pal so soon. You see, my son is missing in action over in the South Pacific, and..." Bill got out his handkerchief and blew his nose.

"Oh, I'm sorry to hear that, Mr. O'Meara. I guess it might be just as well, Meg, that you stay home with your family a little longer."

✒ * ✒

Meg became an instant celebrity at school the next day when a photo of the four winners appeared in the *Record American*. She overheard her mother talking on the phone to her Aunt Grace, "Well, Grace, I'm not disagreeing with you, but I must admit I'm quite proud of our Meg. All the neighbors think it's a wonderful opportunity for her."

Meg heaved a sigh of frustration. "Now she's proud of me! Grrrr."

⍩ * ⍩

The last few months of Meg's senior year in high school were hectic. She had to juggle her school work and her part-time job at Sears Roebuck. Pictures for the yearbook had to be taken. Class rings had to be ordered. Caps and gowns had to be fitted. And on top of all that, there was her social life. She was the editor of the yearbook and the final editing and layout was due at the printers. The book clearly showed the war's influence. There were only seven boys in the photo of the varsity football team. The class history was filled with reminders of the foreign battlegrounds where classmates were fighting the enemy forces. A prominent photo in the front of the book showed the principal and a student holding a poster that urged readers to buy Defense Stamps and Bonds.

Meg was honored to be chosen the most popular girl in the graduating class. Her "club" girlfriends wanted her to slip a photo of Frank Sinatra into the yearbook, labeling him "The dreamiest man of 1943." For the past year, the "club" held weekly swooning sessions while listening to Sinatra's singing. The whole "club" hooked school the day he appeared at the Metropolitan Theater in Boston, and screamed in ecstasy when "The Voice" crooned.

Meg's senior prom was a week away, and she did not have her dress yet. "Mom, Please, can we go to Boston one more time and look for my prom gown.

"I don't understand why you didn't buy that nice yellow taffeta with the puffed sleeves that we saw at Filenes last week."

"Because it was frumpy looking. I really want something special."

They finally found Meg's dream dress in Jordan Marsh. It was quite unique and unlike most of the prom gowns they had looked at. And, it was much more expensive.

"Oh, go ahead and get it, Meg. Next year, you'll be making more money than your father, and you can pay us back." That was the first indication that Margaret might agree to Meg's joining the Ice Capades.

Meg's gown, a white taffeta strapless, was sparsely covered with tiny red embroidered roses on the skirt and the heart-shaped bodice. A pert red velvet bow with long streamers hung down the back, adding a graceful flow to the gown. Her light golden tan was highlighted by the white dress.

Rick picked Meg up in his aunt's new car. He looked handsome in his white jacket, ruffled shirt, red tie and black pants with satin stripes down the sides.

Rick said in an awed tone, "You look beautiful, Meg!" Her long blond hair was shiny and slightly curled on the ends. Rick handed her a corsage box, which she hurriedly opened.

"Oh, Rick, it's absolutely beautiful and perfect."

It was a wrist corsage with a white gardenia surrounded by small red tea roses that matched those on her gown.

"Rick! How could you have known? I wanted to keep my dress a secret from you."

Rick winked at Meg's Mom. "A lady I know suggested it."

Bill put his arms around their shoulders. "You two look like the decoration on the top of a wedding cake."

Margaret opened up her pearl box, "I'd like you to wear these, Meg. Just don't lose them, please."

Meg was thrilled. "I'll take good care of them, and thanks for everything, Mom."

Margaret kissed her cheek. "You deserve it. You're a good girl, Meg." Then she smirked. "Most of the time, anyway."

The nostalgia of that evening at Memorial Hall on May 28 would live forever in Meg's memory. It ended the era that began four years ago, when as a freshmen, she eagerly faced a new strata of education, both academic and social. With her zest for new experiences, she had vied enthusiastically for approval among her peers and for attention from the opposite sex. She had looked forward to the future with great expectations. Then, suddenly overnight, the country was at war. Many of the young men in her senior class who should have been at the prom, were thousands of miles away in foreign lands defending America.

The evening began with the National Anthem and a moment of silence for classmates who were overseas, missing in action or had given their lives for their country.

This small graduating class of 1943 faced a future of uncertainty. Dreams of worldly acclaim, vocations and promising life-styles must now be put on hold for the duration of the war. The dance music tugged at the hearts of the young dancers who clung to each other, singing along with *Don't Sit Under the Apple Tree, I'll Be Seeing You, I'll Never Smile Again,* haunting wartime melodies that would forever stir up sentimental memories.

The strains of *Stardust* signaled the finale, the last few moments before they turned the corner on youth to face a world in conflict. They knew that their lives would never be the same again.

The Monday morning following graduation, Rick left for Fort Devens. He had joined the Army Air Corps. It was a tearful parting. Rick's mother left Meg and Rick alone for their final goodbye.

"Sweetheart, I want you to promise me something. I've thought a lot about this, and I think it's the right thing to do. I want you to date other guys while I'm away. You're too young and vivacious to sit home nights and not have any social life."

Meg was stunned. I don't want to date anyone but you, Rick. I love you!"

"And I love you, and I want you to keep loving me but that doesn't mean you can't go out on dates and have a good time. Write me every day, dream of me every night and pray for me, darling." He quickly broke away from Meg and ran for the train without looking back.

Meg had never felt so lonesome in her life.

Ø * Ø

Meg and Babs got full time jobs at ninety dollars a month as bookkeepers at the Cambridge Trust Company in Harvard Square. "Just think, Babs, I could be making more than double this pay if I were in the Ice Capades, instead of sitting here at these dumb machines every day."

During the first few weeks of their new job, both girls were totally disenchanted, bored and exhausted. They were not allowed to leave work until all their accounts balanced, even if it was just a matter of a few cents. They often thought of quitting. The only good thing about the job was that every day, military officers in the Army, Navy and Marines, on their way to classes at Harvard, marched up the hill past their open office doors on Holyoke Street. The bookkeeping office was in the basement of the bank at street level, and although iron bars prevented entrance, they didn't block the view of the girls looking out, and the military men looking in. At the sound of marching feet coming up the street, the girls would leave their machines and stick their faces through the iron bars and wave to the passing marchers.

Although under orders to keep "eyes front," there was always a marcher or two who couldn't resist the girls' taunting distractions of calling out "Hubba-hubba," "solid Jack," "groovy man." Sometimes, in trying to get a quick look at the girls, one of the men would trip on the cobble-stone street, get out of step or bump into the marcher in front of him. When the girls spotted a particularly good looking man, they'd point to him, and call out, "Ohh! Ahhh! Dig that sharp officer in the third row." Their target usually blushed and had a hard time suppressing a smile.

If the girls' boss, the head bookkeeper, Miss Scully, who was a plain looking spinster, became aware of what was going on out in the bookkeeping department, she'd run out of her office in a rage. "Stop that cat calling you bunch of adolescent bobby-sockers and get back to work!"

One of the older girls, Dottie, always teased Miss Scully, "Come'on, Miss Scully why don't you join us. We're only trying to do our part to keep up the morale of the troops."

"You're all man-crazy! There are more important things in life to think about."

"Name one," Dottie teased.

Slowly, the girls became more proficient at their jobs, and their work load was increased. One day, Miss Scully told Meg to find some old statements from the late 1930s that were packed away in a seldom used vault in a back room of the bookkeeping department.

Peering into the dimly lit vault, Meg saw the outline of two doors at the rear. Meg's zest for excitement was always near the surface and she was a naturally inquisitive person. She thought it might be fun to see what was behind the doors. She reached into her pocket for her cigarette lighter (she and Babs had recently taking up smoking). From the glow of the lighter she could see that the two doors were elevator doors, shrouded in cobwebs. When she went closer, she saw the outline of a button. "I wonder if the elevator still works and where does it go?"

She got Babs attention by "sissing" from the door of the vault. Babs joined her.

"Shall we see if the doors will open?" Meg suggested.

"I don't know if that's such a great idea, Meg, but wait a minute. I'll tell Dottie to warn us if she hears Miss Scully coming back from her meeting."

The two girls got a fit of giggles as they tore away the ancient cobwebs.

"What do you think, Babs, shall I push the button now?"

"We might get in trouble."

"Oh, come on, don't you have any sense of adventure?"

"Not like you!"

Without waiting for Bab's approval, Meg pushed the button. They could hear the sound of an approaching elevator. When it stopped, the ancient doors slowly opened and the girls stared in awe at a modern carpeted elevator separated from them by a brass grilled door. Cautiously, Meg took hold of the handle and slid the door open and stepped inside, urging Babs to follow. There was a panel with buttons alongside the door that indicated five floors. There were "open" and "close" buttons and a red "emergency" button. A lighted panel over the doors would indicate at which floor the elevator stopped.

"Obviously this elevator isn't supposed to come to the basement." Babs said. "This is really spooky, Meg."

"Yeah," Meg said, looking at Babs with a mischievous grin. Then in an uppity voice, she asked, "Would madam like to go the fifth floor where our more expensive dress salon is located?"

Babs answered, "But of course my dear. I buy only expensive clothes."

Meg slid the grilled door till it closed, then pressed the fifth floor button. The two vault doors squeaked shut and the elevator began to rise.

"Wait a minute. Let's go back, Meg. I'm not sure I really want to do this."

"We need a little excitement in our boring day. We'll just look and see what's on the fifth floor and go right back down."

The elevator came to a stop and the outer doors opened to a large blue carpeted foyer. The girls looked through the grilled door and were startled at what they saw. One glance told them they were someplace they definitely should not be. Two soldiers with rifles were standing stiffly at attention facing each other about ten feet apart. Above them was an electric sign that read, "Security Check Point." Beyond the foyer were glassed-in offices with military personnel at desks.

Meg instantly pushed the "close" button and "one" simultaneously and the elevator began descending.

Curious that no one had come out of the elevator, the two soldiers turned to look just as the doors were closing.

"HALT! Stop that elevator!" Both soldiers yelled as they ran toward the elevator. "Identify yourselves!" they hollered into the closed doors.

The girls could hear them, and the sound of a siren coming through a speaker on the ceiling of the elevator. They were terrified.

The speaker came alive again, "Red alert. Red alert. Secure all entrances. Possible infiltration by saboteurs. Suspects in elevator."

Babs began pounding Meg on her back. "They saw us! My God, Meg, we're in big trouble. We'll lose our jobs! We'll be arrested and sent to prison! Quick! Go back up to the fifth floor and give ourselves up before they shoot us," she was hysterical.

"No. I have an idea." Meg scanned the panel praying that a basement button miraculously might appear. "If it came up from the basement, it must go down!" Under the metal panel she saw a very slight circular mark, which had been painted over so well, it blended with the rest of the green walls. "Look, Babs, I think there was a basement button here!" She took off her spiked-heeled shoe and banged fiercely on the hidden circle. Instantly a perfectly round, thick green chip fell to the floor and exposed a brass button with a "B."

The elevator suddenly stopped. They were at the first floor. Meg pressed the "Close" button just as the doors began to open. They closed! She kept her finger on the "B" button and they began to descend. When the elevator stopped, the girls slid open the brass grilled door and the old doors slowly creaked open. Babs ran out but Meg carefully wedged the green chip back over the old "B" button and pressed "close" and "5." She quickly slid the grilled door shut and got out just as the old doors came together.

Terrified, Meg and Babs worked furiously pushing files against the elevator door and retrieving some of the large masses of cobwebs and spreading them around.

Dottie looked into the vault. "Hey, you two! Hurry get out of there. Here comes Scully down the stairs!"

The girls raced back to their desks just as she entered the room.

"Ladies, ladies!" Miss Scully said excitedly. "Let me have your attention. You may not be aware of it, but there are military offices on the upper floors of the building, and they have closed the bank to the public because they suspect enemy infiltrators are in the building. We must stay down here until we get the 'all clear' notice."

Hearing that heightened the girl's fear even more. Meg whispered to Babs. "We have to talk. Let's ask Miss Scully if we can take a cigarette break."

Miss Scully told the girls, "Fifteen minutes only, girls and close the door. I don't want that filthy smoke smelling up the whole department. By the way, Miss O'Meara, did you find those old files?"

"Not yet. I need a break from all that dust. It was making me cough."

"And cigarette smoking doesn't!" Miss Scully raised her eyebrows.

Instead of going to the ladies' room, Meg motioned Babs to follow her up the stairs.

"Hold it, Meg, where are you going?. I'm not getting in any deeper. Let's just leave well enough alone," Babs said in a determined voice.

"Trust me one more time. Please, Babs," Meg urged. "We know something the Army wants to know, and I'm going to try and make a deal with them."

"A deal! Meg, you're talking about the United States Army. They don't make deals with jerks like us."

The two soldiers standing at the top of the stairs saw the girls and came down to them. "Sorry gals, no one is allowed upstairs."

Meg looked them straight in the eye and said in a serious tone, "We want to be taken to your Commanding Officer. We have some information about the spies."

"You do? Ha!" The soldier snorted.

His attitude piqued Meg, and she said, "It just so happens, buddy, that we not only know how the spies got into your headquarters on the fifth floor, but we also know where they are now!"

The soldiers laughed then looked suspiciously at Meg.

Babs muttered softly, "Oh, dear God in heaven."

The older one said, "Hey, girlie, this happens to be a very serious problem. Quit your kidding around and get back to work."

The other asked, "No, wait a minute. Let them tell us what they know? This ought to be good. Come on," he urged.

"We're not talking to anyone but your commanding officer!" Meg said emphatically.

"Oh, yeah! Hummm." The two soldiers stepped close together and talked softly. "I think they know something. Should we take them upstairs to see the old man?"

The other soldier puffed out his cheeks and furrowed his brow. "Ya. Let's take them up. They know more than they should know, I think. Okay, gals, follow us."

Babs looked at Meg in alarm and whispered, "What in God's name are you going to do?"

"Trust me."

"I don't, and I never will again!"

They walked across the main floor of the bank and fortunately, none of the bank officers saw them.

In an authoritative voice, the soldier said, "We'll take the elevator up to the fifth floor. And, for your information, this is a private elevator, and no one uses it without this special key, so don't ever try to ride it, got it?"

When they reached the fifth floor, the doors opened to a very familiar scene, and the girls looked at each other in panic. As the elevator doors opened, the security guards turned quickly and looked at the girls.

Meg felt sure that a momentary flash of recognition crossed their faces, but then they looked away, unconcerned. The girls were given badges, and taken to an office at the end of a long corridor. Meg's confidence was fading quickly, and her heart was pounding so hard, she was sure the soldiers could hear it. She looked at Babs for moral support, and saw tears filling her eyes. Meg grabbed her hand and said through clenched teeth, "We're going to tell the truth, and it will be okay. For God's sake, don't cry. It makes you look guilty!"

Babs looked at her in astonishment. "We are guilty," she hissed.

The soldiers stopped at a desk and spoke to a WAC who went into the room behind her desk. She came back out in a moment and said in a crisp voice, "The General will see them now." Then in a confidential tone she said, "I hope this is important. He's in a rotten mood." She held the door open, let the four of them pass into the office, then shut the door quietly.

It was a large room. The floors were covered with thick blue carpeting, and the walls were paneled in highly polished dark wood. There were no windows. Behind a large desk, sat a heavily jowled, rotund, bald-headed man. He was flanked in the rear by an American flag and an unknown flag. The room was filled with cigar smoke, and the man in uniform was leaning back in his swivel chair, with his arms folded across his broad chest. His bloodshot eyes were underlined with puffy, dark bags. His thick lips protruded like a bulldog's and his teeth were stained brown.

Meg made a quick appraisal and determined he was going to be a tough customer. He already looked angry by the intrusion.

A gold-lettered name plate on his desk identified him as Brigadier General Bartholomew J. O'Malley.

The two soldiers saluted and stood at attention.

"Well, what the hell's going on? What are these civilians doing here?" the General asked loudly in a gravelly voice that bounced off the walls.

The older soldier answered. "Sir. This is Miss O'Meara and Miss Kelley. They work downstairs in the bank, and they say they have information about the infiltrator. They asked to see you, sir."

The General flapped his hands at the girls. "Well, spit it out. What do you know?"

Meg stepped forward, and leaned over his desk and put her face close to his, much to his consternation.

He drew back with a 'how dare you?' look.

In a soft voice she asked, "Please. Could my girlfriend and I talk to you privately?" Indicating with a backward glance at the soldiers that what she had to say should be for his ears only.

The General unfolded his arms, picked up his cigar, took a big drag and blew the acrid smoke into Meg's face.

She willed herself not to cough and blew the smoke upwards, saying with a slight smile, "Oh, you must smoke the same brand of cigars as my Dad. I love that smell!"

The General glared at her, looked at the two soldiers and said, "Outside, soldiers. I'll see these two alone." Then to the girls he said, "And it better be good!"

The soldiers saluted, did an about face, and exited the office, closing the door behind them.

Quickly, before the General spoke, Meg said, "General O'Malley, I'm glad to know you're one of us. I'm Meghan O'Meara, and this is Barbara Kelley. And as you know, we Irish have to stick together."

"Oh, yeah? Who says so?" the General answered. A sarcastic grin formed in the corner of his mouth. He stood up and came around from behind his desk. "All right, O'Meara and Kelley, what the hell is going on here. Spit out what you know and make it fast!"

"Okay, okay. We know who the infiltrators are, how they got in, and where they are right now, but..."

He roared, "For God's sake, girl where are they? They could be escaping while you stand here jabbering!"

"No they're not!" She said emphatically. "But first one thing, General, please promise, as a loyal Irishman, to go to bat for us if the bank tries to fire us? We didn't mean any harm. Honest. We're so sorry. When we tell you what happened, you'll realize that we may have saved all your secret stuff up here from falling into enemy hands. You'll have to thank us for that!"

The General's livid face seemed ready to explode. He grabbed Meg roughly by her jacket lapels. "Just answer one question immediately! Where the hell are the infiltrators?"

Meg broke from his hold and stepped backwards, grabbing Babs by the hand. "You're looking at them. They're us. I mean we did it."

"What the hell are you talking about?"

In rapid sentences, both girls gave him a complete account all that transpired since Meg discovered the elevator door in the vault.

When they finished, the General stopped pacing, sat down, unbuttoned his collar, loosened his tie, and stared at the girls in disbelief without saying a word. He picked up the phone, "Call off the red alert. Tell those sons of bitches on the security staff who supposedly made these headquarters secure to get their asses up here, pronto! Tell Mr. Walters, the bank manager, the alert is over, and he can open up the bank."

"Oh, General, please don't squeal to Mr. Walters about what we did." Babs begged and began to cry. "I need my job desperately."

"Me too," Meg added.

"Naw, I'm no squealer, but you two are ordered to keep your mouths shut about this whole incident. It could have been a very serious security breech if the wrong person found what you two did. For that, we thank you for sticking your nose in where it didn't belong. Now get the hell out of here. And Kelley, you seem like such a nice girl, why don't you find another friend. O'Meara's probably always in trouble. Am I right?"

Nodding her head up and down, Babs said forcefully, "Boy, are you ever right, General."

"Out now," the General ordered, and put an arm on each of the girl's shoulders and led them out the door. "Behave yourselves! And, er, ah, thanks."

They said "Goodbye and thanks" in unison, and the General gave them a knowing wink as he shut his office door. The soldiers probed for what happened.

In an officially sounding voice, Meg said, "Sorry fellows, but it's a military secret."

Babs added, "Remember a slip of the lip could sink a ship."

Nothing more was ever said about the incident except that it was a false alarm. But the next morning, a work crew began sealing up the back wall of the vault. Miss Scully had been told that the building inspector was reinforcing some of the old walls in the building.

TWELVE

*L*ieutenant J.G. Josh Caldwell came into Meg's life on Monday, June 28, and his magnetism captivated her so totally, she instantly lost her heart to him. Of all the officers who passed the bookkeeping office daily, he was by far the best looking and the friendliest. He'd always wave and smile. The girls had voted him "the cream of the crop." Most thought he was the spitting image of Robert Taylor. His jet black hair, dreamy blue eyes, thick lashes, perfect six-foot-tall physique and flirty manner, gave him the kind of sex appeal that all girls dreamed of.

That Monday when Meg left the bank, he was leaning against the building. His arms were folded over his chest, his ankles were crossed, and his visored uniform cap was pulled down low on his forehead. As usual, Meg was rushing and ran right past him until she heard "Hi, pretty girl."

Meg stopped, turned and gawked at him stupidly.

He pushed his cap back and took off his sunglasses.

"Got a few minutes for a lonely sailor boy?"

Meg, momentarily tongue-tied, felt a shiver run through her body, and her heart raced when she recognized who it was.

He grinned. "I'm Josh Caldwell. I've noticed you when I walk by the bank in the morning."

Forcing herself to regain composure, she swallowed the lump in her throat, looked up at his handsome face and uttered a weak, "Hi."

An hour later she knew his name, that he was twenty, and all about his home in New York City. He said he thought she was the prettiest girl at the bank.

She blurted out, "Who me? Well, to be honest, we all noticed you."

"Aw, cut it out," he groaned as if embarrassed.

Meg thought, he can't be that naive about his looks.

They made a date for the following evening. When Meg gave him directions to her house, she thought, Oh, God, I wished we lived in a better neighborhood. Maybe I should meet him in the Square, but I can't do that. Aunt Grace had told Margaret that it was proper for Meg's dates to pick her up at home, and that had become a hard and fast rule.

"I'll be there at six, and because it's our first date, let's live it up. How about the Ritz Carlton for dinner, then the Bradford Roof for dancing?"

Before she could stop herself, Meg answered in forthright exuberance, "Wow, how about that!"

The moment she left him, her thoughts turned to Rick. How could she feel this way about another man? He'd told her to date, but this was different. She was sure of that.

Meg had only seen Josh in his khaki uniform, but when the bell rang at six, and she ran downstairs and opened the door, she was dazzled! Josh was a vision in a white uniform with gold buttons and black epaulets with gold Lieutenant J.G. bars. He was holding his hat in his hand, "Hi, pretty girl. You look, ummm, so beautiful."

Meg grinned broadly, too broadly she knew, but she couldn't mask her feelings and stammered, "You do, too! I mean you look handsome." She felt foolish, blushed and hung her head as she led him up the stairs where her mother and father waited.

Her mother's jaw literally fell open as she looked at Meg's date.

Meg could see shock and disapproval clouding her mother's face and she read her mind. She's thinking he's too good looking and too old for me.

He shook Margaret's hand. "Well, I can see where Meg gets her good looks."

Margaret jerked her head back and stared at him, then forced a thin smile.

Bill shook his hand, and smiled broadly. "Boy, you sure look like a dandy in that uniform. Hope nobody takes you for a Good Humor ice cream man."

Meg glared at her father. "That's really dumb, Dad!" Anxious to get out of the house quickly, Meg kissed her parents and motioned Josh to follow her down the stairs.

"Good night, Mr. and Mrs. O'Meara, I'll have Cinderella home by midnight. Don't worry," Josh said.

Meg pulled him by the hand, hoping to avoid any further embarrassment.

Walking up Newell Street, Meg could feel the eyes of her neighbors watching. Mr. and Mrs. Flanagan got up from their veranda chairs for a better look and leaned over the rail. When they passed nosy Mrs. O'Connor, she called out in a jeering voice, "Well, well, now, will you look at Miss O'Meara and her admiral all dressed in white. Are ye gettin married, luv? Sniff, sniff, ain't I gettin an invite to the weddin?"

"Very funny, Mrs. O'Connor," Meg remarked dryly.

Josh laughed and saluted the old lady.

Meg was upset and thought to herself, Damn neighbors! Talk about shanty Irish! But she had to admit that of all the dates who had ever walked with her up her street, none had ever created as much attention as Josh. She hoped she looked sophisticated enough in her Filene's Basement special. The white crepe material clung closely to her body. The cap sleeves and high shoulder pads were the latest style, as was the v-neckline which showed a hint of cleavage. The slim white dress accentuated her tan and her good figure.

Riding the trackless trolley bus to Harvard Square, a thought kept popping into Meg's head. He's 20 years old. So much older than anyone I've ever dated. He's so worldly. He was almost too good to be true! He rather frightened Meg. She hoped he'd think she was mature enough to ask her out again.

The evening was perfect. He ordered dinner for both of them from a French menu, and Meg sipped his wine. He held her closely when they danced, and he never let go of her hand the whole evening. It was all like a dream.

Just before they reached Meg's house, she hurriedly explained to Josh, her mother's method of making her dates say quick good nights. "She always waits up for me. I'm not allowed to have my own key. The moment she hears footsteps on the downstairs veranda, she starts pressing the buzzer that releases the door lock. Then, if I don't come in right away, she continuously turns the veranda light on and off until I'm inside the hall. And, because of Mom's light and sound show, some boys, especially Dinky Ahearn, got mad because he didn't get a good night kiss, and never asked me out again." Meg laughed.

"Are you hinting that I should give you a good night kiss before we get to your house?" Josh asked with an impish grin.

Flustered, Meg answered, "Oh, no! Well I mean, I just wanted to let you know that my Mom does it to all boys I date."

"I'd think a pretty girl like you would have a steady beau."

A feeling of guilt ran through Meg as she thought of Rick. She still wrote to him every night. "Well I do, or rather I did have a steady boyfriend, but he went into the Air Corps. Actually, he suggested I have dates."

"He must be a great guy."

"Oh, yes, he is."

"Meg, are you trying to tell me you don't want another date with me?"

"Oh, Lord no! I mean, I really had a grand time tonight. No, I hope we'll see each other again, honest."

Just before they stepped on the downstairs veranda, Josh quickly said, "Good night, doll baby, I'll give you a call." He blew her a kiss, and was off up the street with a wave.

Meg was crushed and positive that she'd never see him again because of stupid things she said during the evening.

But, the next evening at supper time, he called and said, "You know something, doll baby, I have a big crush on you."

A tremendous surge of relief filled Meg's whole being and she sputtered, "Oh, I'm so glad!"

That night she wrote to Rick. She felt terrible. She hated to hurt him, but she wanted to be honest. She knew that soon, someone would tell him she was dating a Harvard Square officer. Meg's dating an officer would really gripe him, because he was an enlisted man. Along with that, Josh was stationed at Harvard, and the old antagonism between "town and gown" still existed.

Rick wrote back: "I wish you happiness but please take some advice from someone who cares a great deal about you. Don't rush your new romance. This guy is much older and no doubt more experienced; you know what I mean! I'm Morale Officer of my platoon, and I spend lots of time with the chaplain. We've had long, serious talks, so don't be shocked when I tell you I'm been thinking quite seriously about going into the priesthood when the war is over."

Meg didn't quite believe that at all. She suspected he was just trying to make her feel better about breaking up. He was always so thoughtful. She felt pangs of remorse and yet what she felt for Josh was so much more intense than what she had felt for Rick. It was at times like this that she missed Joe so much. She knew he would have helped her sort out her feelings. Being honest, Meg knew that Joe would have picked Rick over Josh.

For the next month, Meg and Josh dated often. He took her to places she had never been. They went to the races at Suffolk Downs, sailed on the Charles, and often went to dinner at Claverly Hall, his dorm at Harvard. He didn't kiss her until their third date, and by then Meg's anticipation was so great, she initiated the kiss. She had never been kissed like that before. He held her head between his hands, ran his fingers through her hair, kissed her eyes, her ears, and finally her mouth, which excited her so much, she had to draw back to catch her breath.

Josh went home for two weekends in July, and Meg was miserable. Although he never said what his religion was and Meg didn't ask, he usually went to Mass with her. She assumed he may have been a fallen-away Catholic. He did say that he hadn't been to church for a long time. His going to church won points from Margaret and Bill because Meg was not allowed to date non-Catholics.

Within a month of dating Josh, Meg was intensely in love. Her dates with him were emotionally filled, glamorous and admittedly a bit frightening.

She was growing concerned about their relationship because their "necking" became more amorous with each date. She worried that she might not have the will power to stop him if he tried to go "too far." She wasn't sure just how far "too far" might be, but she knew it was waiting in the wings to happen. And, it would be sinful. She dreaded the thought of having to confess "a sin of sex with a man." It was a terrifying thought.

Meg met Jane Baxter in the Square. They hadn't seen each other for quite a while and decided to have lunch in a back room booth at Daly's. Jane, now a sophomore at Wellesley College, had been vacationing at her summer home on Cape Cod. Meg poured out the details of her romance with Josh, trying to explain her dilemma about the sexual feelings that filled her when he kissed her. She admitted that she had never experienced such strong emotions with Rick or any other boy.

"It sounds like you're playing with fire, Meg," Jane said in a concerned voice. "I've had a few close encounters with some boys I've met at frat parties. Take my word for it, Meg, you'll have to be very careful! My roommate has gone all the way, but she makes a guy put on a safe even before they begin. She says it's the only way to avoid pregnancy if you're going to fool around with intercourse."

Meg was stunned by the words "safe" and "intercourse" and shocked to think that Jane would assume that she would ever go that far with Josh. She knew very little about these things. Her "club" girlfriends never discussed the details of sex, because, like her, their knowledge was also very limited. Jane's final words when they said goodbye, although meant to be funny, frightened Meg. "Remember, Meg, pregnancy happens all the time to nice, innocent girls like you. So keep your legs crossed, sweetie!" Jane laughed as she drove away.

Josh had gone home the last weekend in August, and on the Friday before Labor Day, he took Meg out to dinner at the Oxford Grill in Harvard Square. He was unusually quiet and seemed concerned about something.

"Is something wrong, Josh?" Meg asked.

"Doll baby, I have some bad news to tell you. I knew it was coming, but I wasn't sure when. I'm going to be shipped out next week on a minesweeper."

Meg was stunned and quickly reached across the table, grabbing his hands in hers. Her eyes filled with tears and spilled down her cheeks. "Oh, God, Josh, no! Oh, darling, you can't be. I can't live without you. Damn the war! It takes everybody you love away." It was the first time she had said the word, love.

"You know I'm crazy about you, too, Meg, and I hate the thought of being away from you, but maybe it's for the best. I want you so much, and I don't know how much longer I can hold out. You know what I mean."

After her recent talk with Jane, she knew what he meant, and her thoughts were in a turmoil. "There must be another way to show how much we love each other." She blurted out, "I could never do anything like, well...you know." She just couldn't say the words, have sex. "It would be a terrible sin! I could get pregnant," she whispered and was seized with embarrassment at the boldness of her remarks.

"It's okay, doll baby, if you don't want to, then it won't happen." Smiling faintly, he took a cocktail napkin, folded it, and told Meg to put on fresh lipstick and kiss it for him.

She put on the lipstick without the aid of a mirror, never taking her eyes off him. She put the fold of the napkin between her lips, imprinting the outline of a kiss.

She had a sinking feeling that she was losing him, not just to minesweepers, but because she wouldn't go all the way with him.

Josh tore the napkin in half and gave Meg one half of the kiss and put the other half in his wallet. Then he took both her hands in his and look deeply into her eyes. "Doll baby, when the war's over, we'll meet in New York and put this napkin and our lives back together, I promise."

Meg believed him, but her heart was broken that night.

A week after Josh left she received a postcard from him from New York with a short message saying he missed her and would write when he got an address. It was signed with the letter 'J.'

That evening after dinner, Margaret, who obviously had read the card, asked Meg, "Does your friend 'J' have some reason not to sign his full name. Don't you think that's strange, Meg?"

Meg did, but she wasn't about to admit it to her mother. "Why are you always so suspicious, Mom?" Margaret's feelings towards Josh had not changed much. Meg knew her mother didn't completely trust him.

"Mothers have instincts about these things," she said.

A week later Jane was waiting for Meg outside the bank. "I have to talk to you." She said in a serious tone. "Get in the car and we'll drive to my house. They went directly up to her bedroom with cokes and shut the door. "Meg, I stopped by your house about an hour ago to find out what you were doing tonight. I picked up the mail that had been put in the slot and, I really wasn't being nosey. But I did look at the letter on top. It had a 'J,' an APO address, and it was addressed to you. When I handed the mail to your mother she looked at the top letter, and I guess she figured out that I had seen it."

Meg was thrilled. "Oh! So I did get a letter finally. Great!" she yelled.

"Listen, Meg, your mother made me promise never to tell you about the letter, but I can't do that to you."

"You mean she wasn't going to let me have my letter?" Meg was furious.

"I hate to tell you, but you're not going to get the letter. Your Mom asked me to follow her into the kitchen. She lit a match and burned the letter in the sink. She really distrusted him, Meg. I could hardly have stopped her, I wouldn't even dare try."

Meg was astounded. She couldn't believe her mother would do anything like that. Her heart ached, and she began crying.

"I have an idea, Meg. Why not just write to him at Claverly Hall at Harvard, and ask them to forward it. He must have left a forwarding address. Tell him to write to you here at my address."

Meg wrote the letter right away, but decided not to say anything to her mother about burning Josh's letter because she'd be mad at Jane forever. In her letter to Josh, she told him how her Mom destroyed his letter. She thinks that you are too old for me, and wants me to forget you, but I never will, darling. She gave him Jane's address and told him to send his letters there from now on.

Two weeks went by, but Josh never wrote again. Meg feared he was angry, or maybe Harvard didn't forward his letter, but they had.

Jane called Meg. "I have a letter for you at my house with a New York postmark, but no return address. Come and get it!"

Meg rushed there right after work. The handwriting did not look like Josh's but then it was hard to tell because he always printed what he wrote. She tore open the envelope and began to read in elated anticipation.

Dear Miss O'Meara:

This letter will be no more pleasant for you to receive than it is for me to send. I received your letter to Josh which was forwarded from Harvard to his home. I am his wife and he is the father of our two sons.

I find it very difficult to believe the he would deceive you and me. But he did. You sound very young and infatuated. I hope you won't be after reading this letter. Your mother is right. He is too old for you. He's twenty-three and of the Jewish faith. I was stunned that he attended your church. You stated that you missed him at Mass.

Please forgive him. I love him and want him to come home from the war for our children and me. Try not to be too hurt, he's not a bad person. I guess he was just lonely.

Sincerely,
S/Mrs. Joshua Caldwell

Meg felt faint and dazed. Jane, realizing the letter was bad news from the look on Meg's face, held her hand out for it. She felt certain the letter stated that Josh had been killed or wounded because Meg had kept repeating as she read, "Oh, God. No. No. Oh, God, he can't be!"

Meg handed Jane the letter and she cried out hysterically, "Read this! You won't believe it!"

Jane took the letter and sat next to Meg on the bed and patted her back while she read. She could feel Meg's body shaking. When she finished the letter she rolled it up in a ball and threw it across the room. "That dirty, rotten S.O.B. That crummy bum!" Jane yelled to the walls of the room.

Meg looked at Jane as if in a trance. Few things in her life would ever affect her like this. She felt dirty, shamed, but mostly deceived! "Oh, Jane," she wailed. "What am I going to do? Oh, that poor woman and the kids. I'll write to her and tell her how sorry I am, and that..."

Jane interrupted. "You'll do no such thing. She doesn't want to hear any more about his affair. Maybe he's had others. Don't waste any more tears on the rat. Get angry at him!"

Meg leaned into Jane and put her arms around her as if clinging to escape for the pain that filled her. She sobbed, "Oh, God, Jane, how could he do it to his wife and children? And I was sure he loved me. How could he do it?"

"Easy, I guess. He's a selfish person. You were used badly, Meg. Remember that. And remember something else," Jane said smiling faintly. "If you date anymore of those ninety-day wonders at Harvard, check out their marital status before you get too serious."

Recovery was slow for Meg. She had been deeply wounded. Although time eased the pain; the scar would remain forever.

THIRTEEN

*T*he war worsened, and Meg, like most Americans, felt a deep need to do something to help the war effort. The O'Mearas still had no more news about Joe. They went to Mass every day and prayed the he would be found alive.

Meg made a serious, unselfish decision to put off joining the Ice Capades until the war ended. On her 18th birthday, September 12, 1943, She was inducted into the Massachusetts Women's Defense Corps. The Corps was a volunteer female auxiliary of the Massachusetts National Guard. She felt proud in her smart-looking uniform of dark brown twill, khaki shirt, brown tie, and a cap similar to a WAC's hat. The cap had the MWDC insignia, which was gold and cloisonné. A red cord circled the cap band. Meg was now Private Meghan O'Meara. Most of her duties would be at night, so she could keep her daytime job at the bank. She was told, "Cut your hair short or put it up in a rat." She learned that a rat was a rolled pad over which long hair was tucked in with hairpins. She choose the latter.

Bill was so proud of Meg the first time he saw her in uniform, his eyes filled with tears. Meg knew her mother was touched, too, because she hugged her tightly and said, "You're a good girl, Meg, and a good American."

"I'm carrying on for our Joe," Meg said with deep sincerity.

She spent most weekends in various armories in Cambridge and Boston receiving intensive training in "casualty" from a famous surgeon at Massachusetts General Hospital. Her group was trained to recognize fractures and sprains and apply proper splints and bandages. They were instructed in the treatment of burns, shock, bleeding and other medical problems. Their training also included learning the proper procedures for giving medical aid and transport to the injured in a bombed building. They had hands-on training by riding in ambulances and assisting medics in real life situations.

Along with their casualty courses, they were trained in convoy and gas identification. Her squadron drilled with units from other areas and marched in parades. Within three months, Meg made Private First Class, and her mother proudly sewed her PFC stripe on her uniform sleeve.

Meg's social life was at an all time low. She didn't encourage any new relationships but would occasionally date local boys who were home on leave.

Meg's best friend, Babs, had become a secretary at Harvard Law School and spent most of her free time with a girl friend who worked in the same office. Meg felt sad that their close friendship was over, but their lifestyles were no longer compatible.

Meg became deeply committed to volunteering, doing clerical work at the armory across from M.I.T. on Massachusetts Avenue. She did a variety of jobs: typing, filing and making copies of orders and memos on an antiquated hand-cranked duplicating machine that leaked purple ink over everything, including her.

Whenever Colonel Rizzoli, the commanding officer, came into the office, he teased Meg. "Ah, Private O'Meara! There she is with her lovely, smiling countenance smeared with purple ink, most becoming, most becoming."

His ribbing never bothered Meg, because she always gave it right back to him, which he seemed to enjoy. The regulars around the office couldn't have gotten away with it, though. He was considered a tough commander.

One evening, after she had served for three months, Sergeant Thomas entered her office. "Hey, O'Meara, the Colonel wants you out on the armory floor on the double."

Meg assumed it was to pick up a job for the copy machine. It was almost nine forty-five, and she was just about to leave. "I don't want another big job tonight. I'm tired!"

"TS (tough shit), O'Meara. Follow me," the Sergeant ordered.

When he opened the armory doors, Meg could see that about 500 troops from various units were meeting there tonight. They were standing at attention around the outer perimeter of the floor. The Sergeant gestured for Meg to enter and follow him as he marched towards the center of the armory where Colonel Rizzoli was standing.

This had never happened before. Usually the Colonel or others who wanted something typed or duplicated would give her the job, just inside the door of the armory. Meg, now keeping in step with Sergeant Thomas and following him out towards the center of the hall, suddenly realized that 500 men must be looking at her. That thought gave her a severe attack of self-consciousness, causing her whole body to stiffen and her face to turn scarlet and hot. She was completely distraught.

The nipped-in waist of her uniform, along with the wide black leather belt accentuated her bust, making it appear fuller than it actually was. She fought back the urge to cover her breasts by crossing her arms. It was a habit she had developed if she saw a man eyeing her 34B bosom.

Suddenly she realized she was standing in front of the Colonel. Following the Sergeant, she saluted, then glared at the Colonel as she thought, he probably thinks this is funny making me march out here in front of all the men.

The Colonel spoke loudly, "Private First Class, Meghan O'Meara."

Meg was startled and wondered why he was speaking so loudly, and why was he staring at her left breast?

She half-heard what he was saying as he continued speaking, "Her loyalty to our Battalion, her tireless efforts beyond the call of duty for the war effort..."

Suddenly the Colonel touched the lapel of Meg's left breast pocket. Without looking to see why, Meg reacted instinctively and gave his outstretched hand a sharp chop with the edge of her right hand while simultaneously hissing through clenched teeth, "Watch it, buster!"

Stifled laughter echoed off the walls as Colonel Rizzoli withdrew his hand quickly. His face reddened with embarrassment. He handed a medal to Meg, and in a staccato voice, he said, "Private O'Meara, a medal from the Battalion. Then dropping his voice to a whisper, he said to Meg, "Stay in your office until I dismiss the men."

Meg exchanged his salute although her hand was shaking. She did an "about face" and followed Sergeant Thomas across the Armory floor. If Meg thought the walk into the hall had been traumatic, the walk out past the 500 men was total torture. Although she kept her eyes down, she could sense that not only were the eyes of all the men following her, but she could hear them sniggering. Her eyes filled quickly with tears.

When they reached the door, the Sergeant let her pass in front of him. When he shut the door behind them, he stopped, put his hands on his hips and asked in an incredulous tone, "Good God, O'Meara, what in the hell made you do that to the Colonel? And in front of all his men! Couldn't you see he was giving you a medal, you dumb broad! He wanted to surprise you! You...you jerk, you."

The deluge that had filled Meg's eyes now let go and saturated her cheeks. "Oh, my God. I didn't know what he was doing...I ah...I swear to God I didn't know. Oh, he's going to kill me!" She ran down the hall to her office, slammed the door behind her and sat at her desk with her head buried in her arms.

A few minutes later the door opened. Meg looked up and saw Colonial Rizzoli standing there with his arms folded across his chest and his eyebrows furrowed together. His mouth, stretched in a slim straight line suddenly broke into a broad grin, and he started laughing uproariously.

Meg stood, saluted and stared at him in confusion. "Oh, Colonial Rizzoli, aren't you mad at me? I'm so sorry. I acted so stupid! I, I..."

"Hey, kid. Don't start blubbering now. I'm letting you off the hook, okay? And I'll tell you why. I sort of figured you to be a pretty sharp chick, but you know what, O'Meara, you're about as unsophisticated as they come."

"But I had no idea you were going to give me a medal."

"I know, I know. Now I know! You thought, hey, Rizzoli is trying to get a cheap feel in front of 500 men." Then he laughed loudly again. "It's going to make a great story for the men to spread around. What the hell, kid? We need laughs in wartime."

"Oh, I'm so glad you're not mad at me."

"And I'm sorry I embarrassed you. I never gave a medal to a dame before. I guess I better learn how to execute that maneuver before I get a broken arm. By the way, do you like the medal?"

Meg suddenly realized she hadn't even looked at it. It was still tightly clenched in her hand. It was embedded so tightly in her palm, that it left an outline in her skin when she lifted it out. "Oh, it's beautiful, Colonel. I'll be proud to wear it." The medal had the insignias of the three companies stationed at the Armory. Meg asked tentatively, "Colonel, would you do me the honor of pinning the medal on my uniform?"

The Colonel's eyes bugged out. "No way, O'Meara!" He held his hands out defensively and laughed. "Let your old man pin it on. Wasn't he a war hero once? Why don't you hit the road. It's late. See you in a couple of days."

Meg saluted him.

He saluted back and winked.

Meg was teased relentlessly for weeks by the men at the armory. To embarrass her, they'd always make a point to look intently at the medal she wore proudly on her left breast.

She took the ribbing with good humor.

& * &

At five o'clock in the evening on December 14, 1943, the front doorbell rang, and Meg pressed the buzzer. When the door opened downstairs, a male voice called up, "Western Union. I have a telegram for Mr. and Mrs. O'Meara."

Meg raced down the stairs and took the yellow envelope from the young man. The O'Mearas had never received a telegram before. Racing up the stairs, Meg, yelled excitedly, "Mom, Dad we've got a telegram. Shall I open it?"

Margaret came running out of the kitchen drying her hands on a dish towel. Bill hurried into the living room, folding the *Cambridge Chronicle* and tossing it on the divan. Their faces were masked in fear, because in wartime, telegrams meant bad news.

"For God's sake, Meg, hurry, open it!" Margaret cried in a quivering voice, anticipating news of Joe. She grabbed Bill's hand for support.

Meg tore the envelope open and read:

Mr. and Mrs. William J. O'Meara
155 Newell Street
Cambridge, Mass.

Dear Mr. and Mrs. O'Meara:

The Government of the United States of America
has been notified by the Japanese Government,
in compliance with the Geneva Convention, that
your son, Joseph William O'Meara, is alive
and being held prisoner by the Japanese Government. STOP

As the impact of the telegram registered, their tragic expressions turned to astonishment. "Alive!" Margaret wailed. Oh, sweet Jesus, Bill, our Joe is alive!" She leaned her body against his, and Bill clutched her closely, then reached out for Meg.

Squeezing his eyes tight to hold back the stinging tears, Bill gasped deeply, then sobbed out in a pitiful moan, "Oh, dear God, dear God. Thank you, thank you." His whole body shook with emotional release.

Meg tried to soothe him with gentle pats on his back, "Everything's okay now, Dad. Our Joe's alive."

Suddenly Margaret's body went limp in Bill's arms. "Jesus, Mary and Joseph!" Bill cried out. "Meg, Mom's collapsed! What'll I do?"

They gently laid her down on the floor. "What should we do, kiddo? Better call the doctor, quick! I think she's had a shock." Panic seized Meg. "No, she's just fainted. I'll get my MWDC medical kit. I'll be right back, Dad." Within seconds, Meg returned to her mother's side with an ammonia capsule, which she snapped in half. The word "shock" and her mother's pale, clammy face brought back terrifying memories of her Nana and Aunt Nell. Chills ran through Meg's body. She slowly passed the powerful smelling compound back and forth under her mother's nose and within a few seconds, Margaret coughed and the color began returning to her face.

Bill lifted her to a sitting position, pushed her damp hair back from her face, and kissed her gently on the forehead, "It's okay now, darlin! Everything's okay. Our Joe is alive, and here we are all bawling and fainting when we should be the happiest family in the world."

Margaret smiled faintly as she looked from Meg to Bill. Then said in a strong voice, "Oh, yes, thank God, my Joe's alive."

Meg picked up the telegram that she had dropped on the floor. "I forgot, there's more to the telegram. Now don't get nervous. It must be good news!"

"Read it!" Bill and Margaret cried in unison.

Meg read:

You will be contacted by letter with further information regarding your son's physical condition and location. STOP
s/The War Department of the U.S.

Cheers filled the room.

Meg said, "I have to call Eileen this minute."

Ten minutes later, Joe's girlfriend, Eileen, came tearing up the stairs, grinning broadly with tears streaming down her face. "I have to see, touch and kiss that wonderful piece of yellow paper," she squealed with joy and held the precious message next to her heart.

Within the next hour, all the O'Meara's relatives and friends were called, and that evening they had their first real party and celebrated until three o'clock in the morning.

🙂 * 🙂

A week later, a letter arrived from the War Department. It stated that Joe had been taken prisoner by the Japanese on Bataan in the Philippines on April 14, 1942 and was now in a prisoner of war camp somewhere in Japan. His physical condition was reported as "satisfactory." His family would now be allowed to write to him through an Army Post Office address, and he would be allowed to send mail home.

When the O'Mearas finally received the first letter from Joe, it was like a miracle. It was as if they were hearing from someone who had come back from the dead. The letter looked like a lace doily. It had been censored considerably with words cut out about every other inch. It was incoherent, but it was Joe's handwriting. It filled the O'Mearas with a wonderful warm feeling just knowing his hands had touched the paper.

Bill looking steadily at the letter said, "Now we have to pray even harder that God keeps him alive. I hate to think of what the poor kid has been through being a prisoner of those yellow bastards!"

FOURTEEN

*F*rom the time of the attack by the Japanese on the Philippines on December 8, 1941, to the day the O'Mearas received notification from the War Department on December 14, 1943 that he was alive, almost twenty-four anguishing months had passed for Joe and his family.

ଯ * ଯ

On December 8, 1941, close to noon, Joe and his B-17 crew were just waking up after flying early dawn patrols.

"Holy Jesus!" Tiny, the tail gunner yelled as he jumped out of bed and alerted the others. "Listen to that drone! Where in hell are those planes coming from?"

A look of terror froze on Joe's face. He yelled, "Everybody up! "They're Japs!"

The men raced out of the barracks just as the Japanese squadrons of bombers and zeros came into sight. While the zeros strafed the aircraft, the bombers dropped their deadly loads on runways, hangers and buildings. Within minutes, the entire base was in shambles, and there were many casualties. Only a few B-17s and P-40s were in one piece after the raid. Although Joe's B-17 had been completely destroyed, his crew had survived the attack with only minor injuries. He was incredulous that this kind of raid could happen without warning.

ଯ * ଯ

Later that morning, Joe, along with other pilots and Filipino officers, questioned the Base Commander. "Where the hell did those planes take off from?"

"Why weren't we warned?" A Filipino Captain asked.

"They took off from Formosa, we've been told," a sergeant said. "It was a totally unexpected sneak attack. We couldn't have offered any resistance anyway, even if we'd known they were coming. Anti-aircraft equipment here in the Pacific is almost non-existent, and what little we have is outmoded and ineffective. We would never have been a match for them."

Up to now, young pilots like Joe had been confident and cocky about being a match for the Japanese, mainly because the American pilots had never received any reliable intelligence on the magnitude of the Japanese air strength.

An older pilot told Joe, "I've had a feeling all along that the back-up assistance we need, and were promised, to out-perform the enemy, would never reach us in time. The great emphasis of American defenses is geared towards the European theater of war. We're sitting ducks out here."

A week later, the Japanese attacked Nichols Air Base and the Naval Base at Cavite. Now, most American planes in the area had been destroyed. There were more pilots than planes, and only the more experienced pilots would be doing the flying. Joe and many other pilots, navigators, and bombardiers became infantrymen overnight, filling in wherever there was a need.

❧ * ❧

On December 22, eighty Japanese ships, carrying more than 43,000 well-trained troops, landed in Lingayen Gulf. They continuously pursued the poorly trained Filipino and American troops. A massacre was imminent. After two days of resistance, MacArthur gave the order for all troops to retreat to the Bataan Peninsula and to Corregidor. Joe and his crew were still safe. General Wainwright, commander of the North Luzon Forces, also retreated south to Bataan. Manila was declared an open city. Clark Field was deserted as a base. The last troops placed bombs inside all the remaining buildings and destroyed them along with everything they felt might be useful to the enemy. Huge stockpiles of food were destroyed. There was no way to transport it. What little was taken was soon depleted.

When the retreating troops reached the port area of Manila, they took inter-island barges, and under the cover of darkness, anchored under the guns on the hills of Corregidor for protection.

It was Christmas eve. One of Joe's crew turned on his portable radio. *Silent Night* was playing, but the emotional impact was too great, and Joe told him to turn it off.

Before the sun came up, an American submarine surfaced and sent a message to the troops to stay on land because a Japanese cruiser was waiting for them a few miles out. Eventually they made their way to Mariveles Harbor on Bataan and unloaded under fire. Here on the peninsula, they set up a line of defense.

&. * &.

By the end of December most Air Corps units had reached Bataan. The lack of food and medical supplies became a serious problem. Thousands contracted malaria and dysentery as they dug deeper into the jungle. An estimated 80,000 troops had now retreated to Bataan; 16,000 were Americans.

Relentlessly, the Japanese penetrated every pocket of resistance, but the Americans and Filipino forces hung on desperately through January and February, still clinging to the hope of help from the States. It was evident that the Philippines could not be rescued.

On March 12, 1942, MacArthur was ordered by President Roosevelt to leave. He was too valuable to lose. After safely reaching Australia, he made his immortal declaration, "I shall return."

Those left on Bataan and Corregidor felt abandoned. The Japanese renewed their push through Bataan with fresh supplies and troops. Japanese Zeros strafed the island continuously and thousands of Japanese snipers filled the trees. General Wainwright, now the Commander-in-Chief, estimated that more than seventy-five percent of his men needed medical help, or were starving and could not continue to defend themselves. On April 9, 1942, he surrendered his forces.

&. * &.

Joe and his crew had made their way up the hilly terrain to a place called Little Baugie, an engineering depot. For five days they evaded the Japanese, but on the night of the fifth day, they were suddenly surrounded and captured by a search party.

All the prisoners captured in the last few weeks were herded near the only main road on the island of Bataan. There were nearly 50,000 Americans and Filipinos. Before the prisoners were headed out to their destination, San Fernando City, a horrible and sadistic display of Japanese cruelty took place. For no apparent reason, more than 400 Filipino officers were bayoneted and beheaded. Thus began the infamous 85 mile "Bataan Death March."

During the march, prisoners were given little food or water. Many were wounded or suffering from malaria, dysentery, scurvy, scabies, and other tropical, fungus-type, morbid growths, breaking out all over their bodies. All were weak and rapidly dehydrating.

If a man fell, no one was allowed to stop and help him up. It was the most devastating dilemma for those who saw their best buddy fall and make a choice: stop to help him up and be shot instantly, or pass him by and live with the moment forever. To add to the cruelty, trucks drove over the fallen bodies, some dead, some still alive.

Prisoners had to take the attitude, "I refuse to die!" and live by it every waking minute. Those who started out weakened by disease or wounded, didn't stand a chance of survival. Estimates of the number of deaths on the march vary between 600 and 2,300 Americans and 5,000 and 10,000 Filipinos. Most remembered the trip taking about five days. Joe, and all but one of his B-17 crew, survived.

It was 110 degrees the day the Japanese loaded hundreds of starving, sick, and wounded prisoners into freight cars for the trip to Bilibid Federal Prison in Manila. Using their rifle butts, they prodded as many as 100 into each car. There were no latrines and only small slits for fresh air. Within an hour the air was putrid. The men had to stand shoulder to shoulder, back to back or facing each other, holding that position for the trip. There was very little noise except for moans, whispers, curses, the murmuring of prayers, and the constant sound of retching.

Joe was nose to nose with a soldier who was his height and a few years older. He was darkly tanned, and an unruly growth of beard covered his face. His four inch, blond crew-cut hair stood straight up.

Joe teased him, "Good thing you can't see yourself; you'd be frightened to death."

The soldier growled back, "Shut-up, dogface. You've got the baddest breath I've ever smelled."

Joe grinned, "Yeah, I know. Some dirty Nip took my last tube of Ipana and ate it!"

Joe felt a body that had been pressed tightly to his back, begin to slip down. "Hey, guys crowd in behind me! Someone's going down," he pleaded.

"Lucky son of a bitch!" someone said as the men pressed their bodies closer.

The dying man expired in an upright position, thus lending a bit of dignity to his death.

Joe's new friend said without emotion, "Once rigor mortis sets in, he'll stand tall by himself."

"What are you, an undertaker?"

"No, I'm a medic. Name's Chip Johnson. I'm from Oconomowoc, Wisconsin. What are you, a fly-boy?"

"I was," Joe answered. "I'm Joe O'Meara from Cambridge, Massachusetts."

Chip, who had been in the Philippines before the war started, knew the ropes and knew it was wise to have a buddy but not let the Japanese know it. Before the train ride was over, he and Joe made a pact to force each other to go on, no matter how often they were beaten, starved or sick.

At Bilibid prison, beatings and torture were common occurrences. Medical care was never given.

"Listen, Joe, I've got some powdered morphine that I hid when we were captured. I want you to pull out your shirttail and mine. I'll divide the powder, then pour a little water from my canteen over the powder. The cloth will absorb it. If you ever need a pain killer, you can suck the drug out.

It wasn't long before Joe needed the powder badly. A particularly sadistic guard pulled Joe out of the ranks for no reason. He made him drop his pants and bend over. He drew his sword from the scabbard and Joe knew that when a Japanese draws his sword, he has to draw blood. He put the tip of his sword to Joe's buttocks and cut some Japanese figures. Blood streamed down Joe's backside. While the guards laughed hysterically, Joe fainted and fell forward.

If Chip hadn't told Joe about how to handle pain, and how to hold his temper, he never could have withstood this humiliating indignity.

The guards left him lying in the hot sun. Insects swarmed over Joe's bloody bottom. No one dared to go to Joe's aid because they would be shot. Chip worried that the bacteria from the insects would cause a serious infection.

The sun had gone down and there was a change of guards. One of the new guards kicked Joe with his boot to see if he could wake him up. When Joe didn't move, the guard threw a pail of water over him. Joe slowly came to and was in severe pain. He realized that his clothes were wet. He slowly moved his hand down to his shirttail and brought it up to his mouth. He sucked out the pain killing drug and groaned loudly. That seemed to please the guards, and they laughed at him.

Mercifully, he fell asleep. The guards made two prisoners drag him back to his hut.

Chip quickly examined Joe's festering wound that was embedded with drowned insects and dried blood. He cleaned it up as best he could and poured on sulfa powder, hidden in his canteen cap.

Fortunately, Joe didn't get severely infected, but it took a long time for the wound to heal.

Along with two thousand other P.O.W.s, Joe and Chip were moved to a camp called Cabanatuan and were quartered in bamboo longhouses that were infested with lice and fleas. Malaria and pneumonia were common. Some days they were given rice and water, sometimes, nothing. Every day, sixty to eighty prisoners died. Then two miracles occurred. The first was the intervention by a Catholic priest who lived nearby and witnessed the daily tragedies. He convinced the camp commandant that the prisoners could become more self-sufficient if they raised their own food. He donated water buffaloes along with seeds and equipment to grow vegetables. Although it would take time for the vegetables to grow, it gave the men hope.

The second miracle occurred on Christmas Day, 1942. The Swedish Mercy ship, *Gripsholm*, brought three, eleven pound packages for each P.O.W. The packages were from the United States, Canada and South Africa. The prisoners went crazy opening their presents of coffee, cigarettes, sugar, salt, canned meats, powdered milk and vitamins. One young marine was so delirious with joy, he ate everything at once and died next to the latrine.

In March of 1943, 560 of the healthiest P.O.W.s, including Joe and Chip, were shipped to Niigata, Japan to work in a steel mill. Joe stoked furnaces and Chip ran a steam hammer. When it became severely cold, the men were issued Japanese Army overcoats. The only heat they had in their drafty barracks came from whatever they found to burn in fifty gallon drums.

Occasionally, a guard named Nobu Omura, who escorted them daily to and from the steel mill, would smuggle a small supply of coal into their barracks. He spoke English and was the only kind guard they had encountered.

One day on the way to the steel mill, Nobu told Joe and Chip, "I am a Nisei, born and raised in Honolulu, and I'm an American citizen."

Joe and Chip were suspicious of him. They thought he probably was a spy and would try to get information from them. "You expect us to believe that story?" Joe asked.

"Hey buddy, I messed up bad, and I'm here against my will, believe me! My parents are second generation Americans and own a rambling, old wooden hotel, The Hale Omura, in downtown Honolulu. My kid brother, Akira, and me did odd jobs around the hotel. In 1939, when I was eighteen, I went to Japan to visit relatives and fell in love with my beautiful third cousin. But she wouldn't marry me unless I became a Japanese citizen. So, like a real jerk, I did it. Within a month, I was drafted into the Imperial Japanese Army. And you want to hear more shit! I never heard from my beautiful third cousin again."

Chip said, "That's a great story, Nobu, but Joe and me aren't a couple of nitwits. You're wasting your time if you think you'll get any military information out of us."

"Hey, buddy, I'm no spy! At first, the Army thought I'd make a valuable contribution to their spy network because I was bilingual. Hey, I was so bummed out by what happened to me, I began to drink heavily. I was fired as a spy and demoted to prison camp guard."

Joe and Chip were finally convinced that he wasn't a spy when he told them, that because of him, his family, had been interned in a relocation camp in the States.

৯ * ৯

One night while on guard duty, Nobu opened the door to Joe's barracks and stumbled inside, dead drunk.

Joe ran to him and tried to stop him from yelling and sobbing. "Hey, you dumb Waikiki buddahead. Look it's me, your haole buddy. Knock off the noise, pal."

Nobu smiled wanly, "Hey, Joe, what da ya know, I jus got back from a burl-e-que show. How's that for bullshit?" Then he burst out crying and began to vomit.

Chip put a pail under his head. "Listen, Nobu, you're on guard duty, and if they catch you drinking, you'll be put in the stockade. Come'on, straighten up and fly right!"

He passed out.

Joe gathered all the men and reasoned with them to help protect Nobu. "I'll put on his uniform and stand his guard duty while you guys try to sober him up. Remember he's our most valuable asset in this camp!"

Because of the lean diet for the past couple of years, Joe weighed only ninety-five pounds and could easily fit into Nobu's uniform. The only problem was trying to fit into the tight pant legs, because Joe had scabies all over his legs and the scabs were so thick they bulged out. The pain was excruciating when the rough material pulled the scabs off.

Joe slipped out the door and hunched over to make himself look shorter. He strolled in the normal unmilitary fashion of the guards with the rifle slung carelessly over his shoulder. When he'd pass another guard, he'd fake a coughing fit and wave them away. Just before dawn, Chip opened the door and signaled Joe to come in. The men quickly undressed him and put the uniform back on Nobu who was dazed and still slightly inebriated but aware of what Joe had done for him.

Joe handed him his rifle and said, "Hit the road, you Waikiki kanakai (beach boy)."

Nobu grinned sheepishly and looked at the prisoners who may have saved his life. "What a bunch of sad sacks you guys look like in the morning." He bowed. "Arigato, mahalo and aloha!"

From that day forward, Nobu at great risk to himself, kept Joe's barracks supplied with coal, food, and best of all, news about the war, which was beginning to look better for the Allies.

❧ * ❧

In August 1943, in an unprecedented display of generosity, the camp Commandant informed the prisoners that the Japanese Government, in conforming with the rules of the Geneva Convention, would be notifying the prisoners' countries that they were alive and being treated well. And, they would now be allowed to write home and also receive mail. It was the best news the prisoners had ever heard.

But it was five months before the prisoners finally received their first letter from home. Only then, did a sense of hope prevail.

FIFTEEN

Cambridge, 1944. "Please, Meg, go with me to the officer's dance at the Commander Hotel," pleaded Virginia Casey, one of Meg's "club" friends. "It's your patriotic duty."

"I've told you a hundred times before, I'm not going any place where those '90 day' wonders are," Meg said firmly.

"Come'on, Meg, that Caldwell affair happened almost a year ago. It's dumb to believe that all officers are like him. Besides, all you have to do is dance with the guys, not date them."

Meg thought about that. She loved to dance and hadn't had much of any social life for quite a while. "Okay, I'll go. I suppose we have to wear formals?"

"Yup! And we'll have to ride the bus to the hotel unless we can get a ride." Virginia laughed when Meg groaned.

"We'll look absurd!" Meg said.

"Hey, there's a war on!" Virginia chided her.

The ballroom at the Commander Hotel was packed with men in white uniforms and girls in pastel colored taffetas and net formals. The officers outnumbered the girls two to one, and they had to be very aggressive to get even one dance.

By eleven thirty, Meg and Virginia were exhausted. They hadn't missed a dance and were ready to leave. On the way to the coat room, Meg stopped at the water bubbler for a drink.

"May I hold the button for you?" a male voice asked as a hand was placed over hers.

She looked up and saw an attractive Ensign smiling at her.

"Yes, thank you." She now could hold back her long hair with both hands as she drank.

"I was watching you jitterbug. You're a great dancer. Do you think you could keep up with a Californian?" the Ensign challenged.

Meg looked at Virginia and answered hesitantly, "Well, we were just leaving."

"I'll stay longer if you want to," Virginia said smiling. "Why don't you show the Californian how to dance."

They went back to the ballroom. The band was playing a slow song.

The Ensign said, "I'm Jim Wright. I'm from Riverside, California."

"Riverside!" Meg was astonished. "I know all about Riverside. My brother Joe was stationed there before he went to the Pacific."

"He must have been stationed at March Field. My Dad is an electrical engineer there. What was your brother flying?"

"B-17s, but he was taken prisoner on Bataan and is in a POW camp somewhere in Japan."

"That must be hard on you and your family. Uh, are you going to tell me your name?"

"Oh, I'm sorry. My name is Meg O'Meara, and I'm from Cambridge."

They danced until the music stopped. Then Meg looked directly into Jim Wright's eyes. "I'd like to ask you a question. Are you married?"

A shocked look crossed Jim's face. "Married! No way! I just graduated from college and midshipman school. I've hardly had any time to date, much less get married. Why do you ask? Do I look like an old married man?"

"No. It's a long story. Maybe I'll tell you sometime."

"Does that mean that I'll be seeing you again?"

Meg looked thoughtful. He seemed nice. Honest. He was good looking, the virile type. "Would you like to go to the beach tomorrow?"

"I'd love it," he answered enthusiastically.

The band began playing "Muskrat Ramble," and Jim led Meg onto the dance floor. "I'll teach you the Riverside Shuffle."

Jim was a terrific dancer, and Meg had a hard time keeping in step with him.

When the last dance was over, Jim asked if he could take Meg and Virginia home. Virginia lived a few doors away from Meg. Meg's mother no longer did her "light and sound show." She had her own key now.

When they got to her door, Jim tried to kiss her.

She pushed him away with a soft "no." "I'll meet you in Harvard Square tomorrow, in front of the Coop about ten-thirty. I have to go to Mass first."

"Okay, Meg. I'm looking forward to a day at the beach. Good night."

Meg lay awake for quite a while, thinking about Jim Wright. He was attractive, had a great smile, was a groovy dancer, and she had guessed a brain from what he told her. He hadn't bragged about it, it just slipped out that when he graduated from the University of California, he was in the top ten of his class. But he had bragged about California to Meg and Virginia on the walk home. Being a Californian gave him a certain interesting charisma. He brought back memories of Joe's letters when he was stationed in Riverside, because he too had raved about the palm trees, orange groves, high mountains and big surf beaches.

They had a fun day at Nahant Beach, although Jim was not impressed with East Coast waves. They went back to the Square and had sandwiches at the Wursthaus. By the end of the day, they knew quite a bit about each other's lives.

Jim had three brothers and one sister. He was twenty-two years old. Meg liked his strong face with deep dimples. He had a lean muscular build. He was only five feet, eight. He wasn't tall, dark and handsome. She was glad. She'd had her fill of that type.

She thought, it's strange now that I look back at the time I spent with Josh. I never knew anything about his parents or family. Well, naturally he couldn't tell me he had a wife and two sons. Block him out of your mind, Meg, she ordered herself, but it wasn't always easy.

☒ * ☒

Meg and Jim began to date regularly. He had daily and evening classes at Harvard Radar School. He would go on to M.I.T. Radar School when his courses were finished at Harvard. Meg continued her bank job and was quite busy with her M.W.D.C. activities. Because of their busy schedules, they always met in Harvard Square, but Meg wanted her Dad and Mom to meet Jim, and so she invited him to a Sunday dinner.

Margaret set the dining room table with her best linens and china, amenities normally used only on very special occasions, but Meg had insisted.

Bill teased, "This one must be real special if you got your Mom to use her good Havilland china. I thought we only used that on Thanksgiving and Christmas."

"He's very nice and well educated, so don't pull any of your dumb jokes, Dad."

Jim arrived promptly at noon. He was wearing the new summer-weight gray uniform. He shook hands with Bill and thanked Margaret for inviting him to dinner. "My mother is a wonderful cook, and I miss her meals more than anything."

"Well, I hope you won't be disappointed with my cooking. I'm a plain cook, just roast beef, gravy, baked potatoes, and string beans. It's a nourishing meal," Margaret said defensively.

"Oh, that sounds wonderful and smells delicious, Mrs. O'Meara," Jim said sincerely.

The dinner conversation centered around Joe being in the P.O.W. camp in Japan and Bill's WWI experiences. Then Meg bragged about Jim's scholastic skills at the University of California, much to his embarrassment. She could see that her parents, particularly her mother, were impressed.

"Meg says you're going on to M.I.T. when you finish Harvard," Margaret remarked. "You must be pretty smart to go to three colleges. We're real proud that our Joe will be going to Harvard, too, on a city scholarship when he comes home." Margaret bragged.

"What will you do for a living, Jim, when the war's over and you go home?" Bill asked.

"I'm not sure yet, but California is the land of opportunity. There's a great deal of industry there and lots of jobs for mechanical engineers. But, I may just stay in the Navy. I'm going to submarine school in New London when I'm through up here. My brother, Keith, is on a submarine in the Atlantic and my brother, Royden, is in the tank corps in Europe. They're both younger than me, and it really bothers me that they're out there on active duty, while I sit here in Harvard Square fighting the war."

Bill reached over and patted Jim's hand. "Don't worry, kid. You'll get your chance, and if you don't, all the better for you."

Meg sensed good feelings between her parents and Jim. She was glad the dinner was going so well.

Then, without any warning things took a turn for the worse when Margaret asked bluntly, "What religion are you, Jim?"

Meg cringed. Jim and she had discussed religion.

"We're Methodists. My mother is very active in the Riverside Women's Methodist Society. I've been sort of slipping lately and not attending services."

In a holier than thou voice, Margaret said, "We can never miss Sunday Mass. It's a mortal sin if we do."

"My mom would be really upset, too, if she knew I wasn't attending services on Sunday," Jim answered apologetically.

"Protestants don't seem to be as strong about their faith as Catholics," Margaret mused.

"Please, Mom, please," Meg begged. "Let's not talk anymore about religion." She glared at her mother and started clearing the table.

Bill stood up, "How about having a cigar out on the veranda, Jim?"

"Sure, Mr. O'Meara." Then Jim looked back towards the dining room to see if Mrs. O'Meara could hear. In a soft voice, he said to Bill, "My mother never would allow smoking or drinking in our home. Also, we're not allowed to play cards or go to the movies on the Lord's Day. You Catholics have it easy!"

"Geeze, Jim, I didn't know that Protestants were so strict. I'm sure glad I'm Catholic!"

They laughed and lit up their cigars.

In the kitchen Meg and her mother did the dishes in silence. Margaret was offended by the harsh way Meg had spoken to her. She broke the silence, "I don't understand why you got upset with me, Meg. It's important to let Protestants know about our religion. I hope you're not getting serious about this fellow. He seems nice, but he's not our kind. You know what I mean."

"Oh, God, Mom, do I ever! Ever since I was a little kid, all I've heard is how wonderful we are because we're Irish and Catholic, and the rest of the world is no good."

"I've never said they were no good, just not our kind, because they don't believe in God the way we do. It's not good to mix up different nationalities and religions, Meg. It creates problems sooner or later."

"Mom, my grandparents came to America in steerage about seventy years ago. They didn't discover it! Jim's grandparents and great grandparents and probably his great, great, grandparents, all Protestants and English, came to America two hundred and fifty years ago. They made a great contribution to America. They were farmers, sea captains and one was even a Senator. The Irish Catholics are newcomers to this country. Have you ever stopped to think about that? Do you realize, Mom, that before the late 1800's, there weren't even any Catholic churches here? And why do you care what Jim's religion is? I'm not marrying him, just dating him."

Margaret face clouded in confusion. She had never quite thought about the Irish as newcomers to America. She'd have to discuss what Meg said with her sister, Grace.

Meg was a confident and independent eighteen year old. She was never timid about speaking out when she felt strongly about her convictions. A person's religion was of no consequence to her. She believed deeply in her religion but had realized long ago that her parent's bigotry was based on ignorance. She knew that the prestige of being Irish Catholic was recognized only by Irish Catholics, but it had sustained her parents through the hard times.

ॐ * ॐ

From that Sunday on, Meg and Jim saw each other every day, even if only for a short time. They'd meet in the Square after work, often eating at Gore Hall, the Harvard dormitory where Jim lived.

Within a month, Jim began going to Mass with Meg. The first time he went to St. Peters, he told Meg, "It feels good to go to church again. It makes me feel like I've honored God properly, and it's a great way to start a day!"

"Doesn't it make you feel guilty to be in a Catholic church?" Meg asked. She knew she could never go to a Protestant service.

"No. The same God is in your church as in mine. It's just certain beliefs that are different."

All summer, Meg and Jim often double-dated with Jim's roommate, Steve Summers and his girlfriend, Ann Rizzo. Every Saturday they went to dinner and danced at the Officer's Club at the Fargo Building in Boston.

On Saturday, September 2, Meg and Jim went to a party at Ann Rizzo's house in Arlington. It was a lovely home with a swimming pool in the back yard. Towards the end of the evening, Meg and Jim went into the garden and sat on a stone seat near the pool. Seduced by the romantic setting and the full moon, they began embracing each other hungrily, kissing and whispering words of love.

Suddenly, Jim broke away, put his hands on Meg's shoulders and looked ardently into her eyes and said, "Meg, what would you think about getting married?"

Meg was stunned. They had talked quite often about how much they'd miss each other when Jim went to Sub school, but marriage had never been discussed.

"What would I think about getting married? Are you proposing to me, Jim?" Meg was astonished and searched his face for an answer. Was he teasing?

"Yup. I guess that's what I mean." He hesitated a moment, then added, "I mean, why not? We love each other, don't we? Well, what do you think?"

"Oh, Jim, yes," Meg cried, hugging and kissing him so fiercely that they fell backwards off the seat and ended up on the lawn, laughing and squealing like two children.

Steve and Ann came out through the French doors and looked at them rolling on the grass. Steve, smiled and asked, "What in the heck are you laughing about? Come on, share the joke with us."

"It's not a joke," Meg said, her laughing now turning to sobbing. "Oh, Jim, can we tell them?"

Jim looked up at Steve, "Why not? Steve, how would you like to be my best man?"

"Best man! Oh, my gosh! You mean you two are getting hitched? Yahoo! Congratulations, pal!" Steve whooped again, shook Jim's hand, pulled him to a standing position and hugged him.

Jim reached down and helped Meg to her feet. The two couples put their arms around each other making a circle of joy, and Steve began singing in a deep baritone, "Those Wedding Bells Are Breaking Up That Old Gang Of Mine."

They went inside, and Steve told everyone, "Fix a drink. I'm about to propose a toast. Here's to Jim and Meg who just became engaged a few minutes ago. May they have a long and happy life of marital bliss." Glasses were raised and everyone cheered the newly engaged couple.

The impact of the monumental decision Meg and Jim had made became more of a reality as they rode home on the bus.

"Oh, Jim, what will my parents say? What if they say no? I know they're going to object because of your religion. Damn it, why does my church object to mixed marriages?"

Jim held Meg's hand tightly. "Honey, listen, I've been giving religion a great deal of thought lately, and I think I've made a decision, although I'd like to talk it over with a priest."

"What are you saying, Jim? You're not thinking of changing your religion? You can't do that! I don't want you to do that for me! I couldn't do it for you. It's wrong, Jim. I won't let you."

"Meg, listen. I'm not thinking about doing it for you. I'm thinking about doing it for me. I feel good about the Catholic faith. It teaches many of the same beliefs my church does. I'm at peace when I'm at Mass. I can't explain it. It's just a good feeling that comes over me."

Meg's eyes filled with tears. Her whole being welled with love for this very special man. He was a good man, a man of high moral character. She had no doubts he'd be a caring husband and one day a wonderful father.

"When do you want me to tell your parents?"

A sudden sickening feeling surged through Meg and all the happiness disappeared. "Oh, my God, I dread that! There'll be a big scene. It's too late to tell them tonight. We'll tell them in the morning after they've been to Mass. We'll go to a later Mass so we can get out of the house if things go badly, and I'm afraid they will. Why don't you stay overnight? You can sleep in Joe's room."

"That a good idea," Jim said as he looked at his watch. "The gates are locked now at Gore Hall, and I'd have to climb over that ten foot iron fence."

When they arrived at Meg's house and entered the front hall, Meg called up the stairs to her mother. "Mom, are you awake? Could Jim sleep in Joe's room tonight? We had to wait so long for a bus in Arlington that Jim's locked out of his dormitory."

There was total silence at each end of the hall stairs as Margaret weighed the question, and Jim and Meg waited for an answer.

"Well, I guess it will be all right under the circumstances," she conceded.

The next morning after her parents left for eight o'clock Mass, Meg and Jim rehearsed over and over what they would say and how they would counter her parent's objections.

When the front door opened downstairs, Meg and Jim looked at each other, embraced quickly for support, then stood on opposite sides of the room, trying to appear nonchalant.

Meg's heart pounded so fast, she was becoming breathless. Suddenly, she felt like a child again.

When the O'Mearas entered the living room, Margaret frowned and remarked, "You two look like something is wrong. What's going on here?" She reached up and took the hatpin from her summer straw, removed her hat, then placed the pin back in the hat, all the time glancing quickly back and forth between Jim and Meg.

Jim spoke, "Mr. and Mrs. O'Meara, I have something to ask you. Would you please sit down so we can talk?"

Bill immediately sat in his easy chair, but Margaret held her standing position, crossed her arms over her chest, then slowly backed up towards the divan. Her eyes continuously moving from Jim, who was standing in the middle of the living room, to Meg who was sitting on one end of the divan. Margaret then sat at the opposite end. She was openly nervous. She smoothed out the skirt of her dress, crossed her legs, adjusted her position, tugged at her skirt to make sure her knees were properly covered and finally looked at Jim.

Jim held his stance, center stage, patiently. For a moment the four were frozen as in a tableau.

Jim spoke, "I'm sure you must know, Mr. and Mrs. O'Meara, that I love your daughter, Meg."

This declaration of love in front of her parents made Meg's senses throb with excitement.

Jim cleared his throat and continued, "We've been seeing each other for four months and, well I...I, I've asked Meg to be my wife."

Shock registered instantly on Margaret's face. Meg ran to Jim and put her arms around him. Bill stood up, walked towards Jim and put out his hand. "Geeze, Jim, you want to marry my little Meg, huh? Well, I guess congratulations are in order then."

When he grasped Jim's hand, Margaret reacted with the speed of a gazelle, racing from her seat. She interrupted the handshake with her hand and in a shrill voice, ordered, "Don't you dare shake hands, Bill. Meg's not marrying anybody. This is all happening too fast. There's many things to be considered, especially his religion! We don't know anything about Methodists or Californians."

Meg couldn't contain herself. "See, I told you, Jim! I told you so. I told you she wouldn't approve because of your religion, and now she's holding it against you for being a Californian."

Meg and Jim stood locked in each other's arms, unsure of what would be the next step.

Bill standing apart from the others, contemplated what role he should play in this drama. He liked Jim and thought he'd make a good husband for Meg.

Jim broke from Meg and tried to lay his hand on Margaret's arm, but she pulled away. He looked directly into her eyes. "Mrs. O'Meara, please don't be so upset. I know you need a little time to adjust to the thought of Meg getting married. Can we just sit and talk calmly?"

Margaret looked away from Jim and folded her arms across her chest.

Meg suddenly lashed out at her mother, "I don't need your permission to marry Jim. I'll be nineteen in a few weeks and the law says that even eighteen year olds don't need their parents permission to marry."

Jim pulled Meg back to him. "Meg, Meg, come on. Let's not have a shouting match here. Calm down, please?"

Margaret turned and said sarcastically, "Aside from the serious religion problem, just what do you two think you will live on? Love? Ha!" She turned her back on them and walked over to the window.

Jim sat Meg down on the divan and moved towards Margaret. "Mrs. O'Meara, I've calculated all the possible expenses Meg and I would incur as a married couple: housing, food, clothes, and other miscellaneous expenses. And, although we'd have to spend wisely, I think we'd be comfortable. I make one hundred and fifty dollars a month, and Meg makes ninety. That's two hundred and forty dollars. Then I'll get a housing allowance of fifty dollars more. That's two hundred and ninety."

Bill was astounded. "Wow, Jim, that's a lot of money. A lot more than I make. I only get about one-twenty-five a month plus my thirty dollar monthly disability pension."

Meg was stunned that Jim had figured out all this financial information. To her, it sounded like they would be rich.

Without turning around and letting her astonishment show, Margaret presented another argument. "I suppose you think you can just go out find a flat to rent? Well, you're in for a big surprise, young man," she stated authoritatively.

Ignoring her gloomy housing information, Jim said in a somber tone, "Meg and I are going to ten o'clock Mass, and I guess this might be a good time to tell you, Mr. and Mrs. O'Meara, I'm going to see a priest this week to talk about taking instructions to become a Catholic." Emotional quivers filled his last words.

Meg's eyes filled with tears. "Oh, Jim, darling, I can't believe you really want to do that. Please, please, don't do it just to appease my parents."

Margaret was stunned. It destroyed her best argument for preventing the marriage.

Bill took over. "You two had better get going if you're going to make the ten o'clock Mass." He winked at them and mouthed silently, I'll take care of her.

As expected, Aunt Grace became involved immediately. She thought Jim would make a good husband if he turned Catholic. "He's well-educated and has excellent manners. But, I think Meghan is too young, and she should wait a year."

Jim and Meg defended their decision and proceeded with their plans, which Margaret would not discus with them.

She had told Meg emphatically that she agreed with her sister, Grace. "Next year, if you are still serious about Jim, we'll give it some more thought."

❋ * ❋

Jim went to see Father O'Connor and began taking instructions. Jim and Meg selected Sunday, December 5, for their wedding date, but they were told that Catholics cannot marry during Advent, so they changed the date to January 7, 1945.

They went to Long Jewelers in Boston and picked out a beautiful quarter carat, Tiffany-set diamond ring, and matching plain gold wedding bands.

Meg asked Babs to be her maid of honor. Although they didn't see each other often, Meg still considered Babs her best friend. She asked Jane Baxter to be a bridesmaid along with three "club" friends, Virginia Casey, Eleanor Crowley and Carmaline Sheehan. All accepted enthusiastically.

Meg would be the first of the "club" girls to marry.

Margaret ignored all discussion about the wedding as if it were of no concern to her. Meg knew she had been coached by Aunt Grace in hopes that the wedding would never take place. But Meg and Jim wanted it to be as soon as possible, because in March, Jim would finish his radar courses at M.I.T., and he would be sent to Submarine School in New London. He wanted Meg to be with him while he was at school there, because after graduation, he'd be shipped out to sea.

Jim had written his parents the day after he and Meg became engaged. It was a difficult letter to write because he hadn't told his parents much about his relationship with Meg. He found it very difficult to write the words, "I have fallen in love," to his straight-laced parents. He had never discussed anything of a romantic nature with them. And, it was even more difficult to find the right words to explain the drastic news of giving up his Methodist faith to become a Catholic.

Jim's letter had stunned his parents. It was not like their oldest son to do something so rash. He always had been such a serious student, and as far as they knew, he had not dated many girls.

They wrote back to him, "We must caution you about your haste in marrying this girl. Have you given serious consideration to your financial situation? We hope you realize that a severe housing shortage exists all over the country. Where will you live? Does your young lady realize that you will undoubtedly have to go off to war and leave her behind?"

"But we are most concerned about your changing your religion. We are deeply hurt. We don't understand how your religion failed you. You had a proper Methodist up-bringing. How could you change your beliefs so quickly. Because we don't know anything about Catholics, we will try to learn more about them by going to the Mexican section of the city to visit the Catholic church there. Of course, as you know, James, we normally would not go to that area..."

That sentence of their letter would prove to be the catalyst that rallied Margaret and Aunt Grace to join in the wedding plans. Meg knew it would grate on their Irish Catholic pride to think that the Wrights felt that their son was marrying a girl beneath his social level.

Jim had been reluctant to share the letter with the O'Mearas, but Meg knew instinctively that last sentence would anger her mother and Aunt so much, they'd have to approve the wedding.

Meg repeated "the sentence" verbatim at Sunday dinner when Aunt Grace and Uncle Frank were visiting. The reaction was swift.

On Monday, Meg's mother and aunt, visited a printer to select the proper invitation. The following day, they went to the Continental Hotel to begin arrangements for an elegant wedding reception. Then on Saturday, they took Meg into Boston to the Mary Burn's Bridal Salon to select a wedding gown. Nothing could stop the momentum now.

SIXTEEN

ambridge, 1945. Aunt Grace wanted to pay for the wedding so it could be done properly, her way. Everything had to be perfect, and because of her generosity, Meg made a concerted effort to avoid confrontations with her. She really appreciated what her aunt was doing, because her parents could never have afforded such an elegant wedding. Grace, the matriarch, was in her glory. She knew she probably never again would have the opportunity to plan and execute a large wedding.

There was one big disappointment though. The Wrights could not come. Mr. Wright, deeply involved in defense work at March Field, could not get the time off. Aunt Grace and Margaret were particularly disappointed and wondered if that was the real reason for not coming. They had been so anxious to show the Wrights the beautiful Catholic wedding they had orchestrated.

Steve Sumner was to be Jim's best man and four of his fellow officers at Harvard would be ushers. It would be a military wedding with the officers wearing dress blues, white gloves and carrying swords to make the traditional arch for the bride and groom to pass under when they left the altar.

Meg was given a lovely shower by her "club" girl friends. Most of the gifts were lacy lingerie items, some of which they insisted she model.

Two weeks before the wedding, Jim telephoned Meg at work. "Honey, I've got great news! I found a place to live if you agree to it."

"What wonderful news, Jim. Of course I'll agree to it." Meg had been worried that they might have to live with her parents; if they didn't find something soon. "Is it an apartment? Where is it?"

"It's in Cambridge. It's a house on Seville Street. But there's a catch. A lieutenant, Jess Harley, and his wife, Cornelia, live there. He's in my radar classes, but he's in the Army. He said they've been looking for a couple to share the house because of the high rent. But we'd have our own bedroom and share the rest of the house. You and his wife can work out a timetable for the kitchen. What do you think?"

A variety of thoughts raced through Meg's mind as Jim described what possibly would be their first home. It wasn't what she had anticipated. Sharing a house with strangers did not appeal in the least. On the other hand, sharing her parent's home would be the alternative, and nothing could be worse than that. All she really wanted was to be alone with Jim and begin life as a married woman. If she had to share their life together with another couple temporarily, she vowed to make the best of it.

The two-story single family house on Seville Street was about fifty years old and in need of painting. Their knock was answered by a pretty, blond woman. "Hi, ya'all. You must be the Wrights."

"Hi, I'm Jim Wright, and this is my fiancée, Meg O'Meara, who'll be Mrs. Wright a week from this Sunday."

"Congratulations! I'm Corn-eel-ya, and this is ma hubby, Jess. We're from Mississippi. Come on in and sit a spell. Would ya'all like some coffee? I'm 'bout three months pregnant, and I drink nothin' but ice water to keep ma weight down, but ah sho would be happy to make ya'all a cup."

Meg had never heard such a thick southern accent and had a hard time understanding what the Harleys were saying. In turn, within a few minutes of conversation, Cornelia commented, "Heavens sakes alive, I jus have the most awful time tryin' to understand you Cambridge folk, Meg."

Meg laughed and said, "Well that makes us even, Con-e-la."

The Harleys took Jim and Meg on a tour of the house, and pointed out a small back bedroom that would be theirs. The bath was old fashioned, and the upstairs floors creaked. The kitchen was large and had plenty of cupboards.

Cornelia said, "Honey, ah think we can work out a fine arrangement for sharin' the kitchen. Ah don't cook a great deal 'cause the smell of food jus' makes me bilious."

Jess added in his not quite so drawling Mississippi accent, "We pay ninety dollars a month rent, so if ya'all are interested, we'll just split it in half. What do you think Jim?"

Jim looked to Meg, "What do you think, honey? Do you like it?" he asked hopefully.

Meg hesitated a moment, then said, "Yes, I think it will be fine, if it's okay with you."

"Well, I guess we'll be sharing the house with you two," Jim announced, shaking hands with Jess.

ↄ * ↄ

The week before the wedding was hectic. Jim was baptized at a quiet ceremony. Aunt Grace and Uncle Bert were his Godparents.

Meg still had a great deal of anxiety about Jim's changing his religion, and she prayed that he would not regret it. Father O'Connor had assured her that converts usually made the best Catholics.

Jim had applied for a week's leave for their honeymoon but got only a one day pass.

Jim's parents sent two one hundred dollar war bonds so the newlyweds could start a savings plan. They also sent a huge crate of orange blossom buds which had been slightly waxed to keep them fresh. Two days after they arrived, the seventy degree heat of the house melted the wax, and the buds burst into blossoms. The aroma permeated the house. The blossoms would be used on the altar, and a sprig would be put into Meg's bridal bouquet.

Jim admitted to homesickness when he smelled the fragrance. "It reminds me of Riverside."

Co-workers at the bank gave Meg two pieces of luggage, and Colonel Rizzoli and the men at the armory took up a collection and gave her a $25 war bond.

A high energy level saturated the O'Meara's house the night before the wedding as everyone tried to keep each other calm. To lend additional drama, a snow storm was predicted.

After the rehearsal that evening, the entire wedding party knelt at the altar, lit votive candles and prayed for Joe's safe return. His absence at the wedding would cast a shadow on the event. Margaret had decided to set a place for him at the wedding party table at the reception.

Meg woke at six o'clock on her wedding day, hopped out of bed, and looked out the window. Ominous dark clouds filled the sky, and the first sprinkling of snow had begun to fall. Her happiness was so complete that her active imagination turned the snow into a white, fluffy blanket to cover the dark, dreary look of winter.

An hour before the wedding, the phone rang. It was Jim. "Hi, honey. I just wanted to let my Cambridge girl know how much I love her."

"Oh, I love you, too, darling. I'm the luckiest girl in the world."

"Are you dressed?"

"Jim! What a question," she teased seductively.

"I mean dressed in your wedding gown! I bet you look beautiful."

"I hope so. Are you nervous?"

"I've never been so frightened in my life."

"Me too."

"Oops, Aunt Grace says I have to hang up. She's going to put my veil on. See you soon, darling."

"I'll be waiting for you at the church, honey."

Meg's gown was beautiful. The bodice was ivory satin trimmed with duchess lace, and it had an illusion neckline. The skirt and train were marquisette. A cap of seed pearls held her finger tip veil in place.

The snowfall increased in tempo with the tension of the bridal party. The bridesmaids were totally disenchanted with their rented taffeta gowns from Mary Burns Bridal Salon. Bab's gown was light blue. The bridesmaid's gowns, as described by Virginia, were a peachy puke color. Although they had been fitted by a dressmaker at the bridal salon, the bosoms on the dresses had not been adjusted as promised and were at least a size forty D. They sagged to their waists. At least they all liked their finger tip veils which were similar to Meg's and looked pretty on their long hair. They each carried a small nosegay of pastel colored flowers.

The bridesmaids were the first to leave for the church in the limousine with Aunt Grace and Margaret. There was a great deal of pushing and nonsensical chatter as the girls hoisted their long skirts above their snow boots and raced to the limo under the chauffeur's umbrella.

Aunt Grace became impatient with them. "Can't you girls conduct yourselves with a little more decorum?"

Jane whispered just loud enough for the girls to hear, "Decorum, ladies, decorum! Don't you have any decorum at all?" They began snapping their fingers and chanting softly in unison, "We've got de corum, yeah, we've got de corum...."

Their giddiness would have lasted all the way to the church if the chauffeur, a part-time pall bearer for Danny O'Brien, the undertaker, hadn't loudly interceded. "Aw-right girls, knock it off!" he commanded.

After delivering them to the church, he would return and pick up Bill, Babs and Meg. The snow, although soft, was quite deep now.

While waiting for the chauffeur to return, Meg and Babs stood nervously downstairs in the front hall. Babs lit a cigarette and Meg took a quick puff as her father came down the stairs to join them. Her parents didn't know she smoked, and she didn't want them to find out, especially today.

Bill was extremely restless. He kept going up and down the hall stairs. He had insisted on wearing his old gray felt hat to the church instead of the top hat that went with his tails. He carried the top hat in a brown bag. "Geeze, if I get this topper wet, they'll charge me an arm and a leg. Besides, it's too tight!"

Babs teased, "Maybe it's because you have a big head today because you look so handsome."

He smirked and blew cigar smoke in her face.

When the chauffeur arrived, he escorted them one at a time to the limo. "Okay, Maid of Honor, you have boots, so I'll walk you to the car with the umbrella. Then, Bill, you hold the umbrella over Meg and I'll carry her to the car."

The church was more crowded than Meg had anticipated. The scent of orange blossoms warmed the cold interior of the old church. The organist struck a chord, and the *Wedding March* began. The guests all stood and looked towards the rear. A surge of elation filled Meg when her pretty bridesmaids began their slow-paced walk down the aisle.

She put her arm through her father's, breathed deeply, then exhaled heavily to relieve the tension.

Bill squeezed her arm tightly, smiled at her and said, "This is it, kiddo. Here we go!"

They moved slowly down the aisle as the traditional wedding march resounded off the walls. Meg nervously tightened the grip on her father's arm and on her bridal bouquet of Eucharist lilies, sweet peas and the sprig of orange blossom. Nearing the altar, Meg got a lump in her throat when she saw Jim, Steve and the other ushers standing, as if at attention, in their dress blues, white gloves, and swords at their sides. A nervous smile covered Jim's face when his eyes met Meg's. Meg smiled back at him, then all the wedding party smiled and Meg's tension seemed to melt away.

Bill turned Meg over to Jim, and sat in the front row with Margaret, Grace, Frank, Uncle Bert, his wife, Kay and their little sons, Jackie and Tommy. The wedding ceremony began. They could not have a Mass because Jim's ushers were all Protestant. The church did not allow Protestants to take part in a Mass.

Carmaline's sister, Marilyn, sang the, "Ave Maria" beautifully. The ceremony was brief but all the essential questions were asked of the bride and groom. The ceremony ended with a kiss.

Ensign and Mrs. Wright walked through the arch of swords up the aisle, smiling and greeting friends. Now they could relax.

✇ * ✇

The snow continued to fall. It was now almost a foot deep.

The reception line formed immediately when the bridal party arrived at the Continental Hotel. As was the custom, wedding gifts had been brought to the reception, opened and put on display at long tables. Because of the war, there were no gifts of linens or small appliances and only a few gifts of silver. There were many gifts of glass and pottery and a large number of envelopes that held gifts of money.

The bridal banquet began with Father O'Connor saying grace and a prayer for the safe return of Joe. The empty seat for Joe was between Margaret and Bill. Then Steve gave a toast to the bride and groom. Jim and Meg performed all the traditional rituals of a wedding reception. After an hour of dancing to the four-piece band, the three-tiered cake was rolled into the room by two waiters. It was beautifully frosted in swirls and encircled with small roses. On top of the third layer, a naval officer and a bride stood under an arch of flowers. Once the cake was cut and served, the older guests began to leave.

The worsening weather had been the main topic of conversation throughout the day, but it didn't worry Meg and Jim. They were taking a train to Goffs Falls, New Hampshire, to spend their one day honeymoon at a winter resort called, The Elms. They wanted snow.

Aunt Grace urged them to hurry and change into their street clothes in the rooms provided by the hotel. She was concerned that they might miss their train. The guests, now waiting anxiously in the lobby for the final ritual, had been supplied with little bags of rice. Hotel employees were busily shoveling snow to keep a pathway open up the stairs to the street level.

Babs helped Meg take off her wedding gown and get into her honeymoon outfit: a brown and white tweed suit and matching hat. Aunt Kay had very generously loaned Meg her beautiful muskrat fur coat.

"Oh, Meg, you look beautiful," Babs sighed as they hugged. It's all so romantic. Here are your dumb skates, sweetie. Are you really going to take them?"

"Of course. I'll tie the laces together and carry them over my shoulder like I always do."

Jim and Steve knocked on the door and Babs let them in. Jim raced across the room to Meg and enveloped her in his arms. "Oh, honey, are you as happy as I am?"

"I'm in a daze, Jim! I can't believe it! We're Mr. and Mrs. James Wright," Meg giggled.

"No, Meg. We're Ensign and Mrs. Wright."

Steve grinned and said to Babs, "I hate to break up this charming couple, but we've got to get them out of here."

He picked up their luggage, and they took the elevator down to the lobby.

All the wedding guests were waiting near the front door.

Bill and Margaret said goodbye with tears and hugs. Aunt Grace handed Jim a large manila envelope, secured by a string, looped around a disc. "Jim, This envelope holds all your money gifts. It seems like there is a considerable amount in there. Don't lose it, dear."

Meg hugged her Aunt Grace tightly. "I don't know how we can ever thank you for making our wedding so perfect. Everything was so beautiful."

Jim added, "You've been so good to us. We love you very much, Aunt Grace." He kissed her cheek and hugged her.

They then began their run through the gauntlet of guests, and a hail of rice mixed with large snow flakes, to the car waiting for them at the curb.

Babs had borrowed her father's car which Steve would drive. Under normal conditions, it would have taken only about twenty minutes to get to North Station where Meg and Jim would catch their train to New Hampshire. But the deep snow had slowed traffic almost to a standstill.

The tin cans tied to the rear bumper bounced along silently, muffled by the snow. A large paper "Just Married" sign, tied to the trunk, had completely disappeared under a mantle of snow.

They drove the short distance from the hotel to Harvard Square at five miles per hour. The car skidded often. Just as they entered the Square, a trackless trolley passed them, then careened into their path.

Steve was helpless to avoid a collision, and the front of Bab's father's Studebaker accordioned into the engine.

Meg and Babs screamed, " Oh, Jesus, Mary and Joseph!"

"Dammit!" Steve cursed under his breath.

No one was hurt, but the damage to the car was critical. Steam spouted from the Studebaker's radiator and all traffic now came to a standstill. The trolley driver and Steve appraised the crushed front end of the Kelleys' car. It would have to be towed. Traffic in Harvard Square was completely tied up, and angry motorists beeped their horns and yelled profanities aimed mostly at the city for not plowing the streets.

Steve made a decision. "Jim and Meg, you'll have to take the subway. If you don't leave right now, you'll never make the four-thirty train."

"But it's not fair to leave you with this mess," Jim argued.

"I'll handle it. Get going. The best man is supposed to handle every little detail, or big ones, as is the case right now. Leave!"

Jim carried their two suitcases, and Meg carried her skates, makeup case, and the precious money envelope.

They carefully made their way down the slippery subway stairs. At the third step from the bottom, a drunk, swaying and humming to himself almost knocked Meg over.

She braced myself against the railing, recovered her balance, and told Jim to keep going.

The subway train was just pulling into the station when they reached the platform.

The drunk was following them and yelling, "Hey, little lady. Sorry, sorry for, for almos' knocking ya on your bum. Here, take it, take it."

Neither Jim nor Meg paid attention to the drunk. Just as the train doors were shutting, the drunk braced them open and staggered into the car, waving the precious money envelope that must have slipped out from under Meg's arm when the drunk fell against her.

Meg was shocked when she saw it was their envelope that he was flailing in front of them.

Jim quickly retrieved it and thanked the man.

Meg was mortified that she had dropped it and looked at Jim in anguish.

"It's okay, honey," Jim soothed. "We've got it back and that's what's important. Come on, now. Look, your friend is sitting next to you," Jim said with a grin. "Why don't you thank him."

Meg turned her head and saw the drunk grinning at her and humming "Here Comes The Bride."

She gave him a quizzical look. "What makes you think I'm a bride?"

The drunk laughed and began picking rice out of her fur coat. "When I sees the rice, I says to myself, says I, well, she mus' be a bride. How's that fer detective work, huh?" he asked raising his eyebrows and grinning foolishly.

The passengers within earshot laughed, and Jim and Meg looked at them sheepishly. Jim put a two dollar bill in the drunk's hand and said, "Thanks, old timer. You're an honest man. Have yourself a couple of drinks on us."

The newlyweds arrived at North Station at twenty past four and hurried across the station to the ticket window.

Panting heavily, Jim asked, "Could I have two round trip tickets to Manchester, New Hampshire, please?"

"Take it easy, son. Train won't be leaving for quite a spell. Got to clear the tracks up north of snow."

Jim and Meg looked at each other, thinking of all the energy they had just expended to be on time. Now, at least, they could relax for the first time that day. They boarded the train and arranged their luggage in the overhead storage rack.

Although the steam engine started up three times in the next few hours, the train didn't move. The conductor told them that they'd start the engine occasionally to circulate heat in the passenger cars. It was cold, and Meg and Jim snuggled closely.

At seven o'clock, Jim got off the train and bought sandwiches, apples, and a large container of hot coffee. They had made an agreement not to open the money envelopes until the train started, but by seven thirty, their anticipation of the riches sealed in the manila envelope had grown beyond restraint. They decided to open the envelopes.

Just then, they heard "All aboard" and within a minute the train lurched forward. The passengers all cheered. The train was crowded with skiers. Their skis and poles were piled in a storage area at the front of the car. A sense of high spirits and camaraderie grew as the train picked up speed on the outskirts of Boston. It was too dark to see much through the snow-covered windows, except the diffused lights along the roadbed.

"Now, Jim. Please! Let's open it." Meg begged, and began to unwind the string that sealed the manila envelope

"No, let's wait 'til we get there," Jim teased.

"No way! Oh, my gosh, Jim. Look at how many are in here," Meg said pulling out handfuls of envelopes.

"Be careful you don't drop any, Meg. Let's get a system going and..."

Meg interrupted, "You and your engineering mind. I have a feeling it will drive me up a wall someday. Are all engineers so organized?"

"No. Just good ones like me," Jim grinned and kissed her cheek.

They spent the next hour opening sixty-two envelopes. They read each card and put the money orders and checks back in their envelopes, but Jim put the cash in his wallet and wrote the amount of the gift on the cards. He wanted to keep accurate records so they could write proper thank you notes. When finally tallied, Jim said, "We have four hundred and twenty dollars, a fortune."

"Really, Jim!" Meg was startled. "Except for my Dad's Veteran's bonus, that's the largest amount of money anybody in my family has ever had at one time."

"Well, we won't have it long. I want to pay back the loan I got from my mom to get your engagement ring and our wedding bands. That's one hundred and twenty-five dollars."

"And our honeymoon expenses. Oh, well, it was great to be rich for a few minutes." Meg laughed.

The speed of the train had decreased after stopping at Lowell. The farther north they traveled, the deeper the snow became. After the train crossed the Merrimack River near Lawrence, on the Massachusetts and New Hampshire border, it came to a complete stop. It was now eleven forty-five. They had expected the trip to take three hours and by now they would have been eating their honeymoon dinner.

Up to now the delay had not bothered them too much, but after not moving for a half an hour, they were cold and gloomy. Meg looked at Jim and pouted, "Do you realize, darling, we're into our second day of marriage and have yet to be alone!"

"Aha! Does that mean that my bride is feeling amorous?"

"Maybe." Meg grinned.

"I feel the same way, honey," Jim said, putting his arm around her and nestling as close to her as was acceptable in public. They both dozed off.

It was three-thirty in the morning when the train completed the fifty mile trip from Boston to Manchester.

When they got off the train, Jim spotted an old bus with its motor running. "Come on, Meg. Quick! That's our bus."

The driver rolled down the window when they approached. "Only taking passengers to The Elms, folks."

"That's us," they said in unison as the cold air vaporized their breath.

By four-thirty, they settled into their small room. Steam heat was sizzling from the radiator, and a pretty thick quilt was folded back on the canopied bed. They quickly unpacked and took turns using the bathroom to shower and change into their sleepwear. Jim had undressed first and when Meg came out of the bathroom, he was filling two glasses with the complimentary champagne.

"Come over here. You look beautiful and humm, sexy. Let's have our honeymoon toast," Jim urged in a seductive tone.

Meg crossed the room and her lacy white negligee flowed open, revealing the matching satin nightgown that clung to her legs when she moved. Her face began to get hot. She was blushing. She felt stupid, not sophisticated like honeymooners do in the movies.

Jim put his arm around her waist, raised his glass and said, "To my beautiful bride, Meg, my Cambridge girl."

She touched her glass to his. "To my handsome husband, Jim, my Californian."

They drank the sweet, bubbling champagne, kissed amorously and refilled their glasses. They walked to the window, cleared off the condensation and could just see the first light-line of dawn appearing on the horizon. The snow had stopped.

"Oh, Jim, look how beautiful it is."

They leaned their heads together and sipped the last of the champagne. Then, Jim took Meg's hand and led her to the bed. They snuggled under the covers, and joined joyously in the sexual pleasures of love and marriage.

☒ * ☒

By eight o'clock the next morning, they were dressed in their snow clothing and hurried down to the cozy breakfast room where the aroma of coffee and hot cinnamon rolls filled the air. Although they had only a few hours sleep, their anticipation of a day of winter sports made them eager not to waste a minute of their one day honeymoon.

The day flew by. They ice skated for an hour, and Meg was surprised by Jim's ice skating skill. She hadn't expected a Californian to know how to skate; she had looked forward to teaching him. He'd watch her closely when she did jumps and spins, and to her amazement, he made fairly good attempts at repeating what she had done.

Later that morning, they skied down some small slopes, using a rope tow to get back to the top. Jim was a skilled skier. He taught Meg how to traverse and snow plow. It was exhilarating to ski over the powdery snow in a beautiful winter wonderland of trails that took them through snow-covered pine forests. After a late lunch, they joined four other honeymooners on a toboggan slide. Just as the sun was setting, Meg and Jim climbed into a two-horse sleigh that took them back to the train station where they caught the five-o-five o'clock train to Boston.

Certainly enough obstacles had occurred to dampen their honeymoon, but they were riding such a wave of happiness that every moment of their first two days as Ensign and Mrs. James Wright had been magical.

SEVENTEEN

February 1945. Reality set in. The first few months of married life on Seville Street in their shared home was not at all what they had expected. Cornelia was sick more than she was well, and her husband, Jess had very little patience with her. They constantly argued.

One morning after the men had gone to school, Cornelia came into the kitchen. Her protruding stomach was half covered with a loose bathrobe. Her puffy, red eyes showed that she had been crying for quite some time.

Meg felt sorry for her. "Good morning, Cornelia, sit down. Can I make you some tea and toast?"

"Honey, what I'd like to take is a glass of poison right now." Then she burst out crying and buried her head in her arms on the table.

Meg put her arms around her. "Would you like to talk? Sometimes it helps to talk to another woman."

"Oh, Meg, I jus don't feel like livin anymore. I hate being pregnant and havin ma body so distorted. Would ya'all believe that I won practically every beauty pageant in Mississippi once?"

"I would, Cornelia. You're still very beautiful and as soon as your baby is born, you'll get your figure right back."

"Oh, I wish I could go home to ma Daddy and Mommy and Ham. Ham's ma colored nanny, and she's taken care of me since I was born. I'd get waited on and pampered by her for sure, if I was home. She'd wouldn't let ole Jess treat me mean like he does."

"He's mean to you, I agree. Why don't you stand up to him and tell him not to treat you like this. Women have rights, you know."

"Honey, if I back-talked to him, he'd beat me and kick me out, and then what would I do?"

"Go home! Don't let him beat you!" Meg was shocked.

"Honey, he's rich, or at least his family is, and ma family don't have much anymore. So I stay with him. Do you understand now?"

"No! I'd never let a man hit me. I wouldn't care how much money he had."

"We're different, Meg. I hate being poor. Thanks for listenin, honey. I'm going back to bed."

Meg watched her drag her clumsy body upstairs. She's pathetic, Meg thought. I wish she'd go home, I'm sure she'd be better off.

When Meg told Jim that night about their conversation. Jim warned Meg, "Stay out of their affairs, honey, or Jess may kick us out."

Three weeks later Cornelia's colored nanny, Ham, came and took her home by train. Jess stayed on living at the house, but they saw very little of him.

Meg had a great deal to learn about food shopping. Before she married, she hadn't paid much attention to how to use the food rationing stamps or how much things cost. Jim was issued a book because he was now living off base. After the first few weeks of food shopping, Meg was shocked when she realized how carelessly extravagant she had been and for a month, they had to do without many food items.

She knew how to clean a house; Aunt Grace had trained her well. But her cooking was just like her mother's, plain.

Jim suggested she try to be more creative. "Why don't you make a casserole for a change. My mom makes the best casseroles with pasta, vegetables and chicken."

Meg looked askance at Jim. "You mean she mixes them all up together? What does that taste like?"

"Delicious!"

Meg began to make a casserole once a week, trying different vegetables and meat. Her mother came to dinner one night, but she only took a few bites.

🙠 * 🙘

Jim tried to teach Meg to play contract bridge. It was much more complicated than auction bridge, which she had played often with her family. They invited Steve and Ann over for dinner and bridge one evening after Cornelia had gone home. Meg had been nervous about cooking her first meal for company, so she just cooked a roast beef, baked potatoes and string beans with guidance from her mother. She made packaged Royal chocolate pudding and whipped heavy cream for a topping. After dinner, they played bridge.

At first, they forgave Meg her mistakes, but when she and Jim lost the second rubber because Meg led away from a king, Jim got upset with her, "Why in the world did you do that? I've corrected you twice tonight for that same mistake, Meg."

Meg was so stunned, she couldn't even answer him. He had never spoken to her like that. Tears welled. She was hurt. He made her feel stupid. She ran upstairs to their bedroom.

Within a minute Jim was at her side, apologizing and holding her in his arms. Lately she seemed to cry at the least, little thing.

The next day she asked her mother, "If my period is late, does that mean I'm pregnant?"

"When did you have your last period?" Margaret asked.

"Shortly before our wedding."

"Have you felt sick?"

"Mostly when Cornelia was living with us because she was always vomiting, and it made me sick. I'm doing better now." Meg wanted to tell her mother that her breasts were sore, but she thought that was because Jim liked to fondle them when they were making love. She could never talk to her mother about that.

Margaret suggested, "I think you better get up to see Dr. Walker. He'll be able to tell."

A strange gamut of emotions filled Meg when she left Dr. Walker's office. She couldn't suppress the grin that kept involuntarily spreading across her face. She was thrilled. "I'm going to have a baby! Won't Jim be surprised." Meg and Jim hadn't planned on having a baby right away, but wanting to live by the laws of the Catholic Church, they followed the advice in the rhythm pamphlet that explained the "safe days" for intercourse.

"Stunned" was the best way to describe Jim's reaction. "But, honey, how could you be? I mean, I thought we were careful, you know."

"Oh, Jim, you're not happy, are you?" Meg choked out, hostility now filling her voice.

"Sure, I'm happy if you are. I'm just surprised because we had planned to wait, Meg."

Meg glared at Jim and put her hands on her hips. "Well, as Dr. Walker said, 'So much for the reliability of the Catholic rhythm system!' So there's nothing we can do about it, Jim, you're going to be a father whether you like it or not!"

A transformation took place on Jim's face. His serious expression began to change to a sheepish smile that spread slowly from the corners of his mouth. Then he began giggling. "I like it! I'm going to be a father! Wow!" He grabbed Meg in his arms tightly. "Hello, mommy." He kissed her gently, then held her out at arm's length and asked, "Does this mean we can't fool around any more?"

Meg grinned and led him upstairs.

℘ * ℘

The war raged on, although the tide had changed drastically for the Allies. Italy had surrendered, and the Normandy invasion was successful. Patton's 3rd Army and his steel cavalry, as his tanks were called, moved south and west, then north in France, routing German strongholds. Paris was soon liberated. Franklin Roosevelt, despite ailing health, had been elected to an unprecedented fourth term.

By January 1945, the Russians were 200 miles from Berlin. In the south Pacific, MacArthur was making good his promise to return to the Philippines, and by February 3rd, Manila was liberated.

The O'Mearas were still receiving pre-printed postcards from Joe, which, thank God, meant he was alive. When the Allied Forces regained more Japanese strongholds in the Pacific, Joe's release became more of a possibility every day.

℘ * ℘

Joe and his fellow prisoners at Niigata heard the heartening news of MacArthur's return to the Philippines, from Nobu.

The grueling work at the steel mill slowed down and the guards became less abusive. Their new attitude was prompted by a new camp commander.

Nobu told Joe that the new commander had confided in him, thinking he would be a friend because he too was a nisei.

"The dirty rat! Be sure and report him when you guys are freed. He was born in Los Angeles to immigrant parents. He was a lawyer just before the war started but decided to take advantage of being bilingual. He flew to Japan and offered his services to the Japanese government, thinking they'd give him an important position. But he was wrong, the Japanese officials didn't trust him and gave him crummy assignments in remote prison camps. He says he feels guilty. He should! He's terrified that if Japan loses the war, the Americans might find out he's an American defector, and he'll be executed as a war criminal."

Joe smiled and said, "Well, well, isn't that interesting. I'll just have to make sure his dirty secret gets back to the proper authorities."

The best news Nobu gave the prisoners was that American B-29s were intensely bombing the hell out of the Japanese coastline. That caused a serious eating problem for the Japanese. Fish become scarce and then soon the fish disappeared completely. Now the guards weren't eating much better than the prisoners.

On their way to the steel mill each day, the prisoners noticed old men and young boys being trained to march and shoot.

Nobu said, "They're going to be the home guard. That's a joke, huh? We've been ordered to fight to the last man and commit hari-kari instead of surrendering."

& * &

Meg's lifestyle changed completely with her pregnancy. She gave up her job at the bank and reluctantly resigned from the Massachusetts Women's Defense Corps, because she and Jim would be moving to New London shortly.

A very unusual occurrence happened in the last week of February. Both Jim's younger brothers visited Jim and Meg within a week of each other. His brother, Keith, who was Meg's age, stayed for two days. His submarine had come into New London after a long siege of action in the Pacific, and he had been reassigned to another submarine in Portsmouth, New Hampshire. Jim hounded Keith to relate every detail of his submarine experiences.

Then, three days after Keith left, Jim's other brother, Royden, who was two years younger than Jim, surprised them by knocking at their door at ten o'clock one night. He had been injured while fighting in Patton's tank corps and had been sent home on a troop ship that landed at Boston. He was on his way to California and could only stay that evening. His war stories were as harrowing as Keith's.

Jim was deeply depressed after his younger brothers' visits. Having now heard first hand, what they had been through in the war, he felt terrible that they had been in the thick of battle while he was still in school. "The war will be over before I ever get in the fight," he lamented.

Meg tried to console him. "Jim, you should thank God that you're not, after hearing your brother's stories."

"You don't understand Meg. Let's not talk about it any more," he said curtly.

But Meg did understand. She knew, if she were a man, she too would want to be where the war action was.

At the end of February, Jim and Jess Harley graduated from Radar School at MIT. Jim and Meg moved out of the house on Seville Street, and Meg temporarily moved in with her parents until they could find housing in New London. Jim had to report immediately for duty at the sub base.

Two weeks passed, but Jim could not find housing for them. The severe housing shortage in America continued as more and more servicemen came home and got married. Along with that, no new houses could be built. Another factor causing the housing shortage was that the bulk of the population of the United States was concentrated in the coastal and industrial areas of the country and most Navy bases were located there.

Jim's schedule was hectic. He had not started sub school yet, but was assigned to an old sub, the *Pike*, which went out on patrols in the waters off Long Island. He had little time to find a place for them to live. He phoned and suggested to Meg, "Honey, I'd like you to stay with your parents for a while, at least until I start sub school."

Although Jim's suggestion disheartened Meg greatly, her parents' were delighted to have her back home. They were thrilled about having a grandchild. Although Meg and her mother got along much better now, Margaret continuously gave her advice about what to eat, what to do and what not to do.

℘ * ℘

New London, Connecticut, March 1945. Meg finally talked Jim into letting her come and stay at a hotel for a few days to look around and see what she could find for housing. When she arrived at the New London train station, she spotted Jim and ran to him, throwing her arms around him. "Oh, Jim, Jim, I've missed you so much," she cried as she hugged him. She realized that he was pushing her away. She was confused. "Jim, what's..."

"Honey, it's wonderful to see you, but they've got strict rules around here about acting like an officer and a gentleman, and that includes no public displays of affection.

"That's a stupid rule!" Meg said.

"Come'on, honey, we'll take a cab, and I'll hug you on the way to the hotel."

When they got in the cab, Jim took her hand and leaned over and kissed her quickly. "How was the trip, honey?"

"I didn't feel too great. Motion sickness, I guess."

"How about pregnancy sickness?" Jim smiled, patting her stomach, which had begun to show slightly. She was three months along.

"Your uniform smells awful, Jim." Meg sniffed.

"You better get accustomed to that smell if you're going to be a submariner's wife. It's diesel oil. It's the fuel that powers the submarine, and I've been living on the sub more than I have at the B.O.Q. I'll bet all my clothes smell now."

"I guess you could say it's a manly smell. I'll get used to it, I'm sure." Meg said bravely. Actually it was making her sick, but she dared not tell Jim. She was afraid he'd use it as an excuse for her to go back home.

The Crocker House was not, by any standard, a first class hotel. Jim had selected it for its price, because he felt it would take Meg more than a few days to find a place to live. Downtown New London was a depressing area, but it was where Meg had to be to catch buses to go house hunting.

That night they went to the Officer's Club at the base and had a wonderful dinner and danced. When they returned to the hotel, Jim went over a map of the city with Meg. "I wish I could go house hunting with you, honey, but I'm on duty for the next three days, and I'll be out to sea."

"Three days! I'm going to be alone in this hotel?"

"Honey, I've told you, I'm in for three days and out for three. That's why I didn't want you to come. I was afraid you'd be too lonely. It'll be so much better when I start sub school."

Meg's heart was broken, but she had been warned. "Okay. Okay. I'll be fine. I guess I just thought, or maybe hoped, they'd give you a couple of days off. I know, don't remind me, there's a war on!" Meg had never been alone at night.

Jim left at 6:30 the next morning. At 8:00, Meg went to the hotel coffee shop, had a light breakfast, bought the local paper, and went up to her room to look over the rental ads. There was nothing to rent but "rm. with kit. priv." Again, it looked like they would not have their own place. One by one, possibilities were eliminated. They were either rented by the time Meg called or they cost too much. Only one prospect was left, no phone number, just an address.

Meg went down to the lobby and rang the bell to get the clerk's attention. He was reading a paper. He didn't move. His feet were up on a desk. She called out over the counter, "Excuse me, could you tell me where I get the bus to go to Montauk Avenue?"

The clerk reluctantly stopped reading and came to the counter chewing aggressively on a tooth pick. He slowly looked Meg over, "I'll be off in a half an hour, cutie, if you want a ride. It's nice down there on the beach," he drawled in a lecherous tone.

Meg glared at him. "B-u-s," she spelled out. "Do-you- understand-English?" she asked in a slow, exaggerated voice.

Her sarcasm worked. "Down the block to the left. Leaves every half hour." He gave her a dirty look and went back to the desk.

The bus driver was helpful and let her off in front of a neat brown shingled house. She could see the beach at the end of Montauk Avenue and thought how glorious it would be to live here. She said a quick prayer, please, dear God, don't let the room be taken.

She rang the bell. The door was opened immediately by a short stout man with a black beard and a little black beanie hat on the back of his head.

Oh, my God, Meg thought, he's Jewish!

The man's face broke into a big smile. "Shalom. Shalom. Come right in," he welcomed.

"I, a, ah, have come about the room. Ah, the ad here in the paper," She stuttered.

"Ah, I thought so. So come. Come. Follow me, girlie," he said gesturing for her to follow him down a narrow hallway.

Meg had never really known anyone who was Jewish except Josh Caldwell. The thought of him still stung.

"Mama, Mama," the plump man called as they neared the kitchen. "A girl about the room."

A short, heavy-set woman who was spooning a doughy substance into a pan, looked over her shoulder.

Meg thought, she's adorable. She had jet black hair piled neatly on top of her head in a big bun. Her eyes were large and a startling blue. Her cheeks were rosy.

She smiled at Meg. "Shalom."

"Uh, hello," Meg muttered, not knowing how to answer.

"So, Moshe, a goyim to rent the room?" she said, giving her husband a sideways glance.

He shrugged. "So you're not Jewish, huh? I didn't think so, but how can you tell now a days with the nose jobs."

Meg reached up quickly and touched her nose. "Oh, I'm Irish. This is the 'Sullivan nose,' as my mother's family calls it."

"And Catholic?" the lady asked, nodding her head up and down. "Right, darlink?"

"Oh, yes. But it doesn't matter to me that you're Jewish." It would matter a great deal to my mother, Meg thought.

"Listen, darlink, it doesn't matter that you're Catholic. Our best friends next door, the Callahans, are Catholic, but the only ones in this neighborhood. But we're Orthodox Jews, and that's the problem."

"I don't understand. I've never known anyone who was Jewish. Why can't you rent me the room?"

"What's your name, girlie?" The man asked.

"Meg O'Meara. Oh, I'm mean, Wright. We've only been married a short time, and I'm still not used to it."

"So, Meg Wright, I'm Moshe Goldbaum, and this is my wonderful wife, Sarah. I'm a rabbi at the temple on the next block. A rabbi is like your priests, only better. I'm married, and that's better. Right, Sarah?" Moshe stated, and winked at his wife.

Sarah looked kindly at Meg, "Meg, the problem is that because we're orthodox, we keep a kosher house. So, would you cook kosher food? No. So how could you cook here. You couldn't. So how could you live here? You couldn't. Do you understand better now, darlink?" Sarah held Meg's hands.

"Not really. I just don't know what to do. I went through all today's newspaper ads, and yours was my last hope."

"Don't ever give up hope," Moshe uttered in a chanting tone and pointing his index finger.

"Moshe, put the kettle on, and I'll make somethink hot for Meg and let her try my mandel bread. We have to see how we can help her."

Meg looked at them in gratitude, "Oh, thank you both so much. I guess I've created a mess for myself." She told them about Jim and his sea duty, her pregnancy, and the fact that the Crocker House was a terrible place to have to stay. "I guess I should go home," she said sadly.

Suddenly arms were around her, soothing warm arms. "So, come, come, now," Sarah cooed. "You'll stay here tonight. After we have tea, you go back to the hotel and pack up your things. Get back here before dark though. Moshe would help you, but it's the eve of the Sabbath, and he doesn't ride in autos or buses."

Meg devoured the bread in a few quick bites. "It's delicious, Mrs. Goldbaum. Is all kosher food this good?"

"It's the best! Moshe said enthusiastically. "You know the parents of your great prophet Jesus kept a kosher house. Course, he was a great prophet, but he didn't turn out to be such a great Jew."

"Enough already, Moshe," Sarah cut him to silence with a stern look.

Meg looked at Moshe in astonishment. His revelation of Jesus and his parents being Jewish and keeping a kosher house confused Meg. She wondered, when did God stop being a Jew and become a Catholic. Never having read the Bible, Jesus's life as a Jew was almost unknown to her.

Meg thanked them profusely as she left, "You're wonderful people. I'd probably die of fright if I had to stay in that hotel alone tonight."

Later that evening Meg was settled in the Goldbaum's spare room. She had never felt lonelier. She was about to shut off the bed light when there was a knock on the door. "Come in," she called out.

"I just wanted to make sure you're comfortable," Sarah said softly, coming to the side of the bed. Then she leaned down and kissed Meg on the head and said something Jewish.

"Thank you, Mrs. Goldbaum, for making me so welcome. What did you say?"

Sarah heaved a deep sigh. "Moshe and I could never have a child. I couldn't carry. What I said to you was, if I had had a daughter, I'd like her to be just like you. Good night darlink."

"Good night, Mrs. Goldbaum, Thank you for that nice compliment."

❧ * ❧

The next morning Sarah and Meg went next door to talk with Mrs. Callahan, who, Sarah said, had connections all over town. Mrs. Callahan called her friend, Lydia, who worked at Connecticut College for Women, and had her check the bulletin board for available housing. The three women waited anxiously for her report.

Lydia came back on the phone. "There's only one possibility, and it's been on the board for a couple of weeks, which means it's not too hot a lead. The dame that put this notice up is an English professor at the college and lives down by Lighthouse Inn. Probably a swanky house."

"It sounds nice. What's the problem?" Mrs. Callahan asked.

"Well, this professor says she needs someone to cook three meals a day and take care of her invalid father while she's at work, in exchange for board and room. But they must have excellent references," Lydia stated.

Sarah, who was listening to the phone conversation with Mrs. Callahan, yelled, "I'll give her the best recommendation she's ever heard, Lydia."

"Tell Sarah I don't think a recommendation from someone named Goldbaum will impress her, if you get what I mean. This one's probably a real Yankee type, if she lives in that area," Lydia said bluntly.

Mrs. Callahan got the phone number of the professor and thanked Lydia for her help. Sarah had been relaying the conversation to Meg. "Listen, darlink, maybe we have some think, maybe not. Do you know anyone around here besides me, your best friend, to give you a reference? It has to be excellent."

Meg thought for a moment. "Of course! Why didn't I think of this before? When I was in high school, I baby sat for the Hardy family. He's a commander in the Coast Guard and stationed here in New London, I think. I received a wedding gift from them. I hope they are still here. Could I look at your telephone book, Mrs. Callahan?"

Meg was able to contact Mrs. Hardy, who was happy to call the professor. It seemed a lucky omen to Meg, maybe because of her midnight birth, because the Hardys had been transferred to the Woods Hole Coast Guard Station on Cape Cod and were leaving the next day. Mrs. Hardy called the professor and gave Meg such a good recommendation, she told Mrs. Hardy to tell Meg to come immediately.

"Oh, Mrs. and Rabbi Goldbaum, how can I ever thank you?" Meg said sincerely when she was ready to leave.

"We're supposed to do good deeds on the Sabbath, so you helped us do one," Moshe answered matter-of-factly. "Keep in touch with us, Meg. We'd like to meet your Jim, too.

And the little one, too," Sarah added as she held Meg's face in her hands and kissed her forehead.

Meg got in the back seat of the taxi, rolled down the window and waved goodbye to the Goldbaums calling out, "Shalom."

◢ * ◣

Meg was skeptical as she stood in the middle of the beautiful, modernistic kitchen with a list of do's and don'ts that Professor Mary Carter had given her before she left for work. Meg had been elated when she first saw the lovely home and the large bedroom and private bath, which Jim and she would have. The daily responsibilities she was given did not bother her. They would be getting free board and room. That meant a great deal to them; now they could start saving for a car.

What did bother Meg was Professor Carter's condescending attitude. "She talks down to me as if I were a moron, repeating everything she says twice, then following up each statement with, 'You do understand, don't you?'"

Meg's Irish rose to the surface a couple of times, but she held it in. Don't let her know she's annoying you; remember, the Irish don't kowtow to anyone!

A house cleaner would come once a week to do the heavy cleaning, but during the week it would be Meg's responsibility to keep the house immaculate.

"An immaculate kitchen, immaculate baths, immaculate floors, and follow the prepared menus in an immaculate fashion," were the orders Meg was given.

Meg realized that life with immaculate Mary Carter was not going to be easy.

The professor took Meg and Jim's food ration stamp books, because she would do all the food shopping.

Although, Meg was reluctant to turn over the precious books, she didn't have much choice.

"The menus I'll prepare may seem bland to you, Mrs. Wright, but they contain all the nutritional value necessary for a healthy body."

Meg smiled, "Sounds just like my mother's meals."

"Ummm. You are to make sure that my father eats every bit of his food. It's vital to his health, understand? When do you expect your husband to arrive?" The professor asked as she was leaving.

"He's due in from sea tomorrow," Meg answered and smiled. She was so anxious to see him. She had left a message for Jim at the Crocker House with the address and phone number of their new home.

Mr. Carter wheeled himself into the kitchen. "What's your name again, dearie?" he asked in a gravelly voice.

"It's Meg, Mr. Carter."

"I think the damn stroke made me senile, along with crippling me. I can't remember from one minute to the next. Can we go for a walk now?"

"In a little while. Your daughter has given me quite a list of jobs to do."

"Can the jobs! Don't let her push you around. She's a bugger!" the old man hissed.

Meg laughed. She liked his spirit. The stroke had left him paralyzed on his left side. The nurse, who came daily, had arrived earlier and had bathed and dressed him. She also had given him an hour of physical therapy.

When the nurse was leaving, she encouraged Meg to take Mr. Carter out for a walk. "It's a beautiful March day. You'll learn quickly to do things your own way while she's at school, or you won't last a week here, right, Colonel Carter? She's a slave driver, but the Colonel's a doll. See you tomorrow." She kissed the top of his head and left.

"Well, let's get your jacket on, Mr. Carter," Meg said. "You can show me the neighborhood."

When Meg pushed the chair down the ramp in the front of the house, Mr. Carter yelled, "Forward march, Corporal, we're going to inspect the terrain."

Meg stood at attention in front of the wheelchair and saluted. "Yes, sir!"

While pushing him through the streets of lovely large homes, he told her of his war experiences in great detail. He had been a colonel in the Infantry.

Meg enjoyed Mr. Carter's company.

∞ * ∞

When Jim came the next evening, he was quite happy that they were living in such a nice place, but very concerned that Meg would be doing too much. She assured him she was strong enough and felt fine.

"Well the good news is, I'll start sub school next week and be home every night, but I'll have lots of studying to do. I sure hope we can stay here for a long time."

But two weeks later, Meg was told to get out! Two things happened that resulted in Professor Carter's decision to eject the Wrights.

Meg had never used a pressure cooker before, and for some unexplained reason it didn't operate the way the professor said it would. Meg was in the living room with Mr. Carter, when suddenly there was a loud explosion in the kitchen.

When Meg reached the kitchen door, she screamed, "Oh, my God, look what's happened!" The pressure gauge on the top of the cover had blown off and shot up into the ceiling, embedding itself in the plaster. The cover to the pot was lying on the floor, and beef stew was splattered everywhere.

Mr. Carter wheeled into the kitchen. "Holy shit, Meg. The cooker blew its cork!"

"Oh, your daughter will kill me," Meg cried in terror. "I'll have to try and get it cleaned up before she gets home." Meg looked at the clock, "Oh, God, look at the time; it's almost five-thirty." She was panic-stricken.

No sooner had she started spooning the stew back into the pot, hoping to salvage enough for dinner, when the front door opened.

The professor, seeing her father at the kitchen entrance, asked, "What are you doing, Father? Please don't bother Mrs. Wright while she's preparing the meals." She began to pull his wheelchair back toward the living room, but, from the corner of her eye, she saw Meg frantically spooning vegetables from the stove top.

"What's happened here, Mrs. Wright?" she asked, wondering why the cover of the pressure cooker was on the floor. Then seeing that the stove, counter and floor were covered with stew, she screamed, "Oh no!" Catching Meg looking up at the ceiling, she looked up. "You stupid oaf," she yelled as she pointed to the gauge sticking out of the plaster. "Look at what you've done. Do you have any idea how much pressure cookers cost? Do you realize it's impossible to get one with the war on?"

Mr. Carter wheeled himself back to the kitchen door and yelled at his daughter, "Don't you talk to Meg that way. It was an accident. The poor kid's doing her best, considering she's so young and pregnant to boot."

Meg's heart sank. *I never should have told him.*

The professor's face turned purple with rage. "You're pregnant!" she hissed, looking at Meg with disgust as if pregnancy was something dirty. "Pack your bags and leave immediately."

Meg could no longer contain her Irish. "Miss Carter, I'm sorry about your pressure cooker. We'll pay you for it. I wouldn't want to owe you anything. I'll leave immediately. Just give me our food ration stamps," she demanded in a quivering voice.

The professor opened her handbag, took out a book and thrust it at Meg. "That's your husband's. I've used all of yours to stock up. I was expecting you to be a more reliable person."

Suddenly Mr. Carter rammed his wheelchair against the back of his daughter's legs, almost knocking her off balance. "Mary, now you listen to me. I want Meg to stay. She's wonderful company. I need her. Don't I count around here any more?"

Professor Carter turned. Her face looked menacing as she glared at her father. "When you turned this house over to me, and asked me to manage your affairs, I did so willingly. Now this is my house, and I'll manage it the way I see fit." She swung his chair around, pushed him out of the kitchen, into his room and slammed the door.

Meg could hear him sobbing and felt terrible. Oh, God, that poor man, and poor us. Looking at the stew now hardening on the stove and counter, she said loudly, "Good, I hope it hardens, and it never comes off." She ran upstairs to their room, emptied all the drawers and began stuffing their clothes in their suitcases. She knew she shouldn't carry the heavy bags downstairs, so she laid them at the top of the stairs, gave them a shove, and they tumbled noisily down to the bottom.

Professor Carter ran to the hall. Her hands were raised and tightly fisted as if she was going to strike Meg. Her face was pinched into a hateful look. "You idiot, you. What are you doing now, trying to destroy my stairs and walls too?"

Ignoring her, Meg opened the front door and dragged the bags out. Once outside, she turned and looked back at the professor, "You're a mean, miserable old maid, and I'm going to report you to the college for stealing my food stamps." With that, Meg slammed the door as hard as she could. She could hear the professor screaming hysterically. "Whew! I guess I'm lucky to be out of there."

It was dark, cold and windy. Meg settled herself on the bottom front step and cuddled inside her heavy wool coat. Jim should be here shortly, she thought. Sometimes he got a ride but mostly he took the bus.

Looking at their two suitcases, she thought about their household goods now stored in her parents' cellar. How wonderful it would be to have a place of their own and open up all the boxes with their wedding gifts. It would be like Christmas.

She looked at her watch again and shivered. Jim was late. She thought about her marriage. So far, it's not like I thought it would be. My God, I can't believe it! I've lived in five places in just three months of marriage: Seville Street, my parents' house, the Crocker Hotel, the Goldbaum's and the worst, the immaculate professor. And to think that two of those places were "just one night stands!" Meg saw a car coming down the street. It must be Jim.

It stopped and Jim got out and ran to Meg. "Honey, what are you doing out here in the cold with our bags? What's happened?"

Meg threw herself into his arms and sobbed out the details of their eviction. Jim put her in the front seat of the car and loaded the bags in the back."

"Oh, Meg, I'm so sorry you had to go through all that. Pardon my language, but that woman is a bitch!"

"Whose car is this, Jim?"

"Well, I wanted to surprise you, honey. It's ours! My parents loaned me the money, and I picked it up from the car dealer tonight." A sheepish grin crossed his face.

"Oh, Jim, how wonderful!" Meg was thrilled because her family had never owned a car. "How much did it cost? It looks old."

"It's a 1937 Ford. I got it for $350, but it's really in good shape. We had to have one, honey. We were spending too much on taxis and buses."

⸱ * ⸢

The Wrights took a room at the Mohegan Hotel for a week. It was much nicer than the Crocker House. Every day, Jim and Meg searched for suitable housing without any luck. After dinner on Saturday night at the Officer's Club, they joined some friends in the lounge for a nightcap and met a Navy widow named Rose Kirkland. Her husband, a commander, had been killed when his sub was sunk in the Pacific.

When their housing problem came up, Rose asked, "Would you like to move in with me temporarily? My house has been sold, but paperwork for the sale won't be ready for a month. I'm trying to sell my furniture, and it would be a big help, Meg, if you could be there when people come to answer my ads. I work full time."

"We'd really appreciate that, Rose," Jim said. "It will give us time to look around for something more permanent."

Meg looked at Rose, "Are you sure you want someone living with you?" Meg was becoming quite skeptical about sharing a house.

"I've hated living alone, Meg. I'd welcome the company," Rose said with genuine sincerity.

The Wrights' new living quarters were the most pleasant they had had since they were married. Rose was not at home often and seldom cooked.

Jim loved sub school, in spite of all the studying. They made new friends, played bridge and often went to, dinner parties at the Officer's Club at the Base.

EIGHTEEN

*O*n April 12, 1945, President Roosevelt died. Jim and Meg were shopping in downtown New London when the news was announced over the radio. People came running out into the streets sobbing, "The President is dead!" Traffic came to a standstill; the country came to a standstill as crowds gathered and spoke in hushed tones. A great and beloved leader was gone.

Chills ran up and down Meg's spine. She truly mourned the man who gave her father a job when they were so desperately poor.

Never had America been so affected by a president's death. It was announced that Vice President Harry Truman, would be sworn in as president in a few hours.

ꙮ * ꙮ

The month at Rose Kirkland's house sped by, and now the Wrights had to look again for a place to live. They found a room with kitchen privileges in Thamesville on the outskirts of New London. They now would share a home with a Polish family named Lanski. This was Meg's eighth move since she got married.

In spite of many scoldings, Meg often found the Lanski's two young children in their room going through their things. Meg was not allowed to lock the door. Mr. Lanski worried about fire. They usually escaped the close quarters in the evenings, sometimes spending the evening on the submarine, *Pike*, when it was in port. The executive officer, Al Jennings, had become a good friend of Jim's.

Meg had not put on a great deal of weight and could easily fit down the hatch. She would lie on a bunk and read while Jim studied or played cribbage in the ward room.

Because of her many visits on the submarine, her initial fears for Jim's safety on a submarine lessened. She now realized the benefit of being aboard a submarine in war time. It could submerge and get out of the line of fire, unlike surface vessels.

✍ * ✍

When Meg was about five months pregnant, she went to the base hospital for a prenatal visit. The Navy doctor told her everything seemed fine, but there was a possibility she would have to have a cesarean section.

"What does that mean?" Meg asked.

"Well, it means there's a possibility that it might be better to deliver the baby surgically than vaginally." Meg tried to get more information about what that would mean, but the clinic doctor seemed to be in a great rush. His only explanation was, "Although you haven't gained a great deal of weight for five months, the fetus may be too large at full term to be delivered through the normal birth canal. Come back when you're eight months along, and we'll examine you again."

What he had said frightened Meg. She knew so little about birth. She still had a hard time accepting the fact that a baby could come out of her private area. She had seen kittens born at the Lanskis', and Mrs. Lanski had said, "See how easy it is to have kittens? Well, it's just as easy to have kids. A cesarean section," Mrs. Lanski told Meg, "means that they cut your stomach open to get the baby out."

The thought of having her stomach invaded by a knife had brought on waves of nausea. Fortunately one of the girls from the sub school crowd had had a cesarean birth and she assured Meg, "I didn't feel a thing. They gave me ether and it knocked me out."

Still, Meg's fear persisted and would continue until it was time for her to deliver.

✍ * ✍

May 1945. By late April, it became certain that the war in Europe was nearing an end. German armies were surrendering in great masses. Reports of Hitler's suicide and Mussolini's execution filled front pages around the world. But the war in Europe didn't end until May 8. V-E day, victory in Europe, was celebrated throughout the world, but the jubilation was somewhat subdued because millions of lives had been lost to gain that victory.

President Truman strongly advised the Japanese to surrender or suffer devastating consequences. Japanese defeats in the Pacific area were daily events. Okinawa, the principal Japanese base, was surrendering to the Allies after 83 days of fighting. The Allied victory was sealed by the formal suicide of the two Japanese generals in command.

⚱ * ⚱

Connecticut, June 1945. Living with the Lanski family became more difficult each day. Now, every evening just as they were finishing dinner, Mrs. Lanski would hover near the table. If Meg or Jim paused, Mrs. Lanski would ask, "Are you through? If you're not going to eat anymore, I'll scrape what's left off your plates for my mother's pigs."

That usually ended their appetites. She would then take their plates, scrape off the food into a pail and put their dishes in a pan of greasy water in the sink.

"From now on you'll have to wash your dishes in the same water we use to do our dishes. My husband says you waste too much soap and hot water the way you do dishes."

Jim and Meg knew that they had to get out after a week of this new routine. They got lucky. One of Jim's instructors at sub school who was being transferred, asked Jim, "Would you and Meg be interested in sub-leasing my apartment for the next four months?"

It was the perfect solution, because sub school would be over the last week in August, and their baby was due about the end of September or the first of October. Jim hoped to be assigned to a submarine at the base, which meant that they would likely be able to get base housing.

On July 1, they moved into their own apartment on Washington Street in Norwich; it was Meg's ninth move. It was wonderful to be alone at last and not have to share their daily lives with others. There were four apartments in the old Victorian house, which was surrounded by a large yard with beautiful flowering bushes and fruit trees. The Wrights' apartment had a bedroom, living room, dinette, and bath. The furniture was rather old, but it was comfortable. When Meg realized that the couch in the living room pulled out into a bed, she immediately called her parents and invited them to visit.

Confident that they would be in the New London area for a while, they requested the Navy to ship their two sea chests, filled with all their worldly belongings, from Meg's parent's house to their apartment in Norwich.

Margaret and Bill came by train and stayed for a week. Babs and Virginia came for a visit, and the Wrights had their first big dinner party. Jim invited some of his bachelor friends at sub school. According to the men, not only was the dinner great, but they thought the Cambridge girls were beautiful.

Although going into her eighth month and suffering leg cramps and lower back pain, this was the happiest time of Meg's married life.

ᴕ * ᴕ

On August 6, the first atomic bomb was dropped on Hiroshima. When the initial plans were made, the prime target cities were Hiroshima, Kokura, Nagasaki, and Niigata, where Joe was being held prisoner. The United States was unaware that a POW camp was located there. But it was decided to eliminate Niigata as a target; it was too small and too far north.

The United States felt certain that the devastation caused by the bomb would bring about a Japanese surrender. Somewhere between 80,000 and 200,000 were either killed or suffered severe radiation exposure. But the Japanese refused to surrender. On August 9, a second bomb was dropped, this time on Nagasaki, and as many as 100,000 more suffered death or life-long disfiguring burns.

On Tuesday, August 14, the Japanese surrendered. Jubilation spread throughout the world.

Jim and Meg kissed and hugged when they heard the news at seven that evening. They both called their parents. Margaret and Bill could hardly talk, they were crying so hard. "Our Joe will now come home!"

Jim graduated from sub school on Saturday, August 18, four days after the war ended. Jim, like many of his classmates, shared a common feeling of having been cheated out of the chance to defend their country.

A graduation and farewell party was held at the Officer's Club on graduation evening. Most of their friends would be leaving the next day for quick visits to their homes before they reported to their new assignments. Jim, along with many other graduates, got drunk. The next morning when he awoke, he had a horrendous hangover and felt deathly ill.

Because Jim was so sick, Meg called the base to see if he could see a doctor. Jim was sure it was a hangover, but he had never been this sick. The dispensary nurse said she'd call right back after listening to Jim's symptoms, but instead they sent an ambulance. The corpsmen took Jim's temperature and pulse and decided he should be taken to the dispensary for further examination.

Jokingly the corpsman said, "There's a lot of appendicitis going around."

Meg wanted to go with Jim, but the corpsmen wouldn't allow it. "It's a long ride to the base dispensary, and they might keep him overnight."

Meg was frightened. She felt so desperately alone. All their close friends from sub school were gone.

The phone rang two hours later. "Honey, it's me."

"Oh, darling, are you all right?"

"Well, I'm on the way into the operating room to have my appendix out. Take care of yourself, honey. It's no big deal. I'll be home soon. I love you, Meg. Say a prayer," Jim said in a weak voice.

Meg was devastated. The doctor called a few hours later. "Mrs. Wright, your Ensign is doing well, but I don't want you to visit him yet because he's been heavily drugged and he'll be 'out of it' for a couple of days."

Meg called her mother in tears. Margaret wanted to come down and be with her, but Bill was having a bad bout of ulcers and she couldn't leave him. Meg was filled with fear for Jim, and ached with loneliness. She hadn't slept at all. By the second day, she had to see Jim and asked the older couple upstairs if they would drive her to the dispensary.

She was shocked when she saw him. He had tubes in his nose and was not coherent. She was allowed to stay only a few minutes.

By Thursday, she was in a deep depression. At midnight on Friday, August 24, Meg was awakened when a rush of fluid spread between her legs. At first, she thought it was blood, but it was colorless. She called the woman upstairs, who came down immediately.

"Your water broke," Bea said casually. "That means your labor is starting. Nothing to be alarmed about."

"But my baby isn't due until the end of September."

"Then it's going to come early, Meg. You've been so depressed, it has brought on labor."

"I was born at midnight, Bea, and I've always believed that the good fairies were about at that time of night. If my baby is born now, it won't be good because we've only been married eight months. Oh, what will people think?"

Bea made tea. "Listen Meg, you can't stop it now. Just be thankful that you'll be in the hospital with Jim, and you can see each other. You're baby will be premature, but a month early isn't anything to worry about."

"But they don't deliver babies at the base dispensary. I have to go to the Lawrence Memorial Hospital in New London, and a Navy doctor will deliver it."

Bea suggested, "Then I think you should call the hospital. Are you having any cramps?"

"Yes, but not bad."

The maternity nurse who answered the phone suggested that Meg come to the hospital right away when she told her that the Navy doctor had said there was a possibility of her having a cesarean section.

Bea and her husband took Meg to the hospital. They promised to call her mother and to notify the doctor at the dispensary so he could tell Jim.

With each passing hour, the pain in Meg's lower back increased. She knew there would be labor pains but not the agonizing contractions she was experiencing. No doctor had examined her yet. The nurses tried to keep her mind off the pains by having her roll bandages. Over and over she asked if she would be having a cesarean birth; the fear of being cut open terrorized her.

The nurse said, "I don't think so. Too late for that."

"Oh, thank God!"

"We're not supposed to discuss anything about your case with you until the Navy doctor gets here."

Twelve hours later, the cramping had intensified severely. Meg had been placed in a crib-like bed with raised sides because they didn't want her walking any more. Standing up and walking had felt so much better than lying down, but the nurses were afraid she would fall.

Fifteen hours later, Meg was thrashing and screaming for help. The Navy doctor still had not arrived.

The nurses tried to help. "Mrs. Wright. We're so sorry you have to suffer like this. Try to be brave for just a little while longer."

"Please. Oh, God, please. Can't you give me anything for the pain?" Meg begged.

"We've told you, we're not allowed to give you anything without the doctor's orders. We still haven't been able to locate him."

"I've called the base dispensary four times," the head nurse said in an exasperated voice.

A younger nurse added, "We've even called the Officer's Club, 'cause that's where we figured he probably was."

The head nurse gave her a dirty look.

An hour later, the head nurse leaned over the rail and took Meg's hand, "It might make you feel better, Mrs. Wright, to know that your mother just arrived and is downstairs in the waiting room."

"Oh, please bring her up right away. I want my Mom!" Like a small child, Meg wailed, "Please, please. I want my Mom!"

"I'm sorry, honey. No one is allowed to visit patients in labor, not even husbands. It's hospital rules. I'm so sorry, Mrs. Wright," the nurse said sympathetically and walked away. Her eyes filled with tears. She knew Meg was in excruciating pain. There was nothing she could do. Meg was a Navy patient.

Twenty-three hours and forty-five minutes after Meg arrived at the hospital, she was wheeled into the delivery room. The unendurable pains now were coming one on top of the other. Her legs were placed in metal stirrups, and an ether mask was mercifully positioned over her nose.

The Wrights' son was born at the stroke of midnight on August 25. Forceps had been used to extract the six pound baby boy, causing deep, dark bruises on his tiny forehead.

Five hours later, Meg was awakened, "Mrs. Wright, Mrs. Wright, would you like to see your son?"

Meg, opened her eyes and tried to understand what the nurse was saying. Was the nightmare over, or am I dreaming? "Son? Oh! I've got a son! Where's my baby?"

"Right here, dear. Hold him gently now. He's a wee one," the nurse said, handing the tiny bundle to Meg.

Pride swelled through Meg as she unwrapped the tiny form. "I did this? I made this little person? Oh, he's adorable, but his face is all red. What are those black and blue marks on his forehead?" Meg asked with concern.

"We'll tell you about that later. He's fine and healthy for an eight month baby. If he had gone full term he'd probably have weighed eight pounds." The nurse laughed. His birth is unusual though, Mrs. Wright. He was born at the stroke of midnight!"

"Midnight?" Meg was stunned. "I was born at midnight..."

The nurse smiled broadly. "Yes. And I've heard the good fairies were all about you. I'm sure they were there at your son's birth, too.

Here, let me take the baby back to the nursery now. You have company waiting to see you."

A few moments later Meg saw her mother coming through the doorway. "Hello, little mother."

"Oh, Mom! Oh thank God you're here."

They hugged and cried. "I went to see Jim at the base hospital before I came here this morning. He told me to give you and his son a big kiss and to tell you he loves you. He's having kind of a rough time, Meg. He's still bed-ridden and weak, but the doctor said he's going to be fine."

"Oh, my poor Jim. And what a mess for you, Mom. We both end up in the hospital at the same time and to make matters worse, in different hospitals."

"I enjoy playing nurse. Everyone has been wonderful to me."

"Mom, something is really bothering me. What are people going to think, I mean about the baby being born so early? We've only been married a little less than eight months."

"The baby was premature. That's why you had such a hard time delivering. Probably should have been taken cesarean, the nurse said. Don't worry about what people will think, honey. Your neighbor, Bea, told me how upset you were over Jim. She was afraid you might lose the baby. It won't make any difference to the people who love you, and who count in your life. But, in the end, the good fairies brought you a beautiful healthy midnight son. Isn't that remarkable, Meg?"

"It's unbelievable! I hope his midnight birth brings him as much luck as it has brought to me."

"Jim's doctor told him that a midnight birth is rare. He said he'd read a news story that said at midnight, there is no time at all. He also said, according to the nation's official timekeeper, the Naval Observatory, there is no 12 a.m. or 12 p.m., only noon and midnight. Maybe that's why the fairies come around.

"Maybe we better go see a tea reader for little Jimmy and see what's in store for him," Meg said and laughed.

Margaret spent most of her time at the hospital standing at the glass window of the nursery admiring her grandson. She couldn't wait to hold him.

Meg received a telegram. "I'll bet it's from Jim's parents, because I phoned them."

Meg read it out loud.

Dear James and Meg:

*Congratulations. STOP We are happy you have a
healthy son. STOP We hope you carry on
the family name, and christen our grandson
James-Frank-Wright-the-Third. STOP*

Mr. and Mrs. James Wright, Sr.

"Well, how do you like that? They're telling you what to name your baby," Margaret acted annoyed.

"Mom, they're not telling us what to do. Jim and I had already decided to name our baby after Jim and his father, if it was a boy."

"Your father will be hurt," Margaret sulked.

"No, he won't," Meg answered confidently.

⚴ * ⚴

When Margaret visited the next day, Meg told her, "That jerk of a Navy doctor came by this morning. No apologies! Nothing about not showing up when I was in labor. Well, I let go with my Irish and told him off!"

"Oh, you didn't, Meg! You're supposed to be respectful to doctors. I'm ashamed of you. Did he examine you?"

"He checked my stitches; I had quite a few. It seems from what I overheard the nurses saying, I should have had an episiotomy, an incision to help the delivery. But because he showed up so late, I was badly torn, and I'll have a longer recovery because of it. Now, do you still think I should have been respectful to him, Mom?"

"Well, I don't know what to think, dear."

"But now, I have a funny story to tell you. Remember I told you about spending the night with the Rabbi and his wife. Well, this morning, Rabbi Goldbaum came to visit me. He said he was at the hospital for a circumcision. The nurse saw him visiting me. I guess she thought I was Jewish, because about a half an hour later, she asked me if I was going to have my baby circumcised."

"And what did you say?" Margaret asked.

"No! Of course not. Why would I want a Jewish ritual for my baby?" Meg replied in exasperation.

"Well, a circumcision is not just a ritual. And, it's not done just on Jews. Some Catholics have their babies circumcised, too. Didn't you know that? Was Jim? Our Joe was," she stated, looking at Meg as if her statement might solve another fact of life which, of course, she had never discussed with Meg.

"What are you saying, Mom?" Meg asked, now totally perplexed. All Meg knew about circumcision was that Jesus went to the temple when he was twelve to celebrate the feast of the Circumcision. It was a Holy Day of Obligation on January 1 in the Catholic church.

Fortunately, at that moment, a nurse walked in the room. Margaret jumped up and moved towards the door, saving herself the embarrassment of talking about a male's penis. "Nurse, would you please explain to my daughter why her baby should be circumcised. They keep cleaner, don't they?"

Confused, Meg looked from her mother, who was hastily leaving the room, to the nurse. A few minutes later, Meg learned another fact of life.

✠ * ✠

Ten days after little Jimmy's birth, Meg left the hospital in a taxi with her Mom and the baby. They drove to the base dispensary to see Jim who was still quite weak. He was waiting on the sidewalk in a wheelchair. The hospital corpsman pushed him close to the open door of the cab. Meg beamed as she held out their son and offered him to his father.

Jim's eyes filled with tears as he looked down at the baby tenderly. "Oh, Meg, look at my little guy, I mean our little guy. I'm so sorry you had to go through it alone, honey. I feel so helpless."

"So do I, but thank God we have Mom."

"Thanks from me, too, Mom," Jim said sincerely. "I don't know what we would have done without you." He unwrapped the blanket to get a better look at his tiny son. At first he was upset when he saw the deep dark scars of the forceps on the baby's forehead. Then he put his index finger between the baby's fingers and was amazed at his son's strength. "He's really strong!"

Their visit was short. They leaned toward each other, kissed, and said how much they looked forward to their reunion tomorrow when an ambulance would bring Jim home.

For the next seven days, a state of total confusion reigned in their small apartment: formulas had to be made, diapers had to be washed, Jim's incision needed dressing changes, and Meg had to have heat lamp treatments for her stitches four times a day. Margaret was soon totally exhausted, and it showed. By mutual agreement, a decision was made that she should go home. Not only did Margaret need a rest, but Jim, Meg and their son now needed to be alone.

NINETEEN

apan, 1945. Although the news of the Japanese surrender had reached the prisoners at Niigata, they heard nothing about their release. Nobu had kept them informed of everything he heard, but there seemed to be no urgency on the part of their Japanese captors to free them.

They had been told by Nobu about the horrible atomic bombing of Hiroshima and Nagasaki. A sergeant major at the camp gave a talk to the prisoners, condemning the United States for the terrible crime it committed by dropping such devastating bombs.

"America's cruelty knows no bounds! To kill so many innocent people so viciously; those acts will be condemned by the world forever."

The prisoners booed in protest. One yelled, "Hey, Major, you Japs started this war." And in one voice, the prisoners yelled, "Remember Pearl Harbor."

An active demonstration began with both sides shouting insults and condemnations. The prisoners no longer feared retaliation. Life at the camp had changed completely. The prisoners could now walk freely out the front gates, past the armed guards, and stroll downtown. They went in and out of the shops that were mostly bare. There was no food available at all. Joe and Chip walked by a house with the front door open and spotted potatoes lying on the floor. They were stealing them when two old women entered the house and found them stuffing their pockets. The women stared at the prisoners and bowed. Joe and Chip felt badly and tried to return the potatoes, but the women refused them.

When Joe was taken prisoner, he weighed about one-hundred and seventy pounds. He now weighed eighty-two pounds.

There was much talk throughout the camp about how the prisoners would retaliate against the guards who had been cruel to them. But it would be quite a different story for Nobu. Joe and Chip had promised to do all they could to get him set free and sent back to Honolulu as soon as possible.

On September 5, twenty-two days after the war ended, two Navy pilots flying from an aircraft carrier operating off Tokyo Bay, were on a scouting expedition looking for POW camps. When they spotted the Niigata camp, which had been reported to be in that area, they dropped down for a closer look.

When the aircraft approached the camp, Joe stopped dead in his tracks. He looked up. He was so startled he couldn't speak for a moment. Then he yelled, "Oh my God, Christ Almighty. Listen everyone! They're ours! I'd know the sound of that beautiful engine anyplace. I know they're definitely ours!"

The planes approached the camp site on a low pass and tipped their wings. The prisoners could see the markings clearly. They all began to run around the yard screaming and waving frantically.

"Holy shit, Joe, look at those beautiful white stars on those babies," Chip cried. He hugged Joe, and they danced in a circle, crying shamelessly.

A prisoner, punching the air with his right fist, hollered, "They're Navy planes! They're damn Navy planes! Sons of a bitchin Navy Planes." He dropped to his knees, put his hands in a prayer posture, and looked up as the planes made a second pass and tossed out two bundles of food. "Honest to God, I'll never make fun of a swabbie again!"

Pandemonium broke out as the bundles hit the ground and burst open. Food, cigarettes, candy, medications and other supplies spilled out on the dirt.

While the prisoners were reveling in the bonanza, Joe heard the planes getting closer. From the familiar sound, he knew they were about to land near the camp. He yelled, "The planes are landing. The frigin' Navy's landing right here in this God-forsaken prisoner camp."

One prisoner yelled, "Let's give them a big welcome!" All the prisoners who were not disabled made a mad dash for the gate. The disabled followed at a slower pace. The plane had landed on a nearby concrete highway. When the prisoners approached the planes, they began singing "Anchors Aweigh," then sent up a loud cheer for the Navy. The Navy pilots climbed down from their planes and looked toward the prisoners. They were the most beautiful sight the POW's had seen for a very long time.

The pilots were met by the camp commandant who had quickly hopped into a vehicle when he heard the planes landing. The prisoners stopped when one of the pilots motioned them to stay back. They paused reluctantly, wondering what was happening. Then one of the pilots stepped away from the commandant and walked toward the prisoners. He stopped about five feet away from where the prisoners were standing, gave a smart salute, and said loudly in an Indiana twang, suppressing a smile, "The commanding officer of this here prisoner of war camp has just been given an order by the United States Navy to make immediate arrangements to get all prisoners to Tokyo within 48 hours or else answer to General MacArthur." Once again he saluted the men, winked, did an about face, and walked briskly back to the plane as deafening shouts of joy filled the air.

The senior officers among the prisoners walked over to the pilots for further instructions.

"Ask them how the Red Sox did this year," Joe yelled.

"The Yankees beat 'em," A man with a Brooklyn accent yelled across to Joe, giving him a raspberry.

That night a large truck came through the gates. The Japanese driver and his helper jumped out of the cab and lifted up the tarpaulin, exposing cases of beer. The two men bowed to the first prisoners on the scene and gestured for them to help themselves. Although the prisoners thoroughly enjoyed the immediate glow, many got sick when they drank more than two beers. Their systems had been so deprived of a stable diet for so long that the stimulation of the alcohol had severe effects.

The next morning, in spite of hundreds of hangovers, the full realization of their freedom became apparent. At midmorning, B-29s made low passes over the camp and dropped hundreds of food bundles, clothing and cigarettes.

Joe and Chip had shared their beer with Nobu the previous evening and had made a pact to write to each other; it was a sincere promise. "Nobu, if there is anything I can ever do for you, don't hesitate to ask, pal," Joe said looking at the sad Japanese face. Nobu would be lost in a defeated nation, which was not his true homeland.

"Just get me back to Waikiki, Joe baby," Nobu said, shaking hands with Joe and Chip. He stood up, looked at them, and tried to smile while fighting back tears. He saluted them, turned and disappeared into the night. They never saw him again, but they would not forget that he saved their lives many times while they were held prisoners.

The next day the prisoners were put on passenger trains and taken to Tokyo. There, they were transferred to ambulances and taken to Yokohama where they were put aboard a hospital ship, the *Marigold*, for medical evaluation. It was the first time these men had seen an American woman since they were taken prisoner, and they just stared for long periods at the Army nurses who were gentle and kind to them.

The men were allowed to write letters to their families on V-Mail, a very lightweight paper which combined the letter and envelope in one sheet of paper.

After being given extensive examinations, thirty of the men qualified as well enough to travel were put on a C-54 to be flown to Saipan. Joe and Chip were among those lucky thirty, thanks to Nobu, who had played such a heroic role in keeping them fed at Niigata.

On the trip to Saipan, the weather turned bad, and a typhoon developed. The plane shook incessantly and was tossed about violently. They crash landed on Saipan. Miraculously, none of the passengers were injured.

On the next leg of their trip home, they took a PBY flying boat, stopping at Marshall and Johnson Islands. Their last stop was John Rogers Airfield, near Hickham Field, in Honolulu. From there they were taken to a hospital at Wheeler Field where they stayed for several days for further R & R and medical attention.

Joe and Chip very much wanted to visit Nobu's family hotel and talk with Nobu's uncle who was running the hotel, The Hale Omura. They knew Nobu's parents probably would not be back from the internment camp in America, but they wanted to tell Nobu's uncle how Nobu had saved their lives and that they would do all they could to get him home again. But, because they were restricted to the hospital, Nobu's uncle had to visit them.

"I am so happy that Nobu is well and is still a good American. I will notify Nobu's interned parents and his brother, Akira." He mostly looked forward to Nobu and his younger brother, Akira, coming home to help him, because the hotel had become quite run down and was in badly need of repair. The uncle was an elderly man.

Joe and Chip were put aboard a troop ship sailing for San Francisco. On arrival, they were taken to Letterman Hospital where they would stay until they regained most of their lost weight and had recovered from the various fungus infections that had plagued their bodies during their capture.

"The men who refused to die" were home at last.

TWENTY

ambridge, October 1945. Meg made her tenth move in her tenth month of marriage during the first week of October, when Jim drove her and the baby back to Cambridge to live with her parents temporarily. Jim had to return to the base and would live at the BOQ. They hoped to get base housing about the fifteenth of October, when Jim would get his permanent orders to a submarine. They stored their two sea boxes of household goods at the base.

It was fun for Meg to be back in Cambridge and to show off her adorable son to relatives and friends.

A few days after Meg came home, Margaret said, "I want to have a woman to woman talk with you, Meg."

Meg sensed her mother's embarrassment as Margaret sat down quickly, bent her head and looked down at her hands, which she folded and unfolded continuously as she spoke.

"I hope you and Jim are being careful about getting pregnant again. You should practice abstinence for at least six months because you're going to have a hard time making the rhythm system work. You know, because you're not regular."

"Abstinence. Is that the answer?" Meg asked coyly. "I knew the church must have an answer for women like me when the rhythm system fails."

"Well, I certainly hope you would never use any of those...those rubber things! That would be a mortal sin!"

"Don't worry about it, Mom. Jim and I will do what we have to do. It's our personal problem. We want more children just as soon as we get stationed someplace for at least a year. I never want to go through what I just did unless we're together." Meg kissed her mother's head. "Never fear, Mom, we'll do our duty and propagate the faith!"

Jim and Meg had discussed the birth control issue with a priest at length. There was no easy answer; they could play rhythm roulette, abstain, or sin.

❧ * ❧

On Friday, October 5, in the early evening, the phone rang. Jimmy was screaming, and Meg couldn't hear too well.

"Here, Mom, hold the baby, please."

A hollow sounding voice said, "Hello, Hello." The static on the line made it difficult to understand. "Is that my little nephew?" The crackling voice asked. Meg screamed, "Its our Joe! Joe! Oh, my God, it's you! Dad, Mom come quick! It's Joe, our Joe's on the phone!"

They crammed their heads as close to the phone as possible to savor his every word.

"Hi, everybody. I'm in San Francisco at Letterman Hospital. Can you hear me?"

"Yes!" they answered in unison.

"Are you all right, Joe?" Margaret yelled into the phone.

"When are you coming home, Joe?" Bill asked, his voice choked with emotion.

"Soon as they fatten me up, Dad. I can't talk too long, because there are about fifty guys lined up behind me waiting to use the phone. We can make free calls but only during certain hours. Tell Eileen I'll call her tonight, probably in about four hours from now, because I'll have to get back in line when I finish this call. I love you all and can't wait to see you, especially little Jimmy. I'll talk to you real soon. I'm okay. So long for now."

"We love you. Hurry home," his family yelled as the line went dead.

A tremendous sense of comfort filled them as the O'Mearas hugged each other in blessed relief. They were the lucky ones. Many of their friends and neighbors would never hear their sons' voices again, while others would see their loved ones come home with limbs missing or disfigured for life in their bodies and minds.

❧ * ❧

Meg's stay at her parent's home became a stressful situation for everyone. There were always diapers to wash and hang out to dry. Formula equipment had to be sterilized and was usually spread out over the kitchen counter tops most of the time. The every four-hour feedings during the night and early morning hours always woke Bill and Margaret.

Aunt Grace was there constantly during the day. She had been very upset when she heard Meg and Jim would be bringing the baby home in that "that old jalopy," as she called their 1937 Ford. She had wanted to send Uncle Frank down to pick them up in his Caddie.

Her concern for the new baby in the family was understandable, considering what had happened to her only child, John, at birth. But in creating a sterile atmosphere, she had practically remodeled the O'Meara's house. When Meg arrived home, she had found her old bedroom turned into a hospital nursery. All the drawers had been lined with sterilized diapers, and an adorable bassinet was placed near the radiator. The furniture and walls had been washed and new curtains covered the windows. A section of the kitchen cupboards had been sterilized for the baby's food, bottles and formula equipment. She had not only established visiting hours for viewing the baby, but visitors had to stand behind the glass French doors that separated the living room and dining room. Even Meg's Uncle Bert, his wife, Kay and their two sons, Jack and Tom, had to stand behind the glass door.

Meg, not wanting to hurt her aunt's feelings, put up with the excessive sterile situation for a week, but then decided it had to end. "Aunt Grace, I realize you just want to protect Jimmy, but I think we have to let him be exposed to other people a little bit more. I want our friends and relatives not only to see him but to hold him, play with him and feed him. I think the kind of isolation you've set up here could even be dangerous. I have a wonderful book on raising a baby, and it highly recommends exposing the baby to 'well' people so he can develop immunities."

Grace was shocked and hurt. "Well, if that's your attitude, Miss-know-it-all, and you'd rather take advice from a book..." Grace let the sentence hang as she hastily put on her hat and coat, picked up her purse, and said to Margaret, "Call me a cab. I can see I'm not wanted or needed around here."

Meg begged her aunt, "Please don't feel that way; it's not true. I really appreciate what you've tried to do, but we'll be moving quite a bit, and Jimmy will be exposed to all kinds of people while he's little, and we can't quarantine him forever," Meg tried to reason.

Margaret was in a dilemma. She had been amazed at how well Meg cared for Jimmy and saw some logic in what Meg was saying.

Aunt Grace's visits were few and far between after that and she usually commented either that, "the baby looks pale," or, "he doesn't seem to have put on any weight."

℘ * ℘

New London, October 1945. Jim's orders finally came, and he was assigned to a pre-commissioning crew, along with six other officers.

Temporarily, they would be stationed at the sub base in New London. In November, they would be sent to Philadelphia to be assigned to their new submarine, the *Pout*, soon to be commissioned at the Cramp Shipyard.

The officers would be given furnished housing on the base for $37.50 a month. The rows of red brick buildings with white trim were attractive and were surrounded by grassy areas. Each unit had two bedrooms upstairs, and a bath, kitchen, dining area, and living room downstairs.

Jim had waited until they were in the car and on their way to Connecticut before he told Meg that once again, they would be sharing a house.

Meg was angry. She had dreamt about finally having a place of their own.

"Honey, don't be upset. We're lucky just to get housing. I'm a very junior officer, and I'm really flattered because the Exec selected us to live with him, his wife and their year-old son. Their name is Sheehan, and they come from Kansas City, Missouri."

"How old are they?" Meg asked, trying to adjust to the news and not show her disappointment.

"Pat's about twenty-seven. He's a lieutenant commander and has seen a lot of war duty. Wait until you see all his battle ribbons."

It occurred to Meg that probably Mrs. Sheehan would love to have a place of her own, too, especially if her husband had been away for a long time.

Within an hour of meeting Pat and Helen Sheehan, Meg knew she would be both comfortable and happy living with these wonderful people. Helen would be like a big sister who could teach her about babies, cooking, and the Navy life.

Pat teased Meg good-naturedly right from the start, baiting her by using a facade of superiority whenever they had a discussion. Naturally, Meg argued back if she disagreed. It took a couple of days before she realized that he was teasing her, trying to arouse her Irish.

One evening the two got into a vociferous discussion on the merits of ex-Governor James Michael Curly of Boston versus the infamous ward boss of Kansas City, Jim Pendergast.

Finally, Pat, pretending to have been bested by Meg, feigned defeat and said to Jim, "Ensign, your wife has no respect for rank. We'll have to educate her."

Jim chuckled and shook his head, "Good luck, Commander."

A few weeks later while Meg was drying the dishes, Pat said casually, "Meg, please don't just wash the milk bottles. You have to dry the inside before putting them outdoors or they'll crack in the cold." Meg looked perplexed.

Helen had to look away, so Meg could not see her grinning.

Meg slung the dish towel over her shoulder, put her hands on her hips and stared at Pat as if he were simple-minded. Then in a skeptical voice, she asked, "You want me to dry the inside of the milk bottle? Right? Is that what you farmers do out in Missouri?"

Pat looked indignant. "Just do it, Meg. Wrap the towel around a long wooden spoon and put it inside the bottle and dry it completely."

As if to humor him, Meg came back with, "And then what do you country bumpkins do after you put the bottles out, sit around a pot bellied stove, smoking corn cob pipes and talk about the weather?"

Helen and Jim burst out laughing.

Pat's furrowed brow and pursed lips slowly softened and the corners of his mouth began to turn upwards into a smile that instantly became a wide grin. "Okay, okay, O'Meara, you got me that time!" He grabbed the dish towel and snapped it across Meg's butt.

Pat Sheehan was six feet tall. His brown, closely cropped crew cut was sprinkled with gray hairs. His Irish blue eyes twinkled when he laughed, and he often talked out of the corner of his mouth in a rough tone.

In contrast, Helen Sheehan always spoke in a delightful quiet Midwestern voice. Her serene face and manner created an aura of contentment in spite of the fact that she wasn't completely happy as a Navy wife. She was five months pregnant with their second child and had confided to Meg, "I want Pat to get out of the Navy. I want him to be around when I have this baby."

Meg shared her sentiments completely.

Only the *Pout's* skipper, Commander "Pret" Preston, and his wife, Jennifer, had their own house. The other four officers shared quarters. Lt. Jake Dolan and his wife, Kate, shared a house with Lt. Bob Wade and his wife, Jean. Lt.(jg) Al Helm and his wife, Cassie, shared quarters with Lt.(jg) George Johnson and his wife, Ann. Fortunately, the officers and their wives were extremely compatible.

ℒ * ℒ

Submariners are a special grouping of men who are carefully screened and examined extensively by psychiatrists while in submarine school to make sure that they are psychologically suited to withstand the close confinement of life on a submarine.

An even disposition and the ability to stay calm under pressure are the most important prerequisites. Camaraderie among the officers and crew is essential, because little privacy is afforded the crew of a submarine. While the officers have small quarters, the enlisted men sleep in bunks suspended over torpedoes or in crannies just large enough for a man to stretch out. Overly sensitive or undisciplined men would find it difficult to co-exist on a submarine.

ℒ * ℒ

Although Meg was the youngest of the wives, she welcomed their friendships and enjoyed sharing their daily lives. It gave her a warm sense of security to be part of this extended family. Although many aspects of Navy life were foreign to her, she enjoyed the challenge. It was so different from anything she had experienced in her first twenty years of life.

She told Jim, "I sure have a lot to learn. There are so many do's and don'ts and some pretty strict protocols in the social area of this Navy life. We have to have calling cards printed. We leave them on a tray when we "call" at the Skipper's house or other high ranking officer's homes."

"And, we have to go if we're invited, whether we want to or not. And, we can't stay too long." Jim added. "Are you really going to enjoy being a Navy wife, honey?"

Meg answered honestly, "Most of the time, I guess, except when snobby wives ask me, 'What was your husband's class at the Academy?' Then they look down their noses at me when I tell them you graduated from the University of California."

"I get a lot of that too, Meg," Jim admitted. "During the war, an officer's educational background was of little consequence, but now, in peacetime, it seems they're getting cliquish again."

Another policy that disturbed Meg concerned the unwritten rule that officer's wives didn't associate socially with enlisted men's wives. This kind of class discrimination bothered her. She didn't like being told what to do with her personal life, and she decided to let her conscience guide her if such a situation presented itself.

The only major problem with life on the base in New London was the daily invasion of cockroaches. A maintenance man told the wives, "All base housing is infested, and there's no effective method of eliminating them."

The first few weeks on base, Meg had great difficulty coping with the problem. Although not usually skittish about bugs, she began to have nightmares about roaches. They would jump off the walls, hop on her hands when she opened a kitchen cabinet door, and there were always many of them in the bathroom.

The cockroach problem was the main topic of conversation every morning over coffee. Meg told the other wives, "Honestly, I'd never seen a cockroach before. I've always heard that cockroaches were found only in dirty homes. I think we ought to protest to the base commander."

Kate Dolan laughed and said philosophically, "Meg, cockroaches are a way of life in the Navy if you live in Navy housing or in tropical climates. You better get used to it."

On Saturday nights, baby sitters were hired and the two couples went to the Officer's Club. For five dollars a couple, they could have all the drinks they wanted, a steak dinner and a big band for dancing. Aside from the cockroaches, life on the base was good.

TWENTY-ONE

Philadelphia, November 1945. The officers and crew of the *Pout* arrived at the Cramp Shipyard in Philadelphia for pre-commissioning duty. While their new submarine was being outfitted they boarded it daily to acquaint themselves with the new equipment. The commissioning ceremony would take place at the end of January.

Meg and Jim moved for the twelfth time, to Germantown, a section of Philadelphia. By luck, Meg had spotted a lady putting a "For Rent" sign in a row house window. The owner, Mrs. Wald, a kindly widow, not only agreed to rent to the Wrights but also allowed the Sheehans to stay there until they found a place to live. She offered the two couples the complete use of the house. It was a God send, because their sea chests with all their household belongings were again in transit, and they had no idea when the Navy would deliver them.

A week later, without consulting Meg, Jim decided to transfer from the reserves to the regular Navy. Otherwise he would have been discharged. He loved the Navy and wanted to make it his career.

When he told Meg, she was upset, not so much with his decision, but that he hadn't discussed it with her. "You should have asked my opinion, at least."

"But, honey, it's a secure career, and we'll get to see the world. I thought you loved to travel. I really felt you were enjoying Navy life."

"I am, Jim, but please don't ever make any big decisions about our life without talking it over with me. Okay?"

"You're right, honey, I should have, and I will in the future. I hope you won't be angry when I tell you about another decision I made. The Navy gave me a bonus: a 30 day leave. How would you like to drive to California to meet my family? It's time they met my beautiful wife and adorable son." Meg flung herself at Jim, hugging and kissing him. "Oh, how wonderful, Jim!" Suddenly her face looked thoughtful, "How far is San Francisco from Riverside? Could we visit my brother, Joe, at Letterman Hospital?"

"You bet we can, honey." Jim lifted Meg off her feet and twirled her in a circle singing, "California, Here We Come."

Meg was ecstatic. "Oh, Jim, I've wanted so much to meet your family and to show off our Jimmy."

"And finally, I can show you all the wonders of California that I'm always bragging about."

"When do we leave, Jim?"

"How about December 8? I can have the car engine rebuilt for $85 and it will run like new," he said confidently.

Meg usually had blind faith in everything Jim said, but she was skeptical that their 1937 Ford would be like new for only $85.

Neither Meg's nor Jim's parents felt convinced that the old car could make such a long trip. Margaret didn't dare mention it to Aunt Grace.

Jim, an excellent driver and navigator, mapped out their trip on Route 66, a southern route, to avoid snow. Meg wished she had learned to drive. She felt guilty about Jim having to drive the 3,000 miles by himself. She pledged to learn as soon as they got back.

The Sheehans would stay in Mrs. Wald's house until the Wrights returned.

⸮ * ⸾

Across the USA, December 1945. Meg had never been any farther west than Pennsylvania, and every mile was an adventure to her. "I just can't believe I'm actually going to cross the whole country. This has to be the most exciting experience of my life, Jim," she said with child-like enthusiasm the first morning they were on the road.

Jimmy was settled snugly in his bassinet in the back seat most of the time except when Meg took him up front for diaper changes, play time, or to feed him. At three months old, he was a contented baby and seldom cried.

When the dinginess of Harrisburg and the steel mills of Pittsburgh faded from sight, and the quiet rolling hills of Ohio began appearing, Meg marveled at the drastic scenery change. "Jim, how many more miles will we travel today before we stop for the night?"

"About two hundred more miles. If we hope to make my '500 miles a day' plan. We'll go to bed early every night so we can be on the road by 5:30 every morning. We'll start looking for a motel before dark."

Mile after mile, as the sun was slowly setting, they became concerned when every motel they passed had a 'No Vacancy' sign.

The severe housing shortage still existed in 1945. The war had created a severe shortage of building materials, and no new homes or apartments had yet been built. The problem became even more severe as thousands more returning servicemen married and needed homes of their own. Ex-servicemen and their wives also ended up living in motels.

When the Wrights finally found a motel with a vacancy, it didn't have an electrical outlet for the hot plate they used to make Jimmy's formula. They drove on. An hour later they found a vacancy for $4 a night at a rundown motel that had an electrical outlet. Fortunately, a diner was next door. They had decided to eat a hearty dinner and breakfast and not stop for lunch. Instead, Meg made peanut butter and jelly or canned deviled ham sandwiches.

To pass the time, they looked forward to listening to the daily continuing sagas of their favorite radio soap operas: "One Man's Family," "Ma Perkins," and "Mert and Marge." They were amused by local programs of music and the daily news broadcasts in strange dialects.

Although there was no time to stop for sight-seeing as they covered the miles through Indiana, Illinois, Missouri, Oklahoma, and Texas, the panorama of changing terrain never ceased to intrigue them.

The first time Meg saw a cactus, she yelled, "Stop the car, Jim!" She took Jimmy out of the car and stood with him beside the thorny desert sentinel so Jim could take their picture.

The first time a tumbleweed blew across their path, Jim drove slowly, so they could follow its course with their eyes until it disappeared in the desert brush. The vastness of the desert, its flatness, its distant mountain ranges looming on the horizon, its dusty whirlwinds, and mirages that shimmered ahead on the highways amazed Meg.

She had frantically searched the prairies in Texas for herds of cattle and cowboys, but had seen neither. Then early in the morning after leaving their hotel in the outskirts of Tucumcari, New Mexico, her search ended. They parked alongside a wooden sidewalk to have breakfast in a small cafe called "The Pinto." As they got out of the car, they stood still as a large figure loomed towards them from the opposite direction. It was hard to see him clearly, because the rising sun silhouetted his outline. Suddenly, he stepped into the shadows of an overhanging roof covering the sidewalk and a magnificent image appeared.

In whispered wonder, Meg uttered, "Oh, Jim, look, a real cowboy!"

He was the perfect cowboy, over six feet tall, lean build, leathery tanned face, his head topped off with a faded cowboy hat, double holsters with silver guns hanging low on his hips and well worn jeans clinging tightly to his long, slightly bowed legs. His spurred boots clanked noisily along the wooden sidewalk. Covering his plaid wool shirt was a leather vest on which was displayed a six-pointed badge that read, "Sheriff."

Approaching each other, the cowboy sensed the excitement he was creating. Meg stood frozen in wonder, looking up at him with her mouth wide open.

His squinting eyes looked down at her. He grinned crookedly, and touched his index finger to the brim of his hat. "Howdy, folks. That's a mighty cute little fellow you've got there," he remarked, looking closely at Jimmy. He held the cafe door open and gestured for Meg and Jim to enter. "You folks sure picked the best place in town to chow down," he said and sat down at the counter.

Meg and Jim sat in a booth. Meg couldn't keep her eyes off the handsome sheriff during breakfast. She whispered to Jim in a swooning voice, "He's more romantic-looking than Frank Sinatra. I hope you're not the jealous type."

Jim laughed. "I think I am!"

ॐ * ॐ

When they crossed the border into Arizona, Meg saw her first Indians, not on a horse on the top of a hill, but selling souvenirs at a roadside stand. They stopped, and Jim brought Meg a turquoise and silver bracelet. Although it was exciting to talk to a real Hopi Indian, Meg admitted later, "I didn't get the same sensation that the cowboy aroused in me."

"Good! I'll only have to worry about you falling for cowboys, huh?"

The ultimate experience of the trip came when they reached Oak Creek Canyon in Arizona. Soon after they entered the canyon, the red clay hills rapidly materialized into gigantic red spires and peaks. The sudden transformation and magnitude of the foreign landscape frightened Meg. She had never seen mountains this high, and she had never driven on such a precarious road. The patterns engraved by millennia of erosion on the spectacular formations appeared in symmetrical harmony. It was impossible to conceive the forces that had created these wonders.

Meg's fear became paralyzing. She could scarcely speak. She inched away from the window as they climbed higher. The road narrowed and hairpin curves came in rapid succession. She kept her eyes down. She wondered why she was so frightened. She had never experienced this feeling before.

"Meg, look out there to the right. See those buttes off in the distance? Don't they look like cathedrals?"

In a hesitant voice, Meg whispered, "I can't look, Jim. I know it's beautiful, but I'm frightened to death. How much longer will we be in these mountains?"

"Oh, honey. I'm sorry you're so scared. I thought you'd love this. We'll be in Jerome shortly, which is the summit, then we'll start down."

Meg's hands were folded tightly in her lap as she prayed. She looked up for a moment, and her eyes caught a quick view of the steep drop off coming up as they rounded a curve. She squeezed her eyes tightly and prayed, "Oh, dear God, Jim, go slow. Why don't they put guard rails on these sharp turns?" In a desperate tone she asked, "Jim, do we have to come back this way?"

"No, honey, we don't. But I should warn you, you're going to see higher mountains than this in California. Wait until you see our high Sierra."

"I don't mean to hurt your feelings, Jim, but frankly I don't give a damn about ever seeing another mountain."

"You'll get used to them, honey."

Never! Meg thought to herself.

"Look up, honey. We're coming into Jerome. We'll stop for a while, and you can walk on flat land."

When they got out of the car, Meg said, "Jerome could be the eighth wonder of the world, and I wouldn't care if I'd never seen it!" She was standing close to the car as she viewed the little town. It sat on the top of a steep-sided mountain where copper had been mined for years. The entire perimeter of the town dropped off a thousand feet to the desert floor.

"Jim, what a dangerous place for the children who live here. I'll bet a few must go over the edge every year. Look at the condition of the fences on the edges. Most of them are broken and sliding down the mountainside. Let's get out of here," she pleaded.

Meg's panicky feeling did not subside until they reached the desert floor.

When they neared Kingman, Arizona, the radiator boiled over, but fortunately there was a garage nearby. The fan belt had broken, and the mechanic had to call around to find a replacement. It took three hours before a new belt was found and installed. The delay meant that they would not make Riverside by early evening as planned.

Jim phoned his family to let them know approximately when they would arrive, which would be well after midnight.

It was three in the morning when they arrived on the outskirts of Riverside. Meg was both nervous and excited about meeting Jim's family and continuously fussed over her hair and makeup.

Fate dealt them a cruel blow when they were a few blocks from Jim's home. A slow-moving freight train blocked their way as they reached the center of town.

"Damn!" Jim swore. "I can't believe it, we're so close, and there's no alternate route to take."

The noise of the train woke Jimmy and Meg took him up front to watch the train. He was fascinated and moved his head back and forth as each car, carrying oranges, passed.

"Roll down your window, Meg, and breathe in the most wonderful aroma in the world."

Within seconds the smell of sweet oranges filled the car. It made Meg's mouth water, and the scent brought back memories of the orange blossoms at their wedding.

"I'm home, honey! Isn't it beautiful?" Jim asked proudly.

Meg noticed a strange look come over his face, a look she had never seen before. It was not a smile but a far-away stare, as if anticipating something exciting.

Meg looked up and down the wide main street of the town lined with stately palm trees outlined by the yellow glow of street lights. She leaned over and kissed Jim's cheek. "If it's this beautiful at night, I can't wait to see it in the daylight. I wish we could stay longer."

"One day we will, honey," Jim promised. He leaned across the seat and put his arm around Jimmy and Meg and said in a serious tone, "Meg, I know our married life has been rough on you and Jimmy, all this moving around, but hopefully soon we'll settle someplace for eighteen months. I love the Navy, honey, and hope you do, too, because I'd like to make it my career. You've been a perfect Navy wife, and a great sport. Remember, you said you wanted to see the world!"

"Oh, Jim, I've loved our life so far. It's really been exciting, but it would be nice just to stay in one place longer than a month. I'm beginning to feel like a gypsy."

At last the red caboose went by, and the gates lifted.

"It's just a few blocks to my house, honey."

Meg was nervous. She hoped Jim's folks would like her.

Welcoming lights lit up the front of the pretty white stucco house. A giant palm tree stood next to the steps leading up to front entrance. When Jim shut off the motor, the front door opened, and Jim's 15-year-old brother, Kenny, came running down the stairs in his pajamas, hollering. "It's them, it's them."

Before Jim and Meg could get out of the car, Mary Ann, Jim's 16-year-old sister, and his brother, Royden, were on the sidewalk looking into the car at their brother, his wife, and their nephew. Mr. and Mrs. Wright came out of the door onto the porch and waved.

Meg felt a blush of heat come over her face. Her heart was pounding both from excitement and fear. Her normal flamboyant demeanor disappeared, and she suddenly felt severely shy.

"Welcome home, Jim and Meg. Hey, look at the little guy," said Royden, who had visited them in Cambridge. He reached into the car to shake his brother's hand. Kenny came over to Meg's side and opened the door. A sheepish smile covered his face.

"Hi. You must be Meg," he said eagerly.

"And you must be Kenny," Meg said as she got out of the car and turned Jimmy around. "And this is your nephew, Jimmy."

"Gosh, he's cute!" Kenny said, taking the baby's hand.

Mary Ann, Jim's sister, came around the car and said shyly, "Hi, Meg. I'm Jim's sister. Can I hold the baby?"

"Of course, Mary Ann, and you're just as pretty as Jim said you were." Mary Ann had curly blond hair, light blue eyes and a trim build. Jim had bragged about her gymnastic skills. Jim's other brother, Keith, was not home. He had signed on for another four year hitch in the submarine service.

Mr. and Mrs. Wright were anxiously waiting for them at the top of the stairs. Jim and Meg, followed by the others, made their way up to them. Jim ran the last few steps and hugged and kissed his father and mother. Then he turned around, took Meg's hand, and said, "Dad and Mum, I'd like you to meet my Cambridge girl, my wife, Meg."

Mr. Wright shook Meg's hand, grinned and said, "Welcome, daughter," then kissed her cheek. Mrs. Wright held Meg by the shoulders and said in a charming Kentucky drawl, "My goodness, Meg, your pictures don't do you justice. You're mighty pretty. No wonder James raves so much about you." Then she kissed Meg's cheek.

"Thank you," Meg murmured, slightly embarrassed but glad that Jim's mother's first words were of approval. Meg was still skeptical about whether they would like her because Jim had changed his religion.

"Mary Ann, let me hold our first grandson," Mrs. Wright said as she reached out for Jimmy. "My, my, Daddy. Look at this little fellow. Why, he's the image of James when he was this age."

The next morning, Jimmy was the main attraction and was passed from one family member to the other, giving all of them his newly-developed three-month old coy smile and silly gurgles. He was an adorable baby. His little body was chubby and in perpetual motion when he was awake. When he was asleep, nothing would wake him up until he was ready, and he proved that right after lunch. Meg put him down for a nap in the cot next to their bed and propped pillows all around him so he wouldn't roll off.

She was just walking away from him when suddenly the whole house started shaking. She lost her balance and hit the wall. Everything on the bureau was sliding off, and the pictures on the walls jerked back and forth. From somewhere in the house, she heard voices yelling, "Earthquake!" She heard feet running. Then someone yelled loudly, "Quick, get out on the front walk!" Meg grabbed Jimmy in her arms and made her way through the house and rushed out the front door. Where was Jim? she wondered. Jim, Royden and Kenny were on the sidewalk, pointing across the street to the high school playing field. She saw the ground undulating. It looked as though a giant monster were crawling under the carpet of grass. It was an incredible sight, but it terrified her. Never having witnessed an earthquake before, she was sure the ground would open up and swallow them all.

Suddenly, it was over. When Meg's fright subsided, it was replaced with anger and hurt feelings. How could Jim and his family have been so thoughtless, running outside and leaving Jimmy and her inside. We could have been killed.

Jim and his brothers came running up the steps, all talking at once.

"Wow, that was a great one, huh?"

"Did you see that field roll?"

"Must have been at least a 6.0."

"Hey, Meg," Jim yelled. "How'd you like it? Your first earthquake."

Meg glared at him, turned around and walked into the house with Jimmy who was still sleeping. She went to their room and slammed the door. She laid Jimmy on his bed and fought to hold back tears. She had been terrified, but now she was angry and hurt.

Jim opened the door quickly, looking concerned. "What's the matter, honey?"

"The matter is your total lack of concern for your wife and child. You deserted us, you and your family. You left Jimmy and me alone in the house. All you thought about was getting yourselves out safely. This is so unlike you, Jim!"

"Oh, honey," Jim said apologetically, sitting down next to Meg on the bed and putting his arm around her shoulder.

"I wasn't deserting you, Meg. I can see now I should have come and taken you and Jimmy with me. But it happens so quickly. I was so excited, I forgot, I guess."

"That you're now a married man with a wife and child?" she lashed out at him.

"No, Meg, of course not. I just forgot that you had never experienced an earthquake before and, of course, I should have realized you'd be scared. We're so used to them, we always run outdoors to watch the ground roll. I'm sorry, sweetheart," he said in a soothing voice and hugged Meg.

"I wonder if I'll ever understand you Californians! You love real high mountains, thundering waves, and hot rod cars; Now, I learn that earthquakes give you a thrill. What else thrills you that I haven't discovered yet?" She asked in a curt voice, pushing Jim away.

"Beautiful blond girls like you," he said, forcing a kiss on her lips and pushing her down on the bed.

Just then another tremor shook the house.

"Another earthquake," Meg yelled and jumped up.

"Just a tremor, honey. They'll keep happening for a little while." He pulled Meg back down and said, "This is the safest place to be in a earthquake." He began kissing her passionately.

⌀ * ⌀

Mr. and Mrs. Wright had been away when the earthquake happened, but now they heard their car pulling into the driveway, and Jim's mother calling him in an urgent voice.

"Bad timing on my parents' part," Jim said, quickly jumping up, tucking his shirt in and straightening his hair. He blew Meg a kiss and said in a dramatic voice, "I shall return, don't move!"

His mother was standing outside the door. "What is it, Mum? You look worried."

"It's your grandmother. We just came from seeing her, and she's taken a turn for the worse. She asked to see you, Meg, and the baby. The doctor seems to think she won't last out the night. We must get right back there."

When they arrived, 93-year-old Mrs. Hattie Wright was propped up in a large canopied bed. Her thin white hair had been neatly brushed, and her glasses had slipped down on her nose. Her eyes opened when her daughter, Florence, announced their arrival. "Bring my great grandson over here so I can hold him," she ordered in a weak, creaking voice.

Jim and Meg went to her bedside and laid Jimmy in her arms.

"Hello, Gram. It's me, Jim."

"Well, of course I know it's you, James. Do you think I'm blind?" she snapped at him.

"This is my wife, Meg."

"Aah. Certainly produced a good-looking child," she said in her stiff Maine accent, glancing from Meg to Jimmy. With shaking hands, she lifted Jimmy up to her face and kissed his forehead, then laid him on her chest. After a moment, her eyes closed, her head fell to one side, and she let out a sigh.

She had slipped into a coma and never recovered. The doctor said that she had willed herself to stay alive until she could see her only great-grandchild.

⌀ * ⌀

The next two weeks were filled with excitement. Meg met Jim's best friends, Paul Wesson and George Elkins. They visited Laguna Beach, Jim's favorite surfing beach. They drove up to Big Bear, a mountain resort where they ice skated.

Meg insisted that they stop once every day at a drive-in for a coke. "I wonder why they don't have these back East." Meg thought it was exciting to have a pretty car-hop roller skate with their food to the car.

Jim answered her question, " I think it might have something to do with the weather."

They had a wonderful family dinner on Christmas Day. By now, Meg knew it would be a long time before she would ever learn to cook as well as Jim's mother. All her meals were special.

On New year's eve, they went to a party with Jim's friends at the Mission Inn. Meg got quite drunk for the first time in her life on two Moscow Mules. Jim had to carry her into the house. He prayed his parents wouldn't see him. Alcohol was considered evil and forbidden in the Wright's home.

On New Year's day, in spite of Meg's painful hangover, they went to the Rose Parade in Pasadena. Meg was enthralled with the spectacle.

The next morning, Meg and Jim left to drive to San Francisco to see Joe at Letterman Hospital.

ø * ც

Upon arrival in San Francisco, they went directly to the Hospital. Meg was so excited at the thought of seeing Joe, she couldn't stop crying.

A nurse at the reception desk, who seemed to know Joe rather well, offered to escort them to the solarium. "Joe is our very special patient. He's always in high spirits and helps to up the morale of the other patients. Depression is a serious side effect of the war," she said. She also cautioned Meg and Jim, "Try not to look shocked when you first see Joe. He'll look quite different from the last time you saw him. His weight loss was considerable. Positive thoughts and happy family news is the best medicine. He'll be going home soon, and we're really going to miss him."

Joe spotted them first. He was sitting in a wheelchair, talking with a group of men, when he let out a yell, "Yow--ieee! Hey, you guys. Look! It's my little sister, Meg!" He quickly wheeled his chair toward them.

Meg was shocked, but tried not to let Joe see it. She held out her arms and ran toward him.

Joe abruptly stopped the wheelchair in front of her, grinned broadly and stood up. "Ta-da!" he yelled in a bravado voice, throwing his arms out to embrace her.

Their greeting was muffled by sobs. They hugged and kissed, trying to bridge the almost six years of separation in a few seconds. The joy of the moment was further enhanced by a strong round of applause from all the men in the room. This tradition usually eased the drama of a family's first moments with its loved one. It also cushioned the shock a family feels at seeing their relative in such an emaciated condition. It usually worked and brought smiles through the tears. It also elevated the reunion from the maudlin to a more uplifting first encounter.

Jim had stayed back with Jimmy. Now he stepped forward and extended his hand to Joe.

Joe grinned and put his arms around them. "Hi, brother, Jim and my little nephew, Jimmy. Oh, my gosh. Will you look at this adorable little guy? Can I hold him?"

Jim handed the baby to Joe who held him as if he were a piece of delicate china. "Hi, little Jimmy. I'm your uncle. Hey, guys, how's this for a beautiful baby!" Joe bragged, as he held little Jimmy up so the other patients could see him.

"I like his mother," one of the men yelled.

"You've got good taste, Casanova," Joe countered glibly.

Joe led them back to his room, explaining along the way the reason for the wheelchair. "When you've been on a serious diet of rice, like I've been, you lose your stamina, and it takes time to get back in shape. I keep telling them I can walk, but they've put me in a room so far away from everything, it makes sense to take my own cab," he joked. He was very disappointed that his buddy, Chip, who had been with him throughout his POW years, had left for Wisconsin three days ago. He had wanted them to meet. Chip had promised he definitely would come to Cambridge for a visit.

Joe got dressed, and they took him out to dinner at a small restaurant near the hospital. Then they stayed with him in his room until "lights out."

The next morning they checked out of their motel and had breakfast with Joe in the hospital cafeteria. He insisted upon coming out to the parking lot with them to say goodbye. He allowed Jim to push the wheelchair, something he had never allowed anyone else to do.

"I wish we could have spent more time with you, Joe," Meg lamented.

"No, it's good you spent as much time as you did with Jim's family. You may not see them for a long time, but you'll be seeing a lot of me soon. Doc says I'll get another evaluation in about two weeks, and if everything's okay, I'll get my walking papers and be off to Fort Devens and home."

"We missed you so, Joe. Mom and Dad are so excited about seeing you. And Eileen, well, I don't have to tell you about how she feels."

"I'm going to marry her, Meg. I haven't told Dad and Mom yet, but I proposed to her on the phone when I first got back to the States. We decided to keep it a secret until I get home. I figured I'd better get her to say 'yes' before she sees what a skinny blink I've become."

Their final goodbye was upbeat, although tears couldn't be controlled.

"Now I feel the war is really over, Jim," Meg murmured while continuing to wave out the back window until Joe faded from sight.

& * &

The trip back across the country was mostly uneventful, except for the snow storms they encountered in Texas. But their old Ford plowed through and fortunately, it was the only bad weather they encountered. Jim really shocked Meg when he figured out that the trip only cost them $93.

TWENTY-TWO

hiladelphia, January 1946. When they arrived in Philly, they went directly to their house. They weren't sure if the Sheehans were still living there or had found another place. Pat answered the door but stopped them from coming in.

"I've got bad news. Little Pat has a very serious case of measles. The pediatrician warned us that you shouldn't bring Jimmy into the house, because they're highly contagious, and Jimmy is so young. It could have serious side effects."

Jim and Meg were totally disheartened by this news. It was cold, and they were exhausted from the long trip.

But Pat had already made other arrangements for them. I've got you a room at the Parker Hotel on Walnut Street in downtown Philly. It's a nice place and not too expensive. We haven't been able to find another place for us. This is a rotten thing to happen, but it will be at least three weeks before you should bring Jimmy back here. On the positive side, there's a possibility we'll be taking the *Pout* back to New London sooner.

"As you know, the rest of the gang is already sharing houses, and they were willing to let you guys move in with them, but none of their landlords would allow three families."

"It's all right Pat," Jim reassured him.

Meg was fighting back tears.

"God, I feel awful!" Pat said as he walked them to their car.

They drove to the Parker Hotel, their thirteenth home. Jim said, "Meg, there is another alternative. We can stay here tonight, and I could drive you home to Cambridge tomorrow. I could stay on the..."

Meg interrupted him saying harshly, "Don't even suggest it, Jim!"

Their room was on the tenth floor, and life was not easy for Meg. No cooking was allowed in the rooms, so she had to hide the hot plate. She was afraid that if the maids saw it, and reported it, they would have to leave. Meg would have to carry Jimmy everywhere.

"If only I had learned to drive," she lamented. "Now I'll have to wash his diapers in the small bathroom sink and hang them over the radiator to dry."

Because Jimmy was getting too big for the bassinet, they made a bed for him in one of the bureau drawers.

Jim forgot to lock the car doors when he took the first load up to their room, and someone stole the radio and blankets that had been Christmas gifts. Three days later, someone stole all Meg's jewelry from their room, including her prized turquoise Indian bracelet.

Life was bleak for the Wrights.

A week after they moved into the hotel, they had some good news, Jim was promoted to Lieutenant Junior Grade. That meant a pay raise.

One of the colored maids, Lannie Mae, loved Jimmy and always spent a few minutes playing with him when she came to clean the room. She offered to baby-sit if Jim and Meg wanted to go out at night. Within a short time, Lannie Mae became a good friend. She insisted upon taking Jimmy's diapers home to wash and dry. Meg had to force her to accept pay.

She told Meg, "I'm a member of the Salvation Army Church and doing good deeds for folks is what my religion preaches, and I practices." Meg made her agree to take the money and donate it to her church.

✍ * ✍

On January 21, the *Pout* was commissioned at the Philadelphia Naval Base in an impressive ceremony. A bottle of champagne was successfully broken over the bow. The 1,500-ton submarine was a Fleet-type, Perch Class, with a five-inch gun mounted on the forward deck. A commissioning party at the Officer's Club followed the ceremony with many Philadelphia dignitaries attending.

Now the *Pout's* officers, crew, and families anxiously waited for shakedown cruise orders and to find out where their next home port would be. The orders finally came during the first week in February. The *Pout* was to proceed to New London for crew training and adjustment of equipment.

✍ * ✍

New London, Connecticut, February 1946. The Wrights' fourteenth move was back to base housing, in New London, this time sharing quarters with Jake and Kate Dolan and their son, Mike. The two babies, now six months old, loved to play together.

Helen Sheehan had returned to Kansas City to have her second child.

The departure date for the shakedown cruise and its itinerary was not firm, but scuttlebutt had the *Pout* headed for the Pacific.

Meg's mother had sent Jimmy a beautiful new crib and highchair. Kate's mother had sent a playpen. Both Meg and Kate purchased strollers. Life became more normal now.

Once again, the curse of cockroaches invaded their lives. They did their best to ignore them to some degree, but it was a habit to always shake their shoes and clothes out before putting them on.

A newly arrived bachelor officer, Dave Benson came aboard the *Pout*. Lt. Bob Wade had resigned from the Navy, having served on active duty since 1941. The new officer was engaged to a girl from Marblehead, Massachusetts. Her name was Liz Crane, and they planned to be married as soon as the *Pout* was assigned to a base.

It was a busy time for both Jim and Meg. They went home to Cambridge two weekends to see Bill, Margaret and Joe. He was beginning to look like his old self and was making plans to get his high school diploma through special tests. He had applied for the Buckley City of Cambridge scholarship to Harvard and had been assured he would get it. He and Eileen had announced their engagement but decided to wait six months before they married.

& * &

The last weekend in February, the *Pout* went to Newport, Rhode Island for torpedo trials. Kate asked Meg if she would like to drive there with her. Meg still had not learned to drive. They had heard that Newport was a beautiful city. They also heard a reliable rumor that the *Pout* could be leaving on its shakedown cruise as early as the following week; destination still unknown. The wives wanted to spend every minute they could with their husbands. They were invited to stay with Pat Sheehan's sister, Jean, also married to a submariner stationed in Newport. For safety reasons, Jimmy's bed over this weekend was a large old trunk. He had now started crawling, and when awake, he was on the go everywhere.

Meg and Kate were especially glad they had spent the weekend with their husbands, because orders were waiting when the *Pout* returned to New London on Sunday evening.

"I think you girls better sit down while Jim and I tell you about the orders we received when we docked tonight," Jake said, only minutes after they arrived home. "Shall I do the honors, Jim?" Jake asked with an apprehensive look on his face.

Jim put his arm around Meg's shoulder and said in a concerned tone, "Be my guest, Jake."

"Well, gals, there's no easy way to tell you this, so I won't beat around the bush. We're going on an extended cruise for six weeks, making stops in Cuba, Puerto Rico, Venezuela, Colombia, Panama, and then on to Pearl Harbor, where we'll be based for eighteen months."

Kate shouted in elation! "Hawaii! That's wonderful news, Jake! You know I've always wanted to live in Hawaii."

Meg jumped up from the couch and began swinging her arms and hips in a hula motion. "I can see us now on the beach at Waikiki!"

"Hold it, girls, I haven't told you the rest, and this is the bad part," Jake said, giving a side glance to Jim. "No dependents will be allowed to come, at least right away. There's no housing at all, and things are not back to normal yet. All the hotels are being used as R and R centers for the returning Pacific troops. It's a rough place, lots of trouble. I hate to tell you this, but it could be months before Navy dependents will be allowed to go there."

A dead silence filled the room.

Suddenly, Kate jumped to her feet saying, "I've got it! I've got it! We'll just go as tourists! We don't have to say we're Navy wives."

Meg hugged Kate and said, "Kate, you're a genius!"

Jake interrupted. "Wait a minute, how are you going to get there? All planes and ships going to the Pacific are still under government control. And didn't you hear me say there's absolutely no housing available. Come on now, Kate, don't get any crazy ideas."

Meg said, "No housing available has always been the story ever since I became a Navy wife, but it's never stopped me before from being with Jim. I'm with you, Kate. Let's give it a try."

Both men looked at each other in resignation.

"Go ahead. Good luck. But don't say we didn't warn you. You won't be able to do it," Jake said, shrugging his shoulders.

Kate said to Jake, "I think you've forgotten something, mister; my brother Alex works for the Matson Navigation Company, and their ships, the *Matsonia* and the *Lurline* go to Hawaii on a regular schedule."

Jake answered her, "But you forgot, Kate, Alex told us that they're still under government control bringing back servicemen from the Pacific."

"But remember, he also said, that they were going to begin refitting the ships for peacetime passengers." Kate said, looking smug.

The next morning the wives got together. They wanted to start planning right away. The *Pout* would be leaving in one week. The skipper's wife, Jennifer, was four months pregnant, and she was going home to Los Angeles to stay with her parents until the baby was born. Ann Johnson couldn't go, because she was going to be the maid of honor for her only sister in May. That meant there would only be four going: Meg, Kate, Cassie Helm and Liz Crane, the fiancée of Dave Benson. Liz was staying with her aunt in nearby Mystic, Connecticut for the week and had eagerly joined the wives us for this important meeting. Dave Benson's parents lived in Honolulu, so, if Liz could get there, she and Dave could be married sooner.

"Do you really think your brother can do it, Kate?" Meg asked.

Kate looked at her watch. "It's only six o'clock in Vallejo, and I don't think my brother would appreciate being awakened so early. But, if anyone knows anything about how to get to Hawaii, it'll be Alex!"

Kate got through to her brother that afternoon. He said there was a good possibility that he might be able to get them space on a trip in April. He cautioned her, "But don't broadcast it, because service dependents are not being allowed to go. I'll try to get you a firm date as soon as possible. We're still operating our ships under the jurisdiction of the War Shipping Administration, so passenger bookings are done according to priority." Then he teased her, "Is being with Jake a high priority to you?"

"You bet your life it is!" Kate told him.

&. * &.

The *Pout* left New London on its shakedown cruise on Monday, March 4. All the wives were at the dock to see the sub off.

"Jim, I'm going to miss you so much. Let's hope and pray this won't be as long a separation as you guys think it will be."

"Honey, we're going to get you girls there as quick as we can, you know that. I can't stand to be away from my babies any longer than I have to." Jim was holding Jimmy in one arm and had the other arm around Meg. It was windy and cold. "I'll write every day when possible," he promised.

The dock was a scene of tender farewells. Then, one by one the crew filed up the gangway, until the last man was aboard. When the gangway was pulled ashore, and the spring and stern lines were let go, the *Pout's* engines were put in reverse. Orders from the bridge were called out in rapid succession as the sub slowly backed out from its berth. Most of the officers and crew were lined up on the deck, waving their final farewells. Kisses were blown, and last minute messages of endearment were called out across the widening gap. As the order "all ahead two thirds" was given, the *Pout's* bow began to slice swiftly through the waters of the Thames River on her way down to the Atlantic.

Still standing on the dock, the families took their last look at the submarine until it was out of sight. It's an old Navy custom not to look back once you've waved your final farewell.

✍ * ✍

Meg left with, Liz Crane, who was driving back to Marblehead and would drop Meg and Jimmy off in Cambridge. Jim had sold their old car. Once again Meg would move back home with her parents, her fifteenth move in fourteen months of marriage.

Their sea chests of household goods were again put on "hold." Meg wondered if the chests would ever catch up with them. She hadn't seen their things since they moved from Norwich, in September 1945.

Meg's life was not easy, but it was not boring. The excitement of seeing so many different places and meeting so many new people compensated for the lack of normalcy most marriages experience. Meg's Celtic thirst for adventure was still strong. She looked forward to being back home and spending more time with Joe. She would miss Jim terribly, but she knew that he was thrilled to be going on his first real sea voyage.

TWENTY-THREE

*J*im kept his word and wrote to Meg as often as possible. His first letter was postmarked Havana, Cuba.

Dearest Meg:

I miss you and Jimmy already. We're heading for Havana, Cuba. We've been at sea for three days and so far it had been uneventful until today. Now the wind has picked up and the waves are breaking over the conning tower. The Skipper gave orders to secure the boat and prepare to ride out the storm. He felt it would be a good opportunity for the greenhorns, like me, to experience a storm of this magnitude.

The wind became fierce, and at the height of the storm, it was blowing at one hundred miles an hour. The giant waves were cresting at forty to fifty feet, and our sub rolled at seventy-five degrees. It was thrilling!

Pat Sheehan and I were the two officers on duty on the bridge, along with the lookouts. The two of us were lashed with lifelines, so we wouldn't be swept over the side. We were up to our necks in water most of the time as waves broke over the boat constantly. Pat hollered through the roaring wind and asked me if I was having fun. I yelled back and told him I loved it.

A sailor stuck his head up through the hatch and told us that the engine room was flooded and we had electrical damage. Jim yelled at me to clear the bridge because we were going to have to take her down. We untied our lifelines and made our way to the hatch. We were about to descend when a monstrous wave struck and completely buried us under water. When the wall of water drained from the bridge, Pat looked around for me and laughed when he saw me lying spread-eagled in a shallow pool on the deck, I was holding tightly to steel pipes. I lifted my head up out of the flood and blew a steady stream of sea water straight up in the air. Pat laughed and we both quickly climbed below and secured the hatch.

The Skipper rapidly issued orders as the sub prepared to dive. We leveled off at two hundred feet but were still experiencing rolling from the storm. Finally, at two hundred and fifty feet, the sub stabilized. It took twenty-four hours to repair the damage, reset the gyro compass, and pump the bilges. We surfaced the next day and continued on our course to Cuba.

As you can see from the postmark on this letter we arrived safely in Havana, Cuba. I just had to tell you about our exciting voyage. I hope I didn't scare you.

Love, Jim

Havana, Cuba. Our first stop on the list of our sightseeing itinerary of Havana was a rum factory where we drank free samples. We hired a couple of Cuban guides to drive us around in a couple of old Buicks. They took us to Morro Castle, a 16th-century fortress, a cigar factory, their favorite restaurant, and then, at the end of the tour, to a graveyard. There one of the guides pointed out a huge, beautiful mausoleum. He told us in a thick Cuban accent, 'Senors, theese ees where I am being buried. I am member of Taxi trade union,' he stated proudly. Then he added with great emphasis, 'Only union members are buried here.' The rest of the graveyard was covered with shallow graves, many of which had scarcely any dirt covering them, the bones of the deceased were almost completely exposed. The families of the deceased had to pay an annual fee. If they didn't pay, the bones were dug up and stored in a barn-like structure where they were eventually ground up and used for fertilizer. The guide insisted we see the gruesome stacks of bones.

I was surprised by downtown Havana. The cleanliness of the streets was remarkable. It was a beautiful city with buildings of white marble and gold ornamentations. All of us Catholic officers went to Mass at La Catedral de la Immaculada Concepcion de la Virgen Maria built in 1656. It was almost as large as St. Patrick's in New York. The woodwork was inlaid in gold. Its exceptional paintings with lifelike images were draped in rich silks. The entire church was aglow with candles.

Political banners were everywhere, because the elections were to be held in a few days. You could feel the excitement as people with opposing views clashed on the streets. Particularly noticeable was the Communist Party, which had been trying to take over the country and had caused a great deal of unrest. Bombs exploded in public places, and several shootings took place while the Pout was docked there.

When we were ready to get underway, we were delayed for three hours because some crew members had not reported back to the boat. Eventually they were found, intoxicated. When we pulled out of the harbor, two of the more inebriated sailors perched themselves on top of the periscope shears to wave a farewell to the beautiful senoritas who had followed them to the boat.

San Juan, Puerto Rico. Our sub anchored here today in San Juan. Al and I spent most of the day swimming at a beautiful beach. That evening we went on Shore Patrol duty and saw the seamier parts of the town, which were off limits for the officers, but not the enlisted men.

LaGuaira, Venezuela. Here we are now in Venezuela. We were greeted by hundreds of residents who stayed on the dock the entire day just staring at the sub. *The Pout is the first U.S. warship to enter Venezuela since before the war. The crew will spend most of their shore leave in Caracas, about twenty-five miles away over steep mountains with cliffs over 1000 feet high. You wouldn't like it, honey.*

Caracas, the capital of Venezuela, had recently been the scene of a revolution. The Accion Democratica revolutionists had overthrown the government of President Medina and his cabinet, replacing him with Romulo Betancourt. These revolutionists successfully beat the Communists who also had been plotting to overthrow the old regime. There was great turmoil in the country. On the day we arrived, I had duty and had my hands full. Long lines had formed to board the boat. The visitors included members of the Venezuelan Navy as well as some Americans and native civilians. One civilian approached me and said, 'Senor, I major in Venezuelan Army. Want to see torpedo. Okay?'

I told him he could, and asked seaman, Hood to escort the major below and show him the after torpedo room. When he led the major into the torpedo room, the major asked, 'Real torpedo with explosive?' Hood said yes, and the major immediately pulled out a revolver and aimed it at the torpedo. Hood dove for him, knocked the gun out of his hand, and yelled for help. Good old, Hood, our hero! Three of the crew who were nearby raced into the compartment, and the four of them were able to subdue the wild-eyed fanatic, who was screaming in Spanish. They pushed him up the ladder and physically threw him off the sub. He ran off in great haste, probably certain that the authorities would be called. Never a dull moment on the Pout. The next day, the captain, with some of the officers, including me, were invited to place a wreath on the grave of Simon Bolivar and to give a speech. It was an impressive ceremony with President Betancourt, the ministers of war and interior, and the secretary of the Navy all taking part in the ceremony.

Cartagena, Columbia. It was a short trip from La Guaira to Cartagena, Colombia, and two Colombian destroyers welcomed us at the entrance to the narrow harbor. Cartagena had an interesting history of pirate raids. To protect itself the city had built forts and dug tunnels. The tunnels ran for miles under the city, going from fort to fort and from the cathedral to the monastery.

Our first night in port, the officers were given a big party by the Colombian Navy. We started drinking rum punch, which went down very easily but packed a wallop. The party was dull, possibly because of the language barrier.

Barranquilla, Columbia. The city of Barranquilla is situated about five miles up the muddiest river we had ever seen. The stench was almost unbearable. The city was relatively new. A great many of the buildings looked as though they had been hastily thrown together, but not the El Prado hotel. All the officers, including me, who were not on duty spent the afternoon lounging around that hotel's pool.

The next morning we had an official duty to perform. The uniform of the day was dress whites. We were to march in a parade, although neither the officers, nor the crew had marched since boot camp. The skipper thought it wise to put in a little practice along the dock. Even the locals laughed at the clumsiness of the marching sub crew, which was more out of step than in.

"Loco Americanos," the onlookers heckled, pointing and laughing as the crew marched up and down the pier.

Pat called the cadence as the crew of the Pout marched into the area where they were to take part in a ceremony to unveil a statue of Jorge Washington. We had to stand in the one hundred degree heat for an hour and listen to a succession of speeches in Spanish.

We left the following morning for Panama.

The Panama Canal. The officers and crew were told by the skipper to be on their best behavior in Panama because it was a rough place. The trip through the canal was uneventful, but to me, the engineering feat was astounding. That one could sail from the Atlantic to the Pacific through a forty mile canal of locks has to rank as one of the greatest engineering works of all time. Guess what ship I saw there? The battleship, Massachusetts! It made me so lonely for you and Jimmy.

We docked at Balboa, a fascinating spot at the Pacific terminus of the canal.

For the next few days, we anchored off the Perlas Islands. We went out on operating maneuvers daily, firing unarmed torpedos called "exercise fish" at two destroyers. A hit was scored on each shot, which was not unusual for the skipper. He was the best, having been awarded two Navy Crosses during WW II.

After the torpedo training the Pout returned to Balboa to get the sub in shape for the trip to Pearl.

We all had stern warnings from the skipper about the hazards of shore duty here, which was often compared to the port of Marseille in France.

Two days later we left Balboa without anyone getting into trouble, and sailed northwest across the Pacific for Oahu. I won't be able to send you any more letters honey, until we arrive at Pearl Harbor. I miss you and Jimmy and hope we can be together soon. I love you both so much.

Jim

TWENTY-FOUR

 ambridge, March 1946. Meg's stay in Cambridge, her fifteenth move, lasted only a few weeks. She received the following letter from Kate on March 16th.

Dear Meg,

Great news! My brother did it! Hawaii here we come. Alex was able to book the four of us, and Mike and Jimmy of course, on the Lurline, *leaving San Francisco on Saturday, April 13th and arriving in Honolulu on the 17th. Yahoo!*

We'll show the guys. Remember how they insisted there was no way we could get there? They should arrive about a week before us. They can look for housing.

The Lurline *was a luxurious liner before the war but was converted into a troop ship, and it is not completely renovated back to its peacetime luxury. What no swimming pool? I can't stand it!*

Remember, don't broadcast our trip to the wrong people. Dependents are not supposed to be going there. By the way, it's only costing $110. Can you believe it? So get your fanny out here. Come a couple of days early and stay with my mom and me. I'll show you the big city of Vallejo. I'm writing to Cassie and Liz tonight also. Send me your ETA as soon as your plans are firm.

Aloha, Kate

Meg's father and mother were stunned by the news that she would be leaving so suddenly. They had a tough time understanding Meg's lifestyle. It was so beyond their realm of experience.

"I still can't believe you're flying on an aeroplane all the way to California with our little Jimmy. Good God, Meg, I hope you realize what a risk you are taking," Margaret said, shuddering in genuine fright.

Bill was more concerned about crossing the Pacific in a ship. "When I crossed the Atlantic on my way to France in World War I, I was on a really big ship, and believe me, kiddo, I was sick all the way. What if you inherited my sea sickness problem?"

Their trepidations could not dampen Meg's excitement and enthusiasm.

Joe assured them over and over that flying was ten times safer than driving an automobile. He was very supportive and had helped Meg make all her travel arrangements.

Jim's family wanted Meg to spend a couple of weeks with them in California before she sailed for Hawaii. She felt she should, because it would be eighteen months before they would return to the States.

Joe was beginning to look like his old self and was studying for the entrance exam to Harvard. He and Eileen had set their wedding date for August 11. He talked quite a bit about his time in the POW camps, and particularly about Nobu. "Meg, I would really appreciate it if you could look up his uncle at the Hale Omura. I don't think Nobu will get back to Hawaii for quite a while, but maybe his uncle will have heard something. I truly owe my life to him," Joe said, flinching and betraying his feelings about the ordeal. Those feelings were still very close to the surface.

"Maybe if Jim can't find a place for us to stay, we could stay at Nobu's uncle's place," Meg suggested.

"No way, kiddo. From what Nobu's uncle told us, the place has really fallen into disrepair, and the guests who have lived there all through the war are rather unsavory characters. I wouldn't want my little sis around those kind of people. From all I heard about Honolulu, when I was in the hospital there, it's a wild and corrupt place. Lots of prostitutes and gamblers prey on servicemen who are just back from the Pacific. Most of the servicemen have big dough from all their back pay. I wouldn't dare tell Mom these things. She'd never let you go!"

"You're probably right. It's funny, I've always wished I could go to Hawaii ever since Babs and I were little and did a show about Hawaii for the neighborhood kids."

At twenty years of age, Meg was a confident young woman and felt quite capable of taking care of herself and Jimmy. She had matured a great deal in the last two years, having been cast into numerous situations she had never experienced before. A great deal of Aunt Grace's training in manners and social affairs had certainly been an asset in her role as a Naval officer's wife. All the other wives had graduated from college and probably were more sophisticated than Meg. But she was confident that she could hold her own with them.

ﺑ * ﺑ

At the boarding gate at Boston Airport, the O'Mearas were saying an emotion-filled goodbye to Meg and Jimmy. Meg looked very sophisticated in her new, attractive, electric blue wool suit. She had chosen the dark color to hide the many anticipated spills and drooling by Jimmy as they made the long flight across the country. Her blond hair had darkened some, but it was a still a pretty shade. Her hair was very thick, and she was now wearing it in a Veronica Lake style, hanging loosely in soft waves over the left side of her face.

When the moment for their final goodbye came, Joe hugged and kissed Meg. He held her at arm's length. "You're beautiful, little sister. Be careful of the wolves along the way," he said, grinning and pushing her hair back from her face.

Her father and mother, their eyes welling with tears, hugged and kissed Jimmy and Meg over and over. Margaret continuously blessed herself. Meg knew her mother was terrified at the thought of Meg and Jimmy being up in a plane. Bill kept blowing his nose into his handkerchief with his head turned away, but Meg saw him wiping his eyes also.

Meg, too, was extremely nervous about flying but didn't let her parents know it. Her heart was pounding as the moment neared to board.

"Hurry, Meg. Everyone is aboard but you, I think," Joe said as he handed Jimmy to Meg. He put her carry-on bag over her shoulder and led her through the gate.

She walked quickly out on the ramp toward the plane and knew there was no turning back now. The American Airlines DC-4 looked sturdy and sleek. The waiting stewardess smiled, took her carry-on bag, and followed her up the portable steps. She now had a large lump in her throat. When she reached the top step, she stopped on the platform before entering the plane and waved a final farewell to her family. She followed the stewardess, who led her to her seat and buckled her in tightly as the engines started.

"Please hold the baby in your arms until we are airborne and the captain gives permission to release your seat belt. As no one is occupying the other seat right now, the baby can sit or play on it, but pick him up quickly if we hit turbulence. Enjoy your trip," the neatly uniformed attendant said in a pleasant voice.

Meg's heart was now pounding hard and fast. She could feel the beating reverberating through Jimmy's body as she held him tightly against her breast during takeoff. She stayed in that position until she sensed the plane had leveled off. Jimmy now wanted to be released and explore his new surroundings. Meg had not anticipated being this frightened, and had eagerly looked forward to flying for the first time as another great adventure. This onslaught of fear distressed her greatly, and she began praying steadily.

Her fear did not completely subside, but eventually she was able to relax a little and look around at her fellow passengers. Jimmy had crawled over to the window the minute he was released and was fascinated by the billowy clouds.

A matronly woman sitting across the aisle and wearing a funny, flowered purple hat, smiled at Jimmy and Meg.

"What a dahling baby. Are you going to New Yawk?"

"No, we're going to Los Angeles," Meg answered enthusiastically. It calmed her to be able to talk to someone.

"Oh, dahling, what a horrendous trip for you and the baby," the woman stated in a shocked voice.

"What do you mean, horrendous?" Meg asked, confused by her choice of words.

"Well, dahling, I mean so long, you know." Meg knew it would be a long trip but had not been given a definite time of arrival. The ticket agent had said, "Air speed would depend on the weather and the number of stops for refueling and passenger transfers." She had been told it would be an overnight trip.

Jim's parents had suggested that she call them as soon as she arrived in Los Angeles. She'd then have to wait at the airport, until they could drive up from Riverside. Or, she could take a bus.

The lady in the funny hat got off in New York. Her seat and the one next to it were taken by a business man and an Air Corps lieutenant. A burly Marine colonel took the window seat next to Meg. He nodded at her, gave a quick wink to Jimmy, who was smiling at him, and turned his body toward the window and closed his eyes. Within a few minutes he was fast asleep, snoring and exhaling strong liquor fumes. He slept right through the stops in Philadelphia and Baltimore and got off in Washington, D.C. Meg was grateful. She prayed that no one would take his place because Jimmy had fallen asleep after his bottle, and her arms were stiff from holding him for so long. The seat was still empty when the plane began to taxi down the runway, and she laid Jimmy down, strapping the seat belt loosely around his little body.

The lieutenant across the aisle had tried twice to catch her eye by leaning past the business man. Both times Meg quickly turned her head away. She had noticed him when he came on board. He was very attractive, with three rows of battle ribbons below his wings. Now, he was standing next to her, drawing hard on a cigarette and blowing the smoke upwards.

"Where ya headed?" he asked in a soft voice, leaning down near to her, so he wouldn't wake the baby.

"Los Angeles, and you don't have to whisper. If the sound of this plane's engines doesn't wake Jimmy up, nothing will," she said smiling thinly. She hadn't realized that the plane would be so noisy.

"How long are you going to be in L.A.?" the lieutenant asked, staring hard into her eyes.

"Less than a couple of hours, I hope. My in-laws are meeting me at the airport and driving me to their home in Riverside," She informed him smugly, hoping this information was all he'd need to know to deter him from making a pass.

"Riverside! That's where I'm going to be stationed; at March Field."

His penetrating stare made Meg feel uncomfortable. She kept looking away. His face was gaunt but handsome, and he had a distinctive cleft in his chin. His slightly wavy brown hair fell across his forehead and down to his eyebrow.

"My brother was stationed at March Field before he went to the Pacific," Meg told him.

"And he made it back okay?"

"Yes, thank God, but he was taken prisoner in Bataan and was in a POW camp for a long time."

"Then he went through the worst," he said with genuine compassion.

"Yes he did. What about you? You look like you survived the war in good shape, in spite of that Purple Heart and all the battles you were involved in," referring to the three rows of battle ribbons on his jacket.

"I'm A-OK and on my..." Suddenly the plane dropped and shuddered. The lieutenant lost his balance and almost fell on Meg.

"Oh, my God, what's the matter with the plane?" Meg asked in a frightened voice, quickly picking up Jimmy.

"It's all right," the lieutenant said confidently, regaining his balance.

The stewardess braced herself while she made her way down the aisle, telling passengers to fasten their seat belts.

A voice over the intercom got everyone's attention. "This is the captain. We've run into a storm and will have some turbulence for a short time. All passengers are to take their seats immediately and keep your seat belts securely fastened."

The lieutenant went across the aisle to his seat, stepping past the business man. As he was about to sit down, he looked across at Meg and saw that she had her eyes squeezed shut. She was holding her baby tightly. She obviously was praying and was very frightened. He quickly stepped back out of his seat and braced himself as the plane again, made a sudden drop.

Meg gasped and uttered, "Jesus, Mary and Joseph," just as the lieutenant stepped over her knees and sat down next to her.

He buckled his belt and slid his arm through Meg's. He patted her arm in a reassuring manner. "It's okay. It's okay," he said in a soothing voice.

The plane shook so violently that it seemed certain to Meg that the wings would break off. Each time the plane dropped, gasps could now be heard from every section of the plane. When a very severe drop, followed by a series of hard bumps, shook the plane from side to side, Meg turned her whole body towards the lieutenant, burying little Jimmy between them. A hesitant look came over his face, then he quickly put his arm over her shoulder, holding Meg and Jimmy tightly to him.

Meg resisted his embrace, but only momentarily. Her body welcomed the security of his strong confident arms. She was sure they were going to crash. She said an "Act of Contrition," and prayed it would all happen quickly.

Slowly, the plane's chaotic motions began to subside, and Meg pulled herself away from the lieutenant and said, "Sorry I was such a jerk. I've never been so terrified in my life."

He laughed, and in a teasing voice said, "No apologies needed. I love that kind of duty."

Smiling faintly, Meg said, "I can't believe the plane can take that kind of beating without breaking up, or at least the wings falling off."

"There are safety factors built into these modern airliners that allows them to take a lot worse than what we just experienced. Although this was a wild storm! By the way, since we have become so close in the last fifteen minutes, I think we should know each other's names. I'm Greg Wellington, and I'm from Vermont. I've just been home on leave and have signed up for another four years in the Air Corps."

"Hi, Greg, I'm Meg Wright, originally from Cambridge, Mass., but I've have been living at or near submarine bases for the past couple of years. I'm on my way to Honolulu. My husband's submarine is going to be stationed at Pearl for eighteen months.

"Sounds like you have a wonderful life, Mrs. Wright. May I call you Meg?"

"Of course."

During the next half hour Greg sat with Meg and Jimmy while they ate lunch. Jimmy enjoyed sharing bits of turkey and ham from both Greg's and Meg's lunches. He sat between them and drank his bottle, which the attendant had heated.

Greg read to Meg from a brochure, which was tucked in the seat pocket. Our air speed is about 175 mph and we're cruising at an altitude of 9,000 feet."

Meg wasn't sure she wanted to know those incredulous statistics. She had no idea that they were going so fast or were up so high.

Greg told her, "From the looks of this map, we'll be making stops in Knoxville, Nashville, Memphis, Little Rock, Dallas, Fort Worth, El Paso, Albuquerque, and Phoenix before we land in L.A."

Meg was astonished. "I had no idea we would be making so many stops."

"You got booked on the wrong plane. You can get better flights that don't make as many stops. But, hey, you'll be a seasoned traveler by the time we get to L.A., which will probably be early tomorrow morning."

"I can't believe we'll be up in the air that long!" she said in disbelief.

"With the stops for passengers and refueling, it should be about a twenty-one hour trip from Boston. But don't despair, Meg, I'll buy you a few stiff drinks before dinner tonight. Then, about nine o'clock, they'll turn the lights down low, turn on the Musak, and before you know it, you and Jimmy will be sound asleep." Then he grinned at her mischievously. "You better pray that we don't hit any more storms. I'm a heavy sleeper."

"After what we've just been through, I think I'll be able to handle anything."

"This is the captain speaking. We will be arriving in Knoxville in seven minutes and passengers will be allowed to go into the terminal for a half an hour. We'll be changing crews here. It was a pleasure serving you on American Airline's Flagship Toronto. Enjoy the rest of your trip. Thank you for flying American."

Meg was extremely glad to get off the plane. She had to use the ladies' room. She had not, as yet, had the courage to get up from her seat during the flight, but now nature was calling, urgently. Also, Jimmy needed a diaper change.

Jimmy was the object of many of the passengers' attention when she walked with him down the aisle. He looked cute in his little powder blue coat and cap, that he always pulled off. He had chubby cheeks and big brown eyes like his daddy. Jim had given him a crew cut before he left, and it made him look like a little man. Meg never ceased being amazed that she had produced such a darling baby, considering the dreadful birth. But after eight months, the memory of that was slowly fading.

When they got inside the terminal, Meg headed towards the ladies' room. She thought about calling her parents to let them know that she was safe so far, but decided that no news was good news.

She came to the end of the short corridor and there were two doors with an overhead sign that read "Ladies." The door on the left read "Whites Only." The one on the right read "Colored." She stood frozen, rereading the signs. Her mind kept saying, "It can't be." Indignation grew inside her as she thought, colored women are not allowed to use the same toilets as white women. She experienced a flood of mixed feelings: anger, a deep sense of injustice, and a repulsion at the prejudice she was witnessing. She wondered if Indians and Orientals had to use the colored toilets. Welcome to the South, she said to herself. She pushed open the door to the "Whites Only" section. She wondered if she would be arrested if she went into the "Colored" side.

When she stepped through the "Whites Only" door, she was greeted by a colored attendant who came right towards her with a big smile on her face. "Well, look a heah at dis lil' darlin. Here, honey chile, let me hol the yung un while you go do yo duty." She took Jimmy from Meg's arms and held him out in front of her. Her whole face lit up in the widest smile Meg had ever seen. "Oh, he is a lil' rascal, ain't he?" she laughed.

"Thank you very much for holding him," Meg said, hurrying into the stall.

Jimmy didn't object at all to being transferred to the stranger's arms, especially when she sang a peppy song and danced him around the room. He laughed as they twirled, and he tried to imitate her throaty song. He shook his head from side to side, keeping time with her rhythm.

Meg thanked the woman profusely and put a fifty cent piece in her hand when she handed her a towel.

The woman looked at the large coin, then looked up quickly at Meg, a frown covering her face. "Now hole on heah, chile, yo insulten me iffin yo payin me to hole yo yung un. Or, is ah not undastanin? Mebbe dis heah haf dolla is fo da towel?"

Meg was confused. She was afraid she had insulted the woman and felt badly. "It's for the towel, and for the signs on the doors outside. I can't explain it. This is my first visit to the South. I've heard rumors about these things, but where I live, you and I would use the same ladies' room. I didn't mean to offend you," she said sincerely. she took Jimmy from her arms and laid him on the changing table.

The woman placed the fifty cent piece on the dish, which held only pennies and a few nickels. She folded her arms over her ample bosom and walked over to where Meg was changing Jimmy's diapers. A tender look covered her face as she spoke. "Honey chile, don't yo fret nun bout doze signs. It don't matta nun."

Meg looked at the woman, frowning. "Oh, but it does matter! You have to believe that, for your children and their children."

Two women, standing at the mirror across the room, turned and looked at Meg with scorn.

One said, "Damn Yankee!"

The other snarled, "Go back where you belong, Yankee."

Meg's Irish rose up from the pit of her stomach. An angry look spread over her face. She picked up Jimmy and stood directly in front of the two women. In a strong challenging voice, she said, "In case you didn't know it, it's a free country, and I'll say what I think should be said, anytime, any place. You two rebels make me damn glad I am a Yankee!"

Meg spun around, winked at the attendant who had covered her face with both hands in shock, and walked out the door.

Greg was waiting outside the ladies room. "Geeze, Meg, I could hear you all the way out here. What are you trying to do, start another Civil War?"

Meg glared at him, letting out a disgusted groan and walked swiftly to the plane. She took her seat, and started feeding Jimmy his bottle. She was deeply upset.

When Greg came down the aisle, he stopped at her seat. He leaned his face down in front of her. "Hey, Irish, I'm with you on that problem. Don't be mad at me, too."

Meg looked up. "It's such a gross injustice! It's so degrading! Sorry I got steamed at you. I'm going to lay Jimmy down for a nap on the seat. We'll talk later, okay?"

"Yes, ma'am," he said and saluted her.

A few hours later, after stops in Nashville, Memphis and Little Rock, an announcement came over the intercom that the attendant would be taking drink orders, and that dinner would be served shortly thereafter.

Greg leaned past the businessman and looked over at Meg. He was hoping that she'd want to follow through with his plan for drinks and dinner together. The businessman was annoyed as Greg stepped over him, making the man move all his work papers and his tray.

Meg waved him over but refused the martini Greg had suggested, having had a bad experience with martinis once. Instead, she had a rum and coke. The dinner was delicious. Jimmy enjoyed spoonfuls of their ice cream.

After the trays were removed, Greg bounced Jimmy on his knees and got him giggling to a point where he was getting hyper.

Meg was about to suggest that Greg stop, when there was an announcement.

"This is the captain speaking. We'll be turning the main cabin lights off in five minutes for those passengers who wish to sleep. Those who want to read can use their overhead light. We anticipate a few intermittent showers over Texas, but nothing to detain us. There will be no further communications until morning. Good night."

"Well, lieutenant, you heard the captain's orders," Meg said.

Greg gave her a look that would have melted her heart if she had been single. "Don't look at me like that, Greg, please."

"Sorry. My feelings are showing, I guess."

"Greg, there's no room for those kind of feelings between us. I'm really a very happily married woman," Meg said with a tone of honesty that could not be mistaken.

"Yup, I read you loud and clear," Greg said, giving her a final crushed look, which reminded her of her old boyfriend, Tom Souza, who was killed in the war.

Greg got up, crossed the aisle, and once again disturbed the businessman who had just began to snooze.

"Why don't you make up your mind where you are going to sit, with your friend over there (jerking his thumb towards Meg), or here," he said in an indignant voice.

Greg looked down at the man and said in a sad voice, "She won't let me sit with her. I guess she's not my friend anymore." Then he looked from the man to Meg and winked.

Meg shook her head back and forth and smiled at his clownish ploy. She then looked away, determined not to encourage him any further. But sleep was impossible for Meg, even though the flight was now quite calm. She looked up and down the aisle, and all of the passengers seemed to be sleeping soundly. She was envious of them. Greg was stretched out with his back to the businessman, his head leaning on a pillow against the window frame.

They passed through a mild thunderstorm, which caused only minor bouncing. Meg leaned across Jimmy, who was sleeping soundly, and looked out the window. Their seats were over the wing. She thought she could see flashes of lightening that was causing a glow on the wing, but seconds later it was still there. Puzzled, she unbuckled her seat belt, got up, and put her face against the window. "Oh, my God," she said in a hushed, startled voice. The entire wing of the plane was on fire. She unbuckled Jimmy quickly. Fear permeated her so thoroughly, she froze. She forced herself to move. Oh, my God, what should I do? Yell for everyone to wake up? No, no. Don't do that. Get to the attendant so she can tell the pilot. Don't panic! Hurry, hurry! All these thoughts raced wildly through her mind as she sped to the front of the plane where the attendant was napping. She shook the girl roughly and spoke in a hushed voice. "Wake up, wake up. The plane's on fire!"

"What are you saying?" the girl asked in alarm as she hurriedly unbuckled her seat belt, got to her feet, and grabbed Meg.

Tears were running down Meg's cheeks, and she sobbed into the girl's ear. "Look out the window."

The girl slid across the seat and pulled up the drawn shade. Meg watched her intently, hoping that what she had seen was an illusion. But she saw a look of horror sweep across the girl's face. She slid back across the seat, grabbed Meg by the shoulders, and sat her down in the seat.

The girl whispered in Meg's ear, "Don't panic. Don't move. Don't tell anyone else. Keep quiet. Be right back. Must tell the captain." Then she moved swiftly to the cockpit.

It felt like an eternity passed as jumbled thoughts raced across Meg's mind. Oh, sweet Jesus, my baby. Oh, Jim, Jim. I'll never see you again! Oh, my God, I am heartily sorry for having offended thee. She interrupted the Act of Contrition. Jesus, Mary and Joseph, let it happen fast! Suddenly the stewardess was standing next to her, dabbing at her eyes with her handkerchief and smiling lightly. She put her hand on Meg's shoulder just as the overhead lights came on. "It's okay. No fire," she mouthed to Meg as the captain appeared in the doorway of the cockpit and started down the aisle.

"May I have your attention please. There is no need for alarm," the captain said in a calm, casual voice. "I am Captain Blake, and I feel it's worthwhile for our passengers to wake up to witness a magnificent phenomenon."

Everyone became alert immediately. Some stood up, others leaned out the aisle. Greg, seeing Meg's empty seat, immediately got to his feet and quickly scanned the entire plane to see where she was. When he spotted her standing with the stewardess, he yelled, "Are you all right, Meg?"

Meg waved back and forced herself to smile to reassure him.

The captain spoke, "Our plane has just gone through a mild thunderstorm, and we are now experiencing the effects of what is called Saint Elmo's Fire. It is an incredible sight, and one I've never experienced in my fifteen years as a pilot. Although it looks like the plane is on fire, the phenomenon presents no danger. Look out the windows!"

Immediately, everyone looked out the windows and, "Oh"s, and "ah"s, and "Oh, my God"s, hummed through the plane.

"The glow you see on the wings is caused by electrical discharges that have spread across the wings. Absolutely harmless! This young lady," he turned and pointed to Meg. "brought it to our attention in a very brave non-alarming manner, although she had every reason to panic because she thought the plane was on fire."

The passengers applauded Meg.

"Our beautiful phenomenon will dissipate quickly, so we'll turn the overhead lights off so you can see it better. I hope you can get back to sleep. Good night, again."

Before the captain went back to the cockpit, he stopped and shook Meg's hand. "Well done, young lady. We weren't aware of it until the very moment the attendant came into the cockpit. It had just begun to cover the plane's nose. For a second it alarmed us, too, then we realized what it was. It's possible for it to actually come inside the plane, I've been told."

Passengers complimented Meg as she made her way back to her seat. Jimmy had slept through it all.

Greg reached out to take Jimmy when Meg reached their seats. "You're something else, Meg. You must have been terrified! Why didn't you wake me up?"

Jimmy woke up, yawned and cuddled into Greg's shoulder.

Greg told Meg to sit in the window seat and said he would hold Jimmy.

Meg was so drained, she didn't resist.

Greg rocked Jimmy back and forth, while Meg began to replay what had happened.

"I can't believe I didn't scream out. I was sure that we were all going to die. But, something told me to get to the attendant and let her do it."

"You were very brave, Meg. I'm proud of you. I think most people would have panicked. I've flown all over the world, and I've never seen it. Sometimes it appears on ships at sea too. Why don't you try to sleep? I'll take care of Jimmy."

"Thanks, Greg, but I'm too tense to sleep now."

They smoked and talked softly about their lives until dawn.

Meg told Greg about the many moves she had made since they were married and how tough it had been to find decent housing.

"You haven't had a great married life so far, I'd say. Seems to me your old man ought to get out of the Navy and settle down."

Meg immediately became defensive, "Oh, it hasn't been all that bad, honestly. There have been lots of good times. Jim really loves the Navy and wants to make it his career.

"Well if you like to travel then I guess you'll probably enjoy moving around instead of settling down in one place. I'd say that in a way, the Navy is also going to be your career."

"I guess you're right about that." That thought had not occurred to Meg before. "What about you? Have you decided to make the Air Corps your career? If you get married will you stay in?"

Greg didn't say anything for a minute. A troubled expression covered his face. He looked away, then said, "I thought I was going to get married. I got leave, rushed home to Vermont to the gal I left behind and rang her front doorbell. Her mother answered the door. She was shocked to see me. I yelled 'Surprise. Where's my Beth?' Her mother burst into tears and choked out, 'She eloped three weeks ago with a man she met at work.'"

ॐ * ॐ

The sky had turned a vivid blue, and small puffy clouds seemed to part as the plane flew through them, then landed in Phoenix for a short stop.

When they approached Los Angeles airport, Meg felt a surge of relief fill her whole being. She thanked God profusely for their safe journey. Jimmy was banging on the window. He could see houses and buildings now, and it seemed as though he sensed the confining trip was over.

Greg had remained silent until now. He smiled thinly at Meg and said, "Well, pretty girl, I guess we're going to make it. And you know what, Meg Wright, I think your husband is one lucky guy. Listening to your stories last night, convinced me of that." Looking at her intensely, Greg said in a tender voice, "I'm going to miss you." He quickly took her hand, held it up to his lips and kissed it tenderly.

A thrill ran through Meg's body. No one had ever kissed her hand. She was embarrassed, and yet it touched her in a strange way. She tried to make light of it by saying, "My, that was very continental." Then she busied herself by combing her hair, putting on fresh lipstick, and gathering up Jimmy's toys.

Twenty-two hours after leaving Boston, the DC-4 landed. The captain, co-captain and the stewardess once again thanked Meg as she left the plane. It was seven o'clock in the morning.

Greg helped Meg get her luggage, but they had to hire a sky cap. Greg was going to catch the eight o'clock bus to March Field in Riverside. "Let me hold Jimmy while you call your in-laws. I don't like the idea of leaving you here alone. I want to be sure that they are coming to get you."

Meg appreciated his thoughtfulness. "Well, I don't want you to miss your bus either." "If I don't make it I'll cach the noon bus. He held Jimmy, while Meg called the Wrights to tell them she had arrived.

"Meg! How wonderful to hear your voice. Did you have a good flight? We can't wait to see you and Jimmy, but we have a big problem. Dad is still out at March Field, because they had some serious electrical problems. He has the car. But there's a bus leaving the airport for Riverside at eight o'clock. Would you mind catching it? It will get you here a lot quicker than waiting for us to come there. It's at least an hour and a half trip, but we will be able to pick you up at the bus station." Meg's mother-in-law gave her all this information in rapid-fire order, fearful that the three minutes would be up.

"That's fine, Mum. I'll get the bus. See you soon. Bye." She hung up the phone and groaned. "My in-laws can't pick me up. I'll have to take that eight o'clock bus, too."

Greg laughed. "That's great news. You're stuck with me." He signaled the sky cap to follow them. He carried Jimmy, and took Meg's hand as they ran to catch the bus.

The bus was jammed with servicemen. When they got on board, there were no two seats together. Greg stood in the aisle next to Meg.

Meg urged him, "Greg, please take one of those empty seats. I don't want you to stand for and hour and a half."

"I don't mind, Meg. We won't be together for too much longer."

The young serviceman sitting next to Meg, heard what Greg had said, quickly stood up. "Sir, I didn't realize she was your wife. I'll grab an empty seat in back."

Meg opened her mouth to deny the relationship, but Greg saluted the young soldier and said, "I appreciate you kindness, Private. He sat down, gave Meg a smug look and said, "You see, he knew we belonged together." He slipped his arm through hers and took her hand.

Meg tried to pull her hand away. "Greg, please."

"Meg, I'd like to see you again. Please don't say no," he begged, a look of despair covered his face.

Meg looked at him in desperation. "Why, Greg? I'm a happily married woman. I deeply appreciate all the support you gave me during the trip, but I have no intention of being with any other man but my husband. I'm sorry if you thought differently."

"Hey, Meg. Please don't think that I'm just a lonely fly boy trying to put the make on you for a one night stand. I just thought that maybe I could call you at your in-laws and meet you in downtown Riverside for lunch."

"Greg, you're a nice person and, well, under different circumstances…if I weren't married, but I am married and…" Meg turned her head toward the window. She felt so sorry for him. She was exhausted, very vulnerable and came close to saying, yes, she'd have lunch with him.

"Riverside. Riverside," the bus driver called out as the bus slowed down.

Greg looked anguished as he took a deep breath and said, "Goodbye, Jimmy. Goodbye Meg O'Meara Wright. Although I won't see you again, I'll never forget you." He wrapped his arms around them and hugged them tightly.

Meg broke from his hold and kissed his cheek. "I'll never forget you either, Greg." She meant it. He had touched her in a way that made her sad to think she'd never see him again. She stood up with Jimmy, grabbed her carry-on bag, slid out of the seat and made her way to the front of the bus and into the arms of Mr. And Mrs. Wright.

✍ * ✍

The next two weeks, in her sixteenth home with Jim's family, were filled with trips to the beach, the desert, and a visit to Jim's Aunt Marie's sheep farm in Redlands. Jim's brothers took Meg to Hollywood one night to see all the glamour spots.

Greg never tried to contact Meg, and a part of her regretted it. But she knew it was for the best.

On Wednesday, April 10, the Wrights put Meg and Jimmy on a Southern Pacific train at Union Station in Los Angeles for the overnight trip to San Francisco. Kate would meet them and take them to her home in Vallejo, where they'd stay until they left for Hawaii on Saturday, April 13.

Walking through the train to their seat, Meg got whistles and flirty looks from servicemen. She smiled politely. She'd made up her mind that she did not need any more male traveling companions. She was still smarting from her encounter with Greg.

She laughed to herself as she read the notice on the envelope, which held her ticket and baggage checks. It said, "Double up on the train whenever possible. Share your bedroom, compartment or drawing room with a friend. It's everyone's wartime duty to stretch all available accommodations to full capacity."

Meg thought, Greg would have loved this notice. He would have said something like, "It's your patriotic duty, Meg."

I must stop thinking about Greg, she admonished herself.

The overnight train trip cost $7.59. The plane fare was $143.87. The ship fare was $110. Meg thought, it's costing a great deal of money to get Jim and me back together, but worth every penny. Although she loved Jim dearly, meeting Greg had made her realize that it wouldn't be good for them to be apart for too long in the future. She needed to be with Jim.

TWENTY-FIVE

At sea aboard the Lurline, *April 1946.* Kate's mother, Mrs. Rose, drove the wives and babies to the dock and met up with the other two women, Cassie Helm and Liz Crane, who would sail with them to Hawaii.

Mrs. Rose boarded the ship with the wives, and the purser directed them to a small salon for their final good-byes. The purser opened a bottle of champagne, poured, and Mrs. Rose toasted them. "To four brave Navy wives. May your stay in Hawaii bring you happiness. May the bubbles in the champagne help your stomachs adjust quickly to the motion of the sea."

She then reached into her large bag and brought out four lemons and said, "The air on the inside of a ship is filled with peculiar odors. If you feel queasy at all, hold the lemon next to your nose and breath in heavily of the fresh aroma."

The final whistle blew. The wives said their good-byes to Mrs. Rose. The gangway was taken in. The lines were released, and the ship slowly moved out of the harbor.

Meg and Kate took their babies to their cabin. A steward handed them a letter from the Matson Navigation Company and said, "Please read this important message from the captain."

The girls shut the heavy door of the cabin, looked at each other and broke out into laughter. They were sharing the same thoughts. "We made it," Meg squealed, hugging Kate.

"I never doubted we'd do it!" Kate said, a look of triumph on her face.

They put Jimmy and Mike on the floor, which seemed clean enough and looked around at what would be home for the next four days. The cabin was large but had three military type berths on both sides of the room. Foot high slats had been secured on the outside of the bottom bunks so the babies couldn't fall out.

A thought passed through Meg's mind, Jimmy couldn't fall out, but she knew he could crawl out. At eight months he was perpetual motion and climbed on everything climbable.

They had bureaus, a closet and bath with a tub. There was a good-sized porthole for fresh air and an easy chair.

Meg was filled with excitement. She never dreamed that one day she'd be sailing to Hawaii on an ocean liner.

"Let's see what this letter has to say," Kate said as she plunked down on the easy chair. "You keep unpacking, and I'll read."

Dear Passenger:

Welcome aboard. As you can see, at the present time our accommodations are still military. This vessel is operating under the jurisdiction of the War Shipping Administration. The service is not our pre-war standard, but we will endeavor to do our best to make your trip as pleasant as possible.

We feel you will be delighted with our meals, which will be served in the forward dining salon. Breakfast will be served at 8:15 AM, luncheon at 12:15 PM and dinner at 6:15 PM. Passengers with children are requested to leave their children in their staterooms under the care of a steward during dinner.

"Wow! I love the captain for that!" Kate said and continued reading.

Dinner guests are asked to dress appropriately. Please be on time for your meals. It is vital that you not leave your present deck area or enter any of the restricted areas which are posted. Areas below your deck are for Military personnel and Matson personnel only. Your full cooperation in this matter is expected. We sincerely hope that you have made accommodation reservations in Hawaii as the hotel and housing shortage in the Hawaiian Islands is acute. If you have not, you may want to speak with the purser to see if he can assist you with temporary shelter.

Please advise us if we can be of service.

> *Very truly yours*
> *Captain L. M. Goad-Smuthe*

Kate said in a concerned voice, "I guess they weren't kidding about the housing shortage. I hope the guys were able to find us a place to live."

"They will. "They will, don't fret, Kate," Meg said with confidence.

Jimmy and Mike were having fun crawling all over the cabin. The girls decided to take them up on deck for fresh air; the cabin was stuffy.

There was a chain link fence covering the railings, which made Kate and Meg feel better about letting the babies crawl around. There was not much to do. The pool was empty and the shuffle board equipment couldn't be found.

At lunchtime the wives all met at the dining room entrance and were escorted to their table. High chairs were provided for Jimmy and Mike. The luncheon menu offered an outstanding variety of entrees including fish, beef or pork, along with numerous appetizers, salads and deserts.

"If we eat like this for four days, our husbands won't recognize us," Cassie exclaimed.

Meg leaned in close to the others and whispered, "Did you notice those two tables of women sitting over to the right. They look like movie stars."

The wives all casually pretended to be looking around the room, then turned back to each other with looks of surprise.

"Look at the clothes they're wearing; right out of Macy's Mezzanine," Liz said, blowing out a low whistle.

"Did you notice their figures? They could be models," Kate said as she tried to get a better look at them without being obvious.

They appraised the other diners: There were officers from various branches of the service, a seedy looking man and woman, some businessmen types, a continental looking couple who were dressed elegantly, and in the far corner of the saloon, a group of gangster-type men, wearing dark pencil striped, zooty looking suits.

"Get a load of the Chicago mob at that far table," Meg said in a hushed tone.

The wives held their menus up to their faces to follow the direction of Meg's nod.

Speaking between her teeth in a hushed tone, Kate warned, "Lock your doors tonight, girls. I think the fat one is Al Capone."

They got a fit of giggles and had a hard time trying to suppress their flightiness when a ship's officer approached their table.

"Well, well, we certainly have a happy group of ladies here. I'm Officer Dudley Morse, at your service. If you need anything or have any questions please don't hesitate to ask." He was tall and slightly chubby with a baby face. He rubbed his hands together and nodded his head.

Meg asked, "We don't mean to be nosy, but those ladies over to the right." Meg jerked her head and rolled her eyes in their direction. "They're so beautiful. Are they movie stars or models?"

The officer crossed his arms over his chest, and his baby face blushed into red patches. He shifted his eyes left and right and said in a hushed tone, "They're far from movie stars or models. They're ah, er, ah, high-priced ladies of the evening, shall we say. We'll report their presence to the Honolulu police before we land. It's revolting the way these low-life types," (he nodded towards the gangster-types in the corner) "prey on our servicemen. They know there are thousands of men in Honolulu, just back from the Pacific and that they have a great deal of back pay."

The wives all nodded in agreement, trying to appear sophisticated, but actually they were totally intrigued by the officer's news. They knew a little about prostitutes. Their husbands often kidded about the ladies of the evening who were arrested over and over for lascivious carriage in New London. Their real names appeared in the police blotter with regularity, but the sailors knew the women by their more graphic names. But it was difficult to put these attractive, well-groomed women, here in the salon, in the same category as those in New London.

"This should be an interesting trip," Kate said as a look of devilment crossed her face. "Prostitutes and racketeers. Why didn't you ask the officer, Meg, if that's really Al Capone?"

Meg and Kate had not given Jimmy and Mike naps hoping to get them tired enough so they would sleep soundly their first night at sea. They dressed for dinner. Kate looked lovely in a red and white print. Her black hair was softly curled, and she had a dark tan, which gave her a healthy glow.

Meg wore a black sheath and her mother's pearls. The babies had been put into the bunks with the boards up. Mike dropped off to sleep immediately, but Jimmy was still awake.

The steward who was assigned to baby-sit arrived and settled down in a chair just outside the cabin. Meg told him that Jimmy was not asleep yet. The large door was left open in case the babies cried.

"Well, dahling, shall we proceed to the dining salon?" Kate asked. She held out her arm for Meg, and the two women sashayed down the passageway to the amusement of the Steward.

He leaned his chair back against the wall, took a magazine out of his pocket and crossed his dangling ankles.

The dinner was an Epicurean feast, offering entrees such as Filet Mignon, Salmi of Duckling with Risotto a La Turque or Boiled Columbia Salmon with Lemon Butter. There were Pineapple Fritters with Fruit Sauce, Fresh Mushrooms Caruso, Mexican Cole Slaw Salad, and New Garden Peas Francais. The desserts were "sinful" selections of Cream Puffs, Fruit Compotes, Devil and Angel Food Cakes topped with Vanilla Ice Cream, Hot Fudge Sauce and Whipped Cream.

Each wife selected a different dessert, and they gave each other samples. When they had finished dinner and were enjoying cigarettes, their waiter said, "We would like to offer you an after dinner drink. I suggest a very exotic drink which I know you'll like. It's called a 'Kiss of Death cocktail.' Ladies love it!"

"Sounds exotic!" Cassie squealed.

"Bring them on," Kate ordered.

They finished the delicious, but very sweet, drink and were just getting up from the table when the purser announced, "There will be horse racing in the salon at eight o'clock." They all decided to play. Meg and Kate went back to their cabin to check on the babies. Cassie and Liz decided to take a stroll around the deck.

When they reached their cabin, the steward was asleep and snoring loudly. Meg shook his shoulder and said loudly, "Steward, sir, wake up, we're back!"

"Some babysitter," Kate said sarcastically.

They entered the cabin and put on the bathroom light so they could check the babies without lighting up the entire cabin. They were horrified at the sight that met them. The bathroom looked as if a tornado had hit it. The contents of their make-up cases were strewn all over the floor, powder, rouge, bobby pins, curlers and talc. Lipstick was smeared on the tile floor. Toilet paper was piled on the open bowl and scattered everywhere.

"Oh, my God," Meg screamed, looking from the devastating mess in the bathroom to Jimmy's bunk. It was empty!

Kate quickly picked up Mike, who was awakened by the noise and started crying.

"Oh, my God, where's my baby?" Meg shrieked frantically as both women raced around the small room, pulling the covers off the bunks and checking the closet. Meg ran out the door and began looking up and down the passageway.

The steward, now awake, ran into the room. Apologies poured out from him. "I was right here all the time, honest to God lady! I didn't hear anything, I swear! I checked them, I swear I did!"

Kate yelled down the passageway, at the top of her lungs, "Help! help! A baby is missing."

Meg became hysterical when she looked across the room at the large easy chair below the open porthole and screamed, "Oh my God, Kate, he must have climbed up on the back of the chair and fallen out the porthole."

Within seconds a crowd had gathered outside the cabin. Two sailors immediately gave orders for everyone to search the area. They assumed that the baby probably had crawled out the door. They felt sure he could not have squeezed through the porthole opening.

Among the crowd who volunteered to search for Jimmy were two of the prostitutes, a couple of the gangster-types, and many of the ship's personnel, called to the scene by the frightened steward.

The purser and another officer arrived. The purser patted Meg on the arm and said in a compassionate tone, "Mrs. Wright, I'm sure we'll find the baby. He could not have gotten far. As for the steward, he'll be properly reprimanded, I assure you."

The sailor standing next to Meg in the doorway suddenly looked at the heavy metal door to the cabin, which seemed to be flush against the wall.

Meg followed his look. "He couldn't fit behind that door." She sobbed, knowing what the sailor was thinking.

The inside handle of the door was secured to the wall by a locking device so that it would not slam shut in rough seas. It seemed impossible for Jimmy to have crawled into the space between the door and the wall. It was barely six inches wide. The sailor held his flashlight between the door and the wall and shouted jubilantly, "I found him!" He jerked the door out of its locking device, and there was Jimmy, lying stretched out on his side, sound asleep.

A cry went up along the corridor, "They found the baby! He's okay!"

For a few seconds, Meg thought she was going to faint when she took Jimmy from the sailor's arms and held him tightly. She was so weak with fear, she could hardly stand. The purser escorted her to the easy chair.

She smothered Jimmy with kisses and sobbed, "Thank you, dear God, thank you, thank you." His little face, hands, and his Doctor Dentons were covered with smeared lipstick and talcum powder.

When the ship's doctor arrived, Jimmy was screaming. He checked the baby over carefully and said, "He's fine, Mrs. Wright. He's just frightened by all the fuss. Mrs. Wright, I apologize for the trauma you've been through. We'll have a more reliable person tend to your child's care whenever you need the service. Someone will be here shortly to clean up the bathroom. Also, I'm having two large cloth laundry carts, which are approximately three feet deep, sent up. I guarantee the babies won't be able to climb out of them. "Is this little chap always such a rascal?"

Meg looked down at Jimmy who was falling off to sleep and said, "Not usually. Fortunately, he was born at midnight and is protected by the good fairies."

The purser looked amused and said, "Oh, I see. Well good night, Mrs. Wright."

An hour later, both the babies were sleeping in the sturdy cloth laundry carts. Kate had fixed them bottles of warm milk, which she had prepared in the small pantry a few doors down from their cabin.

"Why don't you go to the salon and join the others, Kate? I'm exhausted and ready to hit the sack," Meg said. She gave Kate a peck on the cheek. "I'm sorry about your cosmetics. I'll buy you new ones."

"Don't worry about it, but I must say, I'm really not sure that I want my Mike to be Jimmy's roommate. He'll teach him bad habits!" Kate said and laughed.

After Kate left, Meg knelt down and thanked God for his goodness, undressed, then climbed into her bunk. Eventually she was lulled to sleep by the splashing waves.

ᘒ * ᘒ

The next morning after breakfast, the wives took the babies up on deck because a large school of porpoises had been spotted and were circling the ship. It was a beautiful warm day. The blue green Pacific sparkled in the sunlight, enhancing the rhythmic motions of the gray mammals who rose and dove in unison as if orchestrated by an unseen conductor.

Meg left Jimmy with Kate and went to the purser's office to inquire where she might find the sailor who had found Jimmy. "I didn't get a chance to thank him last evening."

"I'll be glad to give your message to him, Mrs. Wright. I believe he's on duty right now."

When Meg was walking back to join Kate, she saw one of the prostitutes who had helped in the search for Jimmy. She was stretched out on a deck chair. She looked up when Meg passed her, smiled, and said, "I was so happy that your baby was found safe and sound last night. You must have been terrified," she said with sincerity in her soft voice.

She was wearing a brief two piece lavender-flowered bathing suit. Her figure was startling. Her long legs were "pin-up" perfection. The sun spun streaks of gold in her chestnut hair that cascaded gracefully in soft waves to rest on her tanned shoulders. She looked about twenty years old.

Meg was temporarily tongue-tied. The woman's beauty stunned her, and she thought, how could someone this lovely be a prostitute? Maybe that officer was wrong. Should I talk to her? Of course I should. "Thank you for helping. I was terrified." Meg didn't know what else to say. Why did she find it hard to look directly at her? Meg said the first thought that came into her head, "So, isn't it too bad the pool isn't open? But I guess we'll get enough swimming on Waikiki. Do you have housing in Honolulu, or, I mean, like a hotel?" Meg asked. Oh, what a dumb question, she thought. Prostitutes have to have at least a room for their business.

"Yes, we'll be staying at a hotel. My name's Marisa, by the way."

"Marisa! Oh, that's a beautiful name. I'm Meg. My three friends and I are Navy wives. Our husbands are stationed on a submarine based at Pearl Harbor."

"I was a Navy wife. My husband was a pilot." Marisa said proudly. Then she looked down, heaved a sigh, and said softly. "He, ah, crashed over the Pacific in 1942." She turned her head away from Meg and quickly covered her eyes with her sunglasses.

"Oh, I'm so sorry. That must have been really rough on you."

She gave Meg a succinct, "Ya. See you later," she said abruptly and began reading her book.

Meg said, "Okay," and walked away. She couldn't wait to tell the others.

The next afternoon, Meg was walking with Jimmy around the deck. She was holding his hands, so he could pretend to be walking. Although only nine months old, he loved to try to walk. He was moving so fast he tripped and fell, and his hands slipped out of Meg's hold. Before she could retrieve him, he crawled as fast as he could down the metal deck. He giggled as Meg pretended not to be able to catch him.

"Come back here, you little imp!" she scolded.

One of the gangster types stepped out of a passageway door just as Jimmy scooted by. The man stopped and picked Jimmy up, holding him high over his head.

For a moment Meg was frightened that the man might hurt Jimmy.

But he smiled broadly and said, "Hey, yaw a little tie-ga, ain't ya? Heah ya go, Mummy." He handed Jimmy to Meg.

"Thank you," Meg said, giving the man a quizzical look. "Is that a Boston accent I heah?" exaggerating her own Boston accent.

"That's a Southie accent, Miss. Ya know Southie?"

"Of course," Meg said, now smiling. He didn't seem to be a bad person at all.

Then in an Irish tenor voice, he sang, "Brought up on A Street, knocked down on B Street, Southie is my hometown."

Meg laughed. "I'm from across the river. I'm a Cambridge girl."

The man stuck out his giant right hand and tipped his wide-brimmed light gray felt hat with his left. "Nice to meet cha. So, ya one of them classy lassies from Haavahd Squah, huh? Name's Sully," he said, shaking Meg's hand with great force.

"My name is Meg, and this is Jimmy. So, you're a Sullivan? My mother was a Sullivan," Meg said, appraising the man. Somehow he just didn't fit her perception of a gangster. He was a little rough around the edges. He was large both in height and width. He had broad shoulders and a wide chest, but his waist was small. Built like Charles Atlas, Meg thought to herself. He had the dark, good looks of the Irish whose ancestors bred with shipwrecked sailors from the Spanish Armada. He had deep steel-gray eyes, thick black hair, and the dark outline of a beard and moustache, which could never be erased no matter how closely he shaved. Even his skin tone was Mediterranean. He acted cocky, strutted rather than walked. Yet, at this moment, he was gentle, not someone to fear.

He walked along with Meg, offering to carry Jimmy, but Meg declined. He was dressed in a dark dapper suit, which would surely suffer from Jimmy's drooling and dust covered overalls.

"It's windy and cold out heah today, huh? Wished I brung my heavy Aran sweatah. Still as good today as it was the day my Ma brung it over from the old country." He flipped his cigarette over the rail and stuffed his hands into his pants pockets.

"What's an Aran sweater?" Meg asked.

"Aran Island folks, off Galway Bay, ya know? They knit the best sweatahs. They make em with thick white wool yahn with the lamb's oils left in em. It makes em wataproof. The Irish sweah by em, 'specially the fishamen. Ya see, if a dory sinks, and the bodies washes ashoah, they can easily be identified because the sweatahs ah knitted with special pattens for each of the Aran Islands." He crossed his arms on his chest, then in a thick Irish brogue he said, "And that's ya Irish lesson fa today, lassie. I bid ya fahwell as I need a couple of boilermakas befoa we chow down." He tipped his hat, chucked Jimmy under the chin, and walked off in the opposite direction.

Meg was captivated. He had Irish charm! A little rough around the edges, but a real man. He reminded Meg a great deal of her Uncle Frank, Aunt Grace's husband. Oh, my God, Meg thought, now wait until the girls hear about me meeting one of the gangsters. It was almost five o'clock. She would have to rush to shower and get dressed for dinner.

ঔ * *ৱ*

On the last night at sea, dinner was at seven. All the officers were dressed in their white uniforms. The wives wore their best party dresses. They had been invited to sit at the captain's table along with the elegant couple they had noticed the first day. They learned that they were brother and sister and descendants of Captain Cook, the first white man to start a settlement in the Hawaiian Islands. Although aloof, they warmed up to Liz when they discovered she was marrying into an old Honolulu family.

The horse racing began right after dinner. The purser selected Meg to be the jockey and roll the dice. He put a jockey's hat on her and seated her at a head table with two officers and himself. The captain had left as he did not approve of gambling. She knew very little about gambling, but occasionally she had played "liar's dice" at the Officer's

Club in New London. The wooden horses were lined up at the starting post, and the final bets had been made for the first race.

The purser leaned close to Meg and said in a hushed voice, "Bring us luck, Mrs. Wright. If we win, it all goes into the ship's kitty."

By the third race, a trend had developed. Meg seemed to roll sixes and threes more often than other numbers. The Mob sensed this and began betting the limit on the number three and six horses. Sully had looked at Meg more than once, giving her a knowing wink. After the fifth race, he yelled across the floor, "Nice goin, Cambridge," flashing a fistful of bills.

Meg was embarrassed. She was worried that people would think she was helping the Mob win.

The officers kept instructing her in various ways to shake and toss the dice from the cup, hoping to break the "three/six roll" she was on. She shook her whole body, then tossed the dice across the table. Six again! Every second or third roll had a three or a six showing. She shook them easy, then hard. She sensed the officers were upset. They were quickly losing a good-sized pot accumulated over the past few nights. She wished she had never been asked to be the jockey. The Mob was now loudly verbal about her being their "lady luck."

"Atta gal, Irish, baby needs new shoes," the Al Capone look-alike kept hollering.

"This is the ninth, sweetheart. Putting it all on six."

"Make it come three, just for me."

The officers glared at Meg. She looked at them in distress, "I don't know what to do," she uttered softly.

In the last race, the next roll would bring either the six or four horse over the finish line. Everyone was on their feet yelling.

"Come on, lucky six," was the cry from the Mob.

It was evident that the ship's crew and all the other bettors wanted the Mob to lose. They catcalled and jeered across the room at them. In loud voices, they chanted, "Come on home, lucky four. Four, four, four!"

Meg was extremely nervous. The noise was deafening. All eyes were on her as she shook the cup up and down, and side to side. She looked around the room, letting everyone see that she was really shaking up the dice.

Oh, my God, she thought to herself, I'm about to make a lot of enemies. What if the mob becomes my enemy? I could be wiped out!

Please, dear God, let six win. She closed her eyes and spilled the two dice onto the felt.

"Blast it!" were the first words she heard. It was the purser.

A roar went up from the Mob who all converged at the head table to thank Meg, their benefactor. They were handing her one and five dollar bills. "Hey, little lady luck. Tanks a million. Youse is some dame. We oughta put ya on the payroll."

Sully, standing in front of Meg, seemed to be aware of her discomfort. "Hey, kiddo, it's the luck of the Irish, huh? Don't feel bad. They're all grown-ups. They'll get over it."

Without even counting how much had been shoved into her hands, she handed it all to the purser. "I don't want this. Please put it in the ship's kitty." The purser smiled, "That's very generous of you, Mrs. Wright, but we really couldn't take it, in spite of the fact that this last race wiped out the ship's kitty."

The wives now gathered around and teased Meg for trying to give all the money away. "Wait until we tell Jim about Miss Rich Bitch."

"Let's get a nightcap," Meg suggested giving them a sarcastic look. "The drinks are on me."

✍ * ✍

Tomorrow would be a big day. Meg kept visualizing what their arrival would be like. Oh, how she hoped it would be just like the movies. It would be her childhood dream come true.

At eight o'clock in the morning, an announcement came over the ship's speakers. "We will be docking in Honolulu in two hours. Your cabin luggage should now be outside your door for pickup by the stewards. Your other luggage, in the hold of the ship, will be taken ashore after all passengers have disembarked. We hope you have enjoyed your voyage. We are happy to have been of service to you. We invite you to sail with us again, when the *Lurline* is refitted back to its pre-war ambience."

The women had learned from the purser that the *Lurline* and other Matson liners had outstanding war records, carrying personnel and supplies to every important military base in the Pacific. They never had an escort, nor were they armed. Their speed was great enough to outrun both enemy submarines and surface craft.

The Wrights' new sea chest, in the hold, was filled with household goods recently purchased. Their other two sea chests, with all their other worldly possessions, were in transit somewhere and might not reach Honolulu for months. Although Meg still dreamed of a real house with her own furniture, living in the island paradise of Hawaii for eighteen months would make up for it. She still worried about getting pregnant and not being able to travel to be with Jim. One child was quite a job, living this way. She often thought how hard it was on the enlisted families who had two or three children.

Everyone felt the excitement when land was sighted. Kate, Cassie, Liz, and Meg went to the top deck where passengers began lining the rail. A Hawaiian song, "Lovely Hula Hands," was playing over the speakers. Sully moved next to Meg at the rail, and teased, "I'll betcha learn to do the dance to that Lovely Hulahan music, Hulahan's an Irish name, ain't it?"

Kate, standing on the other side of Meg, gave her a dirty look for talking with the gangster.

"Look, we're coming into the harbor," Liz cried eagerly as the ship turned toward the shore.

Meg was so excited. "Oh, Jimmy, we'll see Daddy real soon. He won't even know you, you've grown so." Her heart pounded in anticipation.

Passengers lined the starboard rails on all the decks as the *Lurline* sailed into Honolulu Harbor and the famous Aloha Tower came into view. Then the strains of the nostalgic "Aloha Oe" reached out in welcome. The wives were awed by the huge crowds that were on the dock waving leis and yelling "aloha." Someone touched Meg's shoulder lightly. She turned her head. It was Marisa. "Good luck!" she said and smiled.

Meg made room for her by nudging Sully to move down and his eyes met Marisa's. Their look held for a few seconds. Meg looked from one to the other and introduced them, "Marisa, this is Sully. He's from Boston."

"Hi," Marisa uttered.

"Nice ta meet cha," Sully said, tipping his hat.

Jimmy was jiggling to the music and laughing.

The crowds on the dock were hollering and waving furiously.

"Oh, look, look, Kate," Meg cried joyously. "Isn't this a wonderful welcome. I never would have believed this many people would be here to meet the ship. It looks like there are thousands."

Cassie yelled, "There's a Hawaiian band, and hula dancers, and everyone is wearing leis!"

Meg thought, It's a scene right out of the memorable Hawaiian movie that she and Babs had re-enacted in the old neighborhood garage many years ago.

Everyone was leaning over the rail and peering intently down at the throngs of people crowded so closely together on the dock area.

Meg thought she saw Jim. "Kate, is that our guys in khaki uniforms in the front row to the left?"

Kate leaned over the rail and scrutinized the area where Meg had pointed. "You're right! It's them! Jake, Jim, up here," she yelled. All the girls waved their arms wildly.

Suddenly, everyone who was crowded along the rail, had their attention distracted from the welcoming crowds on the dock. Behind them, they heard the sounds of large numbers of people running up the stairs and out onto the deck from the passageways.

"My God, Japs!" someone yelled.

Passengers' faces froze in panic when the first onslaught of young male Japanese rushed towards the rail.

An angry male voice shouted, "What the hell are damn Nips doing on this ship?"

⚘ * ⚙

Prior to World War II, more than 110,000 Japanese lived on America's West Coast. 70,000 of them were American citizens, many second-generation Americans.

Following the bombing of Pearl Harbor, all Japanese were considered the enemy, and an irresponsible edict was issued by U.S. government officials. All funds belonging to Japanese people on the West Coast were frozen. They couldn't even cash a check. Many stores refused to sell them food. Their insurance policies were canceled, their businesses were closed, the professional licenses of physicians and attorneys were revoked, and most Japanese were fired from their jobs. No specific charges were ever filed against them, but the U.S. Army claimed that they must be evacuated to internment camps as a military necessity.

The Japanese people on the West Coast lost their homes, businesses and billions of dollars. Many claimed the basis of their internment was racism. Anti-Japanese feelings had existed as far back as the early 1900s. Like all immigrants, they were welcomed when they were needed for manual labor jobs, but once their frugality began showing dividends, and they took loftier roles in their communities, resentment set in.

Not everyone shared these anti-Japanese feelings, and many tried to help their Japanese neighbors and friends until they were forced into internment camps.

Most mid-western and eastern Americans had never seen a Japanese person except in war movies and newsreels where they were depicted as evil and cruel, stereotyped as slant-eyed, buck-toothed fanatics. Only occasionally, newsreels showed the 442nd Regiment, which was made up entirely of 8,000 Nisei who fought for America with honor. They had an outstanding military record in every battle and won every possible award for bravery.

Hawaii was different in that it had a greater ethnic and racial mix tolerance. Of the 158,000 persons of Japanese ancestry in Hawaii, fewer than 2,000 were interned, most of them at the Jerome Relocation Center in Arkansas. Most of those interned were Japanese language teachers, Buddhist priests, commercial fishermen, merchants in the import-export trade, or those who received an education in Japan or played a leadership role in the Japanese community. Being a Nisei, (second-generation American citizen) did not prevent internment.

Immediately after the bombing of Pearl Harbor, it was thought that all Japanese in Hawaii should be interned. But before long, reality set in, and General Delos Emmons, commanding general in Hawaii, looked at the situation in practical terms. He saw the Japanese in Hawaii as productive citizens in all communities and foresaw a severe labor shortage if they were interned.

Little was ever heard about the loyal American citizens of Japanese ancestry who were enduring persecution, living in barracks on remote federally-owned barren land in harsh weather states such as Utah, Washington and Wyoming. The public rarely heard about those who were housed in such uninhabitable places as the Santa Anita and Tanforan racetracks where they were assigned horse stalls as homes. They were subjected to inexcusable indignities. They were penned in behind barbed wire under constant surveillance by Army police, much like prisoners of war in concentration camps.

❧ * ❧

The passengers at the rail were perplexed when the young Japanese men were joined by others: young girls, small children, middle aged men and women, and some frail, elderly citizens. Although the elderly were stoic, the young men, women and small children were smiling. The children were neatly dressed, their beige skin was flawless, their almond shaped eyes twinkled, and their thick jet black, shining hair was cut short and in bangs. They craned their heads past those at the rail to get a better look at the crowds on the dock. But, the passengers at the rail did not move. The two groups stared at each other as if an impasse was at hand.

Meg whispered from the corner of her mouth to Sully. "Are they really Japs? Maybe they're Chinese."

"They're Japs, they sure as hell are. I've been face to face with them in the Pacific," Sully whispered.

"What are they doing on our ship?" an indignant passenger demanded to know.

The authoritative voice of a ship's officer answered the passenger's question. "These folks are residents of Hawaii and are returning home."

At that moment, the ship came to a complete stop, and the passengers at the rail quickly turned their attention down to the dock. The Japanese immediately pushed forward, crowding in close behind them, so they, too, could see the cheering crowd. Many passengers at the rail hunched up their shoulders and elbowed the Japanese back. Some cursed obscenities at them.

A young Japanese man about seventeen eased his slim body in between Meg and Marisa. He smiled at them. They parted quickly and stood sideways, making room for him.

Suddenly, Joe's stories of the torture by the Japanese flooded Meg's mind, and anger seized her momentarily. Then she thought, but this young man wasn't old enough to be in the war. And he doesn't look evil.

In an excited voice, he began calling down to someone on the dock. Then he began climbing the chain link fence. He was about a foot from the top, with both of his feet fitted snugly into the small openings of the chain link. He let go of his hold on the top of the rail and flailed both arms to attract the attention of someone below. Within a second of raising his arms, he lost his balance and began teetering forward and back. His body swayed out of control.

"Oh, my God," Meg screamed, quickly handing Jimmy to Kate with one arm and reaching out for the swaying boy's leg with the other.

"He's going to fall!" Marisa yelled, and she, too, reached out, grabbing for his legs.

Sully stretched out over the rail and just barely hooked his large hand onto the young man's belt as he fell forward, and yanked him back. The three rescuers now had the young man safely engulfed in their arms, and lifted him down to the deck.

Fright covered his face as he looked at the trio of rescuers. They loosened their hold and stepped back.

Someone along the rail yelled, "Should have let the son of a bitch of a Jap fall!"

The young man looked in the direction of the voice with cold, hard eyes but said nothing. He looked back at Meg, Marisa and Sully. His eyes softened, and he said in a quivering voice, in perfect English, "Thank you so much. That was a stupid thing for me to do. I saw my uncle in the crowd below. And, well, it's been a long time since I last saw him," he explained.

A middle-aged Japanese couple broke through the crowd and ran to the young man. They embraced him, while thanking the three rescuers.

The father reprimanded his son, "Who do you think you are, Superman? What a stupid thing to do!"

A jeering voice called out from along the rail, "Hey, Japs, we'll never forget Pearl Harbor!"

The boy's father looked in the direction of the taunt, then turned back to the rescuers and said, "It might interest you to know that my wife and I are second generation Americans, of Japanese ancestry. Our son is a third generation American, maybe like many of you. We are very grateful to you for saving our son's life."

Speaking articulately, the father raised his voice slightly, "As the ship's officer said a few moments ago, we are being returned home. Like many other Americans of Japanese ancestry, we were interned and sent to a relocation camp right after the war began. We have been prisoners in a camp in Jerome, Arkansas for the past five years."

The ship's officer now stood next to the man. "It's all right, Mr. Omura, you do not have to explain your presence on this ship to anyone."

"I know that. But I want to speak out, now that I'm free to do so." He turned away from the officer and slowly scanned the faces of the passengers along the rail. "We have endured internment because of the pride we have in our heritage, which teaches us to respect authority.

Please remember we were, still are, and always will be loyal Americans. Enjoy your stay in my hometown. Aloha."

There was complete silence from the passengers.

Meg felt both pangs of sympathy and admiration for the undaunted loyalty the man still held for America. She had known nothing of the internment of Japanese Americans except what she had heard from her brother, Joe, about Nobu's family. She watched them leave. Although their clothes were shabby and their battered luggage was tied with rope, there was no doubt about it, their dignity was intact.

Sully said to Meg, "Jeeze, that Jap kid is more American than me. I'm only a first generation American."

Meg was curious, "I wonder where all these Japanese people have been during the trip. I've never seen any of them. Have you?"

"Nope. But I bet all my hoss racing winnings that they were housed a few decks below us."

TWENTY-SIX

onolulu, April 1946. The wives hurried down the gangway juggling their luggage and babies towards their husbands who were waving leis and blowing kisses. When they reached the dock, the men hung beautiful orchid and ginger leis over their shoulders, while kissing and hugging them. It was a memorable, romantic reunion Meg would never forget.

Jimmy looked at Jim without recognition and held back when Jim tried to kiss him. He kept trying to get back into Meg's arms.

"I can see I'd better not stay away too long from my little son. I'm a stranger to him, aren't I!" Jim remarked in a forlorn tone.

"I'm afraid so," Meg answered. "But you two will have lots of time to get reacquainted."

Dave Benson's parents, who also had come to welcome the wives, invited all of them to their home that evening for cocktails, followed by dinner at the Halekulani Hotel.

The group, making their way through the crowds on the dock, witnessed many touching scenes of Japanese families being reunited. One very elderly man was helped to kneel; he wanted to kiss the ground.

Dave Benson's father, who was born and raised in Hawaii, was aware of the Niseis' situation during the war, commented to the group, "Some of our Japanese American friends were interned. It's a terrible blot on American history, which should never be forgotten."

Meg told Jim about how many of the passengers resented the internees and said cruel things to them. She told Jim about the young Japanese boy who almost fell overboard, and how she and two other passengers had saved him. She didn't elaborate on who the other two passengers were. She'd tell him the details later. But she did comment loudly to the group, "I think if they interned me, and I was an American, I'd sue the government."

Dave Benson said, "Actually, Meg, the government finally got a guilty conscience and released quite a few early because they were willing to sign waivers stating they wouldn't sue the government."

Kate asked in a voice loud enough for all to hear, "Speaking of the government, I'm sure we don't have Naval housing, but we do have a place to live, don't we, boys?"

Jake answered, "Right, Kate, no Naval housing. But you gals knew that. Jim and I found nice rooms at a small hotel called The Na Pua. We were really lucky to find anything, there's so little available."

"It's a nice place," Jim commented. "It was a Red Cross Center during the war, and the owner has just renovated it." Jim squeezed Meg's shoulder protectively and looking sideways at her to see how she was taking this news.

"Kitchen privileges?" Meg asked hopefully.

"Uh, no, honey, but there's a nice, inexpensive, family restaurant a few doors away. There's even a nice park next door with swings and slides. Jimmy'll love that!"

Kate and Meg exchanged exasperated looks.

When the Dolan's car was finally unloaded from the ship's hold, they crammed their luggage into the trunk and tied the rest onto the roof.

When they took off from the dock to their new home, Meg commented, "My sixteenth move is coming up, not counting the two weeks I lived with Jim's parents in Riverside or the four days aboard the *Lurline*, although actually, come to think of it, they were the only homes I had at that time. I think I'll call the Na Pua my eighteenth move."

That reality stunned Jim. He knew Meg must be disappointed that they would be living in a hotel, although the wives had been warned about the housing situation.

Riding through the palm-lined streets of Honolulu, Kate asked Meg, with a trace of sarcasm in her voice, "So, Meg, big surprise, huh? Ending up with one room and no kitchen privileges?"

"Come on, Kate," Jake answered before Meg had a chance to say anything, "Knock it off! You gals were warned about housing here. You're not even supposed to be here. You drive around the island. See if you can come up with something better. We couldn't!"

⚬ * ⚬

The Na Pua was a two story, freshly painted wooden building on Kapiolani Boulevard, not on the beach at Waikiki as Meg had dreamed about. They had a small room and a private bath for $21 a week. The owner didn't supply cribs for the babies, but gave them small mattresses and suggested that they put them in the old fashioned high-footed bathtub.

Jim commented, "The bathtub seems like an excellent idea, Meg, after what you told me about Jimmy's frightening escapade on the ship."

"It'll have to do," Meg said caustically as she thought of the beautiful new crib that her parents had bought for Jimmy. The Navy would now ship it to Honolulu, but it would be weeks, maybe even months before it arrived, Meg feared.

They unpacked and settled Jimmy with a bottle into his new bed. He was cranky from all the excitement, but nestled right down in his new sleeping quarters. He was such a flexible baby, he adapted to each new environment quickly.

Suddenly, Meg put her hand up to her mouth and looked alarmed. "Oh, Jim! I just remembered. That's the last bottle of milk I have. Will you go to the store? The hotel owner said we could keep the babies' milk in his fridge."

Jim frowned. "Oh, my gosh, Meg, I never thought of it. Jimmy will need milk every day, won't he? Milk is always scarce. There's not many cows on the island. Servicemen and restaurants have priority on all the fresh milk that's available. Islanders mostly drink powdered milk. But it really tastes terrible. You wouldn't want Jimmy to drink it. But I'll bring home fresh milk from the boat whenever I can. Why did you take Jimmy off formula?"

Meg said sarcastically to Jim. "Because I thought it would be too difficult to make formula aboard the plane, the train and the ship." Annoyance showed in her eyes. The charm of the paradise she had so looked forward to was quickly diminishing. She suddenly felt alienated, sad, even homesick. She sat down on the edge of the bed and buried her head in her hands as she fought back tears.

Jim took her into his arms. "Everything will be all right, honey. I'll get you all the milk Jimmy can drink. I wish I could give you a better life. You've been through so much since we've been married. We'll find a better place to live." He held her chin in his hand and said enthusiastically, "Wait 'til you see Waikiki! They call it the "skinny beach," because it's not too wide, but the surf is unbelievable. And, we get to use a private area called Grey's Beach right in front of the Royal Hawaiian Hotel. The hotel isn't open to the public yet. They're using it as an R & R stopover for the troops still returning from the Pacific."

He began kissing Meg with great fervor, arousing her. They had been separated so long. Meg tried to put all the disappointments out of her mind. She was with Jim, and she loved him. He began nibbling on her ear, and then her neck. He picked her up and laid her on the bed, and they made wonderful love. They had been married sixteen months.

The hotel manager's daughters babysat for the two couples when they went to the Benson's home that evening.

On the way, the men pointed out the highlights of the busy city of Honolulu. Beautiful flowers grew in abundance. When they approached Waikiki and spotted the surf for the first time, Meg and Kate yelled, "Oh, stop, Jake!"

They got out of the car for a better look at the famous beach. The red sky on the horizon contrasted magnificently with the turquoise ocean that was frosted with funnel-like waves. A red-sailed catamaran outlined in the sunset cut a swift path to shore. Young kanakis (beach boys) in colorful bathing trunks, expertly maneuvered their surfboards, which carried them on the crests of the waves back to the beach.

"It's a scene right out of a travel poster," Meg exclaimed exuberantly.

A Hawaiian woman wearing a muumuu and a large straw hat pushed her lei cart up to them, and in a lyrical voice said, "Kanes (men) buy beautiful leis for beautiful wahines (women). Only one dolla. Yes?"

The women selected leis to match their dresses. And, once again, following the custom, Jim and Jake placed the leis on their shoulders and kissed them on each cheek.

Kate commented. "Beats corsages!"

The Hawaiian magic captured Meg completely. Tears filled her eyes. She thought, I'm here, Meg O'Meara from Cambridge, Massachusetts, on the beach at Waikiki, with a beautiful lei, and looking out at a Pacific sunset with the man I love. She held her arms out to the ocean and exclaimed dramatically, "I think I've now decided that it's going to be so easy to be in complete harmony with life here in Paradise. I could stay here forever!"

They all laughed, and Jim grabbed Meg around the waist and said, "How poetic, Meg! That's the spirit; that's my Cambridge girl!"

As they drove along the beach boulevard, it became evident that servicemen made up a large proportion of the population. Traffic was heavy and the streets were crowded.

Jim told them Oahu's population includes only a small number of full-blooded Hawaiians because of the many intermarriages over the years with people from the Polynesian Islands. There are many haoles (Caucasians), Japanese, and Chinese, and other nationalities."

They reached the Bensons' house. It was a lovely old home on several acres in a beautiful residential neighborhood. Dave's parents were charming hosts, and following cocktails, they all left for dinner at the Halekulani Hotel.

Crossing the lobby of the hotel, the women spotted three of the prostitutes sitting around a small table having a drink. It was impossible not to notice them, they were so fashionably dressed and exceptionally pretty. The men's eyes were also drawn immediately to them. When they were out of earshot of the three women, Meg told Jim and Jake who they were. The men glanced back for a second look.

Jake said, "Not like the ladies of the evening in New London, hey, Jim?" Both men laughed.

Just as they reached the dining room, the "mob" was leaving. When they saw Meg, they all smiled, waved and called out, "Hey, there's our gal, hey, lady luck, how are ya?" Sully just smiled and winked.

Meg was embarrassed. She had told Jim about them, but never expected to see them again. She gave them a weak smile. Mr. and Mrs. Benson glared at the men with a "how dare you," look. Right now, it was not funny, but later, all of them would get a kick out of Meg's role as the jockey.

The evening's exotic dinner under palm trees and stars, easily changed any adverse opinions of Hawaii.

❧ * ❧

An event the next day should have been a harbinger to Meg of what life on the island was to be like. Jim had gone to the boat early. Meg lifted Jimmy's mattress out of the bathtub to change the sheet and screamed. At least twenty large black beetle-like bugs were crawling in and out of the drain and on the mattress. Shivers ran through her body. It was the most repulsive sight she'd ever seen.

The owner's only remedy was, "I could have sworn I told you to be sure and put the plug in the tub. Those are only what we call palmettos, yard roaches. Nothing to worry about. Hawaii has lots of insects, but no snakes!" Their first few weeks in Honolulu went by quickly. When the women were not out exploring the island for decent housing, they spent their time on the private beach in front of the Royal Hawaiian. When they wanted to swim, they kept the babies in playpens on the upper beach deck, and Filipino steward mates watched them until they returned.

Saturday nights were spent at the Officer's Club at Pearl Harbor, where, for $3 per person, they had drinks, dined, danced, and played the slot machines all evening. The only drawback to this weekly affair was that it was formal, and none of the women had more than one long dress.

Meg used her wedding dress. She had redesigned it into a strapless gown last New Year's eve. But, after wearing it three Saturdays in a row, she knew she had to do something. She had taken her sturdily built toy Singer sewing machine with her for hemming things. Now she used it to create long sarong-type dresses made of inexpensive flowered material that she purchased at Sears Roebuck in downtown Honolulu.

On Sundays, all the officers and their families went to Kailua beach on the other side of the island. On the way, at the Pali pass, they'd stop to view the spectacular vista below the historical cliff. The wind was always fierce, adding credence to the story that King Kamehameha and his men, forced to the brink by enemy invaders, jumped off the cliff and floated safely to the floor of the valley below.

Kailua was a beautiful white sand beach reserved for the use of service personnel only and sometimes the Marine band played for several hours. On their way home, they'd stop for dinner at their favorite Chinese restaurant, Trader Vics. After dinner, they'd all have a nightcap under the big banyan trees at the Moana Hotel on Waikiki.

⍦ * ⍦

All the officers and their wives attended the wedding of Dave and Liz, which was followed by a lovely reception at the Oahu Country Club. The newlyweds were lucky, they had found a nice house to rent in Manoa Valley when they returned from their honeymoon on the big island of Hawaii.

ø * ⱷ

The *Pout* got a new skipper, B.J. Hallett, a handsome, gregarious bachelor. He had been a prisoner of war for four years in Japan, after his submarine was sunk. The evening of the day he took command of the *Pout*, a party was held in his honor at the Officer's Club at Pearl. He sat next to Meg, because he had heard that her brother had been a POW in Japan. He wanted to know more about Joe. Midway through dinner, Meg was talking to him, and as usual, dramatically gesturing with her hands. She hit her tall glass of claret lemonade, and it splashed all over the front of the captain's white uniform. Everyone glared at her, especially Jim. She was so embarrassed, but the captain was a perfect gentleman. He patted Meg's arm and said, "It's okay, dear." Then he looked at the others, grinned and said, "No big deal, I have two sets of whites!"

He went upstairs to his room at B.O.Q., put on a fresh uniform, and rejoined the group, again sitting next to Meg. "You're very brave to sit next to me again," Meg said. "I think you should know that I have a bad reputation for spilling drinks."

He laughed and said, "I know that now. I like to live dangerously. How about a dance? "

When they returned to the table, the captain held Meg's chair. When she sat down, she picked up her napkin from the table, not realizing that the corner of her napkin was under a new glass of claret lemonade that had been brought while she was dancing.

The inevitable happened. The captain's white uniform was pink again. Meg was so humiliated, her eyes filled with tears, and she rose to go to the ladies' room, but the captain stopped her.

"Oh, no you don't, Meg Wright! I have no more white uniforms, therefore, you will dance with me again and explain to the other dancers, why I'm wearing a pink uniform." The captain never sat next to Meg again, but he often related the incident with good-natured teasing.

ø * ⱷ

One day, Meg, Kate, and the babies stopped at a drive-in restaurant called, Kau Kau Korner. They couldn't believe it when the carhop came to take their order. It was Marisa!

"Hi, there, how are you?" she said, smiling faintly.

"I'm fine. How about you?"

"I'm fine." She held out her pad and pencil as if ready to write, and said, "What'll it be?"

Somehow she didn't look as glamorous as she had looked before. She took their order, but another girl delivered it.

Meg thought a great deal about Marisa after that, but saw her only one more time in downtown Honolulu. She and another girl were stopping servicemen, asking them if they wanted to buy a subscription to a magazine. "We're trying to work our way back to the mainland," Meg heard them say.

A month later, Meg had Jimmy out for a walk in his new stroller. A car pulled up alongside them.

"Hey, Irish, how ah ya?" It was Sully from "the mob."

In the course of conversation, Meg asked him if he had seen Marisa.

"Ya, she's gone back to the states. The cops kept on top of them. Well, ya know what I mean, hassled them, and their pimp skipped out on em. I met her downtown one day and gave her a couple a hundred to get home. She was strung out on somethin and depressed. Hope she makes it."

"That was really nice of you to help her. You're a good guy, Sully."

"Hey, she needed a friend, that's all." See ya around." He touched the brim of his hat and sped off.

℘ * ℘

The Wrights and the Dolans were given a one week notice to vacate their rooms at the Na Pua. The owner didn't want babies in his rooms anymore. They were too noisy. They quickly searched for another place. As a last resort, Meg suggested to Jim that they look at the Hale Omura that Nobu's family owned. From what Joe had said, she knew it was not a place to live because of the clientele. Maybe things had changed. She had called Nobu's uncle several times as Joe had asked her to do, but he never returned her call.

The Hale Omura was a large rambling two-storied wooden building. It had a wide veranda with rocking chairs and a dining room. Meg and Jim went into the lobby where a maid was sweeping the woven grass carpet with a broom. Meg was fascinated with the speed at which she worked. She dunked the broom in a pail of water, to hold down the dust, Meg assumed, and swiftly swept a large area. At the reception desk a young man was sorting mail in slots. He turned, and his face broke into a wide grin. "Hello, hello, you're one of the passengers who saved my life on the ship!" he said in an exuberant voice. He reached out his hand and shook Meg's hand.

Recognizing the young man, Meg said, "That's right! You were trying to get your uncle's attention, as I recall."

"Yes, my uncle who has been running this hotel for my parents while we were away. Ah, speak of the devil, here he comes now. I want him to meet you."

A rather obese Japanese man with gray thinning hair and hooded eyes walked towards them. "Well, Akira, are you helping these customers properly? My nephew is learning the business, and sometimes he does stupid things, but he's a good boy."

"This lady knows I do stupid things; she's one of those who saved my life when the ship was docking," the young man said in an impish tone.

"Ah, so!" the man said, shaking Meg's hand. "I thank you very much. Is there anything I can do for you?"

"Well, we need a place to live right away, but first, I want to introduce myself and my husband. I'm Meg Wright and this is my husband, Jim, and our son, Jimmy. You have another nephew named Nobu, in Japan, don't you?"

Both the uncle and the young man looked at each other in alarm.

"Why do you ask that question?" the uncle said in an startled voice.

"Do you remember visiting an Air Corps Lieutenant named Joe O'Meara at Wheeler Field hospital right after the war?"

"Joe O'Meara? Sure! You know Joe?"

"He's my brother."

"Nobu is my brother!" Akira said excitedly.

"I thought so!" Meg said, smiling at the young man.

"Well, your brother saved my brother's life when he was a prisoner in Niigata, Japan."

"And you save Nobu's brother's life in Honolulu," the elderly uncle said, pointing his index finger at Meg. "The spiritual powers of Gautama Buddah have intervened in our family's lives. Our home is your home."

The entire Omura family came to have lunch with Meg and Jim that day. Akira's parents, whom Meg had seen on the ship, now looked healthier and younger than they had earlier. They made Meg tell them over and over, the stories Joe had told her about Nobu. They were proud that their son was still a good American. They had been trying without success to find ways to get him back home since they returned to Honolulu. They had accepted the fact that it would be quite some time before they would see their oldest son again.

Although the hotel was not as clean as the Na Pua, and the Omuras did not deny that the clientele was not the most desirable, they assured the Wrights that they would be safe. They promised to do all they could to make them comfortable and didn't want to charge them, but Jim insisted.

The Wrights moved into a large second floor room, which the Omuras felt would be cooler than the ones below. All the furniture was extra large for some unexplained reason. They could not reach the top of the bureaus, but they decided instantly that they would use one of the deeper drawers for Jimmy's bed. There were no glass windows, only screens. The door was louvered. It was their nineteenth move.

They hesitated when they heard that they would be sharing a bath, but they were assured that they would not be putting anyone in the next room except if the hotel was filled, which was unlikely.

Joe's assessment of the clientele was still valid. The Omuras explained that many of their present guests had lived in the hotel throughout the war, providing the only income the hotel had received. The Omuras felt badly about asking the undesirables to leave now. But, once they started to refurbish the hotel, they would raise their rates, and they felt that those people probably would then leave voluntarily.

On the Wrights' floor, two prostitutes lived with their children. Two homosexuals had the room next to them, but not the room they shared the bath with. The Wrights knew they were homosexuals because the thin walls and the screened windows allowed the sounds of their love-making into the Wright's room. The first time this happened, Jim banged loudly on the wall and told them in a strong voice that their obscene talk was embarrassing his wife. He used a threatening tone and warned them to hold it down, or he would call the police.

They yelled back, "Sorry," and rarely disturbed the Wrights again. But another tenant was determined to get the homosexuals to move. One evening about a week after the Wrights moved into the hotel, they were walking up the dimly-lit stairs to their room. Out of the darkness someone slipped a note into Jim's hand and disappeared. It frightened them until they were safely in their room and read the note.

Dear Neighbors in Room 210:

Like you, I am a family man and expect my wife and child to arrive on the Lurline next week. Let us band together and do something about the disreputable low life on this floor. I have been threatened by the two fairies next door to you. Please come now to my room across the hall (room 211). Please knock on my door three times. It is dangerous here.

s/ Otto Schumann

Jim and Meg found the note intriguing, and out of curiosity, they decided to visit Otto Schumann. They realized he must be the man with a guttural voice who opened his door and screamed at the two men every time they walked down the hall. It seemed to Jim and Meg that he had been itching for a fight.

Grinning at Meg, Jim softly knocked three times. The door was opened by a slight elderly Japanese who was introduced as Mr. Schumann's man servant. It was he who had slipped the note to Jim. Otto was a German who had been in a prisoner of war camp in the United States and had just recently been released. He told them that he had been a chemistry professor at a university in California and had been wrongfully accused of sabotage. He confessed that his imprisonment had turned him into a hypochondriac. To prove his point, he opened his refrigerator, which was filled with medications.

In an agitated voice, he told Meg and Jim, "I told those two queers they were incomplete men. They threatened to hang me out the window by my balls."

Jim and Meg had to suppress smiles.

Jim told him, "I've let them know they'd better behave. They know I mean business. It's really best if you don't argue with them. Just ignore them."

But every time the homosexuals left their room, Otto opened his door and screamed vulgar accusations at them.

The Wrights avoided Otto as often as they could. He was much more frightening than the homosexuals.

✄ * ✄

When Otto's wife arrived with her daughter, she visited Meg one afternoon. She described her relationship with Otto, which wasn't very good. "My father was in the prison camp with Otto. He became terminally ill and was very worried about me. He asked Otto to take care of me and my daughter when he was released. I'm really not his wife, and my daughter by another man was born out of wedlock. I'm only eighteen; Otto is fifty-five. He says he'll provide for me financially if I take care of him. I'm stuck with him."

Meg was sympathetic but really didn't want to get involved.

A week later, Otto's Japanese man-servant knocked on the Wright's door. He handed them a beautiful bird of paradise plant and a note and disappeared.

The note said,

Dear Friends in 210:
This is top secret information. My wife, child and I have secured passage on a small ship to the island of Maui. We will be safe there. I hope the queers don't injure you. I have to move to be rid of them or I'll have a heart attack.
s/ Otto Schumann and family"

Oddly enough, three days after the Schumanns left, the homosexuals had a violent fight and one threw the other's suitcases and belongings out through the screens to the driveway below. They were asked to leave immediately.

⚥ * ⚥

The Omuras were kind to the Wrights. They made sure that there was always milk for Jimmy's bottles. They prepared special baby meals, and allowed the Wrights to make coffee and toast in their room on a hot plate. They offered to have their laundry man do Jimmy's diapers. Meg was thrilled about that. It was difficult to wash diapers in the tub and hang them all over the room to dry. But the first time Meg went to the laundry room in the basement and saw the two prostitutes with baskets full of laundry. She turned quickly and left.

Often, Meg and Kate would spend the whole day at the beach. Kate and Jake were living much like Meg and Jim in another hotel. It wasn't easy. The men were gone a great deal of the time for a few days at a stretch. But if they had the duty, the wives might join them on the submarine for the evening. Meg was not comfortable being alone in their hotel room at night, especially about the "things" that crawl in the night.

Keeping small lizards in their room was a necessity because they ate the numerous insects that infested the islands. Exterminating insects was a very lucrative business in Hawaii, and no house or building escaped the most destructive of all insects, termites.

A strange phenomenon occurred precisely at six o'clock on Saturday evenings at the Hale Omura. Usually the Wrights were dressing to go out for the evening when the termite invasion occurred. Flying termites by the thousands filled their room. The first time it happened, Meg called down to the desk to complain.

The Uncle answered, "Ah, so, no problem; happens every Saturday night now. It's the season. Turn all lights out for half an hour, and termites will disappear."

He was right. At six thirty they turned the lights on, and the termites had disappeared, but what they saw was thousands of termite wings covering their bodies and everything else in the room. It was an unbelievable sight. They dusted off Jimmy and his bed clothes and took a shower together. The wings seemed to disappear in a few days, but the termites stayed, and while in bed at night, you could feel them sprinkling you with their borings from the wooden ceiling.

ଓ * ଓ

At the end of June, the *Pout* was ordered to join a squadron of U.S. submarines to conduct a six-week-long maneuver in the Arctic. Meg was frightened at the thought of Jimmy and herself staying alone that long in the hotel room. But, a wonderful solution came about almost immediately. Dave's new bride, Liz, also didn't like the idea of staying alone in their rented house and asked Meg if she and Jimmy would stay with her. Meg was thrilled with the idea of living in a real house.

Liz's house had the usual force of insect-eating lizards, which were welcomed guests, because Liz had discovered scorpions and centipedes in the damp basement where she did the wash. Meg knew the scorpion's bite could be poisonous, especially to children. The radio often made announcements cautioning mothers to look for red marks on a baby if they cried continuously for no apparent reason.

ଓ * ଓ

The wives and children of the *Pout's* crew saw the submarine sail away from Pearl Harbor for their "Blue Nose" expedition to the Arctic. Like the other wives, Meg was despondent about this unexpected separation. That night after she went to bed, she lay awake thinking about their marriage. Am I beginning to become disenchanted with being a Navy wife? Do I still love Jim? Does Jim love me? Does he feel as badly as I do about these constant separations? These were questions she had mulled over for quite some time now. Although she loved the sense of adventure it offered, she also needed Jim around to share it. They had wanted another child, but Meg wanted to be sure that Jim would be stationed in one port for at least two years and be with her. The officers and wives often had frank discussions about enlarging their families. Six out of the seven officers were Catholics. Some were seriously thinking about getting out of the Navy. Many of the enlisted men had one or two children. It was especially difficult for them to find housing that they could afford.

The *Pout's* crew had good reasons to be skeptical about the future. The new skipper was a bachelor with no family to worry about. Also, because he had been a POW for so long, he was "gung ho" about volunteering the *Pout* for any deployment opportunities that came along.

♋ * ♋

Meg was very content living with Liz in a real house, her twentieth move in eighteen months. She never let Jimmy out of her sight and rarely let him play on the floor because of the dangerous insects that proliferate in Honolulu.

But one day, while washing dishes in the kitchen, she let Jimmy play with pots and pans on the floor next to her feet. Suddenly, he made a strange noise and Meg looked down. Jimmy was making a sour face and brushing his mouth with his hands. She quickly picked him up and smelled a strange odor coming from his mouth. She looked on the floor and spotted a small tin can filled with a yellow, salve like ointment. The bottom of the can said, "Insect Killer." A skull and cross bones with tiny printing showed on the label.

Meg screamed for Liz. They rushed Jimmy to the hospital, wiping at his mouth all the way.

The doctor swabbed the inside of his mouth carefully. "I don't think we'll have to pump his stomach, but I'll give him a dose of syrup of ipecac to make him vomit, just to be sure. I think the poison is so bitter that Jimmy wasn't likely to have swallowed it. He probably spit it out."

At times like this, Meg felt anger towards Jim for not being near to give her support. Then, just as that nightmare was fading, a terrifying situation confronted Meg in their bedroom. One night, Jimmy, who was almost a year old, slept in the bottom bunk bed with a railing so he couldn't fall out. Just to be safe, Meg always kept a night light on and the bedroom door shut in case he awoke and crawled out of bed. She had climbed into the top bunk, closed her eyes and began saying her prayers. She stopped when she sensed a barely audible sound near her. She listened more intensely. She couldn't determine what it was. She opened her eyes wide. They were immediately drawn to a large dark blot on the ceiling directly above her head. It was alive. It moved slightly. It was big, black and had big, hairy-legs, lots of them! Oh, dear God! Meg realized it was a giant spider hanging upside down on the ceiling right over her head. She was so frightened, her heart stopped for a second. She was frozen with terror. She couldn't even close her eyes. He just stood above her, upside down waiting to lunge. I have to get a grip on myself. I have to move. I've got to get Jimmy out of here. But if I move, that black repulsive thing will jump down on me, and I'll die of fright. I know it! That thought brought to mind a scene from a horror movie she'd seen long ago. A big black hairy spider crawled over a woman's face, bit her throat and killed her! Oh, my God, I remember now, It's was a tarantula! Move Meg, move!

Never taking her eyes off the hairy legs above her, she eased very slowly and quietly across the bed until she was on the edge. She slowly moved her right foot over the side of the bunk bed. Then in one swift motion, she jumped to the floor, grabbed Jimmy, and raced out of the room, slamming the door and screaming, "Liz!"

Liz raced from her room, fear flooding her face when she saw Meg standing in the hall clutching Jimmy, who was screaming. Liz shook Meg. "What happened? What is it, Meg? Quick, tell me, are you or Jimmy hurt?"·

Meg kept pointing to the door of her room. Liz started towards it. Meg grabbed her and screamed, "No, No, No, don't go in there."

Chills ran through Liz's body as she sat Meg and Jimmy down on the sofa. "Quick, tell me, Meg, what's in there?"

"It's a gruesome-looking giant spider. I'm sure it's a tarantula! I've seen them in the movies. They can kill you."

Liz tried to soothe, Meg, "No they can't, Meg. The lady next door found one in her yard a couple of weeks ago. She showed it to me. She had put it in a jar for her son. It's not poisonous, Meg, honest, but it sure is gruesome-looking, I agree. Liz's first thoughts was for them to go to her in-laws for the night. but once they calmed down, they decided that they just might be able to kill it, if it was still there. They came up with a plan. They put Jimmy on the living room sofa with a bottle of warm milk. They then wrapped kerchiefs tightly around their heads, put three pairs of socks on their feet, then put on sweaters, coats and gloves.

Slowly, Liz opened the door. The tarantula was still in the same spot on the ceiling. Shivers ran through Liz's body. Meg turned away momentarily. Liz signaled her that she was ready to swipe him with the broom to the floor. Meg stood poised with six heavy books, ready to slam him when he landed on the floor.

"Now!" Liz yelled and swiped at him, but missed. Both girls screamed and froze in position as the spider began to lope swiftly across the ceiling.

Liz swiped at him again as he came down the wall. And again she missed! Meg began firing her ammunition of books at him, never hitting the mark or, even coming close. Screaming, they retreated swiftly as the hairy monster headed towards them across the floor. They slammed the door and stuffed towels under it. They spent the rest of the night on the couch, which they had moved to the center of the room where it faced the bedroom for better surveillance.

The next morning Liz called the exterminator. They had to move in with Liz's in-laws for two days until the toxic fumes dissipated. Although they wished he hadn't, the exterminator reported finding a centipede and a nest of scorpions in the basement.

After a while, the girls laughed about the tarantula encounter, but Meg never went to bed again without first checking around the room.

Liz and Meg seldom went to Waikiki any more. It was too dangerous. Returning American servicemen, lonesome for female companionship, would make obscene overtures to every woman they saw. One morning, Liz, and Meg, who was pushing Jimmy in a stroller along the beach, were accosted by two soldiers who kept trying to put their arms around them and kissing them. They couldn't make the men stop, so the girls screamed for help. The soldiers ran off laughing.

TWENTY-SEVEN

The *Pout* returned on August 10, coming into Pearl with the bullnose of the bow painted blue. The exercise had been called "Operation Bluenose" because their mission took them under the Arctic icecap. Along with a Navy Band to welcome them back, the wives had made many multi-flowered leis for the whole crew.

The excitement of the reunion was short-lived. That evening at a welcome home dinner at the Officer's Club at Pearl Harbor, the captain announced that the boat was ordered back to New London. It was to be converted into a "Guppy II" design. That was a real blow to all, especially the wives. They had been in Hawaii only about four and a half months, not eighteen months as expected.

Jim decided that he and Meg should be alone for their last few weeks in Hawaii, so he rented a rather expensive apartment, a block from Waikiki, her twenty-first move. He knew that Meg was despondent because they had to move again so soon and be separated. This time she didn't try to hide her feelings. They had serious and angry discussions about the state of their marriage. Jim loved Meg and his son, but he also loved the Navy and wanted to make it his career. "Meg, all this moving around we've done is really unusual. It can't keep up. I've looked into it, and I can tell you that a Naval career will give us financial security for the future. I'll keep going up in rank every few years and when I make captain, we'll live in a big house on the base with all kinds of privileges. I'm positive that we'll be in New London for quite a while because the boat will have to be in dry dock for the conversion repairs."

Meg reluctantly agreed to give it a chance.

All the officers and crew were in a depression about the sudden transfer to New London. Dave submitted his resignation. He and Liz would now live in Hawaii permanently. George Johnson also resigned his commission.

⚘ * ⚘

On August 25, Jimmy celebrated his first birthday. He had been across the country and back by auto. He had flown across the country, taken a train to San Francisco and a ship to Honolulu. He had moved at least ten times. He had slept on floors, in drawers, trunks, laundry baskets and bathtubs. In spite of all that, he was a happy-go-lucky baby.

⚘ * ⚘

Getting transportation back to the States presented a serious problem for the wives. Most planes and ships were booked solid to accommodate servicemen returning from the Pacific. The wives were really in Hawaii illegally as far as the Navy was concerned and therefore the Navy was not responsible for their transportation to the mainland.

Fortunately, Jake knew an admiral who was able to get them free passage on an APA, a troop ship, the *President Hayes*. It would leave on September 2, four hours after the *Pout* got underway for New London.

⚘ * ⚘

September 1946. As the *President Hayes* sailed out of Pearl, the wives tossed their leis overboard. It is believed that if the leis float ashore, you will return one day.

During the six days aboard the troop ship, Meg felt it certainly was her home and called it her twenty second home. Life aboard the APA was quite different from life on the *Lurline*. The wives' quarters were spartan, and they shared a bathroom with six other passengers. Meals were very punctual. They had to take their babies to meals, and if they weren't seated at their place when the waiter came by to serve them, they didn't eat. A chain link fence separated the men passengers from the women.

⚘ * ⚘

The women made friends with two of the ship's officers, and when they were off duty, they often played bridge, that was about the only entertainment outside of old, old movies, which usually broke half way through. The two officers, Ed Weis and Tom Blanchard, offered to drive Kate's car, which was in the hold of the ship, back to New London. They were getting their discharge papers when the ship docked in San Francisco, and they wanted to drive across the country. Ed lived in Ohio, and Tom lived in Indiana.

When they docked in San Francisco, Meg said goodbye to Kate and Cassie who were met by Kate's mother. Meg planned to take a train to Los Angeles where Jim's family would pick her up. She would live with them for a while before flying back to Boston. She called Southern Pacific from a booth on the dock to find out what time the next train left for Los Angeles. All trains that day were booked solid. She couldn't get a reservation until 8 AM the next day. Dismayed, she spotted Ed on the dock and asked him to recommend a hotel where Jimmy and she could stay for the night.

"My God, you didn't make a train or hotel reservation, Meg?" Ed asked in astonishment.

Meg reacted tersely, "How would I know that the trains would be so crowded? I didn't think I'd have to stay overnight."

"Well, kiddo, the war may be over, but the troops are still trying to get home you know."

"I guess I goofed. Can you recommend a nice hotel where Jimmy and I can stay tonight?"

"That's a big problem. Hotels in Frisco are usually jammed. Our hotel, the Pickwick, where Tom and I stay when the *Hayes* is in port, always has a waiting list."

Ed offered to hold Jimmy while Meg made calls to the hotels that he recommended.

Meg came out of the booth after trying seven different hotels without any luck. She was desolate. "Now what am I going to do?"

Ed said, "Well, I can't leave you standing here on the dock all night. We'll go to the Pickwick. I'll bunk in with Tom and give you my room, but you'll have to register as my wife. We have standing reservations, but we're not allowed to transfer them to anyone else except wives or parents."

Meg accepted his generous offer and insisted on paying him for the room. They walked into the Pickwick lobby. Ed carried Jimmy and a suitcase, and Tom helped Meg carry the rest of her luggage. The bellhop who knew Ed and Tom greeted them. "Hey, who's the cute little guy, Lieutenant?"

Ed hesitated, then mumbled, "Ah, er, ah, it's my son, little Eddie," Then, nodding towards Meg, "And this is the wife."

The bellhop grinned broadly, "Geeze, I didn't know you were married Lieutenant. Big Eddie and little Eddie. How about that? Hey, he looks just like you!"

Ed was quite rotund, and Jimmy was a chubby baby. They both had crew cuts, but the resemblance stopped there.

Ed signed the register, Lt. and Mrs. Edward Weis. The bellhop put the bags on a cart and led them across the lobby to the elevator. While waiting, a Marine came running through the lobby with a duffel bag over his shoulder. He stopped suddenly, looked at Ed and said, "Eddie Weis? Sandusky, Ohio? Right?"

"Hey, Skip Moran! Gee, I haven't seen you since 1942. You've been around! Look at all those battle ribbons."

"Ya, I'll have to tell you about it sometime. I'm rushing to catch a bus home at the station next door, otherwise we could have painted the town red, like in the old days. Hey, I'll call your Dad and Mom and tell them I saw you."

The bellhop interrupted, "Hey, don't forget to tell them you saw his cute baby, and his missus, too!"

"You're married, Ed? The big bachelor is married! I'll call your folks when I hit Sandusky and tell them I ran into you and your family! Gotta run. See you and the baby back in Sandusky, Mrs. Weis!" And with that he raced out the door to his waiting bus. Ed's mouth was hanging open as he raised his hand to stop the Marine. He yelled, "Hey, wait a minute, Skip," But the Marine had disappeared.

Ed looked at Meg, rolling his eyes up towards his head and said, "Oh, boy oh, boy." The bellhop took them up to their room.

Meg cringed. "Gosh I'm sorry, Ed. I'm sure you can explain it to your folks, can't you."

Glaring at Meg, Ed said, "Good Night, Mrs. Wright. We'll meet you in the lobby at seven AM. We'll then deliver you to the train station and out of my life!"

Ed walked out the door. Tom looked back at Meg, grinned, winked and said, "He's always bragging about being a confirmed bachelor."

Ed and Tom took Meg and Jimmy to the train and got them aboard. When they were leaving, Ed put his hands on Meg's shoulders and said, "I thought you'd like to know, trouble maker, what my mother said when I called her last night to explain."

"Was she upset?"

"Upset? On the contrary. She said if it had been true, it would have made her the happiest woman in the world."

Meg laughed. "Maybe you ought to do something about it when you get home, Ed."

"Never!" Ed said with determination.

❧ * ❧

Soon after the train left the station, Meg and Jimmy went to the dining car to get some breakfast. Jimmy was hungry, and began to whine. There were many civilians waiting in line. Meg asked if she might go up to the head of the line just for a minute. "I'd like to ask the porter if he could fill Jimmy's bottle with milk."

The porter, blocking the entrance to the dining car, bluntly told Meg, "No civilians eat until all the servicemen aboard are fed."

A tough looking sergeant standing just inside the dining room door heard the porter. He looked at Meg and asked, "What do you need, ma'am, just some milk for the little guy?"

"Yes, please. Here's his bottle, and thank you so much," Meg said gratefully.

"Here, give me the little tyke. I'll get his milk and take him for a walk. I got a couple of kids of my own that I haven't seen for three years. I'll get a little practice."

Meg hesitated for a second, but the big sergeant held out his hands in such a gentle way, and his face had such a wistful expression, she couldn't resist. "His name is Jimmy," she said, handing her baby to the large man who held him aloft as if he was a prized possession.

For the next fifteen minutes, Jimmy was a celebrity and loved all the attention. The sergeant paraded up and down the aisle while feeding him his bottle. He stopped at every table so the soldiers could get a better look at Jimmy. Some asked to hold him. The sergeant always looked towards Meg through the dining car door for permission. It tugged at Meg's heart to see the way some of the men looked at Jimmy, obviously anticipating the thrill of holding their own children soon.

❧ * ❧

When the train arrived in Los Angeles, Jim's two brothers, Royden and Kenny, were waiting for them.

Meg and Jimmy stayed with the Wrights for three weeks, their twenty-third move, until they flew to Boston.

ℬ * ℬ

Meg and Jimmy had an uneventful trip on American Airlines until they reached Washington, D.C. There they were "bumped off," along with other passengers, because servicemen needed their seats.

Fortunately, Meg was able to get a train reservation right away for the trip to Boston, where they were met by Meg's parents, her brother, Joe, who had just started his first year at Harvard and his wife, Eileen. They were happy that Meg would be home for a while.

Meg lived with her parents, her twenty-fourth move, for almost a month until the *Pout* arrived in New London.

TWENTY-EIGHT

ew London, Connecticut, November 1946. Good things began to happen to the Wrights. They were assigned a two-bedroom housing unit on the base for one month. Their twenty-fifth home in less than two years; after that they would have to find civilian housing.

Jim gave Meg a wonderful present. He put a blindfold on her and led her outdoors. "Honey, I have a big surprise for you." When he got her to the sidewalk, he took the blindfold off and yelled, "Surprise!"

"Oh, Jim! A black convertible with a white roof! It's just what I've always wanted!"

"Yup, it's a 1940 Mercury convertible, and you're going to have your first driving lesson right now. Get in."

Three months later Meg had her license. It was wonderful not to have to depend on others for rides.

ᾨ * ᾨ

They found their twenty-sixth home in Waterford, Connecticut, a lovely, furnished three bedroom house in a rural neighborhood. It felt like a palace to Meg.

Their next door neighbors, the Berninos, adopted them from the day they moved in. They had three young daughters, Ellie, Glo and Katie. Helen, the mother, was expecting a fourth child. The father, Gene, had a wonderful sense of humor. The Wrights were often invited over for delicious Italian dinners and card games. The young daughters loved to take care of Jimmy, and he was seldom out of their arms. He was like a doll to them. They taught him to walk and talk.

Helen was the Girl Scout leader for their area, but it became too much for her and she asked Meg if she would take over the troop. Meg was thrilled, having been a Girl Scout as a child. She had twelve girls in her troop and held the meetings at home. This new responsibility gave her a great sense of belonging to a community for the first time in her married life.

☒ * ☒

After two months of blissful living, the word was out that the *Pout* was not going into the shipyard yet. The captain received word from Washington that the "Guppy II" design plans wouldn't be completed for another couple of months.

That was good news to the officers and crew, until the captain decided that it didn't make sense to have the *Pout* just sitting in New London doing nothing. He volunteered for eight weeks of exercises in the West Indies, operating out of the naval base at Guantanamo Bay, Cuba, and going out on maneuvers as far away as the Canary Islands off the coast of Morocco.

Jim, like the other officers, was furious with the captain and made a promise to Meg. "I'm not going to have you putting up with this anymore, Meg. If we don't stay in New London, when we get back, I swear I'll get out of the Navy. The captain assured us that we definitely would be in the shipyard for six months when we got back."

Meg was not appeased by the promise and in an angry voice, lashed out at Jim. "I'm going to hold you to your promise of getting out, Jim, because I really don't believe a damn thing the captain says, and I don't want to go on living like a gypsy. I want a normal married life and so far I've had nothing even close to that!"

☒ * ☒

Although Meg and the other wives saw the *Pout* off, their farewells were subdued and indifferent.

Two new officers had come aboard, one a bachelor, Ensign Tim Allen, and Bart Richardson, whose wife, Mary had just arrived and was staying at the Mohegan Hotel. She had considered going home when she found out her husband was going out to sea, but Meg asked her to come and stay with her and Jimmy. Meg knew she'd enjoy Mary's company. She had liked her from the first moment they met. Mary, five years older than Meg, was a very relaxed, easy going person who loved children but had been unable to have a baby.

She told Meg, "I want you to know, I'll probably spoil Jimmy rotten, so don't say I didn't warn you."

Actually the two women were very compatible and thoroughly enjoyed each other's company.

◊ * ◊

Jim wrote almost every day about his adventures in the tropics. Meg also wrote regularly about her adventures in the cold, snowy weather of Connecticut.

Helen Sheehan, the exec's wife, who had stayed in Kansas City because she was pregnant with their third child, called Meg with some bad news. "Hi Meg, how are all you lonely wives doing there?"

"As well as can be expected. We're all furious with the skipper, though. I think he's going to lose all his officers if he keeps changing ports. How are you feeling, Helen?"

"I'm fine and glad to be in Kansas City, but I miss Pat terribly. Meg, I'm calling you because my brother-in-law, Pete, he's a commander stationed in Washington, just called with some bad news that I think you gals should know about. Maybe I shouldn't be telling you, but if I were there, I'd want to know."

"What is it Helen? Has something happened to the *Pout?*"

"No, everything's fine except that it won't be coming back to New London."

"What? Are you sure? Where are they going this time?"

"They'll go directly to Portsmouth, New Hampshire, into dry dock at the shipyard there for the conversion work instead of in New London."

"Oh, God, I can't believe it! Another move! Are you sure it's not just scuttlebutt?" Meg asked hopefully.

"Unfortunately, it's not. Pete said he saw the orders."

"Well thanks, Helen, for letting us know. I guess I'd better tell the other girls so they can make plans to vacate their houses here. We'll keep in touch with you. Hope to see you in New Hampshire."

Meg had all the wives over for coffee and dessert that night and broke the news to them. They were devastated and surprised that their husbands hadn't told them about the change.

Kate said sarcastically, "I'll bet that SOB of a captain hasn't even told the guys. I think this is where Jake and I'll get off the boat."

The others had the same thought.

The most ironic part of this change of orders to Meg would be that their two long-lost sea chests filled with their wedding gifts and household things had just caught up with them. The one that was aboard the *President Hayes* was due to be delivered at the end of the month, the day she would now have to move out of their wonderful home in Waterford.

In bed that night, Meg thought, maybe we won't have to move if Jim gets out of the Navy. We could continue to rent here in Waterford. But, what if he doesn't resign? She agonized over that thought all that night. She had never seriously contemplated ending their marriage, but she knew that she didn't want to go on living like a nomad any longer. These constant separations from Jim caused another problem for Meg. Lately, when he'd come home after being away for a month or two, he seemed like a stranger not only to Jimmy but to Meg as well. He acted as if he had only been gone for a day. He was anxious to make love, but Meg didn't share his enthusiasm. She needed a little time to adjust to him being back. It was a curious feeling that she couldn't explain to Jim.

✍ * ✍

Portsmouth, April 1947. The *Pout* returned from its eight weeks of exercises in the West Indies and went directly to Portsmouth. None of the officers or crew could get leave because it was necessary for them to be on duty as preparations were made for the boat to go into dry dock.

Jim called Meg before she moved out of the Waterford house and apologized profusely for the change in plans. "We were as shocked as you were when the skipper told us about the port change. But you know what, honey, it won't be too bad living in New Hampshire. You'll be a lot closer to your folks and friends. One thing's for sure, Meg, once the boat goes into dry dock, we'll definitely be staying here." He assumed that she and Jimmy would be coming right away to New Hampshire to look for a place to live.

He was shocked when Meg said, "I'm not sure what I'm going to do. Didn't you promise me that you were going to put in a request for your resignation if we had to move again? Have you done it?"

Jim was stunned, "You're right, Meg, I did promise you that." In a faltering voice he said, "I'll talk to the captain tomorrow, but it will take time, Meg. It has to go through Washington."

☙ * ☙

Meg's brother, Joe, took the train down to New London and helped Meg pack up and move back to Cambridge to stay with her mother and father. Her twenty-seventh move in two years of marriage.

Meg's parents shared her discouragement with her marriage. They had never been able to understand how Meg could live the way she did. "It's a terrible atmosphere for a child to be raised in," Margaret said.

Her parents loved Jim but agreed that he should get out of the Navy and devote more time to his family. It was hard for them to remain unbiased, because they could see that these long separations had taken a toll on their Meg. She needed a sense of security.

☙ * ☙

New Hampshire, June 1947. Jim's request for resignation was denied. He was informed that his skills as radar officer would be vital during the conversion work as an advisory technician. He was considered indispensable.

There was a severe shortage of Naval radar officers now because so many of them had retired and had sought lucrative civilian employment.

When Jim called Meg and told her why his resignation request was denied, he prayed that she would realize that it wasn't his fault and reconsider moving to New Hampshire. "Honey, if I can find us a nicely furnished beach house, would you consider coming up here?. I'm guaranteed to be here for at least six months."

Meg admitted to Jim that living at home with her folks was not an ideal situation. She felt so confined because her parents treated her like a child. Most of her friends were either married or going steady, which left her with little to do. Her life seemed empty. "I'll think about it, Jim."

A week later, Jim called, "Meg, you won't believe this wonderful beach house I found! We can rent it until the end of September, maybe longer. You'll love it! It's right on the water with four bedrooms, a big fenced-in back yard for Jimmy with a swing and a slide. It even has a rowboat! And guess what? It has a player piano with a whole trunk of rolls. You'll have a ball with that."

"It sounds great, Jim. But once the boat is out of dry dock, you will put in your request for resignation, won't you? I need you to promise me that and mean it."

"I will honey! Oh, I miss you and Jimmy so much. I don't want to live without you any more. I love you. I can't wait to see you."

✍ * ✍

Their twentieth-eighth home was in a lovely setting on a bay with a beach close by. It was an old house but fully furnished with everything they needed. It was a perfect place for entertaining Meg's family and friends, and they all came often. Her Dad loved to go out fishing in the row boat. Meg's mother spent most of her time at the player piano singing the old songs. Life was the best it had been for Meg for a long time and the future looked hopeful.

✍ * ✍

In keeping with the excitement level that seemed to prevail in Meg's life, two near-crises happened involving Jimmy.

The first occurred one afternoon when he'd been put down for a nap in his upstairs bedroom. Meg was sitting on the veranda reading. Suddenly, the elderly man across the street began yelling at her and pointing to the second story of the Wrights' house. "Holy mother of God. Look at that!"

"What's the matter?" Meg yelled as she raced down the steps and looked up. Jimmy was hanging out over the window sill. The screen was hanging by only one corner.

With lightening speed, Meg raced into the house, and upstairs into Jimmy's room. Her heart stopped. His little body was hanging out of the window. His little hands were tightly grasping the window sill. She grabbed his arms and pulled him inside. She was limp with fear as she hugged and kissed him. Her heart pounded frantically as she thought, Oh, my God, in another minute, he would have fallen to the street below. She saw that he had unscrewed three of the screws that held the screen onto the window frame. This was the first time he had crawled out of his crib. Holding him tightly, she said, "Thank you, God, and thank you good fairies too! I'm glad you're still around."

That night, Jim secured all the screens on the second floor with reinforcements. But now that Meg knew Jimmy could get out of his crib, she'd have to keep a closer watch on him.

About a month after this incident, another frightening episode occurred. Kate was visiting with Mike, who was one month younger than Jimmy. The two boys were playing in the back yard while the women had a coke in the kitchen. It was a safe place to play because the high fence was not climbable, and the gate latched from the outside. The women were alerted to trouble when they heard Mike crying loudly, "Mummie! Mummie!"

"My God, Kate, he's not calling from the back yard. His voice is coming from the water side."

The girls fled out of the house and raced to the water. Jimmy was standing in the teetering row boat and pulling on Mike's legs, which were slipping off the metal ladder that went down to the boat.

Meg jumped into the water and Kate leaned over the sea wall and rescued the screaming Mike from the ladder. Meg reached into the boat and moved Jimmy towards the bow where Kate grabbed him.

When they got the two howling babies up to the house, Kate said to Meg half seriously, "I don't think I'm going to let my Mikey play with Jimmy anymore. He's always in trouble."

"Oh, Kate I'm so sorry. I just can't understand how they got out."

"Let's go look and see," Kate suggested.

The mothers discovered a hole under the fence which was hidden by tall grass. There was just enough space for the two babies to squeeze through.

Jim filled in the hole that night and had a long talk with his two-year-old son.

& * &

Their landlord, Mr. Garrett, had told them he would extend their lease until the end of the year, but he changed his mind. "I want you out the first of September."

Meg immediately began to search for a house. The boat was still in dry dock, and probably would be for at least another couple of months. Jim would have to stay until the job was done. If Meg could find a place to live, she decided that she and Jimmy would stay until Jim heard from Washington about his retirement status.

Jim and Helen Sheehan had rented a large six-bedroom house in Rye Beach and invited Jim and Meg to stay with them until they found something. It was always fun to be with the Sheehans, and Jimmy loved living in the same house with other children. The Wrights had to stay with the Sheehans, their twenty-ninth move, for only two weeks. Luckily, when Meg was shopping in the small neighborhood grocery store, the owner, Mr. Carbury, said, "Mrs. Wright, if you're still looking for a house, there's a real nice furnished one across the street that's for rent."

Meg immediately inquired, and the owner agreed to rent to the Wrights on a month to month basis. Three days later, they moved into their thirtieth home just off Route 1 in Rye Beach, New Hampshire. It was a delightful neighborhood, with many children. The town had built a skating rink nearby, and Meg taught Jimmy how to skate on double runners. It was a wonderful feeling to be skating again. Meg hadn't realized how much she missed it. Soon she was teaching all the little neighborhood girls how to do spins and jumps.

It was a frigid winter with many fierce snowstorms, which seemed even more ferocious because the Wrights lived about 500 feet from the ocean.

The people next door had just bought a new chair and had put the large box outside because it wouldn't fit in the trash barrel. The neighborhood kids played in it. An older girl who was twelve was babysitting Jimmy while Meg went to the store on the corner of the street. When Meg came out of the store something caught her eye on Route one, the highway in front of their house. A large box was moving slowly down the highway. A car passed it on the ocean side. It now moved faster.

The babysitter that Meg had hired, came running up to her. "Mrs. Wright, I can't find Jimmy! He was here just a minute ago, honest."

"Were you playing with a big cardboard box?"

"Yes, we were putting it over our heads to keep warm."

Meg didn't need to hear more. She handed her groceries to the girl and raced up the highway to where the box was still moving. She saw a car coming in the distance. Quickly, she raced to the box and pushed it off the road just as the car passed. Jimmy was crying because he couldn't get out of the box. Meg lifted the box off him and held him tightly in her arms and carried him home. There was no doubt that between the good Lord and the good fairies, Jimmy led a charmed life.

♌ * ♋

The Wrights celebrated Thanksgiving and Christmas with Meg's family in Cambridge. It had been so long since they had this kind of a family reunion.

On January 7, 1948, they celebrated their third wedding anniversary at a lovely old country inn and had dinner next to a roaring fireplace.

"Happy third anniversary honey, we made it," Jim said with exuberance as they toasted with champagne, and kissed.

"Just about," Meg said with a sly smile. "Let's hope our fourth is in our own home, and you are happily employed in an exciting civilian job."

"In California," Jim said enthusiastically.

"I'll drink to that," Meg said with hope in her heart.

⚘ * ⚘

The "Guppy II" conversion work on the *Pout* was nearing completion. This type of submarine was unique because of the snorkle, a large telescoping tube that supplied air to the engines. It was located to the rear of the periscope shears, extending slightly out of the water when submerged, continuously opening and closing. Other "Guppy II" modifications included streamlining the superstructure and increasing the battery capacity. These two improvements allowed the sub to stay submerged longer and go faster.

Jim was electronics and communications officer. The captain thought very highly of his electronic and mechanical skills and decided to give him a new title, "Snorkle Officer." That meant more responsibilities, and it also meant that Jim's chances of having the captain approve his resignation were zero. He dreaded having to tell Meg. Their life seem to be so contented right now.

The *Pout* was taken out of dry dock the second week of January and went out for a week of sea trials around the Portsmouth area.

When it returned to port, the captain called Jim into his quarters and tossed Jim's resignation request across the desk at Jim. "This bullshit has just come back from Washington. What the hell's the matter with you? You knew damn right well that I wouldn't approve it, couldn't approve it! Where the hell am I going to get an officer to replace you in a hurry? On Friday, we're shoving off for a thirty-day undersea voyage to our new home port, Key West. Request denied, Lieutenant Wright." The captain left the cabin without another word.

Jim was speechless. His stomach tightened in a knot. A new home port. Oh, God, how can I tell Meg? She'll never go for another move so soon. Jim had known that they would probably be changing home ports, but not so soon. Why couldn't the Skipper have given us a little more warning?

Over the boat's loud speaker came a message, "Now hear this, the entire ship's officers and crew will assemble dockside at thirteen hundred."

At thirteen hundred, the captain announced, "I've been advised by COMSUBLANT that the *Pout* has been transferred from Squadron Eight to Squadron Four. At zero eight hundred on 9 January we will leave Portsmouth and will proceed to our new home port of Key West, Florida. No leaves will be allowed at this time."

Shock covered the faces of the crew. To the married men, especially those with children, it was a catastrophe. The officers glanced sideways at each other. When they were dismissed, they all gathered in small groups and began discussing the startling news.

"The son-of-a-bitch just loves to keep moving."

"What are the chances of getting housing there?"

"Key West is the pits. It's four miles wide and four miles long and the population is all Cuban."

"I'm getting out!" Jake said.

"Me too!" Al agreed.

Pat Sheehan, who was the executive officer and second in command to the captain, said, "Jake, Jim and Al, come'on, let's go to the O.C. for lunch and a drink. We have to talk."

The men took a table in the corner for privacy. Their biggest concern was telling their wives.

"Hey, Pat, you know how Meg feels. How the hell am I going to tell her we're moving out again?"

"I don't know the answer to that question, but I'll tell you this, I'm putting in my resignation. I should have done it when the war was over. I'm sending Helen and the three kids back to K.C."

Jake said, "I'm with you, Pat. Kate has been on my back for the last couple of years to get out. This will do it!"

Al Helms added, "Me too."

Jim then told them what happened that morning when the captain saw his request for resignation. "I think the main problem is that I'm not one of the good old boys from the Naval Academy and therefore I don't have the privileges that you guys do."

Pat looked at Jim and nodded his head up and down in a knowing way. "That could be the case, Jim, but aside from that, I know the skipper thinks your an electrical genius and he probably couldn't make this trip if you weren't aboard."

🖎 * 🖎

Meg knew the moment Jim came through the door that he had bad news. He put his arms around her and held her tightly. When he let go and looked at her, his eyes were filled with tears. He said, "Meg," in a choked voice...then looked away, squeezing his eyes to hold back the tears.

Meg look at him in dismay, "You're shipping out again..."

"Yes," Jim uttered.

A terrible sense of abandonment filled Meg. She felt like her whole life, her marriage, her whole world was collapsing. She clenched her fists and forced back the anger that was building inside her. "Go on, tell me what's happening; no sense in putting it off."

They sat down at the kitchen table across from each other. Meg lit a cigarette with shaking hands.

Jim repeated word for word everything that had transpired since the boat returned to Portsmouth this morning.

Meg never interrupted. When he was through, she got up, lit another cigarette and walked to the window with her back to Jim. She knew there was nothing he could do about the situation. The question was, what was she going to do?

🖎 * 🖎

In a silent protest to the captain, the wives decided not to see the *Pout* off at the dock. Instead the officers, their wives and their children all had a seven A.M. breakfast at Pat's house to say their farewells. It was a very emotional morning; it was the end of an era. Within the next week, one by one each of the wives packed up and left. None went to Key West.

🖎 * 🖎

Exhausted and depressed, Meg loaded up her car with all she could fit inside, and tied the crib, high chair and stroller onto the roof. Yesterday, the Navy had picked up the crates she wanted shipped to Cambridge. When she and Jimmy left New Hampshire, it began snowing and continued until they reached her parent's home in Cambridge, her thirty-first move in three years of marriage.

TWENTY-NINE

*C*ambridge, January 1948. Harvard Square began to look like it did in the pre-war days. Happy-go-lucky college students in civvies were again dashing to classes through the square. Cambridge servicemen came home to a different world than the one that they remembered and dreamt about while they fought for their country in foreign lands. Maturity had been swift for them, and they soon realized that the good old days with the gang in Harvard Square could never be recaptured. But many needed that familiar solace and often headed to the old meeting place in the square, the Georgian Restaurant. But now, instead of "shooting the bull" over cokes and coffee, they would go around the corner for beers at the Oxford Grill on Church Street or at Cronin's on Dunster Street.

Jobs were scarce now that all the defense plants had closed down. Some had begun converting to peacetime production. Servicemen were encouraged to set up their own small businesses with government loans and their separation pay. Many went back to finish high school or took advantage of the GI Bill of Rights, which allotted them $500 a year for college tuition along with a living allowance. Out of work ex-servicemen could collect financial aid from a government program called "the 52-20 club," which paid them $20 a week for 52 weeks.

ø * ⍥

Meg's life in Cambridge seemed dull. Usually when she came home, she was filled with a warm feeling of belonging, but this time, her anxiety over the future with Jim, continuously troubled her. The days were not bad because usually, Meg, and her sister-in-law, Eileen, did things together. It was the evenings that were depressing. Many of her old "club" girl friends were married or had moved away. Her old best friend, Babs, was dating a law school student, and they didn't seem to have much in common any more.

A next-door neighbor, Ann Foley, who was single and a year younger than Meg, asked her to go bowling down the square one night.

Meg's mother encouraged her to go. "I'd wish you'd quit moping around the house with that sad face. You should be with your husband. That's where a wife belongs."

"Mom. Why do keep saying that? I'm sick of hearing you say it! You think Jimmy and I should go to Key West to live in some filthy bug-infested hotel room, and probably see very little of Jim? No thank you, I've had enough of that life."

Meg's father stood up and yelled, "Hey, cut it out you two. How the hell do you expect me to hear the radio? I don't seem to have any peace around here any more between you two fighting and Jimmy jabbering all the time."

Meg was stunned and hurt. Her father had never talked to her like that before. In the past, she had always felt that she could come home anytime and be welcomed with open arms. But things weren't the same this time. Bill had been having more frequent ulcer attacks; he was not his usual jolly self anymore.

Meg apologized, put Jimmy to bed and called her next door neighbor, Ann, to say she'd like to go bowling. Staying with her parents obviously was not the answer to her housing dilemma.

Ann was a very popular, pretty blond girl who had a wonderful glib sense of humor.

After bowling, the girls joined some of their old high school friends at the Oxford Grill for a drink.

On their way home, Meg was feeling maudlin and said, "I'm glad I came with you tonight, Ann. It feels good to be with my own kind of people again. It sort of reinforces the feeling I've always felt about Cambridge. We really enjoy being with each other. Right?"

"Right! You planning on joining Jim in Key West?" Ann asked bluntly. Meg had not discussed Jim with Ann.

Hesitating, Meg answered slowly, "Ah, I don't know. Honest to God, Ann, I really don't know what I'm going to do. I really want Jim to get out of the Navy. He says housing in Key West is awful, but living with my folks isn't working out too well either. Jimmy gets on my dad's nerves, and my mother gets on mine."

"Boy, if I were you I'd swap all that and this freezing weather for Key West in a minute even if I had to pitch a tent."

Meg laughed, and then became thoughtful. "Hey, I just had a crazy idea, Ann. Could you take off work for, say a couple of weeks? Maybe we could drive down to Key West together for a little vacation. I could look around and see just how bad the housing situation is. I'll pay for the hotel room, or the tent!"

"I'd love it, Meg! Let's do it! Of course, you know I don't drive, but I'm a hell of a navigator."

"Great" Meg whooped. It felt like a giant weight had been lifted from her shoulders. When they pulled up to Ann's house, Meg asked, "When could you leave, Ann?"

"Well, I don't want to seem overly anxious, but keep the motor running, and I'll be back in a flash with my toothbrush and pajamas."

⚬ * ⚬

Jim had been both surprised and happy when Meg called. "We're coming for a vacation only, Jim. I don't know how long we'll stay, but try to find us a clean hotel. We should arrive in Key West on February 24."

"You couldn't make it the 25th, could you, because..."

Meg didn't allow him to finish his sentence. "Oh, of course, naturally, you'll be out to sea. That's okay, just leave the name of the hotel at the sentry gate. We'll manage. We usually do."

Meg's sarcasm jarred, Jim. "Sorry about that. We'll be back in on the 25th, and I'll see you the minute I get in. I love you, Meg, and thanks so much for coming to Key West."

⚬ * ⚬

On February 20, Meg, Jimmy and Ann left snow-covered Cambridge in the Mercury convertible for the southernmost city in the United States. They had made a play area for Jimmy in the back seat. He seemed to enjoy the whole idea of "hitting the road" again. Hopefully, Meg would be able to continue Jimmy's potty training during the trip and had brought along a few coke bottles with corks. Jimmy liked this new method.

Meg had an AAA "strip map" for the trip. Ann's job would be to guide Meg onto the correct routes.

Driving through New York, Ann exclaimed, "Wow! This is so exciting. Here we are, two Cambridge girls, making our way through the great metropolis of New York. But I must say it's a little confusing now." She studied the map.

Meg had never driven in this kind of traffic before and after crossing the George Washington Bridge, Meg asked, "What do we do now?"

Ann said, "Now we have to go through the Holland tunnel."

"Are you sure, Ann? I think we're already in New Jersey."

"No. Well, that's the way it looks on this map. Both the bridge and the tunnel are at the bottom of this page, and the next page is New Jersey. So I think we have to go through the tunnel."

When they got to the end of the tunnel, Meg spotted a sign that indicated that they were back in New York! She stopped the car as they came out of the tunnel, rolled down the window and yelled to the attendant directing traffic, "Are we in New Jersey or New York?"

He looked at her like she was crazy. "Ya just come from Joysey, lady! Where do ya wanna be?"

Meg put her head down on the wheel. "New Jersey."

Ann apologized, showing the markings on the map. "Honest to God, Meg, it looked like we had to do both the bridge and the tunnel."

The attendant yelled at them, "Move it!" The agonizing look on Meg's face, softened the gruff man. "Okay, okay. I'll get youse turned around. Cut ya wheels real hard to the left. Okay. Now youse ah gonna go right over da curb, and back into da other side of da tunnel which is going to take ya to Joysey. Go!" he commanded loudly.

Meg made the maneuver expertly, and Ann leaned out her window, blew him a kiss and yelled, "We love you!"

"Ya, ya, ya, sure," He yelled, resuming his forceful hand motions which directed the heavy traffic.

Now it was five o'clock, and Meg faced the greatest driving challenge of her life, Pulaski Highway at peak traffic. Meg didn't tell Ann how frightened she was being trapped in the middle lanes. Once the traffic thinned, Meg edged her way to the right lane. The mixture of fear and fumes had made her nauseated. She pulled off the highway and vomited.

That was the worst of the trip. They stayed at motels every evening and splurged on dinners. As they drove farther South, they were shocked at the poverty of both colored and white families along Route 1. When they entered Georgia, they were horrified to see the chain gangs working along the highways. They had only seen this kind of penal punishment in movies. The inhumanity of it revolted them. The way the men were connected and confined to each other by heavy chains made them seem like animals. They couldn't get out of Georgia quickly enough.

The last 120 miles of the journey across the Overseas Highway was spectacular. Sometimes it was just them on the bridge road surrounded by the Atlantic Ocean with nothing in sight. Every now and then they'd come to a key with little villages.

About 50 miles out to sea, the radiator began to boil over. Meg stopped the car, got out and lifted the hood. The rusty water was sizzling out from the radiator cap. There was nothing they could do but wait for it to cool down and hope someone with water would stop and help. It was an eerie, lonely feeling being so far out to sea in an automobile. A half an hour went by, and the only car that passed did not even slowed down.

"Meg, did you take biology in school?" Ann asked.

"Sure. I dissected a frog and a worm."

"Do you remember that we learned that urine is one of the purest liquids in the world because of all the filtering it goes through in the body before it comes out?"

"And, it's ninety-five percent water! Are you thinking what I'm thinking--Jimmy's wee-wees," Meg said and burst out laughing.

"Worth a try!" Ann said. "There are two filled bottles back here" Meg unscrewed the radiator cover and Ann carefully poured Jimmy's urine into the opening.

Meg hopped back into the car. "Say a prayer!" She turned on the ignition and to their delight, the engine turned over and the temperature needle stayed on normal. "It worked! Come'on, get in, Ann. Key West, here we come."

When they got to the next Key, they stopped and had the radiator filled with one hundred percent H2O.

THIRTY

*K*ey West, Florida, February 24, 1948. They arrived in Key West at noon and went directly to the base. The guard at the gate asked for their pass.

"I don't have a pass. We just arrived here from Massachusetts. My husband is stationed here aboard the *Pout*. He was to leave a message for me here at the sentry box with the name of the hotel where we would be staying. My name is Mrs. Wright."

"I'll look, Ma'am," the Marine guard said and went into the guard house.

The hot sun felt wonderful as they waited in the open convertible.

"Ma'am, the *Pout* is out to sea, Ma'am. Won't be back until tomorrow, Ma'am. I can't find any message here for you, Ma'am."

"Could you call the chaplain's office for me?" Meg asked, getting more upset by the minute. I'm sure he'll be able to help us."

The Marine returned in a few minutes and said, "The chaplain's office is not answering, Ma'am. He's probably out to lunch, Ma'am. Why don't you come back at one o'clock, Ma'am."

In exasperation, they drove off the base towards downtown Key West. Ann, in her usual good humor said, "Ma'am, you have to admit, Ma'am, that Marine is the most polite person you've ever met, Ma'am! Let's find a hotel, Ma'am, have lunch, and go back to the base later, Ma'am."

Ann always made light of any situation. She had a great attitude, and Meg needed her moral support right now.

They found a small, reasonably clean hotel on a main street of the quaint little island, where all the stores and homes were covered with peeling pastel paint and filigreed trim. Giant palm trees grew everywhere.

The three fair-skinned blondes were in the minority. They saw only dark-skinned Cubans who were handsome people and who smiled easily but moved very slowly.

They walked into the hotel and were stared at by the men sitting around in the lobby. They were exhausted and hungry and went into the small dining room and bar. The men at the bar turned and stared at them. They were all Cuban except for one. He was a very handsome man with a square-jawed face. His brown hair was curly and closely-cropped. He was wearing a three-piece glen plaid suit but had removed his jacket. It was slung over his shoulder where it hung by his thumb. His white shirt-sleeves were rolled up, and his tie was loosened. He lit a cigarette and turned to blow the smoke away when he glanced at the women, nodded and smiled. His cheek dimples matched the deep cleft in his chin.

They smiled back. They ordered BLTs and cokes for themselves and a jelly sandwich and milk for Jimmy.

When they finished lunch, they picked up the small bags they had taken into the hotel and began to leave.

The attractive white man at the bar got up and came toward them and said, "Ladies, I'm assuming you have just arrived (pointing to our small bags). I don't want to seem bold, but I just thought I'd caution you about this hotel, if you were thinking of staying here. It's not one of the better places on this island for two young ladies and a baby."

"Well, thank you," Meg said. We had already made that decision."

"Just thought I'd warn you. Do you have a place to stay?"

"I hope so. My husband is on a submarine here, but it's out to sea. He said he'd leave the name of our hotel with the sentry at the gate, but the sentry said there was no message. We just arrived from Massachusetts. I'm going back to the base and get my Irish up if he won't let us in to see the chaplain."

"I'm staying at the base. I'm sure I can get you in. I have a pass. If you feel comfortable about it, I'll drive back with you."

"We'd appreciate that," Ann said giving him a coy smile. "Are you a submariner too?"

"No, I'm just on an assignment here. Are you both Navy wives?"

"I am. I'm Meg Wright, and this is my son, Jimmy, and this is Ann Foley, my friend who was my navigator on our trip down south."

"Nice to meet you. I'm Tom McAvoy, another Irishman."

When they got to the gate at the base, Tom McAvoy got out of the car and walked over to the Marine. They talked for a few minutes, and both went inside the guard house.

Tom came out a few moments later waving an envelope in his hand and grinning broadly. "Mrs. Meg Wright, here's a letter from your husband, I presume. It was tucked away neatly under a coffee cup and a half eaten donut."

Relieved, Meg said, "I knew he wouldn't go out to sea without letting us know where to stay."

Jim's note said that he had made reservations for them at the Overseas Hotel and that he'd be back tomorrow around five. He'd said they'd have a reunion dinner at the Officer's Club.

They thanked Tom for his help.

"I'll probably see you girls at the swimming pool at the Officer's Club. That's where we hang out. Say, why don't you come into the base now, Meg, and go see the chaplain about a temporary pass."

"That a great idea. We'll do it."

The Marine sentry saluted them as they drove through the gate and said to Meg, "Sorry, Ma'am."

They let Tom off at the BOQ.

The chaplain gave them a pass and directions to the Overseas Hotel, their thirty-second move.

❧ * ❧

The nice things about the hotel: the room was large and clean and had a laundry cart for Jimmy's bed. But the tell-tale spray can of roach killer under the sink upset Ann.

"You'll get used to them," Meg assured her. "Insects are standard equipment wherever the Navy goes."

Meg had planned that she, Jimmy and Ann would stay at the hotel and Jim would stay at the BOQ, unless they found an apartment that could accommodate the four of them.

It was extremely hot and humid in Key West. They unpacked quickly, got into their bathing suits and cover-ups, and took off for the base swimming pool.

This time, the Marine guard recognized them, saluted and waved them through. The girls smiled at him, and Jimmy saluted him back.

The recreation area at the submarine base was beautiful. Besides the enormous pool, there was a kiddie pool for Jimmy, a sand box, shuffleboard, tennis courts, a snack bar, and an air conditioned cocktail lounge called "Echoasis," with slot machines. A poster outside the lounge advertised a "Penny Cocktail Hour Every Evening from 5-7. Buy One and Get Another for a Penny."

After reading the sign, Ann said, "Hey, Meg, I'm going to like this life. Maybe I'll join the Navy."

Only a few other women were at the pool when they arrived, and quite a few men who all seemed to know each other. For several obvious reasons, Meg was certain that they were not submariners. They were probably in their forties and older.

Within ten minutes after their arrival, Meg noticed two men talking to Jimmy, who was playing in the kiddie pool. Jimmy pointed to Meg several times and said, "Mommy."

Meg and Ann were just enough out of earshot not to hear what the men had asked Jimmy, but Ann commented, "Obviously they want to know which of us is his mother."

The two men sauntered past the women, smiling politely.

"My God, they're obviously looking us over," Ann remarked under her breath.

A handsome man carrying a tennis racquet, walked past the women, nodded and said "Good afternoon."

Meg said softly, "Wow, is he handsome. I think I've seen him before."

Ann added, "For a minute I thought he was Errol Flynn."

Laughter came from directly behind the women's lounging chairs. Then a man faced the women and said loudly, "Errol Flynn. That's a hot one. Boy, will his head swell when I tell him what you women said. That's Frank Bourgholtzer. You've probably seen him in the newsreels. He's an NBC newscaster."

The jovial man had a happy face and a bit of a pouch above his baggy bathing trunks. He extended his hands outward and said in a bravado voice, "And, you lucky ladies are looking at none other than Tames of the *Times*, the *New York Times.*"

Just then a loud voice called out, "Thar she blows," and a huge man who must have weighed at least 300 pounds jumped into the pool right near the women, causing a splash that completely soaked them.

"You louse, Rous, you've ruined my coiffure," Tames of the *Times* yelled as he pushed his thinning, wet hair back with his hands. Everyone around the pool was laughing.

"Is he a friend of yours, Mr. Tames?" Ann asked as she rubbed her soaking hair with a towel.

"That's Johnny Rous from the Associated Press. He just did that to get your attention. He's about as subtle as a ten ton truck. Loves to show off his beautiful body. And by the way, call me, George."

"George, what are all you newsmen doing here? Are you having a convention or something?" Meg asked.

George turned around and yelled out, "Attention, please. This lovely lady wants to know what we're all doing here. Let's hear it, fellows!"

In unison, the men around the pool yelled, "Harry brung us!"

"Harry who?" Ann asked.

"The one and only Harry, our president, Harry Truman!" George said, grinning broadly.

"The president's here?" Meg uttered in a startled voice. She looked around the pool area to see if he was among the men.

Another man sauntered over, extended his hand to Ann and Meg and said, "Hi, ladies, he's not here. The president has his own private beach. I'm Frankie Cancellare from *Acme News Pictures*. Is this guy bothering you?"

Within the next hour the women met most of the newsmen. They learned that the president loved Key West and when he wanted to get away from it all he would fly to Key West on the presidential plane the *Sacred Cow* and take along what he referred to as his "circus," which consisted of his staff Secret Service personnel, cronies and newsmen. The president stays at the commandant's house on the base, and calls it the Little White House. The rest of his circus stayed at the BOQ.

During the afternoon, the women heard fascinating stories about President Truman, President Roosevelt and "off the record" information about world events.

The women learned that Harry Truman was the newsmen's favorite president, and in turn the president loved them.

"Especially the White House News photographers!" George bragged. "Do you know what *Coronet Magazine* said about us? They said, 'We're the boys who boss the president. We've been known to frighten foreign visitors, intimidate provincial politicians, reduce statesmen to a confused gibberish, and publicly shout orders at the president himself.' We've been accused of being brassy and irreverent."

"Don't forget handsome and great lovers," someone added.

Meg and Ann enjoyed the banter tremendously. Ann's clever, quick retorts were thoroughly enjoyed by the men. She coquettishly asked, "So, if you're on such intimate terms with the president, how about introducing us?. Maybe you could arrange just a little tete-a-tete."

"I'll see that you meet him," a familiar voice said as he pulled up a chair next to the ladies. It was Tom McAvoy.

George looked at Tom and said, "Let me introduce you to these lovelies."

"We've already met, George," Tom answered and grinned.

"You couldn't have met them; they just got here!" George challenged.

"Ah, but I did. I saw these two damsels in distress downtown, and helped them out, and in return, they drove me back to the base."

"These women have a car? At last, we have transportation!" George cried dramatically.

It was true. The press corps didn't have a car available to them, only taxis which were none too reliable.

Ann asked Tom, "So, Tom, are you famous like the rest of these guys?"

"Not as famous as Tames of the *Times*, of course," Tom quipped.

Then, George, expounded on Tom's accomplishments, "Tom is *Life Magazine's* most famous photographer. Noted for extraordinary assignments in WWII. It's been said that he photographed President Roosevelt more than anyone else. He's..."

Tom interrupted him, "Knock it off, George. You're embarrassing me."

"I was just going to tell Ann that you're too old for her."

"Geeze, George, I'm a kid compared to you."

Most of the congenial men were at least fifteen to twenty years older than Meg and Ann. All had outgoing personalities and loved to tease and kid with each other. Most were married with children. Their assignment to cover the President's stay in Key West was boring. Harry Truman made very little news while vacationing on the small island.

They told the women that the biggest excitement they'd had so far was watching a cockfight and a striptease called the "Marijuana Dance."

Before the afternoon was over, Ann had been asked out by a Secret Service agent and several newsmen who were all single.

Later in the afternoon, Meg and Ann enjoyed meeting and talking with two Bostonians, Matt Connelly, first secretary to the president, and James Nickerson, who was with the Secret Service and had, at one time, been a close associate of James Michael Curley, the infamous Massachusetts governor.

By four o'clock, the women and Jimmy were ready to go back to the hotel. They were tired and sunburned.

As they were leaving, they were invited by Tony Vaccaro, president of the White House Correspondents Association, to a dinner with the entire presidential party at the Officer's Club the next evening.

Meg said, "We accept, If I can bring my husband."

Jokingly, Tony gave Meg a bored look, "Well, okay, if you insist."

When they were driving back to the hotel, Ann asked Meg, "Do you think Jim will mind the change in plans for dinner tomorrow night?"

"No, I think he'll enjoy it, but I hope we can find a baby sitter for Jimmy."

ᴂ * ᴂ

Meg asked their talkative waitress at the Overseas Hotel dining room if she knew of any houses to rent on the island.

"There's not much that you'd want to rent, but I know about a place that might work for you. It's in an all Cuban neighborhood. Mr. Morales, the owner, built an addition onto his house for his son who was to be married, but the wedding's been called off. I'll give you the address, and you can go take a look. Tell him Rosa sent you. Just don't expect too much."

The women drove to the Williams Street address. Mr. Adolfo Morales was a big man with dark olive skin, large black eyes shaded by bushy eyebrows, a full curly beard and large white teeth. He spoke English with a strong lyrical Cuban accent and never stopped smiling. The apartment was connected to a two story house that went off in many different directions it seemed. Mrs. Morales, a pretty but tired looking woman, hovered behind her husband as he showed the women the apartment, which didn't take long.

The front room, which Mr. Morales called the living room, was about fifteen feet long and ten feet wide. There were no windows, just screens, although Mr. Morales did point out, in the corner of the room, a small blue pane of glass he called a "voodoo" window. "You know, to ward off evil spirits," he shrugged and smiled. The walls were unpainted, and the floors were bare concrete.

The room had a couch, a table and four unmatched chairs. Behind this room was a combination kitchen/bedroom. The kitchen consisted of a combination two-burner gas stove and oven, a sink, and a small refrigerator. The bedroom had a small closet with a colorful drape for a door, a large bureau, a double bed and, a crib. The bathroom had a toilet, stall shower and sink. It was in good shape except for the fact that there was no ceiling.

Meg asked Mr. Morales about the missing ceiling.

"I'm making a trap door so we can get up to a storeroom up there," he assured her, "I'll do ceiling for you, manana. Don't you worry bout that, Missus."

Mrs. Morales said, "We'll keep it clean and give you linens, towels, dishes, pots and pans, whatever you need, okay?"

Although Meg was tempted, she told Mr. Morales, "I want my husband to see it first."

"You better hurry up, Missus. Lots of people want to rent it. It's good rent, only fifty-six dolla for month. You stay as long as you want, okay? But, you gotta tell me by manana or too bad for you."

"Okay. We'll let you know manana, Mr. Morales," Meg said, getting with the local lingo.

Meg and Ann broke up laughing once we were out of earshot of the house.

"My God, the place is a catastrophe," Meg said.

"But you have to admit, it's unique," Ann said. "It's air conditioned. You'll never have to wash windows. There's a great view of the storeroom from the bath, and you'll never have to vacuum carpets."

⚹ * ⚹

The next day Meg and Ann went to the few real estate offices in town. Only unfurnished houses were available, and a few rooms with "kit. priv." were advertised in the *Key West Citizen,* but Meg refused to go through that again. Besides, she wasn't sure if she wanted to stay after Ann left.

⚹ * ⚹

The women and Jimmy were on the dock when the *Pout* arrived. None of the other wives had come to Key West. Excitement filled Meg when Jim ran down the gangway and took her and Jimmy in his arms. He thanked Ann for coming down with Meg. The other officers except for the captain joined in welcoming Meg and Ann.

Pat Sheehan asked Meg, "Where are you staying?"

"I haven't found a place yet."

"This place is the pits. Are you going to be okay here?"

"I'm not sure I'm staying, Pat."

"Yeah, Jim told me. I'm sorry that the captain didn't let Jim resign. You knew that he sent in his resignation again, and I'm going to help him get it this time. Jake and I have put in our resignations, too."

The captain walked by and gave Meg a cursory, "Hello, surprised to see you here."

"Just visiting," Meg said in an aloof tone.

⚓ * ⚓

Jim was astonished that Meg might consider living in the Morales' apartment after they "toured" the two rooms. They sat out in the car to talk about it. In Meg's mind, there was a lot at stake here. She didn't know if she was going to stay or go back with Ann. If she stayed, she'd rather have the apartment than a hotel room.

"Well, Meg, It's up to you. I want you and Jimmy here, but only if you're sure you want to live here. You know I'll be out to sea a lot."

"I'm not making any promises, Jim. I know I'd feel safer in the apartment than the hotel." Meg held her chin in her hand and looked pensive. "Let's see, this will be my thirty-third move if I include the Overseas Hotel, in a little over three years of marriage. I wonder if that's a record."

"You're a wonderful sport, honey," Jim said and wrapped Meg in his arms. "God, how I hate being away from you and Jimmy. But I feel sure that with Pat's help, I'll get out this time, then we can be together forever."

⚓ * ⚓

Delores, the Morales' married daughter, who lived in a room in the main house with her husband and their four-year-old son Frederico, had offered to baby-sit for the Wrights. She had told them, "I need to earn money because my husband, Miguel, can't find work."

The Morales also had two sons. Tomas, who was twenty, and out of work also, was to be married to a beautiful girl from Cuba, where they would live. Their wedding was delayed because the girl's family had not, as yet, made the customary prenuptial visit with gifts for the Morales family. The other brother, Carlos, a senior in high school also did not work. He was handsome, and quite flirtatious with Meg and Ann. Mr. Morales was also unemployed. It occurred to Meg that the rent from the apartment would come in very handy.

⚘ * ⚘

The Wrights moved in that afternoon. Meg and Ann didn't tell Jim about their new found friends at the base, or who they were. They thought it'd be fun to surprise him, especially after he said, "You'll never guess who is here at the base."

"Who?" the women asked in unison.

"President Truman!" Both women showed appropriate awe.

"Maybe we'll see him at the Club tonight," Meg said.

Ann added, "And, oh by the way, Jim, we met some very interesting guys at the pool yesterday, and they invited us to dinner at the Officer's Club tonight."

"A date already, Ann!" Jim exclaimed. "Well, from what our bachelor officer tells us, there aren't too many eligible women around here. You're going to be mighty popular, Ann!"

"I already am," Ann said, fluttering her eyelashes.

When they arrived at the Officer's Club, Meg said to the Maitre d', "Mr. Vaccaro's table, please."

They were directed to a private room where men were milling around.

George Tames spotted them, came over and welcomed them with his usual exuberance, "Ah, here's the lucky man. Nice to meet you, Lieutenant! I'm George Tames of the *New York Times*.

Soon, Jim realized who they were having dinner with. Besides the men the women had met at the pool, now they met more notable members of the presidential party, including Dewey Long, a presidential aide; Bill Hassett, the president's corresponding secretary, Jessie Sabin, *NBC Television Newsreel;* Bryson Rash, *ABC* newscaster; Bob Nixon, *International News Service;* Jim Rowley, Chief of the United States Secret Service; Stew Stout, U.S.S.S.; John Adams, *CBS*; Ted Berrier, a vice-president with AT&T, Bill McEvoy, a vice-president of Pan American Airlines; "Duck" Benson, *INP*. Everyone was there except Harry.

At dinner, Jim told the women that the president was going to inspect the *Pout* and would spend a little time with the officers and families. Tames of the *Times,* said they'd try to get a picture of Jimmy shaking hands with the president and put it on the wire service.

By the end of the exciting evening, there was no doubt about it. The Wrights and Ann had been adopted by the presidential party. During the course of that evening they had been invited to participate in some upcoming parties, a baseball game against the crew of the presidential plane, the *Sacred Cow*, and tennis matches.

⊗ * ⊗

Jim had very little time off because the *Pout*, which was still one of a kind at present, was always busy with special assignments. Also, he had the duty every third night.

Meg wanted a phone, but there were no lines on their street. Half in jest, she had asked Ted Berrier, the A.T. & T. vice president, "Mr. Berrier, could you use your influence and get a phone put in our apartment?"

"Write me a reminder, dear, and put it in my pocket and I'll see what I can do."

Within two days, a pole and lines were installed. Not only was Meg thrilled, but the Morales family was ecstatic. They had never had a phone. No one in the neighborhood had. When the Wrights' phone was being installed, the serviceman had asked Mr. Morales if he'd like to be hooked up.

Mr. Morales bragged to Meg, "Now, next to you, we are the most important people in the neighborhood."

⊗ * ⊗

The first time Meg used the oven, the wallboard behind the stove became so hot, it was smoking. She ran next door to get Mr. Morales.

"It's not a problem, Missus. It's not on fire, just hot! I'll do something about it manana."

Within a very short time, Meg had a long list of manana jobs that Mr. Morales had promised to do.

Jimmy enjoyed being around the Morales family, because he always had someone to play with. He particularly enjoyed playing army with Mr. Morales and Frederico in the back yard under a makeshift tent. The three of them would pretend they were on guard duty with homemade wooden rifles for the revolution.

"Revolution" became Jimmy's favorite word. He would imitate Mr. Morales by holding his right arm out, and yell, "Come the revolution!"

Mr. Morales would ask the two boys, "Are you ready? Here comes the Russians!"

The boys would answer, "Yes, sir!" Then they'd run around the perimeter of the yard shooting their rifles.

⊘ * ⊵

Jim told Meg and Ann to be down at the dock on Wednesday because the president was going aboard the *Pout.* They waited with the small crowd. When the president and the newsmen arrived, everyone applauded and the president waved. George Tames told Meg to stay put with Jimmy, and he'd get a photo of him with the president when he came over to shake hands with the civilians.

To fool the press, the president went down a forward hatch and came out a hatch on the stern. The newsmen raced to the other end of the sub to get a photo of him coming out of the hatch, but they were too late. He laughed at their dilemma and went back down the hatch, but came back up and paused for photos. That's why the press loved him.

At the same moment, Jimmy said, "I have to do wee wees, Mommy."

Jim quickly picked him up, "I'll take him in the building."

"Hurry, Jim," Meg urged.

Within minutes of their leaving, the president came down the gangway and headed toward the crowd. Jim had not returned.

George asked quickly, "Hey, where's Jimmy, Meg?"

"Had to go potty," She groaned.

"Shall I ask the president to wait until he gets back?" George asked good-naturedly, sensing her disappointment.

The president shook hands with everyone.

The Wrights were disappointed. It wasn't that they wanted the notoriety, they wanted their son to have the honor of being photographed with a president that Jim and Meg had admired greatly since the day he took office.

George said, "There might be another opportunity." But there never was.

⊘ * ⊵

A traumatic event took place the first Sunday they were in Key West. Jim had the duty and left early. Meg decided to go to Mass in town instead of at the base. Ann was not feeling well and said she'd stay home with Jimmy.

As was Meg's custom when she went to Mass for the first time in a new church, she'd sit in the last row. Just as she knelt down to say a prayer, a woman walking down the aisle touched her shoulder, and said, "You're sitting in the colored section, Miss. You don't want to sit there."

Meg was stunned! Her heart felt like someone had driven a knife into it, and she momentarily lost her breath. She was horrified. Tears flooded her eyes. There was no mistaking what the woman had said, white and colored people could not sit together in that church, that Catholic church. Meg was aware that in the South, white and colored used different public toilets and sat in different waiting rooms in train and bus stations. But in a church?

A gamut of emotions raced through her. She was enraged and deeply hurt to think that this kind of prejudice could take place in church, her perfect Catholic church.

At that moment, a colored woman and a little girl began to enter Meg's pew from the other end, but stopped. Their eyes met Meg's, and a puzzled look covered the woman's face. Meg motioned for them to come sit in the pew. The child looked wide-eyed at Meg, then up to her mother. At that moment a man leaned down close to Meg's head and said in a gruff voice, "Move, lady, this is the colored section!"

Meg sat stiffly in her seat. She would show them she didn't mind sitting with colored people. The shock of having this conflict of color happen in her church, strengthened her resolve to stay put.

Other colored people had now joined the woman and child. Their eyes moved from Meg to the front of the church. It was as if they were trying too signal her to move.

Meg wondered how they could just stand there so passively? How could they just accept the humiliation? Meg realized that most people in the church had now turned around and were whispering and staring at her.

Suddenly, a nun pinched Meg's arm, twisted the skin and said in an angry tone, "You've been told twice to sit somewhere else. Now get up! You're causing unnecessary trouble. Move! Mass is about to begin!" She squeezed Meg's arm more forcefully.

Childhood memories of another nun flashed through Meg's mind. Anger overwhelmed her. She clenched her fists tightly, rose and looked towards the altar as the priest and altar boys came out from the sacristy.

Meg looked back at the nun and literally snarled, "Take your hand off me, Sister." She broke from the nun's hold and said loudly. "I'm leaving! I don't want to be in a church that makes colored people sit in the back of the church. She pointed to the altar and yelled, "What kind of a priest are you to allow this to happen in God's house?"

Two men now grabbed her under the arms and began to drag her out of the church backwards. Something nagged at her as she took a last look at the colored people now filing into the pew. What was it? What's wrong? Suddenly it dawned on Meg that most of the people in the church were Cubans and dark-skinned, much darker skinned than the colored people.

The two men literally dropped Meg onto the sidewalk and went back into the church.

She was devastated. She was filled with the kind of painful emotion she had felt when her Nana and Aunt Nell had died. She got up, brushed her dress off and walked to her car. Tears were now running down her cheeks as she sat in the car and smoked a cigarette. Suddenly, she thought, Oh, my God, I can't miss Mass; it's a mortal sin. I'd better go to the base and wait for the next Mass.

When she arrived at the base chapel, Father Sparrow, the chaplain was just leaving. She called out to him, "Father, wait! I have to talk to you for a minute."

"Sure. What can I do for you?"

"I just walked out of Mass at St. Mary's By The Sea church."

"How come?"

She expected him to be shocked when she said, "Did you know that they make colored people sit in the back of the church there?"

"So..."

"Don't you think that's terrible?"

"Come on, Mrs. Wright, you're a big girl. What do you want to do, start another Civil War? That's the way it is down South."

"Is that all you can say? Do you think it's okay for the Catholic church to do such a disgraceful thing?"

"Mrs. Wright, my advice to you is either put up with it or go back up north."

"Do you make the colored people sit in the back of the chapel?"

"I don't have to. The colored servicemen know their place and sit in the back without being told."

Meg was outraged. "I'll never go to church again as long as I live here. My Catholic church doesn't exist here. And, it won't be a sin, Father. Or, maybe it is in your color-blinded eyes, but not in the eyes of God. Of that I'm sure. I'll never go to a church that separates colored and white people."

Storming out of the chapel a stinging message flashed across her mind, "Go home Yankee!" Meg never went to Mass again in Florida.

◟ * ◟

The president decided to leave Key West earlier than was planned. He missed his wife, Bess, and, daughter, Margaret. He would go back to Washington on Friday.

The word got out quickly around the pool. Most of the men were glad about the change in plans. It was getting too boring in Key West. They began planning a farewell party and invited Meg, Jim and Ann.

George Thames commented to Meg, "Hey, kiddo, you know you've never showed us your beautiful hacienda."

"Yeah," Johnny Rous added. "I want to see the wall smoke when you light the oven."

"And I want to see the ceiling-less bathroom and the blue voodoo window," Frankie Cancellare teased.

Tom McAvoy said, I want to have a little talk with your landlord, Mr. Morales, about the Russian invasion. I think I smell a story there. Cuba would be an ideal place to set up a Communist government."

"Seriously, Meg, why don't you invite us to dinner? Nothing elaborate, just a simple meal," George suggested.

Meg talked it over with Jim that night. Jim was reluctant. "The place is such a disaster, Meg. I just can't imagine inviting such important people to such a dump."

Meg asked him, "But it's good enough for Jimmy and me, huh? Aren't we important?"

"I'm sorry, honey. No, it's not good enough for you and Jimmy..."

"Never mind, never mind. It was my decision to come here and stay in this dump. They know all about this place, Jim. They'll think it's a kick."

Meg decided to have a spaghetti dinner on Wednesday night. The following night, Thursday, the presidential party's farewell affair would take place at the Officer's Club, and they'd leave for Washington on Friday.

Meg and Ann prayed that it wouldn't rain. Not having windows (just screens), meant flooded floors, sometimes with water up to their ankles. They would have to move everything up on the beds and pull all the electric cords out of the wall.

Key West rain was always torrential and usually ceased as abruptly as it began. But, it usually took about an hour for the rain to slowly go down the drains that had been installed in the concrete floor. And, the deluge was always followed by the arrival of huge hard-back cockroaches or palmettos as the locals called them. They were forced out of hiding by the water. Some were dead and floated on the tide, but others came out swimming for their life. Usually, Mr. Morales helped Meg and Ann use the mops and brooms and sweep the critters out the front door while singing, *Manana*. He did a hilarious imitation of the singer, Peggy Lee, snapping his fingers over his head and singing.

ぬ * ぬ

Meg borrowed pans from Mrs. Morales to cook the spaghetti, and Ann made a huge tossed salad in a borrowed bowl. Jim bought four loaves of Cuban bread, two gallons of Cuban red wine, paper plates, cups and napkins. He had to make two trips to the base to transport the twelve guests to the apartment.

Mr. Morales was thrilled at the prospect of having such distinguished guests at his house and put on a shirt, tie and jacket for the occasion. Mrs. Morales cooked a huge platter of fried bananas. Within minutes after the newsmen's arrival, Tom McAvoy engaged Mr. Morales in conversation about the possibility of a revolution and an invasion by the Russians. Mr. Morales was in his glory as he elaborated on his political opinions and an upcoming revolution, offering Cuban cigars to all the men.

Meg had sliced the Cuban bread lengthwise and buttered and sprinkled it with garlic powder. She folded the halves back together, and having no other place to keep them until dinner was ready, stored them in the oven. When she was ready to broil them, she took the loaves out and lit the oven.

Johnny Rous had just stepped into the kitchen to test the spaghetti for the fourth time and to watch the wall smoke.

When Meg opened the loaves of bread to put them in the oven to broil, she screamed in hushed panic! "Oh, my, God!" Two giant roaches were eating away at the center sections of the loaves.

Johnny Rous looked at the bread and said, "Yuck!"

Meg was mortified. "Oh, Johnny, quick, throw the bread out!"

"No way, Meg," Johnny said in a secretive voice. "I'll just take these monsters outdoors and be right back to cut out the sections they were eating." He came back in, winked at Meg who was still standing frozen, looking at the bread, and said, "See, I'll just kiss it up to God and slide it in the oven." Which he did.

Meg begged him, "Don't tell anyone. I'm so embarrassed."

"Mums the word, kiddo!"

🔖 * 🔖

The presidential farewell party on Thursday was at the Officer's Club, and everyone had to entertain, standard procedure at all their parties. Ann and Meg heard Tony Vaccaro announcing, "Now, we will have a song and dance by those two lovely Dolly Sisters from Boston." (The Dolly Sisters were an old vaudeville act, the women were told later.) They went on stage and began gesturing in cheerleader style and singing their old high school song.

Oh, that Cambridge girl is quite discrete
She's just a hundred per from head to feet
She's got that style, that smile, that winning way
And say, now there's a girl I'd like to know
And just to look at her, you'd recognize her way,
She's got that good old Cambridge vim and go
And just to look at her it's quite a treat,
She can't be beat, a Cambridge High and Latin girl!

The piano player had picked up the melody instantly, and when the song was over, he continued playing, and the audience boisterously yelled and whistled for more. Ann and Meg had practiced the waltz clog and began with a time step. They were doing fine until Meg kicked to the left and Ann kicked to the right. They cracked each others ankles so hard, they couldn't continue and limped off the stage to a standing ovation.

🔖 * 🔖

It was lonesome after the presidential party left. They certainly had given the Wrights, and Ann, many memorable fun times that they would never forget.

The following week, Ann had to fly home. Meg would really miss her. Up to now she hadn't suffered from the confinement of living on such a small island, but now she began to feel trapped and lonely.

They had been living in Key West for only eight weeks, when Jim came home early one afternoon at the end of March.

He had that look that Meg now recognized instantly. "I don't want to hear it, Jim!" she said before he had a chance to say anything.

"I know, honey, and none of the crew can believe it either," Jim said taking her into his arms.

Meg stiffened. "Just spill it out, Jim. Nothing you say will surprise me! What's the dope?"

"We're going back to Portsmouth, New Hampshire, and then on to Portsmouth, England. We're going to be involved in a joint operation with the British Navy off Northern Ireland.

Meg was shocked. "Why? The war is over!"

"B.J. volunteered our sub to take part in what he calls a plum assignment."

"For You, of course it is. You men. Good. I want to go home! When can we leave?"

"Honey, I, ah, have to go to Portsmouth with the boat. I don't have a choice. We'll ship the car to Cambridge and you and Jimmy can fly home."

Like a religious revelation, Meg suddenly knew that she couldn't go on living like this anymore. Their marriage was floundering seriously. She had played a game with the number of moves and houses since they were married and most often joked about it. But now, somehow she knew that game was over. She was worn out. She had reached her limit of tolerance for this kind of life that offered her nothing more than loneliness and uncertainty. She would again go home to Cambridge to the security and comfort of her family and friends and do some serious thinking about her future life.

Divorce was out of the question. It was forbidden by the church, and those who got divorced were automatically excommunicated and could not receive the sacraments. Along with that shame, the stigma of being divorced meant alienation from friends and many times from family. It was a step Meg would never even consider. The alternatives were an annulment of the marriage, which was not possible because they had a child, and a legal separation. That she would even think in terms of leaving Jim was potent proof of her state of mind.

THIRTY-ONE

Cambridge, April 1948. Meg and Jimmy arrived home in Cambridge on April 3. It was her thirty-fourth move in three and a half years of marriage.

One of the first things that Meg did when she got home was to go to confession at St. Peter's church. She was very nervous because it was a serious sin to have not gone to Mass for such a long time. She entered the confessional and began, "Bless me Father for I have sinned." Then she sobbed out, "I haven't been to Mass for three months."

"Did you have a good reason, dear?" The priest asked in a gentle voice.

"I think I had a very good reason, and I hope you think so too," Meg said, now feeling very apprehensive.

"Tell me why. What's your first name?" the priest asked.

"It's Meg."

"Okay Meg, let's start from the beginning now and take your time."

Meg related the entire incident from when she walked into the church in Key West and what the Navy chaplain said. She was sobbing quietly.

The priest said, "Okay, Meg, it's okay. I'm so glad you came to my confessional, because I'm not sure the other priests would have absolved you of the sin. But I forgive you, and I'll tell you why. I was stationed at Walter Reed Hospital in Washington, D.C. during the war. The ambulance brought a colored woman into the emergency room. She was hemorrhaging severely. Actually they said she would die if the bleeding wasn't stopped quickly."

He paused, then continued, "The head doctor told the ambulance driver, "You know we don't take colored patients here. Take her downtown.""

The priest sighed heavily, "I ah, protested moving her. I should have been more forceful, but I wasn't. I drove with her in the ambulance. I held her hand and prayed. She died before we reached the city hospital. I hated myself for allowing it to happen. I became greatly disturbed over the incident and began drinking heavily. I became a drunk."

Meg was astonished at his story and said, "Oh, Father, I feel so badly for you. It wasn't your fault."

"Oh, I thought it was. It's okay now, Meg. I haven't have a drink for six years. You put up a much better fight for the rights of the colored people than I did. I forgive you for missing Mass for three months. I think you did the right thing. You honored God's house. For your penance say three Hail Marys and three Our Fathers. God bless you, Meg."

"Thank you, Father." Meg blessed herself and left the confessional feeling cleansed.

*⊘ * ⊗*

Margaret had not said anything to Meg on the phone about her father's ulcer problem, but when they arrived, Meg saw that he had lost quite a bit of weight. He was on a strict diet and no beer! He wasn't his usual jolly self and appeared to be extremely nervous.

A few days later, Meg got a letter from Jim. He wrote that he had met the skipper of another submarine stationed at Key West who said he was looking for an engineering officer and offered Jim the job. Jim put in for a transfer that day. The skipper had four children, and his sub was to be stationed in San Diego for eighteen months, for sure.

Meg was so skeptical of this kind of promise, she wrote Jim that she'd believe it only when it happened.

After a few days of being home, Meg realized that Jimmy's constant running around and jabbering was upsetting her father. About the third day, he yelled at Meg. "Can't you keep Jimmy toned down a bit. Geeze, kiddo, he's driving me up a wall."

That night, Meg had a talk with her mother. "I think I better try to find an apartment for Jimmy and me. He's making Dad too nervous."

"I know. But your Dad would be hurt if he thought you had to move out because of him. I don't want him upset anymore than he is. Why don't you send Jimmy to that nursery school on Garden Street where Joe and Eileen's Elizabeth goes every day now that Eileen is working. I'll bet Jimmy would love being with other children."

"Mom, that's a wonderful idea! And I think I'll look for a job too."

* & ∗ &

Joe had been asked by the government to testify at the war crime trials in Tokyo, but he couldn't afford to be away from college that long. His buddy, Chip, had also been invited and wanted to testify at the trials. Joe wrote a letter in praise of Nobu Omura for all he had done for the prisoners and asked that Nobu be giving assistance by our government to return to Honolulu. Joe asked Chip to hand deliver it to the highest authorities.

∗

Jimmy loved nursery school, and played so hard all day that he was usually in bed and asleep by seven o'clock every evening.

Ann got Meg a job at Touraine's dress shop in Harvard Square. She loved working and having lunch with her old friends. It gave her a sense of what she would face if she ever left Jim. It hurt to even think about it. She missed him very much, and knew she had to keep busy to keep her mind off the ever-gnawing feeling of desolation that filled her lately.

∗

Meg's old friend, Jane Baxter, offered her a wonderful opportunity. She and her family were going to Europe for July and August, and she asked Meg if she and Jimmy would like to use their summer home on Cape Cod, on the ocean in Falmouth. Meg was thrilled at the prospect of spending the hot summer days on the beach, even though she'd have to quit her job. She knew it would be good to give her Mom and Dad a rest from Jimmy. She moved for the thirty-fifth time. It was wonderful to wake up each day to the fresh salt air, to hear the sea gulls' plaintive cries, and eat meals on the long porch that faced the ocean. Jimmy tanned quickly and looked so healthy with his blond crew cut and little brown body.

Meg's loneliness subsided there. Many of her friends from Cambridge visited regularly and her family spent many weekends with her. She was able to stay in Falmouth through the month of September. Jim was due home any day now.

⚥ * ⚥

Meg had heard from Jim regularly, and he even called from Londonderry, Ireland. He had not had any word on his transfer, but felt it probably would be waiting for him when he got back to Key West in September. But it wasn't.

B. J. had denied the transfer. When Jim found that out, he immediately went to see B.J. and said, "Captain, I'm resigning from the Navy!"

Meg probably would never know the depth of Jim's feelings at this time. She knew that he gave up his passionate love for the Navy for her. She had come to regard the Navy as Jim's mistress, glamorous and exciting. It was September 30 before she saw Jim again. They had been separated for six months this time. Now the challenge of civilian life faced them.

THIRTY-TWO

ambridge, October 1948. After much discussion, they agreed that Jim would have a much better opportunity to find work in the Los Angeles area than in Boston. Meg was so happy that he was out of the Navy that she didn't object to the California move, their thirty-sixth. But she was melancholy the first few days of the trip.

"I want this move to be good for us, Jim. I don't want you to have any regrets about getting out of the Navy. I feel guilty because I've griped so much this past year. I feel like I have forced you to get out."

"Honey, if you think you feel guilty, forget it. I'm the one who should feel guilty. When I look back on all the terrible places you and Jimmy have had to live, I'm surprised you didn't take off and leave me. Sure, I loved the Navy life, but this last year has convinced me, it's not for us. We've got to get going on that family we've talked about for four years, and I have to find us a nice house you can fix up with new furniture of our own."

∅ * ଧ

They arrived in California on October 10. It had been a tiresome trip. Jimmy didn't enjoy being confined for so long. Jim's folks had invited Meg and Jimmy to stay with them in Riverside. Jim would look for a job in L.A., seventy miles away, and stay with his brother, Royden and his wife, Jean, during the week in their tiny efficiency apartment.

Things had changed in the Wrights' home. Mrs. Wright had found a job teaching and was gone most of the day. Jim's younger brother, Kenny, was a senior in high school, and his sister, Mary Ann, was a freshman at a local college. It seemed only reasonable that the household chores of cleaning and getting meals should be Meg's responsibility, which she didn't mind at all. She was thankful for being able to live there free of charge in exchange for running the five-bedroom house. Unfortunately, the kids were always comparing Meg's cooking to her mother-in-law's.

After two weeks of job hunting, Jim found a position at Airesearch in Los Angeles as a preliminary design engineer. His salary was $75 a week. But finding a place to live was another story. Hundreds of thousands of servicemen who had been stationed in California, or had passed through during the war had now come back to live. There were rooms with "kit. priv" available, but Jim knew that Meg would never live like that again. He looked at efficiency apartments like his brother and wife had, but they were so small, and very few allowed children. Three months went by, and still Jim couldn't find a place for them to live. Quite often now, he would have to work on Saturdays. That left only Sundays together. Meg's depression deepened more every day. Jim knew that her patience was wearing thin when she lashed out at him one Monday morning before he left to go to L.A.

"I want to cook meals in my own home, Jim. I want to clean our house. I'm sick and tired of picking up after your brother and sister and their friends."

Jim's father had overhead this tirade and when Jim came home the next weekend, his father said, "Jim, I want to talk to you and Meg." After an hour of discussion, they all came to the same conclusion. There was no easy answer. They would just have to tough it out.

About a week and a half later, Meg got a phone call from her mother. "Honey, I just called to let you know that Dad has to have a serious operation. His ulcer has become so bad, he going to have a large portion of his stomach removed."

"Oh, Mom, I'll come home right away."

"No, honey. Joe and Eileen will be here with me. I just want you to say prayers for Dad," she sobbed out.

Meg called Joe later that evening. "Joe, please tell me the truth. How serious is Dad's operation?"

"Well, Meg, it's very serious, but I'm sure he'll make it. He has one of the finest surgeons from Mass General Hospital."

"Joe, I want to come home. I want to see Dad before he's operated on. I want to be able to help Mom. Oh, Joe, I'm so homesick! I'm miserable here. I want to be there with all of you," Meg couldn't hold back the tears and began sobbing in a pitiful tone.

"What's happening there? It sounds like you are not getting along too well."

"Oh, Joe, Jim still hasn't found a place for us to live in L.A., and I'm so depressed. Our life is just like it was in the Navy. Nothing is different."

"Come on, honey. Where's your Irish spirit? Since when does my little Sis let things get her down? Have the good fairies deserted you, kiddo? Come on now, we're not quitters. Geeze, Meg, I wish I were closer. I'm sure Jim is doing everything he can to give you a good life. You must believe that."

"I do. I guess there's nothing more he can do."

"Meg, I promise I'll call you if Dad gets worse. Okay? Now, chin up, kiddo. Remember, Cambridge girls can handle anything. You know that!"

Three days later, Joe called. "Meg, Dad was just rushed to the hospital. He's hemorrhaging very badly. They won't be able to operate until he's stabilized. Maybe it would be a good idea, kiddo, if you did come home."

In panic, Meg called Jim in L.A. "Jim, I have to fly home right away. My Dad is hemorrhaging severely and I want to be there. I'll take Jimmy with me."

"Okay, honey. I'll leave work right away and be home in about an hour, depending on traffic. Meg, your Dad's strong. He'll pull through. Don't worry. Call American Airlines and get a reservation."

Three hours later as Meg was flying across the country, she thought, my thirty-seventh move, I wonder how long I'll be there.

🙷 * 🙷

Margaret, Meg and Joe kept a vigil at Bill's bedside for the next twenty-four hours. Two days later they operated successfully.

"He's a tough old soldier," the surgeon said when he came out of the operating room. "I think he'll be fine."

The O'Mearas went to the hospital chapel and thanked God.

Bill came home ten days later, and although weak, the doctor really lifted his spirits when he told him, "Bill, in a couple of months, you'll be able to drink all the beer you want."

🙷 * 🙷

Meg put Jimmy back in nursery school and thought about getting a job. Jim called often, always hoping that Meg would say she was coming back. But lately, she'd tell him, "I think I'm going to stay here until you find us a decent place to live out there, Jim."

Meg knew she'd be miserable if she had to live with Jim's folks again. Just the thought of it made her despondent.

Eileen was alarmed about Meg's depression and encouraged her to talk about it. "Everyone is worried about you, Meg. You've lost so much weight and you seem to be so tense all the time." Eileen made her promise to see Doctor Walker.

That night, Meg felt particularly depressed and after she had been in bed for a while, she began hyperventilating. It frightened her, but she had learned in the MWDC how to stop it by blowing in a paper bag. She took the incident as a serious danger signal and made an appointment with the doctor the next morning.

Doctor Walker gave her a complete physical and convinced her that she was heading for trouble if she didn't resolve the problem that was causing her depression. She told him about their housing problem. He didn't have an easy answer for that, but prescribed a green tonic which would keep her less tense. After completing her physical, he asked her, "Did you know that you are about three and a half months pregnant?"

Meg had suspected that she might be pregnant because they hadn't been overly cautious when Jim came home after being away for six months. They had fully expected their lives to become normal then, like most married couples.

She asked Doctor Walker not to say anything to her parents. "Let me tell them." She didn't want them to know because she was sure her mother would tell Jim. She also felt sure that he would quit his job and come to Cambridge right away. She didn't want that on her conscience. He was so enthused about his new position. She was still feeling guilty about insisting that he get out of the Navy. She decided, I'll tell him about the baby when he tells me that he's found a nice place for us to live. Dear, God, let it be soon.

Meg didn't show much at all because of having lost so much weight.

About a week later, Meg and Jimmy had finished dinner with Joe and Eileen and were getting ready to leave. Suddenly a severe pain raced through Meg's lower body. "Oh My God", she screamed, bending in half and holding her stomach.

Joe grabbed her to prevent her falling. "Kiddo, where do you hurt?" he asked, panic filling his voice.

Meg grimaced in pain. "Oh, my God, Joe, it's my baby. I think I'm going to lose my baby,"

"Your baby!" Joe and Elizabeth cried in unison.

Writhing in pain, Meg blurted, "I'm almost four months pregnant. I didn't tell anyone. I was afraid you'd tell Jim, and he'd come, and, oh, my, God, I think the baby is coming out," she screamed hysterically as they laid her on a bed.

Eileen quickly put a towel under her. "Quick, Joe, call an ambulance."

As Meg was being placed into the ambulance, Joe kissed her forehead and tried to soothe her, "Everything is going to be okay, kiddo. I'll call Jim."

No Joe! Don't call Jim and tell Mom not to," she begged. "You mustn't. Promise me, please."

The four-month fetus was delivered on the way to the hospital. Meg was treated for a miscarriage and stayed in the hospital overnight.

When she came home, Margaret began force feeding her at every meal. "I'm going to get some meat back on your bones." She made Meg drink three egg nogs every day and hovered over her as if she were a child.

Meg assumed that her family had not told Jim because he never mentioned the miscarriage when he called.

THIRTY-THREE

ambridge, 1949. About three weeks later, on a Sunday afternoon, Meg and Jimmy were playing Lincoln Logs on the living room floor when the front door bell rang.

Margaret called out from the kitchen in a strange, shrill voice, "Answer the door, Meg, I'm busy out here."

Jimmy yelled, "I'll get it, I'll get it." He loved to press the buzzer. He ran down the first few steps, and stopped short. He looked back sheepishly, at Meg who was getting up off the floor. He stuck his tongue in his cheek and cast his eyes downward and said softly, "It's Daddy."

A shock wave seized Meg's body. She ran to the head of the stairs and looked down at Jim now racing up the stairs carrying Jimmy and grinning broadly.

She cried out plaintively, "Jim!" She opened her arms and ran to him, embracing both him and Jimmy tightly and letting her tears flow freely.

Jim covered her face with kisses then pressed his mouth against Meg's ear and murmured between sobs, "Oh, my Meg, my Meg, I'll never leave you again. Why didn't you tell me about the baby? Why did you go through all of that alone? Don't you know I love you and care about every little thing that happens to you? You know I would have come immediately."

On the sidelines, Margaret and Bill watched the joyful reunion. Jimmy, not understanding what was happening, jutted out his quivering bottom lip, looked at his Nana and started to cry. Margaret reached out for him and said the magic word, "cookies," and took him to the kitchen.

Meg suddenly pushed Jim away and asked in a startled voice, "Oh, Jim, you shouldn't have come. What about your job? Aren't you afraid you'll lose it, taking time off?"

Jim grinned and said, "Oh, you mean the Airesearch job? I gave it up!"

"You what?" Meg was shocked.

"I've got a new job, honey. It's great. I start tomorrow." Meg was confused. You mean you're flying back tonight?"

"No way, Honey. You're looking at a Combustion Research Assistant who will be working in the Chemical Engineering Laboratory at MIT starting tomorrow."

"MIT? Our MIT, in Cambridge?"

"Right down on Mass. Ave., across from your old Armory."

"But, Jim, I don't understand. How? I mean, how did you get a job here?"

"Well your resourceful brother, Joe, has been sending me the classified section of the *Boston Globe* for about two months now. I didn't want to say anything to you, in case I didn't find a job. But I applied for this job at MIT and they called me on Thursday. I quit Airesearch on Friday, packed up on Saturday, sold my car to my brother, Royden, flew here today, rented a car at the airport, and here I am."

Stunned, and wide-eyed with joy, Meg looked up and uttered, "Oh, dear Lord, thank you, thank you."

Jim stood in the middle of the living room, raised his arms up and said, "Could I have everyone's attention, please. I have an important announcement to make." An impish grin covered his face, and he said loudly, "Everybody, get your coats and hats on, we're going for a ride. I have another surprise."

"What are you up to, Jim?" Meg asked, looking to her parents for a clue.

Their smug smiling faces told her they knew but were not about to give away his secret.

✍ * ✍

They rode west, out through Newton and Wellesley. Meg, still in a state of shock, kept asking, "Where are we going, Jim? Come on, someone tell me."

"We have no idea honey, honest," Margaret answered and laughed.

When they came to the junction of Route Nine and Speen Street in Natick, Jim pulled off the highway and stopped in front of a house that said, "Model Home." He then ordered, "Everyone out! I want you to come over here and read this sign"

They all stood in front of a large billboard and read.

ATTENTION VETERANS!!!!
Buy Your Dream House Now. No Down Payment.
Twenty Year Mortgage with a G.I. Loan. Low 4% Interest.
ONLY $9,850.
Pinewood at Natick. An Innovative Development.

Meg looked from the sign to Jim. "Jim! You aren't thinking of buying a house. We could never afford to buy a house."

"Why not? You read the sign; no money down. Come on, let's take a look inside the model home and see if you like it."

Meg couldn't believe this was really happening. She was stunned. "Jim, how could you have known about this?"

"Your brother bird-dogged it for me," Jim said as he led them inside the beautifully furnished model home. "It has two bedrooms, a bath, an enormous kitchen with sparkling white cabinets, and a large living room with a fireplace!"

Meg and her parents were awe-struck. It was so modern. The living room wall that faced the back yard was all one big picture window. The attic was expandable. There was no cellar. The floor was a concrete slab covered with pretty vinyl tile. There was wall-to-wall carpeting in the living room.

The salesman joined them and asked, "How do you like it, folks? These houses are going as fast as hotcakes. Developments like Pinewood are going up all across the USA. We want to take care of our veterans. I've got a beauty on the corner of Bough Lane. Just cost you $350 extra for the corner lot. Makes it nice to have only one neighbor next to you; more privacy; you know. It will be ready for occupancy within a week or so."

Meg was flabbergasted. "Wait until I see my brother Joe!"

"Yup, thank him," Jim said and laughed. "I took his word about this place. He said he was sure it would put the smile back in your Irish eyes, and the roses back in your cheeks. So my city girl from Cambridge, what do you think about becoming a country girl."

In a sassy voice, Meg answered, "You know that this Cambridge girl can adjust to any situation, especially moving!"

The salesman gave them directions to number two Bough Road and said, "If you like the lot, hurry back here to sign the mortgage papers. I'm sure it'll be sold today."

Margaret was skeptical and whispered to Jim, "He's a little too pushy. I don't think I'd trust him."

They drove down a dirt road, past both completed and unfinished homes. They were all the same design, but those that were finished had different appearances. Various paint colors and wood textures made each one unique. When they came to the corner of Bough and Pineneedle, Jim stopped and said excitedly, "Here it is, honey."

Meg put her hand over her mouth to hold back a sob, "Oh, Jim, It's beautiful."

The house, surrounded by trees, was sitting in the middle of a square lot. The roof was shingled and the outside was finished in brown wood trim with white shingles.

Jim picked Meg up and carried her across the threshold. Her heart was pounding fast. She couldn't believe this was happening to her. She fought back tears and whispered to Jim, "My dream's coming true at last. This is what I've always wanted, Jim. We'll have our own furniture and Jimmy can have his own room. We'll live like normal human beings. I'll finally be able to unpack our sea chests once and for all! "Oh, Jim, I love it! Can we really afford it?"

"If you like it, honey, we'll buy it!"

"I love it!" Jimmy yelled as he raced in and out of every room and ran upstairs yelling, "I want my room to be up here, Dad."

Jim took Meg's hand and led her up the stairs, "Let's look at that expandable attic. I'll build two bedrooms up here so we'll have room for that large family we've talked about so often." Then he whispered in her ear, "Won't it be nice not to have to go to confession every week?"

"Can we light a fire, Dad?" Jimmy yelled as he ran down the stairs. "It's kinda cold in here."

"Not today, son, but real soon!"

When they came downstairs, Meg went into the kitchen and ran her hands along the smooth, white cabinets. She envisioned herself cooking at the new stove and thought about what kind of furniture she wanted.

Jimmy flushed the toilet for the third time.

Bill was looking out the big living room windows. "Boy, you veterans sure have it better than we did. College loans, house loans, twenty bucks a week for a year. Geeze, we were really robbed," he said as if talking to himself.

In a plaintive tone, Margaret said, "You're going to be so far away, again, Meg."

"Only about 20 miles from Cambridge, Mom. You'll see plenty of us," Jim consoled her.

There was a knock on the front door. Jim opened it. It was the man, woman and child they had seen earlier out in front of the house across the street on the opposite corner, on Pineneedle.

"Thought we'd come over and introduce ourselves if we're going to be neighbors. I'm Ed Jones, this is my wife, Kathleen, and our daughter, Jean."

The little girl stood in front of Jimmy and said, "Want me to show you all the big lumber piles in the back yards?"

Jimmy hesitated, "Well...okay, I guess so. I'll let you show me."

Everyone laughed. Jim said, "I think we've pretty much made up our mind that we are going to buy it. Right, Meg?"

"Positively, Jim!" Meg answered enthusiastically.

Jim introduced the O'Mearas and Meg.

"Will this be your first home?" Kathleen asked.

Jim and Meg looked at each other and burst out laughing.

Meg said, "It will be our first home, but our thirty-eighth move in a little more than four years of marriage!"

"My, God! This calls for a celebration." Ed said. "I just happen to have a half bottle of Johnny Walker Red Label out in the car. I think we should toast this momentous occasion. Kay always has a supply of paper cups in our picnic basket. I'll be right back."

"Johnny Walker! You have expensive taste, Ed," Jim said as they walked outside. "I think we'll be living on a beer budget ourselves, for quite a while."

"I didn't buy it," Ed said, "I'm a salesman in the optical business and just came back from a trade show. It was left over in our hospitality suite. I always get to do the cleanup. I'm the new man. Just got out of the paratroopers. Not bad duty, huh?"

The men came back with the bottle and cups and poured everyone a shot, except for Bill, who was still on a bland diet.

Ed raised his cup. "Well, here's to all of us. May we have many years of happiness and friendship. Cheers!"

"Cheers," everyone responded. The pungent scotch warmed them, for it was very cold in the unheated house.

Kay asked Margaret, "Do you like these houses?"

"I like most everything about it except that wall of window. Everyone can look in, and they'll know all your business."

"Margaret, you don't understand," Bill said in a patronizing voice. "The guys that buy these houses are all veterans. Veterans stick together. They like the same things. They help one another. They'll all know each other's business anyway. They'll be like just one big happy family."

ℨ * ℨ

Bill was right. Within six months, as he predicted, the entire neighborhood was one big happy extended family that shared and cared for each other. No one had much money. Most of the men had their first real job. Only one family, the Kileys, had a seven-inch television. Every Friday night all the men went to their house to watch the fights. The women played Canasta.

Meg, like many of her neighbors, became pregnant within a few months of moving in. Every child had playmates and there were wonderful woods to explore. No one ever had to go through a crisis alone. Doors were never locked. Joe, the milkman, went in and out of each house at five o'clock in the morning and put the milk in the refrigerator. Lennie, the bread man, also carried cigarettes, aspirins and Alka-Seltzer. Angelo, the postman, sorted the neighborhood mail on Meg's kitchen table.

The neighborhood used any excuse for a party, and everyone brought their own drinks. Children's birthdays always had a theme. With help, Jim cut down some trees and turned their backyard into a volley ball court for summer fun. Then, in the winter, it became an ice rink for skating. Within a few months, Jim and Ed formed a committee to begin building a Catholic church for the area. New schools were nearing completion.

Every day was a new adventure for the veterans of Pinewood and their families. The horizon looked so promising, and, although they didn't have much, they felt like they had it all.

The End

ℨ * ℨ